CALL HOME THE HEART

"A romantic, well-drawn story."　　　　　*—Booklist*

❧

"A fine tale, encompassing emotional depth and histori-
cal authenticity."　　　　　*—Publishers Weekly*

❧

"Poverty and wealth, love and hate, and warm, believ-
able characters. I thoroughly recommend it."
　　　　　—Dorothy Eden

❧

"Jessica Stirling reminds one of that other great creator
of family sagas, R. F. Delderfield."　　*—Daily Express*

CALL HOME
THE HEART

Jessica Stirling

BALLANTINE BOOKS · NEW YORK

Library of Congress Catalog Card Number: 76-28059

ISBN 0-345-27331-1

This edition published by arrangement
with St. Martin's Press, Inc.

Manufactured in the United States of America

First Ballantine Books Edition: June 1978

Contents

CALL HOME
THE HEART

PART ONE

***

Travellin' Folk

One

⚜

THE MAN HAD been looking at her for five minutes or more. At first Mirrin ignored him, but his persistence was so curious that, capitulating, she pushed herself away from the cornstore wall and, with hands on hips, stared pointedly back at him.

He laughed.

Laughter was the last reaction Mirrin Stalker expected. In spite of her annoyance, she found herself smiling ruefully. That was invitation enough. Sauntering through the ranks from the labourers' benches, the stranger tipped his hat and eased into conversation as if he had known the young woman all his life.

"Tell me, what does a handsome lass like you hope t'find at Lanark Hiring Fair?"

"Employment," Mirrin replied.

"On the land?"

"I'll take what I can get."

"Let me guess, then, what you're best at."

"I'm best at fendin' off the attentions of men like you."

"Where's your common sense?" the stranger demanded.

"What?"

"You'll never get work talkin' that way. Meekness is a sterling virtue in this market. Aye, you're too bold for the sleekit wee farmers in this part o' the world. God, their wives would have a fit if they toddled home wi' you on a string."

"I'm an experienced servant," said Mirrin. "A housekeeper, in fact."

3

"Then try the bureau in Glasgow," the stranger advised. "This is a bad fair for soft hands."

"Call these soft?" Mirrin held out her palms for his inspection.

"Aye, I have seen softer," the man admitted.

"What about you?" Mirrin said. "I haven't noticed you bein' plied with offers."

"I've had my share," he said. "But, t'tell the truth, my heart's not in it this time of year. Besides, the gowks round here are wary o'givin' papers t'the likes o'me."

"What's wrong with you, then?"

"They can spot a tinker a mile off."

Now that she looked at him more closely, Mirrin could see the strain in him. But there was little physical difference between the gypsy and the short dark-haired men that made up most of the population of her village, some twenty miles away to the north. In Blacklaw, Northrigg and even Hamilton, she had encountered many men more obviously robust. This man was only a couple of inches taller than she was, though compact, tamped down like a buckram wallet for neatness in the carrying. His hair and eyes were dark brown, and his skin tanned like nutwood.

"A tink, are you?" Mirrin said. "I should have known by the hat."

Tipped raffishly back from his face was a flop-brimmed felt, ornamented with a crop of small coins and medallions stitched to the ribbon. His shirt was cut full, clean patched cream flannel, his leather waistcoat shrunk like a bolero. The kerchief around his throat was polka-dot red, matching the handkerchief loosely tucked in the vest pocket. He still seemed to be laughing, though his lips were pursed as he studied her in turn.

She knew how she looked, tired still after the long, hard winter. Her pallor was pasty; any collier in the country would have marked her as a coal-picker at a glance. Even so, though she was no more than average vain, she had to admit that she was the most attractive girl in the square, tall and full-figured and not—as the stranger had pointed out—meek.

On the women's benches, the other females, even

the young ones, waited with hang-dog submissiveness. Their persons were neat but their characters were somehow drab, showing a hopeless, almost belligerent, resignation. The next job, they seemed to say, can only be worse than the last. They changed fees as often as their terms allowed. None, however, were true migrants, as the tinkers were, or the new breed of manual workers who charged about Scotland and the North of England in search of high wages.

The hiring fair was for farmers—growers, herders, berry-men, drovers. The work offered was hard and dull, the annual fee small. The stranger was right. Mirrin did not belong here. Though some men cast speculative glances in her direction, no one dared approach her. No one responded to her smile and her murmured advertisement, "Servant, sir? Experienced servant? I can cook an' sew. I'm strong and healthy."

Those qualities, undiluted, were, she realised, enough to put any traditional farmer off.

"The name's Thomas Armstrong. You can call me Tom, if y'like," the stranger said.

"What do I call you if I don't like?" Mirrin asked.

"I've the price o' two teas an' a bridie between us."

"I told you, I'm not here for a picnic. I'm here for work."

"Where are y'from?"

"Blacklaw."

"A dreich hole, that."

"It's my home, Mr. Armstrong."

"Is Lamont's pit in full production again?"

It was not a particularly perceptive question. The Blacklaw mining disaster of 1874 had been the talk of Scotland.

Mirrin nodded, not willing to be drawn.

"Did you lose somebody in the explosion?" the man asked.

Mirrin nodded again.

"A husband?"

"Two brothers an' my father, if y'must know."

"Aye, I'm sorry," the stranger said. She sensed his sincerity. It was not hollow commiseration like that usually offered to the folk of Blacklaw by those who

did not understand the depth and breadth of the tragedy and imagined that such wounds healed in time.
"Was it that drove y'out?"

"Partly," Mirrin replied.

"Are you . . . alone?"

"I've a brother in Edinburgh, an' my Mam an' two
sisters still live in Blacklaw. No, Mr. Armstrong, I'm
not without a place t'go back to, if an' when I choose."

Armstrong sighed. "What *are* you doin' here?"

"Escaping, I suppose," Mirrin said.

"Had enough of sortin' black gold, then?"

"More than enough."

"But y'said you were a servant?"

"Just what is your interest in me, Mr. Armstrong?
Have you a contract of hire in your pocket?"

"No."

"Then away back t'your side of the square an' hope
that some blind drover comes along that's got no aver-
sion t'tinkers."

Armstrong shook his head, clapped his hands together and glanced off down the lane that debouched
from the square of stores and two-storey cottages.
Trees, laden with May blossom, lay very close to the
small town, and the road dipped and rose again on to
the breast of the green, sheep-speckled hill. The spring
sky was big with sunlight and the flight of clouds, open
and inviting.

"I've no stomach for this county, really," Armstrong
said. "I just dropped by in the hope of seein' a friendly
face or two."

"But you didn't."

"Just yours," Armstrong said. "It's bonnie, but no'
that friendly. So, I think I'll toddle on my way again."

"Where to?"

"Ayrshire, like as not."

"Good luck t'you, then," Mirrin said.

"Listen, it's too late into the mornin' for a hire now,"
Tom Armstrong said. "In the afternoon, maybe the
gentry'll have a factor or two on the scout for a servant.
Right now, most landlords are only thinkin' of dinner
an' a dram."

"Tea an' a bridie will do me fine," Mirrin said.

"Half a bridie," Tom Armstrong said.

"An' I'll pay my share."

"I knew it."

"Knew what?"

"That you were a lady at heart."

"Aye, that'll be right," Mirrin said. "Now where's the tea-stall. I'm starvin'."

"This way," Tom Armstrong said.

Two

FLORA STALKER PAUSED on her trudge up Blacklaw's steep main street. The shawl which protected her head and shoulders from drizzling rain was beaded with moisture. When she halted a single droplet gathered and splashed, like a tear, to her cheek. Impatiently she brushed it away.

Before her, jutting on to the pavement which fronted the row of miners' cottages, a pair of thin legs barred her progress. The legs were humped inside a shiny cotton skirt and presumably connected to a trunk, arms and head somewhere within the tiny lobby of the house. As Flora watched, the creature inched backwards like a snail lured from its shell by the smell of rain.

"Not much of a day, Georgina," said Flora to the legs. "The start of a wet winter, like as not."

Georgina McKenzie's head appeared, plastered with ragged wisps of hair. "Is it yourself, Flora Stalker?"

"Aye."

Stiffly the woman sat back on her heels, the skirts negligently flopping into the suds that oozed down the worn steps, dabbed her scrubbing brush on to the bar of carbolic and propped it on the edge of her bucket.

Flora sensed what was coming. Georgina was by no

means the most malicious woman in Blacklaw, but, this last year, Flora had become fair game for gossip-mongers.

"How's your lad, then, Mrs. Stalker? Doin' well at school?"

Fine well Georgina McKenzie knew that Drew was at Edinburgh University.

As if by rote, Flora answered, "Drew's doin' just grand."

"An' Mirrin: what's she up to these days?"

"Domestic service," Flora intoned.

She was sorry that she'd stopped for a blether: it was a habit she must learn to break.

"Oh, a *housekeeper* again, is it?"

"Parlour maid," Flora lied.

"I heard a rumour she was workin' on a farm." Georgina peered like an oracle into the depths of her bucket, not meeting Flora's eye. "Is it a dairy parlour maid she is?"

"No, it's a big house in Ayrshire," Flora said curtly. "She likes it fine."

"Aye," said Georgina in a tone that signified dis-belief. "Hughie—m'son: he's articled to a very good carpenter, y'know, in Hamilton—Hughie was sayin' there's been some changes up at Lamont's place since Mirrin left."

"I wouldn't know anythin' about Lamont's," Flora Stalker retorted.

She had never had much interest in the coalmaster's private life or what went on in his mansion. She real-ised that her daughter, Mirrin, and Houston Lamont had been close, but shut her ears to the scandal. Out-with the Ewings and one or two of Alex Stalker's old cronies, Flora and Kate had no close friends in the vil-lage now. Flora wanted her son and daughters to live much as she had lived, to grant her the things that a woman of her age had a right to expect, acceptable, unoriginal sources of pride. How could she be proud of her children when she did not know what they were doing with their lives?

Brusquely, she said, "I've an appointment, Geor-gina. I must be on my way."

She turned and started uphill again, ignoring the McKenzie woman's anxious cry, "An appointment, Mrs. Stalker? At the pit, is it?"

Precious little privacy had been left to Flora; what remained she would protect to the letter. It was none of their business what she did. She would die before confessing that she had no idea where Mirrin was, or that she had not had the scrape of a pen from Drew since he'd left Blacklaw in May. Not even today.

Today was her birthday.

She hurried on. The familiar landscape of Blacklaw no longer protected her: the graceless sweep of Main Street topped by colliery gates and winding towers and, on a green knoll across the shallow valley, the coalmaster's handsome mansion. Between these poles stood unbroken rows of cottages, a couple of ships, the schoolhouse, the pub, the kirk, and the kirkyard where her husband Alex and her sons, James and Douglas, lay buried, together with all the stability which had been blasted away in the black spring of '74.

Flora Stalker had lost more than her menfolk in the explosion in the damp-ridden underground seams. One by one, after that, through circumstances she could not fully grasp, she had lost touch with all her children, even with the girls who had remained at home.

Today was Flora's birthday. She was fifty-two.

Nobody had remembered.

Kellock's Good Bread Bakery stood at the upper end of Main Street, tucked back from the cottage rows and overshadowed by loud tin hoardings on the gable of the *Lantern*. Though Willie Kellock did his best, mere bread could hardly compete with the glamour of Four Crown Whiskey and Tencher's Heavy Beer. Bakehouse and shop shared a shallow yard with a rickety shed in which a local cabinetmaker stored timber. Men on 'change shift' declared that the scent from Kellock's ovens was appetising enough to *compel* you to blow a couple of pence on a big paper bag full of piping hot rolls.

The bun shop was as bright and clean as a Salvation Army cornet, with a wee square window and a deal counter the colour of a crusty brown loaf. One shelved wall led through an arched corridor into the bakehouse at the back. In addition to bread and rolls Willie baked and sold parkins, meat pies, bridies, sponge cakes and a black bun so rich that one slice would keep a man nourished for a week.

William Kellock was a kindly widower in his mid-fifties. Under a scant sandy-grey thatch his nose and chin would have done Punch proud. After his wife's death Willie was faced with the choice of shrugging off his dingy memory-haunted house in Polmadie or of hitting the bottle. As boozing had never been his vice, he gathered himself together mentally and physically and sought redemption in the hinterlands of Lanark-shire.

Blacklaw was the fourth of the half dozen sites that Willie had marked as worthy of investigation. Careful survey satisfied him that he need search no further for Nirvana. The bakehouse was broad enough to accom-modate a couple of ovens and the retail shop—though not large—would suit the scale of enterprise he origi-nally had in mind. Domestic quarters above the shop were too large for a single man, but the fact that the courtyard was only a couple of hundred yards from a gate which regularly disgorged three hundred hungry miners was the clincher.

Business got off to such a flying start, however, that in the first month he had been obliged to hire a laddie to grease the tins and sweep out the shop. Now, in his second month, he felt it necessary to relieve himself of selling and concentrate on the baking, which was really where his skill lay. Besides, he had a notion to press the boom in trade while the going was good.

A brass bell tingled cheerily as Flora Stalker pushed open the door of the shop and stepped hesitantly over the threshold. Brushing raindrops from her face, she carefully folded her shawl and primped her hair.

"Well, well, Mrs. Stalker!"

In a white apron and striped shirt, the baker ap-peared out of the brick corridor on a blast of hot air, like one of his own pastries sliding from the oven. His smile and tone were warm, conveying the impression that Mrs. Stalker's presence in his shop was all that he required to fill the day with sunshine.

"Is this not terrible weather?"

"Aye, terrible." Flora kept her large, red-knuckled hands below counter level. "Still, they tell me the harvest's all in an' that's good for the farmers."

"Good for us all, the Lord be thankit," said Willie without a trace of piety. "And now, how can I serve you today, Mrs. Stalker? The usual crusty?"

"Not . . . not today, thanks, Mr. Kellock."

"Parkins, then?" asked Willie hopefully "Light, or well-browned. Take your choice."

"No, I . . ." Flora hesitated. "It's the card in the window."

"The card?"

"In the window, Mr. Kellock. About the job."

"*That* card!" said Willie. "Aye, Mrs. Stalker. What about it? Have you somebody in mind that might suit?"

"Me, Mr. Kellock."

"You, Mrs. Stalker?"

"I'd like to be considered for the job."

Bemused, Willie shook his head. "Oh, no, now, I don't think that would be right at all. It's not just for the shop, ye'see."

"Aye, I know what it's for."

"It's really for the van. What I'm after's a big raw laddie, not a . . . a lady like yourself."

"Your consideration does you credit, Mr Kellock, but I need to earn a wage, an' I'm stronger than I look."

"The shop . . . oh, aye, you'd be fine for the shop, Mrs. Stalker. I couldn't ask for better. But not for the van. An' I'm fixed on the notion of a van. It'll be out in all weathers, too, without much protection."

"I promise I'll hap up well, Mr. Kellock."

The baker bit his lip. "I don't know. It's nothin' personal, Mrs. Stalker, but . . " A fresh thought occurred to him. "Does Kate know you're here?"

Flora's features firmed. If there had been less need for diplomacy she might have snapped out her answer. As it was her tone was barely civil. "No, Mr. Kellock,

Kate doesn't know I'm here. It's what in a younger person you'd call 'initiative'."

Willie stuck his tongue in his cheek and contemplatively tapped his nose with his forefinger, thoughtfully.

"Please, Mr. Kellock," said Flora, but not plaintively.

Throwing up his hands in capitulation, Willie smiled. "Well, why not, Mrs. Stalker? But it'll be *hard* work."

"The Stalkers aren't afraid of that, Mr. Kellock."

"Six o'clock start, to catch the night-shift coming off, then again at two o'clock, for the . . ."

"For the day-shift, an' the back-shift," Flora said. "An then the night shift again."

"No, no, I'm no slave driver, Mrs. Stalker. I wouldn't ask those hours of anybody. I'll do the final run m'self."

Flora said, "As you wish, Mr. Kellock."

"The wage as advertised," Willie said. "Plus a mixed bag of cakes an' pies an' a loaf per day." Seeing Flora's eyes harden again, he added hastily, "Bakers always do that. It's tradition, I assure you, not charity."

"Thank you, then, Mr. Kellock," Flora said. "I'll see you at a quarter to six tomorrow mornin'."

"Can you . . . er, drive a van, Mrs. Stalker?"

"A van?" said Flora, then promptly added, "I can drive anythin' if I have to."

"Good, good." Willie watched the woman leave the shop, so lost in thought that he neglected to step forward to open the door for her. He wasn't thinking of the mother, though, but of the daughter. He hoped Kate Stalker wouldn't blame him for what had happened. He wouldn't want to do anything that would cause him to lose face with Kate.

Still, he thought, as he returned to his mounds of dough, there might be advantages to both sides in hiring Flora Stalker. He just hoped that Wallace would take to her, that was all.

The Stalkers' house was not as it had been when the menfolk were alive. Kate's return from work at Lamont's sorting tables and Betsy's arrival from Dalzells' Emporium in Hamilton did not dispel the hollowness, though on that late-September evening there were diversions to keep depression at bay. Firstly there was Flora's news that she had taken the job advertised in Mr. Kellock's bakery; then there were presents to open and admire—for the girls had not forgotten her birthday after all. Lastly, and most important, Kate had received a letter from Drew. She had collected it from the postie on her way to work and had saved it unopened to add to Mam's birthday treats.

The news that Flora had taken work, though, put the letter momentarily out of Kate's mind.

Eldest of the family, it seemed that Kate was destined to remain a spinster. In the last year she had become drawn, her gaunt features accented by neatly braided hair. On the other hand, Betsy Stalker had blossomed. Her features were refined, her hands delicate, her hair frivolously groomed into loose sausage-shaped ringlets which, bobbing and tossing, drove the impressionable young men of Hamilton quite wild. Mirrin was the handsome sister; Kate, the plain; Betsy pretty as a picture in a storybook, and fully aware of the value of such natural endowments.

Tonight, Betsy suppressed her disdain for the working women. It would only be a matter of time before Drew honoured his promise to introduce her into Edinburgh society. This dream sustained Betsy. She had not, however, expected to be informed that her mother would soon be driving a horse and cart round Blacklaw's streets. Outrage overwhelmed self-control.

Betsy blurted out, "Well, I think it's *disgraceful,* so I do."

"Nobody asked you, miss," Kate warned.

Potatoes chugged inside the iron pot on the stove. From a smaller pan broth released an appetising steam. None of these creature comforts made the least impression on Betsy. She tried to imagine how the changed domestic circumstances would affect her, what village gossips would say about her, how the staff in Dalzells' would sneer at her if it ever got back to them that her aged mother had become a common carter.

"When they hear of this in the shop," Betsy cried, "I shouldn't be surprised if I'm asked to leave."

Once, Kate would have humoured her sister. But

Kate had no energy left to expend on the spoiled child.

"Well, if you're asked to leave," said Kate, "I dare say I can find you a job at the pit. How would that do?"

"But my friends . . . !"

"It isn't your fine Hamilton friends that put the bread on this table, Betsy," Kate reminded her.

Flouncing, Betsy rose to retreat to the sanctuary of the back bedroom. There she would salve her injured pride by brushing her ringlets or experimenting with alluring perfumes from the collection of cheap vials which she wheedled from the silly lads who thought themseves madly in love with her.

"Sit down at that table," Kate commanded.

"I'll . . ."

"You'll *sit.*"

Biting her lip, Betsy obeyed.

The birthday treat for Mam had been spoiled now. Hoping to restore some sense of occasion, Kate quickly extracted the letter from her pocket.

"This arrived today," she announced.

Immediately Flora's eyes lit up. She was seated at the table, the two gifts on the plate—mittens from Kate, a cheap handkerchief from Betsy—forgotten in the excitement of hearing at last from one of her prodigals.

"Is it from Mirrin?"

"No, I think it's from Drew."

Betsy clapped her hands, squealing, "From *Drew!*"

Solemnly, Kate lifted a knife from the table and slit the long envelope. She slid out a sheet of parchment-like paper—appropriate for a budding lawyer—and scanned the manuscript. Mastery of copperplate script had been one of Drew's minor accomplishments during his year of private study with Dominie Guthrie, headmaster of Blacklaw school.

Betsy cried, "Give it to me, Kate: you read too slow."

Still studying the letter, Kate swung it out of Betsy's reach.

Pouting, Betsy said, "Well, go on then, read it aloud. What does he say? Does he say anythin' about *me?*"

It was the first communication the family had received since Drew had departed for Edinburgh five months ago. Though Kate tried to convince herself that her brother was simply too occupied with his studies to spare time to write home, she felt slighted by his ingratitude. Only Kate's drive and Mirrin's sacrifices had enabled Drew to assume his place on the benches of the university. But every penny of his fees and livings had had to be earned, scraped out of thin air. Even then it would not have been possible if Mirrin had not obtained a patronage for her brother from Houston Lamont. It was Lamont's twenty pound annuity that had finally given Drew his chance and fulfilled the rash promise that Kate had made to her father just before his death.

The promise had been kept. But the doing of it had splintered the family. Would it be worth it? Idealism had been Alex Stalker's motivating force. Opportunism, unadorned, spurred Drew.

At the back of her mind all that day had been a nagging doubt about the sentiment which had prompted Drew to write on his mother's birthday. She had forgotten how callous Drew could be.

Tracing the words with her finger, Kate read aloud.

Though Drew sent stilted greetings to his mother and sisters, he did not mention the birthday. He excused his long silence by explaining that he had been studying very hard to make them proud of him. Gow Havershaw, Lamont's Edinburgh lawyer and Drew's reluctant mentor had, so Drew said, obtained his pound of flesh by using him during the vacation as a jobbing clerk in the offices. Magnanimously, Drew admitted that the experience had been quite valuable. Then, abruptly, as if he had suddenly wearied of the filial charade, he moved to the point of the letter. In spite of the flowery phrases Drew's demand was crystal clear.

"Notwithstanding that Mr. Havershaw pays my quarterly emolument precisely on time, mainly, I suspect, to avoid antagonising Mr. Lamont, he did not see fit to recompense me for the many hours spent jobbing. As I had not anticipated that I would be expected to donate my labour entirely from charity I failed to adjust my five pounds accordingly for the period in ques-

tion and have thus been obliged to borrow from a classmate to purchase food. I fear that, with the onset of winter, lack of nourishment and anxiety incurred by being in debt to a fellow, will have an adverse effect upon my concentration and that I may . . ."

Kate let the letter slide to the table.

"He wants us t'send him more money," she said. "That's why he wrote."

Betsy shot to her idol's defence.

"You don't understand him, do you?" she shouted. "None of you have *ever* understood him. He *must* get proper feeding or he won't be able t'study. He wouldn't have written to *you* if there'd been any other way."

"He'll have no more from us, Betsy," Kate said. "We don't have it to give. Let him struggle on his allowance."

"An' what about the debt, then?" Betsy said.

"It'll only be for a shillin' or two," said Kate.

In fact, the debt disturbed her. Debt was a phantom which haunted all colliers' families, the desire to keep a ha'penny ahead, secure in the knowledge that nobody could press for payment at an awkward time and ruin the flimsy structure of domestic economy.

"He can work for that, if he's so worried about it," Kate added.

"He *must* be worried," Betsy cried, "or he wouldn't't've written to *you*. Send him *somethin'*, Kate."

"*You* send him somethin'," Kate snapped. "Stop buying that trash you spray on yourself an' send your precious brother the savings."

Flora Stalker pushed herself from her chair. Her brow was creased and the set of her mouth indicated that she was learning to arbitrate between her two remaining daughters as once Kate had had to act as peacemaker between Drew and Mirrin.

"I'll have no more of this bickerin'," Flora said. "Not on my birthday. Kate, how much is in the stone jar?"

"Six shillings and five pence."

"Send six shillings to Drew."

"But Mam, we're saving to buy you a warm coat."

"Send that money to Drew, I tell you," Flora insisted.

In the past Flora had always deferred to Kate or Mirrin, but tonight she felt unusually confident.

Startled by their mother's authority, Kate and Betsy fell silent.

Flora said, "I'll make it up out o'my week's wage."

"All right, Mam, if that's what you want," Kate said. "But I must make it clear t'him that there's no more."

"You'll do no such thing," Flora said, adamantly. "If Drew needs help then he'd best come t'us. We're still his family, remember."

Slighted, Kate turned to the stove. Noisily she slid bowls from the rack and ladled broth into them, planting them before her mother and sister. She lifted the potato pot and laid it to simmer on the hob. Her hands were ingrained with dirt from the streams of coal that rattled and slurried endlessly down the shutes. Even if she ceased such labour tomorrow, her fingers would never again regain their smoothness or mobility. At twenty-six, she was already marked for life. Why should Drew escape? Mirrin had gone, too, taking care of her own destiny, disgracing them in the manner of her going. At the time Kate had felt sorry for Mirrin, but that sympathy had dwindled. She envied her sister now.

Plucking Drew's letter from the table she tossed it on to the mantel. No doubt Betsy would filch the letter for her tawdry collection of mementoes, to pore over by the light of a tallow dip in the safety of her room, feeding her dreams of satin and silk and eligible, wealthy young bachelors that, in her inflamed imagination, made up the citizenry of the capital.

Deliberately Kate kept her back to the table. She could hear the clink of spoons, the shifting of Betsy's dress on the chair, the creak of the table, the peevish crackle of dross in the chimney's throat and, faintly, the multitude of sounds that filtered in from the street and the colliery. Each individual sound was identifiable yet so familiar that the ear no longer took heed. Poverty and grief were like that, so familiar, so constant, that they dulled the senses and, worst of all, numbed the will.

Kate was sensitive to the changes in herself but totally unable to counter them, to return to what she had been half a year ago. She had lost contact with an enduring source of strength, the struggle of keeping the family secure and intact. In that striving, however hard, there had been life and hope. But what dared she hope for now? Precious little! In a year or two Betsy would fly the coop and Drew would have no need of them, not even to borrow money. And Mirrin—Heaven alone could tell where Mirrin was now or where she would wind up. For sure, it would not be Blacklaw. So what would happen to her, a useless spinster chained to meaningless habits. She would live on in this cramped house, slave daily at the troughs, pinch to hold soul and body together, until Mam died: then she would live on again until some winter the icy wind would spear holes in her lungs and she too would die —here alone.

Kate performed the routine suppertime chores without conscious thought, feet shuffling her across the room from stove to sink to table, a treadmill in miniature. As she turned, her eye involuntarily caught her father's chair, deep and sagging, larger than the rest of the sorry collection of furniture. Her Mam's chair now, more comfortable than the others. She would inherit it, if she waited long enough; payment for patience and dutiful humility. Beyond the chair was the alcove bed in which her father had died. He had died peacefully in the night, after months of pain and struggle. He had died content, soothed by the promise he had extracted from her in his last hour. Kate recalled that burned and ravaged face and heard again the words he had murmured in her ear: "It'll not be easy, nothin' is ever easy, but you'll do it, will y'not? You'll see that it's done, just as I ask?"

Now it had been done, her father's will. Drew had been set on his royal course, equipped to better himself, the lot of the favoured son.

She had loved her father, yet she found that her love was diluted by a kind of hatred, a loathing for the ideal that had robbed them of respect for each other and shown up the family's loyalty as shallow and fraudulent.

Aye, she would send Drew his money. She would have sent it anyway. She would not have left him in debt. Debt was a thing she understood.

She ranged the plates to warm and seated herself to eat her soup. Hunger had gone. She ate listlessly.

After an awkward pause, Mam said, "Willie Kellock gives his employees a free loaf every day."

"That's nice," Kate said, flatly.

"Charity," Betsy remarked, sipping from the nether edge of her spoon as they did in Hamilton restaurants. "It's just an act of charity to the poor Stalkers, don't y'see."

A violent, seething impulse possessed Kate like a demon. She yielded to it as Mirrin would have done, tempestuously, regardless of consequence.

Saying not a word, she lifted her hand and smacked it twice across Betsy's cheek.

The girl's astonished wail was deafening, choking into a breathless sob of disbelief. The keening brought Kate sudden, absolute relief and Betsy's petulant weeping moved her not one jot towards contrition. She regretted only that Drew had not been there to receive his share of retribution; and that Mirrin might never know how alike their characters had become, shaped by strife and tragedy and change.

Three

THE MEN SQUARED up to the last row in the field. Corn stubble lay clean-scythed behind them, the earth relieved of its burden, ready to be revived again by sun and rain before next year's sowing. There was no need

now for the reapers to hone their oak-backed whet-
stones along the blades. It was no more than a gesture
of respect to the farm's last standing stook, a 'touch
wood' that this profitable hiring might lead to another
of the same before the fruitful season waned.

The summer of 1876 had been late in coming. But
slow bloom was best bloom and in the end all
Ayrshire's tillage had run heavy with grain, a grand
harvest promising full bins and bread-crocks, cheaper
meal in markets and corner shops. Prudent farmers
like Maclean would hold back enough grain to nourish
the tupped ewes to drop sturdy lambs on the snell
March pastures. There was little work for casual hands
at the lambing time, Mirrin Stalker had learned. Few
travellin' folk had much truck with mutton except as a
lining for their stomachs. Besides, spring was a long
haul yet and the harsh winter months had first to be
endured.

Already many families had shifted from the land,
drifting away with their packs and cuddy-carts, aban-
doning cold camps for the pleasures of cheap communal lodgings and rowdy pubs in the cities of the
central plain. The exodus had become something of a
tradition in itself. Nobody thought much of it except
die-hards like Mag Marshall who railed against the
deserters, called them mongrel *gorgios* and spat con-
temptuously into the pot fire to flavour her curses.

Mirrin paid little attention to the matriarch's rant-
ings. She considered the discomforts of the gypsy life
small beer compared to the struggle for existence in a
pithead village in the sump of Lanarkshire. Never had
she looked or felt better. She was slimmer and more
lithe and her hair had a sheen to it. Though Betsy
would have disapproved of the freckles which sprin-
kled the bridge of her straight Stalker nose, the grime of
Blacklaw's dust had been bussed from her skin by the
sea breezes which laved the coast from Ballantrae to
Largs.

Stretching to slacken her shoulders, Mirrin watched
the reapers and binders tackle the last of the rigs with
superstitious zeal.

Suddenly an arm slipped about her waist and hoisted

her from the ground. Snaring her playfully, Tom Armstrong ignored her struggles.

"What are you grinnin' at, m'lad?" Mirrin demanded.

"Yourself, m'flower," Tom answered. "You draw breath as if you'd suck in the stooks, the rooks and half the damned firth as well."

"God's good air is free for all, as far as I know," Mirrin retorted. Contact with Tom's arm rested her. She leaned back against his chest.

"Aye, but of highly variable quality," Tom said. "The sniff here is better by far than the soot where you came from, is it not now, Mirrin?"

"You make it sound as if I'd sprung through a trap door in the roof of Hades."

"I'll tell you this, Mirrin," Tom said, "if Auld Nick himself was fashioning an ambassador to tempt a man from the straight and narrow he could do a deal worse than take you for a model."

Mirrin jabbed her elbow into the man's midriff and, as he released her, spun round to challenge him. "I think that's an insult, Tom Armstrong."

"I meant it as a compliment, for once." Tom grinned again, in the arrogant manner Mirrin had come to know well over the past months.

Over tea at the stall in Lanark back in the spring, Tom had soon persuaded her to try her luck out of the county. They had travelled to Ayr to meet with Mag Marshall's clan and soon Mirrin found herself learning to harrow and hoe and pick over dreels of early spuds shoulder to shoulder with the weatherbeaten tinker women. The life seemed romantic and free. The warm summer weather encouraged her to stay.

Life for Armstrong, however, was a slack tidal process. It was typical of him to assume that she would be content to float with him like flotsam in a backwater until the quickening current of opportunity tugged them apart. Mirrin realised that she could not allow herself to drift into a lasting relationship with this man, that common-law marriage was not for her. The hurt of losing Houston Lamont was too recent to tempt her into giving away her heart again like a Valentine trinket. To do him credit Tom did not regard her as a casual woman. He showed no signs of seeking to cajole her into his bed sack. He treated her as an equal, a fellow spirit, so different from Rob Ewing, the collier who had been daft in love with her. She might have married Rob if he had not been so priggish. Tom was different too from her father and brothers, men steeped in the work ethic, however much they rebelled against its obvious injustices. The past rode easy on Tom Armstrong and the future was a cuckoo-land behind tomorrow's hill—or so Mirrin thought at the time.

"Take a rip at that row with the rest of them, Tom," Mirrin said. "It's a luck-bringer, is it not?"

"Aye, but it's pagan luck."

"Well, since you're no God-fearin' Christian, maybe you'd best lay in stock with the other side.

"You're a real adder-tongue, Mirrin."

"Are you requirin' a hand t'lift that blade?" the girl asked sweetly. "It'll maybe be a wee thing heavy for a skelf like yourself."

Stepping to the rig, Tom bullied into the rank, arched his scythe, paused to catch the rhythm and shuffled on with his mates, their blades devouring the last golden swathe.

No, Mirrin told herself, as she tucked a spray of binding straws into her belt and stooped among the gathering women, Tom Armstrong is not the one for me.

When the last of the harvest was bound and stacked, the tinks and farm hands wended up the land above the bay of Creagan. Drystone dykes defined the contour, leading the eyes to majestic Arran, whale-backed Kintyre and out to the lonely pyramid of Ailsa Craig, blue and insubstantial on the horizon. The sun was veiled by cloud now and only the gaudy voices of gulls and crows and the chittering of sparrow flocks relieved the melancholy. Inland the rowans burned yellow and red-berried in a slant of sunlight, the oaks, elms and beech trees that ringed Lord Scales' estates vivid as braid against the plain brown Holland of the hill, sad too with the soft day's waning.

Mirrin and Tom walked side by side, dusty, sticky, and in need of a sluice at the yard pump before they joined the others in the barn for a feed and the ceremony of totting up the wages. Trestle tables had been set up, laden with potted meats, hugh loaves, butter tubs and a cheese the size of a cartwheel. Kegs of home-brew and gargantuan teapots steaming on hot bricks promised to slake the deepest thirst. For all their anticipation, only the youngest children were entirely insensitive to the sadness of the evening and the end of the long summer—the youngest plus Colly, Mag Marshall's daughter.

Last summer Tom had been indiscreet enough to play the gallant to Colly, and reap the profit of being the apple of Mag's eye. The heavy Melton jacket which warmed his back on cold nights had been the pick of a bundle scrounged in Ayr. All the men in camp had squabbled for it, but it had gone to Tom. The medals and coins which decorated his hat had mostly been presents from old Mag. His surrogate mother-in-law fed him the best gobbets of meat from the pot and, when times were lean, sacrificed others' shares to make sure that her Tom Dandy was fed like a fighting cock.

What the old woman wanted in return for such favours was a husband for Colly, a strong raffish young stallion to breed grandsons out of Colly's loins, grandsons who would assume the name of Marshall and preserve Mag's very tenuous connection with the famous tinker tribe of Galloway. Tom would be a useful addition to the family in his own right, of course. She would soon mould him to her will when she had her claws in him.

"*Tom! Tom!*"

"God!" Tom exclaimed, rolling his eyes heavenward.

"*Tom, it's me!*" Colly insinuated herself between Mirrin and the man, using her plough-handle hips to shove her rival out of step.

"Are you hungry then, Colly?" Tom asked pleasantly. "Ready for the feed?"

"I'm takin' a walk up t'the loch for a dip after supper, Tom," said Colly directly. "Are y'for comin'?"

"I'll see," Tom said.

"It'll be dark b'then, so nobody'll see," giggled Colly.

"It's dangerous swimmin' the loch in the dark."

"Ach, we'll not do much swimmin', if y'know what I mean."

"No, Colly," said Tom, innocently. "What d'you mean?"

"Y'ken fine, Tom," said the girl, slyly.

Pregnancy would be one means of trapping Tom, Mirrin thought. He was probably daft enough to do the honourable thing. After all he was half-tinker and did treat Mag's ravings with a certain respect. Surely he would draw the line at wedding Colly, though. A blind carthorse would draw the line at that.

Ignoring Mirrin, the tinker girl grabbed Tom's arm and threaded it through her own. Mirrin dropped back. Tom glanced over his shoulder, a pained expression flitting across his face as he gave in to the situation that his own lazy opportunism had helped create. Though Mirrin was unaware of it, there was danger in thwarting Mag Marshall's plans, in treating Colly as a dolt. Tom had often witnessed knife-play in the camps in the past and knew only too well what could happen to an outsider—man or woman—who invoked the anger of the matriarch.

The barn supper was almost over before Tom had a chance to free himself from Colly's clutches. Farmer Maclean was doling out the wages, the last act of that year's harvest: five shillings a day for the men, half that for the women, and a sixpence each for children over ten.

Mirrin knotted her silver coins into a cotton scarf and wedged it into the waistband of her skirt. Four shillings of her hard-earned cash would find its way into Mag's scuffed satchel in camp later that night, the matriarch's tithing. But there would be quite enough left over. Some to spend, some to jingle, as her Da used to say, though, God knows, there was seldom enough left to jingle in the Stalkers' house. The coins made a lump against her stomach. She would not squander her earnings. She was too much a collier's daughter to fritter her money away on betting or boozing or on buying gaudy scarves and rings.

She glanced round the barn in search of Tom. As if in answer to her summons, he stole up behind her and gently touched her arm.

"For God's sake, Mirrin," he whispered, "let's away out of here while that damned girl's busy countin' her haul."

"Not goin' for a swim, then?"

"I'm disinclined t'joke about Colly Marshall," Tom said. "Listen, we'll slip away t'the Creagan Inn. It's only about a mile from here."

Conspiratorial glee came over Mirrin. Frustrating Mag and Colly Marshall was just a game to her. She could not take the tinkers seriously. Life was too lax, too rich, too promising to sully with quarrels. Colly was a joke, that was all, and Tom the butt of it.

Ducking behind the ranks still waiting to be paid, she said, "Come on then, m'lad. I'm in the mood t'be plied with gin and lugged home on your shoulder."

The expected quip did not come.

Tom had already slipped out of the barn into the twilit safety of the yard.

The Creagan Inn was a long, low cottage with a thatched roof. It reminded Mirrin of engravings she'd seen of Robert Burns' birthplace, though that was in another part of the county. The inn squatted on the old highway, the traffic largely gone now, tapped off by the new broad road which followed the coast. From the Inn, though, the view was magnificent, out over the raw fields to deep jade waters and the Arran peaks silhouetted by the sun's loitering reflections on the underbelly of the cloud.

Mirrin sighed and settled on the bench in the side garden, back to the whitewashed wall, skirts spread, boots unlaced. Life was good here, a far cry from Blacklaw. Here in the benign countryside she felt at home. Her mood of depression had passed.

She sighed again.

"Is the brew not t'your taste, Mirrin?" Tom asked.

"The brew's fine, Tom. In fact, I'm just thinkin' how good it's been here in Creagan."

"Aye, but we'll be leavin' tomorrow—travellin' south."

"I've no doubt it'll be just as much fun elsewhere."

"Fun? I've heard the rovin' life called many things but never 'fun' before."

"It's fun for me, after what I've been used to."

"Heartless places, mining towns," Tom agreed.

"No, there's as much heart in Blacklaw as anywhere, maybe more," Mirrin said. "It's just the dirt, the sameness of things that makes it ugly."

"The sea's the same the whole way round," Tom told her, crooningly. "All wet. And farms: there you're bound by the needs of the beasts and the changes of season and the arrival of renting day and the markets an' . . ."

"You're not locked in by walls all the time, though."

"You know little of life, I'm thinkin'."

"I know more of life than you'd credit, Tom."

The man shrugged. Clearly he did not believe her.

"I *chose* to hitch on with you," Mirrin said. "I chose t'stick with the Marshall clan an' I'll string along only as long as it suits me."

"Do as you please, y'mean?"

"Aye, an' why not?"

"You're wide of the mark in judging the rovers. We're no more free than your colliers. A winter on the road'll soon show you that, Mirrin. In a twelve-month we'll be back here, harvestin' for Maclean again. It might be a lean year or a fat one, rain or shine or wind, but that'll be all the difference. You should be content, Mirrin."

"I am: very content."

"Aye, but can you be content with insecurity as a way of life? There may seem to you now t'be a wisdom in it, a healing maybe, but that's an illusion."

"For me, or for everyone?"

Tom did not reply immediately. She studied him by the light of the lantern on its bracket by the inn gable. Inside the public bar a man laughed, a bray as gritty as chaff.

At length, he answered her question lamely. "I follow the work, that's all."

"An' I chose the work," said Mirrin. "Until now I lived my life on a rail between the house, the pit and the kirkyard. Tomorrow I'll sleep in a fresh field."

"In the rain, maybe."

It had rained before and the huts and tents had remained snug and dry. Mirrin said, "I wonder why you stick with the tribe, Tom, if you feel that way about it?"

Armstrong shrugged. "It's only a habit. To tell the truth I'm thinkin' of changing my style."

"How?"

He shrugged again. "I might go back to sea."

"I didn't know you'd been a sailor."

"Just a couple of short jaunts as a deckhand, to Denmark an' the Low Countries; but enough to whet my appetite for more. My Daddy was a sailor."

"I thought he was a gypsy."

"He was that too, but there's no law that says a man must be permanently labelled from birth," Tom said. "The old man, my Daddy, didn't take to the road 'til after he met my Mam.

"He wanted her from the moment he clapped eyes on her. At first her family wouldn't put up with a sailor for a suitor. There was fightin' and bloodshed—but he got her in the end. The tinks have always admired persistence, even in *gorgios*. Father gave up the sea and took t'the road and became well known among the travellin' folk."

"When did he die?"

"Nine years ago. I'd just turned seventeen—old enough to look out for myself. Soon after, Mam married a crofter and went t'live on the Isle of Harris where she is still, last I heard."

"So what do you plan to do with your life, Tom?"

"Maybe I'll away t'sea." Tom sipped his ale. "On the other hand maybe I'll try for a farm somewhere an' put down roots. Buy a table t'stick my feet under. It depends on you, Mirrin."

Startled, Mirrin sat forward. "On me? What have I to do with it?"

"I've already saved a bit," Tom said. "If the pair of us worked hard for a year or two and salted away our silver we could start out with a patch of ground of our own."

"We?" said Mirrin. "Are you askin' me t'live with you?"

Enigmatic as ever, Tom grinned. "Unless you feel it'd cramp the style of a free woman like yourself."

Mirrin shook her head in bewilderment. *"You'll* never settle, Tom. Aye, we might go through some sort of tink betrothal, but one day you'd find the pull of the road too strong an' that would be an end of us. You'd be off with a whistle an' never a glance back."

"Don't you trust me, Mirrin?"

"Don't sound so grieved, Tom."

"I'm a man o'my word, Mirrin."

"Aye, but which word, Tom?" Mirrin said. "Anyhow, if you're minded t'settle down, the perfect candidate for a mate's right here in camp."

Tom looked blank for a moment, then his eyes widened in horror. "Colly?"

Mockingly, Mirrin said, "Maybe you'd not get that farm patch, Tom, but you'd have the right t'sling your tent on the driest ground and all the juiciest pickings from the pot. You could even invest your savings in a cuddy-cart for the old woman to drive while you sat in the back an' puffed your pipe like a real tinkie lord."

"Don't jest with me about . . . about Colly Marshall," Tom said. "God, but there's a cold streak in you, Mirrin Stalker. I never noticed it 'til now."

"You're sayin' that just because I refused t'share your bed. Have you never been refused before?"

"I've never asked before."

"Do you usually just take what you fancy?"

"Mirrin, I asked you t'share my life, not just my bed," Tom said.

He finished his ale and rapped the mug down on the bench. She had insulted him, but did not know if that was perhaps part of a devious plan too. She was sure of nothing at that precise moment.

It was almost full dark. An owl was screeching over the hedgerow quite close at hand and a bat, like a fragment of cloth, was flittering in the boughs of the blackthorn.

"I can see you've been hurt in some way, Mirrin," Tom said.

"I told you, I lost my Da and my brothers in . . ."

"I think you've been hurt by a man."

"No man you know, Tom Armstrong."

The tinker was motionless, hands folded in his lap in an attitude akin to that adopted by the old women of the tribes, patient, perceptive and prepared.

"So *that's* it, you're runnin' away from a man," he murmured.

"Maybe I am runnin'," Mirrin said. "But it's not from a man. No, nor to a man either."

Lifting his hat from the bench he shook it to make the coins jingle, studying it and not the girl. He got to his feet.

"We'd better go back," he said. "It'll rain soon."

Mirrin rose too.

"Rain'll not matter now the harvest's in."

"It matters to us," Tom said. "You'll find that out before the year's end."

Lamont's mansion on the knoll outside Blacklaw had changed hardly at all since the days when Mirrin Stalker had been housekeeper. The rooms were still grand and gloomy, heavily varnished like oil-paintings preserved for their heirloom value. In the coal-master's study, the tall coffin-shaped clock still ticked sonorously. The desk was littered with papers, bills and balanced ledgers, a quarry of facts and figures out of which a cloverleaf of liquor decanters and a coal oil lamp jutted like landmarks.

The view from the window behind the desk had a more honest aspect of decay. The first autumn storm had stripped down twigs and leaves, leeched green from the grass and irrevocably puckered the last of the border blooms. Within the mansion the withering was more subtle and insidious and not confined to any particular season.

Neglect showed too on the owner of the house who slouched in his leather chair, boots carelessly propped on the debris on the desktop.

Houston Lamont was handsome in a dark, dour,

doomed Scottish manner that hinted at nobility dishonourably mixed with peasant coarseness. Under a hopsack morning coat his shoulders were as menacingly broad as a coalheaver's, though stooped now as if the effort of hauling a hundred thousand measures of coal out of the earth by proxy had finally caught up with him. His features were furrowed beyond the point of dignified restraint. It was a visage that would have frightened children with its unyielding introversion. But the solitary child of that household had died many years ago, and there would be no others now to rekindle affection and sweeten the bitterness of middle age.

Even Houston's sister Dorothy, whom he loved without fault in spite of her feyness, had been transformed into a sinister threat and, in a sense, stolen from him, though she still lived in a shuttered room upstairs.

Lamont sat motionless, head cocked, gaze riveted to the study door, listening.

The mutter of voices told him that his wife Edith and her housekeeper, Anna Thrush, were hard at work, conspiring. In a minute or so Edith would release Anna to her duties, admit herself uninvited to the study and plunge into the topic which had obsessed her for the past four months.

He held his listening pose until tension prompted him to move. His eyes smarted from the cigar smoke that drooped like withered wreathes within the room. He had not been out of the house in four days, had hardly left this room in all that time, sleeping here two nights out of three.

Rising stiffly he took a few aimless turns around the study, his head pivoting always towards the door, the cigar spilling ash on his jacket lapels and waistcoat beneath. He nursed a kind of rage, tamed by indifference to his own selfish suffering, as a zoo-caged bear will adjust to the wild and savage urges which trouble its cramped captivity.

The women's voices dwindled, then gradually returned, to end in a duet of polite twittering laughter.

Lamont returned to his chair and dropped into it just

as the door opened and Edith entered the room. He watched her warily.

Edith's oval face had become plumper and her body had thickened. In the past months, however, her choice of dress had become less sober and she had even taken to boning to show off her bosom to best advantage. The display of cleavage was not for his benefit. He understood, as he was supposed to understand, that it was for another man, any man, an additional personal fillup to the power that Edith sought in the arena in which she had finally chosen to make her stand.

"My goodness, Houston!"

She held a cambric handkerchief over the lower part of her face and crossed with rapid clipping little steps to the window. She grasped the brass handle, yanked at the sash and eventually raised the frame several inches. The cool dampness of the garden seeped into the room gradually dissipating the tobacco smoke. Edith waited, back to her husband, until streamers of blue-grey smoke thinned then, forcefully, she pumped the sash shut and seated herself on the hardwood chair opposite him.

"I confess, Houston, I am at a loss to understand why you behave in such a manner."

Lamont crossed his feet at the ankles. His boots were drab and unpolished. One lace was frayed. He studied the woman.

Time and events had altered Edith too, but the manner of it was different. Burnished: that was what Edith had become. Others suffering damage found the essential part of themselves dulled: not so Edith. If anything she would appear to have passed over, rather than through the tragedies of the past eighteen years. Aware of his silent scrutiny, Edith's eyes narrowed and her fingers linked in her lap.

"I wish to talk with you, Houston."

Lamont did not respond. How many hours of conversation would be required to change one iota of the past, to restore one fraction of what had been lost?

"Donald Wyld called last evening and you refused to see him," Edith said. "That was hardly the act of a responsible person, Houston. Do you no longer care about what happens at the pit?"

"Donald called here on your instructions, Edith, not on mine. I had nothing to say to him."

Edith simpered. "Wyld's more your man than mine, Houston. He is, I believe, an excellent colliery manager. You have extolled his virtues often enough in the past."

Lamont nodded: Wyld *was* an excellent manager, trained and experienced, seasoned now by the horrors of full-scale disaster and its aftermath.

"Wyld is fast losing patience, Houston," Edith said. "He is, after all, *only* a manager. He needs to be given instructions to function. There are limits to what he can take upon himself, particularly in such an erratic climate."

"Donald knows what to do."

"He has even taken advice from me," said Edith.

Six months ago such an admission would have been unthinkable. It was true that he had neglected the manager, and the management, of the colliery. In the past months, using the determination and fervour which she had formerly applied to social climbing in Edinburgh's aristocratic monkey-puzzle tree, Edith had acquired considerable knowledge of the economics of colliery administration. In fact it would not be too much to say that, recently, she had become almost as much a coalmaster as he was. He regretted, vaguely, the insult to Donald Wyld.

Collecting his wits, Lamont gave the woman a little more of his attention.

"I appreciate that it has not been easy for you, Houston," Edith was saying. "It's because I care deeply for you and for the colliery that has been your life that I am compelled to bring up this matter again."

"What matter, Edith?"

"To implore you to see Sydney Thrush."

"I do not require another manager," said Houston, wearily. "I cannot afford another manager."

"Examine the figures, Houston." The invitation was plangent with irony. "You will find that management of a high order yields high returns. Why, Lord Blaven raised this question only last week before the Commission on Mines. The report was in *The Times*."

Edith had all the half-baked fanaticism of a convert, seizing on every wayward pronouncement as if it was relative to the stink and filth of the seams. Textbook management must seem simple to Edith, stripped of dirt and damp, props, ponies, barrows, engines, cages and, most of all, of men.

Bluntly, Lamont plucked out the most hypocritical phrase from her talk. He said, *"Do* you care deeply for me, Edith?"

"Of course, my dear."

"In consequence, you must also care deeply for Dorothy?"

"I have . . . great sympathy for poor Dorothy."

"Enjoying your regard, Edith, is a dangerous habit."

After a pause, Edith said, "Not so dangerous as it might have been, my dearest."

"Please do go on," Lamont said, acidly.

"I could have blackened the Stalker name and have brought scandal not only to that miserable colliers' family but into our drawing room, into this fine house, the 'mighty' house of Lamont. But I did not."

Smouldering hatred in her husband's eyes did not halt the flow of recriminations and self-justifications.

"What cause have *you* to be bitter?" she continued. "We forged a bargain. I have kept my part of it to the letter. Do you not suppose that the doctor would have been most interested in the degeneration of poor Dorothy's condition? Do you not suppose, Houston, that the medical consultant from Glasgow would have read significance into the fact that Dorothy was rescued from an open window only last Friday—rescued by me, I might add—and that it was obviously her intention to . . . I dare hardly say it."

"Kill herself?" Lamont snapped. "She sought only to escape from the room. Besides, *she* didn't open that window. She hadn't the strength. That window, that second-floor, roof-level window was opened by another hand—*deliberately*."

"Dorothy is stronger than you imagine, Houston,"

said Edith. "Anna Thrush carries bruises from struggling with her."

Lamont could not ignore the possible truth in Edith's claims. His sister was a large woman, gaunt but sinewy. He sank back into the chair, cowering from the doubts that Edith had raised. At length he said, "What more do you want of me, Edith? You run the mansion as you please. You staff it with pallid little skivvies who scamper through the corridors like frightened mice. You entertain such members of society as are prepared to overlook the unrefined source of your capital for the pleasure of helping you spend it and who are polite enough not to raise an eyebrow at my non-appearance at the dinner table. You have found a stalwart companion and highly efficient housekeeper in Anna Thrush. You have banished me . . . "

"No, Houston, I will not allow you to be so hard on yourself. You have *chosen* this ridiculous housebound exile. I did not foist that upon you."

"No matter: no matter," Lamont said. "Just tell me what you want now?"

"Interview Sydney Thrush."

"God!" Lamont lunged from the chair in irritation. He leaned on his knuckles on the debris on the desk, scowling. Her singlemindedness was intense enough to be classed as a vice. *Ennui,* fostered by will-power, took him again and, fishing a cigar from the box, he sank heavily back into the leather and spent some moments with match and tobacco, concentrating his attention on the proper igniting of the cigar. He had hoped, vainly, that Edith would have sense enough to let go. He should have known better.

As he exhaled a cloud of smoke, Edith sat forward in her chair. "Please, Houston," she insisted. "See Mr. Thrush. Judge him for yourself. If you find him as praiseworthy as I believe you will, then you would do well to engage him."

"As what?"

"As colliery manager."

"Over Donald Wyld?"

Lamont watched Edith's struggle. Even her superficial examination of the colliery's financial state must have told her that Wyld would not hold with a downgrading; that if Wyld left there would be trouble, trouble more serious than the general dissatisfaction with wages and conditions that had already resulted in many lost hours of work, pithead scuffles and even the vandalising of surface gear and offices.

"Under Wyld, of course," Edith answered.

"What makes this Sydney Thrush so extra special?"

"His experience."

"Donald Wyld is experienced enough."

"Not in dealing with men."

"Hah! Donald is a wizard with the men, a quieting force."

"Mr. Thrush has more experience in that area, I assure you."

"More?"

"He was employed by Lord Howden."

"Ah!" said Lamont. "You did not include that information in your last anthem to Mr. Thrush."

"And by Mr. James Finnie at Barrowgill in Fife."

"So—Thrush is a strike-breaker."

"He is a rescuer of collieries in trouble."

"A strike-maker, and a strike-breaker," said Lamont. "Where did you acquire the catalogue of his virtues? From Anna?"

"Partly."

"Have you met him?"

"I . . . I have."

"Where?"

"In Hamilton. I was adequately chaperoned, of course."

"Yes, of course," Lamont said. "He impressed you?"

"Yes, Houston. Must I tell you a thousand times. Sydney Thrush is the person we need right now. He could forestall a desparate situation. He could be a great boon in the difficult times that lie ahead. He would take the weight of responsibility from your shoulders, give you more opportunity to enjoy life."

"And if I interview him," Lamont said, "may I ask him how many heads he has cracked, how many families he has cast into the gutter, how many sick children he has helped to the Better Land Beyond?"

"You are *impossible,* Houston!" Edith rose to her feet.

"The pit is not in profit, Edith."

"I know that, you fool."

"It's the profit that concerns you, is it not?"

"The pit is your life, Houston. I am only concerned with saving it."

The hypocrisy was smoothly applied, ire and concern whisked into a bland wifely application. Lamont considered the effects of agreeing to Edith's proposal. He knew that if he interviewed Sydney Thrush he would be obliged to engage him. Wyld would chafe against sharing managerial responsibility but perhaps he would not jeopardise his position by threatening to resign. Edith, for her part, would keep her sharp eye on everything, her protégé Thrush included. And he, nominal owner of Blacklaw Colliery, would hardly have to stir himself out of his chair, only reach for his pen and scribble his signature to the documents that Edith slid before him from time to time.

"I have no need to interview him, Edith," he said, evenly. "If you advise Thrush's employment then I will sanction it. For all it matters to me, you and he and that sister of his, can run the house *and* the pit straight to hell."

Edith showed no trace of triumph.

"But," he said, thinly, "if Dorothy is harmed in any way—d'you hear me, my dearest?—if Dorothy is harmed, then I will contrive to destroy you and your accomplices, aye, and this mansion and all that's in it."

Edith sniffed and lowered her eyelids demurely.

"Are you stating terms, Houston?"

"I am."

"I will send for Mr. Thrush on Monday."

"I have no need to interview him, I tell you."

"Come now, Houston. Such formalities are expected of a coalmaster. They are part of *my* terms."

Lamont rose from his chair and walked lumberingly around the desk towards her. For an instant it seemed that he intended to strike her. She did not quail from him, standing by the door, chin tilted. In him, however, was no aggression, only fatigue and resignation.

"Very well, Edith," he murmured. "On Monday, I will meet with Sydney Thrush."

Four

NONE OF EDINBURGH'S aromatic flavours escaped Andrew Stalker that summer of '76. Fascinated by the capital, he measured its anomalies subjectively. He balanced George Street's wealth against the abject poverty of the Royal Mile's closes, the dignity of kirks and colonnaded banks against the ramshackle decrepitude of the Cowgate, Princes Street's frock coats and pompous toppers against the barefoot tatters of Leigh Walk's scrofulous urchins. With considerable dejection, he was finally obliged to place himself in the company of the lesser mortals of this world. Lamont's annual grant of twenty pounds and tuition, however bountiful it sounded back in Blacklaw, lacked elasticity in the city and could not be made to stretch Drew away from the brink of penury. In his more disgruntled moods, Drew debated if Lamont's parsimony reflected the coalmaster's true regard for Mirrin, and if his passion had, all along, been similarly niggardly.

Whatever the way of it, on the basis of his background and low financial standing Drew found himself excluded from the company of the elegant, roistering bluebloods whose favour he coveted. He was also coldshouldered by his fellows in poverty, lads quite perceptive enough to sense his disdain and be wary of his ruthless superiority. Every passing day, every perambulation through Edinburgh's genteel streets, every imagined slight or prick of envy, served to stiffen Drew Stalker's determination not only to merge with the upper classes but to scale to the summit of their artificial pyramid, via the stout, well-chiselled blocks of the legal profession.

Jobbing for Gow Havershaw had given him insight, indicating that beneath the murmurous courtesy of legal affairs were certain exploitable frailties which an astute young gentleman, shielded by an established firm, might turn to his personal advantage. He salted away such knowledge as raw material which, when he had mastered his letters and acquired the protection of a degree, he might exploit with all the dogged zeal that his father had once applied to pithead politics.

Even Gow Havershaw's niggling refusal to fee him for his services only steeled his resolve to wring wealth and respect from the diffident city.

Gow Havershaw's musty chambers were well suited to business of shady triviality. Around the walls of the inner sanctum, spilling out into the wedge-shaped tank, records of all the Havershaws' past dealings reposed, machinations mummified in dreich rows of lichen-grey box files and liver-coloured cardboard 'melodeons'; interminable correspondence, court reports, deeds, wills, municipal actions, parchments more ornate than Royal decrees, documents fox-spotted with senility, bills, claims, appeals and muted threats—stuffy lawyers' blackmail, twenty thousand tracts on the art of circumlocution. The ceiling friezes were of tartar-yellow plaster, the panelling cracked like dark brown ice-floes, the floorboards warped, the clerks' tall desks stained and upright as town gibbets.

Havershaw had crouched at his desk, back to the leaded window with its four inset panes of bullseye glass which distorted the view of the sober frontage of Dowdall's Temperance Hotel, as if the lawyer could not bear to donate even *that* vantage to his clients clear and unimpaired. A circular wooden chair with a leather cushion, like a cow pat, was aligned before the desk. Havershaw's carved oak throne towered over it, a shelter for the man. He had peered out of a lattice of smokey sunlight, out of shadows of the chair's fretwork and, plucking his lip with his thumb, had hummed and hawed his way to an explanation.

Standing, Drew had not moved a muscle, nor uttered a word in protest. One part of his mind was collecting phrases for the future, another was rioting furiously at the injustice of such legal robbery.

"Ah, Stalker, yes, even during the course of, ah, a single term of instruction, one would have, ah, supposed that you would have, ah, become familiar with the principles attendant on jobbing, and, ah, general clerking and would, ah, have appreciated the inestimable value of taproot training in, ah, procedures not in general covered by the, ah, learned professors. The law student is, of course, ah, expected to undertake such menial work to inculcate in him a respect for the, ah, minutiae of procedures and to, ah, inculcate in him habits of obedience, punctuality and neatness and, ah, all the graces, shall we say, of subservience to the needful disciplines of the law, to which we, ah, are all bounden. But, ah, in apprenticing, shall we say, oneself to a placed member of the profession, the student, ah, is given benefits far beyond those that could be purchased for a fee. Ah?"

Gow Havershaw's eyelids drooped over his pale, sandy eyes as he reclined in the chair and crossed his arms over the lapels of his slope-fronted morning coat. The lawyer's voice reminded Drew of kirk sermons and, by a strange analogy, of port wine and pork with apple sauce.

"Such opportunities are not, ah, scattered upon the cobbles of the Canongate, young man, as, aha, I'm sure you'll agree."

"Sir," Drew had said, tightly.

"Your, ah, patron, Mr. Lamont, will be gratified to learn of your diligence and, ah, co-operation. I shall, as is your due, write him to that effect and assure him that, ah, he is not throwing his silver down the, ah, proverbial stank, if you take my, ah, meaning, Stalker."

"I am not to be paid."

"That is correct."

"But, Mr. Havershaw, I did not expect to be paid."

"Did you not now?" Havershaw's intransient smile had indicated that he knew Stalker to be lying. "You have your personal accounting, ah, in good order,

Stalker? Is it prudently apportioned through the current quarter?"

"Yes, sir." Drew had lied again without a blush.

Drew had hoped that Havershaw would pay him on the last day of the vacation. Indeed, he had counted on it. But he had been quick enough, in the sparring match into which the interview devolved, to evade the lawyer's more cruel jabs and, with that single inspired blow, rob his mentor of much of his advantage.

The lawyer did not like Drew Stalker. Few folk did, as it happened, but Havershaw's dislike stemmed from motives that, oddly, Drew would have upheld as right and proper if the shoe had been on the other foot. Havershaw disliked Drew because he had marked the boy as a social kangaroo and was, perhaps, a little afraid that *he* would be clouted by a clumsy foot as the lad leapt up the ladder of success.

"I am, ah, gratified to learn, Stalker, that you are not given to squandering your subsistence on, ah, tobacco, wine and the, aaahhh, pleasures of the flesh."

"I have more respect for myself, Mr. Havershaw."

"I am, ah, glad to hear it, Stalker."

God knows, the wine had been cheap, a penny per quarter bottle; two cheroots for the same sum and, probably, if he had scoured the stews long enough he might have found a woman willing to educate him in 'the pleasures of the flesh' for the same trifling amount.

Apparently Havershaw had heard rumours of his fondness for sampling the joys of the bottle and the tobacco jar, indulgences which went hand in glove with manliness through all ranks of society. Was the lawyer taking him to task, or merely warning him that such spendthrift ways might mitigate against his success in the years to come? Drew had itched to petition Havershaw for a loan on his next quarter's grant. Logic, and pride, killed the impulse. He had scored well by denying his need for more money. He could not now drop into an unsophisticated stance, even if it meant starving for a week or two. That was how his first jobbing vacation had ended, in an armed truce between lawyer and student.

By the end of September, however, Drew was be-

ginning to regret his rash gesture of pride, to wish that
he had a crown in lieu of satisfaction. He had already
written home, a hopeful procedure now that Mirrin
was not on hand in Blacklaw to spread her spiteful
poison against him. Kate would see him right. He could
depend on the family's weakness, their loyalty.

Cheered by his faith in Kate, Drew Stalker saw no
reason to economise excessively and, as was his habit,
continued to eat his evening meal in the *Cockerel*
tavern—and let October take care of itself.

On the cobbled stoop of the Lawnmarket close to the
dive of the West Bow the houses scrambled up in careless tiers like tattie boxes plastered together with
pitch and buckram and roughly faced with stone. High
lofts jutted precariously over the pavements and elon-
gated ochre and coke-black chimney stacks protruded
like mitten fingers through the uncertain slates. The
whole conglomeration of Shannon's Close was perched
on a row of porous wooden posts behind which shops
and warehouses cowered in timid self-effacement as if
they doubted their ability to withstand the tilt and
would, some gusty night, shrug off their superstructures
to a toss of wind from the Forth. In one of the attic
summits Drew Stalker pored over his volumes of Scots
Law and, occasionally, slept. Comparatively speaking,
it was a fairly respectable lodging, though it shared in
the general sleaziness which spread round the Castle
Rock and the High Kirk of St. Giles.

A mile downhill towards Holyrood, tucked into
Geddes Wynd, Drew had discovered the *Cockerel*
tavern. It was conveniently close to his lodgings, to the
Law Courts, and to the 'New' University on the South
Bridge, and to Havershaw's High Street chambers.
Unless the inclination took him, he had no need to
travel beyond the confines of the Old Town. But the
Cockerel had other advantages. Few students patronised it, and it was cheap and strident enough to provide an antidote to the arcadian stuffiness of the
university and the isolation of his Shannon's Close attic.
Within a month of his arrival, Drew regarded the tavern as his second home.

The *Cockerel's* alcoves were lit by sooty lamps clamped to hamhooks in the brown brick walls. The uneven flagstones were strewn with butchers' sawdust. Furnishings consisted of solid rectangular tables and priory benches through which blowsy serving girls weaved their hazardous courses. Drew enjoyed the coarse repartee although, tucked away at a small table in a draughty nook far from the hearth, he took no part in it. Nursing his supper or tipple of wine, he remained an inconspicuous onlooker. When he became a lawyer no doubt he would have dealings with such folk. Studying them now, he tried to fathom motives for behaviour so irrational that no legal system in the world could take account of it.

Drew had another reason for patronising the 'cauld corner' of the *Cockerel*. Unwittingly he had attracted the attention of an admirer, a useful contact for a young man short of the readies.

The girl's name was Heather Campbell, a slightly-built Highlander of an age with himself. Heather's contribution to Drew's welfare came in the form of double helpings of shepherd's pie, stovies, broth and rice pudding. The high-handedness with which the student treated the serving lass—while graciously accepting her charity—only served to strengthen her conviction that Drew was somebody very special who would, some day, rise above squalor. Heather had been orphaned at the age of seven, a ward of the Inverness Parish Council who, in their wisdom, had judged her fit to earn her own living at the age of fifteen. As she was a personable, quiet-spoken girl, if not too robust, she had been earmarked for something out of the ruck of farm or parish work and duly 'found' to act as companion to an elderly lady who had need to make the arduous coach journey from Inverness to Edinburgh. Heather was assured that when she reached the capital, if she had performed her duties in a satisfactory manner, she would be given permanent employment as the lady's companion. It all sounded too good to be true—and it was.

The elderly lady's indisposition was the result of insatiable thirst. At every stop on the way south

Heather had found herself involved in squabbles with
the landlords of various inns. Once the lady had evaded
her guardian completely and had run cackling into the
bracken clutching a bottle under each arm. It had
taken the entire coachload of passengers, plus crew,
to winkle her from her lair and drag her, bawling
boisterous ditties, back to the carriage. The experience
had terminated in Edinburgh. The old lady had been
whipped off by her daughter to a Home for Inebriates
in Liberton, Heather being summarily discharged on
the grounds of gross negligence.

Destitute and homeless, Heather had flinched from
throwing herself on the mercy of the parish in this unfamiliar and frightening city. She had no desire to come
under the thumb of another official body, to be treated
like refuse again and swept quickly out of sight. She
had been near to starving when she had chanced on the
Cockerel and learned that the position of skivvy was,
not surprisingly, vacant. At least she was assured of
three shillings a week, a square meal a day and a
mattress in the slum tenement adjacent to Geddes
Wynd. She shared a cupboard-sized room on the back
upper floor with four other working girls and received
from them, in short order, a theoretic education in the
ways of the world. It was remarkable that, up to the
time she met Drew, her innocence had remained un-
curdled, that she had not followed her companions'
advice to find herself 'a chap or two' to supplement her
income.

It was immediately obvious to Drew that Heather
Campbell's naïvety was mixed with self-pity, a for-
givable quality however that had no trace of melo-
drama to it but rather a weird, prophetic, inimitably
Celtic melancholy. She was safe enough from the
Cockerel's seducers; too shadowy a presence to excite
them, too skinny to appeal to bluff rogues in off the
streets who preferred a sparkle in a girl's eye and a
broad beam to occupy their knees.

That Heather liked Drew was patently obvious. He
had remarked such behaviour in other girls, coyness
and blushing which, in Blacklaw at least, soon had
them tumbling into bed, with or without the benefit of

a wedding ring. Pride had no place in his relationship with the servant. Until that evening, he had never deigned to explain his exact situation to her. As she approached to take his order, however, he saw in her a saviour and, for the first time, turned on the poor-lip in the hope of exploiting her sympathies.

He put a single penny on the board between his half-closed fists and, looking down at it, said, "That's all I have. What'll it buy?"

The frank admission of poverty had its expected effect.

Heather gave a little crooning groan.

"It's not even enough for a bowl of broth, is it?" He glanced up at her. Her eyes were round, her cheeks flushed. She looked, he thought, as if she might weep for him.

He waited.

The girl said, "I'll . . . see what I can do."

It took her an hour, piecemeal, to secure him the kind of supper that a healthy young man required. But in the end Heather supplied, at no charge, a brimming bowl of kail soup, a broken cob loaf, a plate heaped with potatoes and pork belly and a slice of currant cake which another customer had abandoned. She even managed to thieve him a short tipple of red wine to wash down the meal. Drew rewarded her by giving her more than a cursory glance. . .

She was not unattractive, really. Slender rather than skinny, her movements, as she threaded between the tables, light and graceful. He sipped his wine. He could not imagine what he had done to so stun this highland waif that she would risk her job to keep him fed—but he had no conscience about it. Until that evening, he had done nothing to invite her charity. She seemed to like being of service to him. Clearly, out of human decency, he ought to provide her with further opportunities—being careful to preserve his dignity, of course.

When Drew quietly suggested that he might walk her home to her lodgings when the tavern closed at midnight, Heather Campbell needed no second invitation. He waited for her at the mouth of the Wynd, standing in the shadows away from the lamps while buxom girls and their beaux for the night hurried, laughing and giggling, past him, and weazen wee men, pickled in whiskey, reeled gently away over the cobbles to their nests. The Old Town of Edinburgh, pickled in history, seemed to stagger too, toddling uphill into the dry, cold sky. A skit of moonlight was caught in the cloven shadows of pots and turrets. A salt breeze whispered in from Leith and Portobello, Musselburgh and Aberlady, from the Bass Rock and the North Sea beyond, stirring the rubbish in the yard and neglected washing which still hung in pale hanks from the bows of the houses opposite.

Heather wore a man's flannel jacket, stitched up at the cuffs and tuck-sewn at the waist to make it fit at all. It swept away from her bodice and soiled skirts in a style that, in the wan moonlight, mimicked the fashions of those society ladies who were going in for rational dress that year. Drew bowed as she hesitantly approached and, from instinct, not courtship experience, took her hand and inserted it formally into the crook of his arm. He heard her catch her breath.

"Which way?" he asked.

"It's not far."

"That's unfortunate."

"Why do you say that?"

"It gives me less opportunity to talk to you, Heather."

It was the first time he had called her by name.

To cloak her confusion, she said, "It's that house, just there."

"Conveniently situated for the tavern, I see."

"Aye," the girl said, adding, "It's not much of a place. I don't earn much, you see."

They were strolling along the cobbles adjacent to the building in which Heather had her lodging. The night was still full of sly and stealthy sounds, perforated now and again by more raucous shouts or peals of laughter or the clatter of a post-chaise carrying some raffish gentleman in search of pleasure.

Drew was inclined to play the part of man-about-town. Common sense decided him against it. After all, he was cultivating this girl in the hope of obtaining free meals. Trading on her sympathies would serve his purpose best. He injected a certain wistfulness into his tone. "I don't earn anything at all, Heather."

"How do you live, then?"

"I . . . ah, I have an annuity which covers my tutorial fees, but apart from that . . ." Tactfully he stopped, too noble, too modest to burden her with his personal troubles.

Gratified, he felt her hand tighten on his arm; then, unexpectedly, his gratification was tinctured with another emotion, novel and not altogether pleasant. With less aplomb, he said, "Good of you to give me food tonight. First I've had for a couple of days, in fact. Keep me going for a week, it will."

"You've no money, Drew?"

Anxiety for his welfare caused her to use his name without embarrassment.

"A temporary state," Drew said, airily. "I'm used to making sacrifices for my career."

Heather said, "What is it you're studying at the university?"

"The Law," Drew answered, importantly.

The girl was so impressed that she could think of no further conversation for a moment.

Sighing, and patting her hand on his arm, Drew said, "Aye, the law: a damned hard taskmaster."

She stopped him gently, staring at him. He knew that he had impressed her. Whatever else happened in October, he wouldn't starve—not unless she was careless enough to be caught pilfering. He must advise her on that. Later, not now.

The girl said, "But you're not . . . not . . . ?"

Smiling, Drew said, "Not a gentleman, do you mean?"

"No, I . . . You're not like the other student gentlemen, Drew."

"My father is dead," Drew said. "My mother struggled to give me my opportunity. It was only at the insistence of my schoolmaster that I tried for a place on the faculty bench at all."

The girl smiled too, suddenly. "You'll not need to go hungry, Drew, not while I'm still in the kitchens."

"I can't allow that," Drew warned. "It's dreadfully risky. Besides, I have some pride, you know."

"You can pay me back."

"How?"

"You can be my escort some nights, like this. See me safe to my house—that's if you want to."

"That isn't repayment," Drew said glibly. "That is a privilege an' pleasure."

The girl blushed and turned her head away so that her fair hair swung across her face, screening it.

"Now," Drew said, "it's late and you must be weary. Which house?"

"That one."

Drew led her across the cobbles into the pend. Externally, it was not so different from his own lodging but lower, older, more rank. Rats scuttled in the common middens which mounded up one corner of the yard. A fractured gas-mantle gave dim light to the scene. The breeze wheezed asthmatically in the closes and wynds and crankily rotated a chimney-cowl high, high overhead.

Heather loitered in a dark corner just under the arch from the street.

Drew hesitated. He knew—or thought he knew—what she expected of him. What disturbed him was not the gesture itself but the fact that he wanted to take her in his arms. Roughly, he tugged her towards him and slid his arm about her waist. He drew her closer than he intended, crushing her against him so that he could feel her breasts even through the bodice, pressing softly against him. Abruptly he was no longer in control.

Astonishment possessed him almost as much as hunger for the girl. Heather's hair was soft, her lips soft, the swelling of her breasts soft. At that moment, Drew wanted to hurt her for being more to him than he had ever intended. Confusedly he kissed her mouth, long, hard and unrelentingly, arms rigidly about her, her body pliant against his.

"It's . . . it's late: I m . . . m . . . must b'gettin'

back now," Drew Stalker stammered. "I . . . I . . . I've got work t'do t'night: studies."

As he pivoted away from her, harried and anxious, she caught at his sleeve. Furiously he glanced back over his shoulder, the anger melting instantly at the tenderness in her eyes.

"Come tomorrow," she whispered. "Tomorrow night."

"Co . . . come where?"

"For your supper, Drew; to the tavern."

"Aye: yes: I'll do that," Drew Stalker promised and, without another word, hurried out into the cobbled street and, veering west, ran for the top of the town.

Wallace was no summer stallion, no russet-maned quality high-stepper with fetlocks like daffodil stems and a brisk gentlemanly nature. Wallace was three parts Clydesdale to one part Shire, with a stubborn streak that had ruined the temper of three ploughmen and four leathery carters in a mere decade of endeavour. Recalcitrance had reduced Wallace to the kind of bargain that Willie Kellock could not resist in spite of the fact that the bloody animal had champed the banknotes out of his fist even as he tried to pay the knacker for the privilege of hauling his purchase away.

Wallace was too healthy a lump of horseflesh to fall prematurely to the knacker's spike, too wicked a brute for much else. In that first night in his new home he had baptised his nice clean stable in the bakehouse yard with a sufficient quantity of urine to float a coal-barge and had hoofed a hole in the back planks large enough to admit the Northrigg band marching in column of route. But Willie admired spirit in men, women and four-legged animals and stuck to Wallace grimly. He finally reached an uneasy truce with the nag by pampering his manic fits and feeding him hugely on hay, choice oats, greenbite and the odd currant bun.

Maybe it was the buns that persuaded the stallion that he was better off bending a bit to the wee man's will than winding up as the filling in a batch of so-called mutton pies. For whatever equine reason, Wallace eventually allowed himself to be cajoled into the shafts of Kellock's van and coaxed into pulling the flimsy thing round the streets of Blacklaw. Wallace could even be bribed, with currant buns, of course, into standing still long enough for Willie to press a few sales before taking it into his head to look for a less draughty stance and clumping off without warning, leaving a shoal of protesting colliers and a trail of breadrolls scattered in his wake.

Flora Stalker, however, did not subscribe to bribery. She gave the huge iron-shod frosty-maned stallion no quarter in the campaign. In fact, Flora was not even aware that war had been engaged until the morning's run was almost over that first day of her employment, Monday, October second.

Flora had arrived early at the bakehouse to find Willie already easing his second batch of rolls from the ovens. With trepidation Willie had led the woman to the stable and, shielding her, had lifted the bar and opened the door. Wallace had remained passive, anticipating his usual breakfast treat. Instead of Willie heaving an oatbag or bond of hay, though, in strolled an empty-handed stranger, a big-boned female with a look in her eye that Wallace instantly distrusted. Being wily as well as truculent, he did not rebel at once. He bided his time, snorting a little when the woman buttered him up with the sort of phrases that wifies reserve for babies. In spite of her flattery, the woman paid him no serious attention as she lifted his collar from the stall hook and, on Willie's instructions, put it and all the leather and brass tack onto the horse.

Wallace restrained himself. He sized her up. It was her eye that he really didn't like. There was no temper in it, no trace of the wary baker's patience. It was like no eye Wallace had ever encountered, indifferent to his stature and reputation, suggesting that the woman thought of him as nothing more than a horse.

Still brooding, he was led from the stable and hitched to the cart. He looked back then, past the blinkers, along his bulging flanks, to observe the woman climb

on to the seat in the cart's cowl which was usually reserved for the wee man. When he experienced the tug
of the reins, Wallace realised that he had a novice on
board. With a whinny of amusement, he pretended to
obey her commands and went out of the yard like a
lamb.

Plodding like some blown old dray-drudge, he swung
right. That was the usual route; no positive guidance
came through the leathers. Besides, the wee man was
tramping along close to his crupper, alert for any sign
of rebellion and toting, unusually, not a bag of buns
but a barrel-slat heavy enough to indent even Wallace's well-tanned hide.

Mildly, Wallace pulled into the collar on the steep-
ening hill, like so many of the giants of his breed who
seemed to crave human approval and affection, past
the *Lantern*, past the last of the rows. He stopped at
the gates, watched them open and disgorge a shower
of dirty colliers who made for the hatch in the tarpaulin, but steered wide of him as if he was a basket-
ful of snakes and not just a poor humble old horse. He
waited motionless, moved on when told, and waited
again.

At the third halt Willie gave the woman some final
instructions in cartmanship, and murmured advice—
so Wallace couldn't hear—on how to cope with an
emergency. Aye, an emergency! There would be a
proper time and place for that, Wallace told himself.
And he would pick both.

Willie Kellock returned to his bakehouse, leaving
the woman in sole charge.

Wallace whinnied softly to himself.

High and mighty on her perch, the woman *cleeked*
at him as if he was a pussycat. She waggled the reins.
Obediently Wallace rounded the butt of the yard
where stout sleepers made up the fencing. He went on
between mounds of dross across the spur of the pit
rails. He didn't even pretend to be frightened when
a shunter whooped, a noise which usually provided
him with an excuse to practise his lion rampant act
and spill a few more bakings to crop up on the return
journey.

Languorously Wallace clopped up to the row of ancient earth-coloured cottages on a flat hillside over-looking the pit workings. Here a clutch of old-biddy widows lived on the bounty of their families, a laza-rette of discarded grannies who appreciated the con-venience of Kellock's service and bought rolls and sweet things every morning as part of their planned communal economy. They were much surprised to see Flora Stalker—her that was Duncan's lass, and Alex's wife—sitting on the board, and kept her blethering a while. Wallace waited, his big belly rumbling, think-ing not of reward but of revenge.

It was only when the woman had flapped the reins and he had brought the vehicle round and down the gradient towards the dirt patch that spread out from the rees where his hoofs would have grip and traction and no cobbles to skliff upon that Wallace elected to show his mettle—and ran away.

Gradually he picked up the pace. The cart bounced over muddy ruts, slithering on its clench. Flora sawed at the reins and shouted at her charge, ordering him to *Whoa*. Wallace snickered, filled his lungs with air, snapped his neck into the collar and let the pull of the hill take him. Churning the ground with his hoofs, he accelerated until he felt his mane flick out and the strap-tabs stiffen like oak. He passed the sleeper fence but did not wheel left. The shunter shrilled, in panic now, for Wallace, the woman and the cart shot under its buffer with only feet to spare.

Clinging to the reins, Flora's thick legs locked under the seat, feet splayed to hook into the wrought-iron struts. Behind her, under the tarp, rolls, loaves, pies, bridies and buns were hopping in confusion like peas on a hot girdle and spewing from the loosened hatch flap on to the ground. Her rump ached already. Her arms felt as if they were being torn from her shoulders. Her head shoogled forward and back. It was all she could do to keep herself from shutting her eyes to blank out the rush of the workings and the rise of palings which separated the backs of the miner's rows from the waste ground.

At any moment Flora expected to be hurled to the dirt and killed outright. Her past life danced before her eyes. She called out to Kate to save her. But there was no slackening, no idleness to encourage subconscious nostalgia. The fragments of her past were shaken and thoroughly dispersed as the stallion galloped into the sagging fence and trampled it flat on its rusty wires, forming a gap through which the van hurtled, leaping on to the rank grass sward.

Women were running out from the houses, bawling in fear, searching for their toddlers, snatching away the baskets in which their infants slept, though the runaway was past by that time. Wallace headed on through the strings of washing which draped the drying greens until he was caparisoned like a knight's charger in a jousting tournament, caped in sheets, stockings and shifts. A pair of navy-blue drawers flew from one ear.

Strangely, Flora's initial terror had diminished. She sensed perhaps that the horse was not mad, nor truly scared, and that his rampage was controlled enough to cause no damage to himself. Precariously she raised herself on the board and flung all her weight on the reins, canted backwards into the mouth of the tarpaulin tent which, swaying on its bindings, threatened to tear loose at any moment. A peculiar elation gripped her as, yard by yard, she felt the stallion weaken and hesitate, though the ride was far from over.

Women and men were pouring on to the grass which separated the rows, night-shift workers dragged from their beds to help avert disaster, the usual legion of adventurous bairns who had no more sense then to run in the cart's wake salvaging the cakes and pies which fell like manna from heaven. In a cloud of flour, Willie Kellock puffed into the backs, far up in the lane's end by the kirkyard wall. Barrel-slat in hand, he panted after his property as fast as his legs could carry him.

Wallace's tour of the cottages took in the entire length of the backs, a half mile or more down the arena of grass and stunted shrubs. He might have gone on past the rear of the Stalkers' house, out on to the tongue of moorland by Poulter's burn if he had been a few years younger and had less girth.

As it was, the horse suddenly called a halt to his flight. Slewing wide to give the woman at the reins a final lesson, he slammed the van broadside into a tangle of thorn bushes; then he stopped, braced to collect the brunt of the van's weight along the shafts. But, cushioned by the thorns, the van did not yield. After a quick peep to ensure that the woman had been discarded, Wallace bent his neck and nonchalantly nibbled the weeds as if nothing at all had happened.

On all fours Flora Stalker crawled from the rear of the van. Canvas was torn, trays broken, counter lids askew, the floor slanted so she had no need to lower the little wooden ladder to climb, sore and shaky, to the ground.

"Mrs. Stalker! Oh, Mrs. Stalker, are y'all right?"

"What a thing t'happen!"

"Flora, are y'hurt?"

Women who had not exchanged a civil word with her all summer long were solicitous now. Gathering in a wide circle, chary of coming too close to the wild brute that had done so much damage to the drying greens, they offered anxious condolences from a distance.

Flora leaned against the tail-board. She plucked a bridie from the neck of her dress. Could she trust her legs to carry her? Spots jigged in front of her eyes for an instant, but, when she inhaled, cleared away. In spite of throbbing muscles and jangled nerves, she experienced a vivid awareness of the world about her, a refurbishment of the all-too familiar environs of Blacklaw and, in that precise instant, a lurching strength. Danger, terror and triumph melted into conscious self-reliance. When Callum Ewing, first man on the scene and an old friend, tried to take her arm to lead her away, she shook him off.

"I'm . . . fine, Callum."

The old miner was clad only in shirt and trousers, braces dangling, feet bare. He peered into her face.

"Flora, come away t'our house and lie down."

Before she could reply, Willie Kellock broke through the ranks and waving his slat like a claymore, shouted,

"Mrs. Stalker, how can I apologise enough. I'll kill that damned animal, so I will."

"Aye, you've a damned cheek sendin' an old woman out alone wi' that four-legged devil," Callum snapped.

The baker drew up as if shot. "I told her in advance what to expect, but she . . . she insisted."

"A bloody mad stallion," Callum retorted. "Should be put down, both you an' the horse, if y'ask me."

A chorus of agreement rose from the women and miners, though the men, by and large, were too interested in returning to their beds to become involved now that danger to life, limb and property was past.

Callum wagged his finger in Willie's face. "Bloody irresponsible, that's what it was."

"No harm done," said Willie, shrilly. "No harm done, though. You're not injured, Mrs. Stalker?"

"I'm fine, I tell you."

"Get rid o'that horse."

"I'll . . . I'll do that," Willie capitulated. He looked over at Wallace who, with ears pricked, pretended to crop the weeds. The baker lifted the stave threateningly and said, without genuine conviction, "I'll . . . eh, teach him."

"Wait," Flora said. "Leave the beast t'me."

The men stared at her.

She had composed herself, mouth firm, hair tucked back in place under the shawl, crumbs of ruined stock brushed from her dress. She put her hands on her hips.

"I suppose I'll get the sack now, Mr. Kellock?"

Willie hedged. "Well, no, I . . . I'll find you other work, Mrs. Stalker, that's the least I can do."

"I should bloody think so," Callum added.

"And the van?" asked Flora.

"I'll . . . I'll have to give that up."

"That's what I thought you'd say."

Without another word, Flora walked past the men, down the side of the couped cart and the stallion's flanks. She stripped off remnants of clothing which still draped him and threw them aside, then placed herself in front of him so that, blinkered or not, the horse could not help but notice her. Wallace raised his head until his face slowly came level with the woman's. Before he could even think about another tantrum, she caught him by both ears and held his head like a sack of barley, steadying his muzzle and compelling him to look her straight in the eye.

Of course, Wallace did not understand what he saw there.

It is doubtful if a man could have fathomed the depths which lay below the authority of the Stalker woman's gaze, the hurts and the healings, the bone-hard will developed in youth, tempered by the sufferings, large and small, of life in a pithead village. It was all in her gaze now, an indifference to something as banal as a wilful horse, something as transient as the physical pain he had caused her, a fleabite beside the real wounds of grief and loneliness which she had endured and survived.

Wallace read none of this. But she informed him by that fixed stare, that she had only contempt for him, scorn for the thought that he could dissuade her from her purpose. When he had the temerity to snuffle and chaffer and try to lift his head, she thumped him on the muzzle. Not a savage blow, it was pronounced enough to assure him that *she* was the boss and *he* the servant in the circumstances which had thrown them together. He was nothing but a Clydesdale, and he had better not forget it again.

Flora released the ears.

The stallion remained as still as a monument in chastened acknowledgment of her superiority.

Flora said, "Pull that van out of the bush, an' straighten it up. Mr. Kellock, would you be good enough to check the fastenings?"

"But . . . ?"

"If you will, please."

Callum Ewing grinned, "Do as she says, Mr. Kellock."

The old collier had often wondered how much of her husband's fighting spirit had rubbed off on Flora. Now he had an answer. It happened that way with some women, a late flowering of an independence that they never knew they possessed. He had no need to worry about Flora Stalker any more.

Rounding up help, Callum Ewing put his shoulder to the wheels and righted the van in minutes.

Alone, Flora Stalker climbed into the cowl and seated herself square on the bench. Ashen beneath his flour coating, Willie handed her the reins. She flicked them, waking Wallace from his trance, and tugged right to lead his head round.

As she drove the bakehouse cart slowly up the drying greens, the citizens of Blacklaw cheered. Flora smiled to herself. She was no longer afraid.

The bad-tempered horse had been broken and, it seemed, much else besides. She felt that she could face the prospect of the rest of her life now with equanimity.

The wind had changed. Skating down from the north, it caused the Blacklaw folk to huddle deeper into their threadbare overcoats and dig out their scarves and gloves for darning. In the early morning greasy ice slicked the main street's cobbles. Weather-sages grumbled that it was too soon for frost and that the winter in consequence would be severe. Flora Stalker was of that opinion and, Kate reflected, her mother wasn't often wrong these days.

Kate pulled the shawl round her ears and tucked the little parcel under her arm. In the parcel were three squares of sliced sausage, three rounds of black pudding and a scrag-end of mutton. The butcher's bill had been cheap—as life itself, so Kate thought, was cheap in this sad, black village. Only her mother, of all the elders of Blacklaw, seemed happy these days.

A weird transformation had come over Mam since she had found work at the bakery and, even more odd, since her fracas with Kellock's horse. The incident had caused laughter in the village but Kate could only shiver in horror at the thought of how close to tragedy the Stalker family had sailed again. Mam could have been killed or maimed, then what would she—Kate —have done? She *could* do no more. The effect of that wild charge had been a tonic to Flora, however. She

defended the awful stallion now the way some colliers
defended their scrawny whippets, talking of Wallace
as if he was nothing but a big unruly lad.

Worry, Kate thought, was becoming a habit. Close
consideration of their current circumstances showed
that the Stalkers had little to fret about, not compared
with previous years or the state some of their neighbours were in. They had free tenancy of the narrow
house. Together they were pulling in a wage totalling
more than one hard-working miner could extract from
Lamont in a week's graft at the face. For all that,
Kate fretted. She picked at the prospect of disasters
that *might* befall them, vague fears for Mirrin and
Drew and Betsy, though all three, and Mam, seemed
more than able to take care of themselves.

"God, Kate, you look right down in the mouth."

The speaker had been leaning against the wall of
the public house. Kate had hardly noticed him as she
approached. He pushed himself away from the brick
and, taking his hand from his pocket, caught her
shoulder. The gentleness that had once been in Rob
Ewing's touch was gone. There was an almost desperate anxiety in his grasp, as if he needed assurance
that she wouldn't spurn him. As if she would! In spite
of his quarrel with Mirrin, Rob Ewing had always
been her friend. She hadn't seen him for months,
though, not since the early summer in fact. Though the
village was small and both worked at the pit, the division of shifts and—with the drawing in of the community's belt—the absence of social events had kept
them apart. Kate had no interest in politics, Rob
Ewing's hobbyhorse until his marriage to young Eileen
McMasters back in the spring, a marriage which,
through no fault of the bride or groom, had rapidly
turned sour.

It was Sunday morning, early. Chapel bells clanged
for mass, the sound drifting forlornly over frost-
white fields. It would be three hours yet before the
kirks wakened the sparrows in their towers, and colliers' families, those who still professed faith in God,
would troop out into the streets in sober, mothball-
reeking Sabbath garb and make for their chosen place

of worship, the Church of Scotland, the Baptist, or the tin shed that served the Evangelical Society, a livelier, if more demanding Christian band.

Though it was frowned upon by the 'unco guid' the village shops sneaked open for a spell on early Sunday morning and the *Lantern* would unlock its doors to a 'registered clientele' from one o'clock until two-thirty. Rob could hardly be waiting for the pub to open.

Kate said, "How's Eileen now, Rob? Stronger, I hope?"

"Aye," Rob said, still holding Kate. "The doctor seems pleased with her progress."

"You're . . . out early," Kate said, tentatively.

"Fresh air," said Rob.

"Walk down with me an' I'll make us some tea."

Rob hesitated, then nodded.

His bluff boyishness was gone now. His blond hair was as lank as his ungroomed moustache. His high colour—more suited to a farmer than a miner, Mirrin used to say—had paled to fishbelly grey. He had lost much weight. Of an age with Kate, almost to the month, he looked much older now. She wondered if she appeared as haggard to him.

"Have they indicated what the trouble is?" Kate asked. "With Eileen, I mean?"

Kate had heard rumours, some of them nasty, about young Eileen Ewing's affliction. The girl had lost a baby in the third month and had been a semi-invalid since. There were many questions that Kate wanted to ask Rob. Mam had had news from Callum, Rob's father, for the old collier still came about the house to do small chores for the women. But Callum, normally forthright and frank, was defensive about his daughter-in-law's illness and pooh-poohed the Stalkers' concern.

Rob released Kate's shoulder. "Aye, I would like a cup o'tea," he said, leaping her question about Eileen's health.

It pained and embarrassed him to talk of it. Many miners considered that there was shame in sickness, a lack of the innate strength which was the boast of every working man. Kate let the subject lapse and conversation as they walked on down the hill was disjointed. Rob's troubles eroded the communion between them, and they scratched for common interests.

Rob said, "Goin' to the kirk later?"

She shook her head. "Are you?"

Rob said, "For what? To be told about Heaven? I've little enough credulity left, Kate, but what I have I'll save for believin' in a better world here on earth."

This bitterness was new in Rob. It mirrored her own disillusionment.

Rob laughed mirthlessly. "John Kerr thinks paradise is t'be found in America."

Jumbled snippets of information regarding the huge continent on the far side of the Atlantic had come to Kate through items in the *Hamilton Advertiser*. It did not strike her as paradise, though maybe it was manly enough to appeal to youngsters like Johnny Kerr— and even to staid Rob Ewing.

"Is he going?" Kate asked.

"He's savin' for the passage. He wants t'farm."

"Farm?"

"But he's got a job open," Rob sneered. "A job in a Pennsylvanian coalmine. Does the stupid bugger not see that he'll be trapped there just like he's trapped here?"

"Maybe you're wrong, Rob."

"It's not wrong." Rob spat on the pavement. "He'll never work on a bloody farm. He'll die wi' a lamp in his hand just like those of us who stay home."

Kate was dismayed at the change in Rob. He had valid reason for bitterness, for hating the colliery. Not only was his wife ailing, but Callum too was ill, a victim of anthracosis caused by inhaling coaldust year after year. It was a major cause of death among miners, more damaging, though less dramatic, than accidents. She'd seen sufferers—two out of every five men above the age of forty—gasping for breath, hawking up phlegm so filthy that it didn't seem possible for the human system to contain it. It had been inevitable, Kate supposed, that Callum would fall heir to colliers' blight: her father too would have contracted it if he'd lived. It was part of the price of survival, of living longer than one should. She had no need to press

Rob for details. The insidious nature of anthracosis was all too familiar. Callum would work for another six months or a year before the strain told on his heart, then he would be dismissed to become a ward of his son's charity, a wheezing, choking cripple fit only to crawl from the bed to the fireside chair until he was strangled by black dust clogging his lungs. A year ago Kate would have wept for Callum Ewing; now she regarded such happenings as the starch which stiffened the loose and shapeless fabric of village life.

When they reached the door of the Stalkers' house, Rob paused. He looked up at the attic window where Drew had once burned his candle far into the small hours.

"I . . . I won't come in after all, Kate," Rob said. "I'd better get home. Eileen wearies for my company."

"What is it?" Kate asked once more. "Can't you tell me what's wrong?"

"A thing called angina," Rob said. "Her heart's damaged. It was an illness she had when she was a child. Carrying the baby, I suppose, brought it back."

"I'm sorry, Rob. She'll maybe be all right."

"Aye, as long as she rests. No . . . no excitement. No bairns, Kate," Rob said. "At nineteen, she's finished as a wife."

Kate touched his arm. "You shouldn't . . ."

"Shouldn't what? Shouldn't say things like that: give up hope of a miracle or face up to facts. It's the truth, though, Kate, an' I'm man enough t'acknowledge it. I should've heeded Mirrin. I should not have married. I should've packed it in here and set out for a cleaner country."

"In America?" said Kate quizzically. "In Pennsylvania, maybe?"

"Have you heard from Mirrin?"

"Not lately."

"Where is she?"

Kate shrugged. "I'm not certain. In the Borders, I think."

"Happy t'be shot of this dungheap, I'll wager."

"Mirrin can look out for herself."

"Aye," Rob said. "I must go, Kate."

"Give my love to your father an' your wife."

Rob nodded curtly. "An' if you hear from Mirrin," he said, "be sure pass on my . . . fondest regards."

"I will," Kate lied. She would not mention Rob to Mirrin. The collier was married now and must, like the rest of them, shoulder his burden without the illicit pleasure of harking back to what might have been.

Five

THICK AND GLUTINOUS clay clung to Mirrin's arms and oozed under her fingernails. It dobbed boots and makeshift leggings so heavily that the tinks shuffled up the drills with a ponderous mechanical gait that quickly wearied them. Steered by Mag Marshall, the tinker clan had drifted south out of Ayrshire and on over the Scottish-English border, picking up a day's hire here and there, turning between whiles to the traditional winter chores of collecting old clothes, weaving baskets and peg-making. Now, though, it was turnips, three large fields, the last farm job liable to be undertaken by the collective tribe for the year.

The weather had broken a fortnight ago, a week into October. Rain rolled off the Cumbrian Mountains traced with sleet in the dawn rising. All the turnips had already been unearthed, topped and tailed by men wielding sharp crooked knives. The soil was too wet to bear farm carts and the womenfolk filled hempsacks which they lugged or dragged to the hard pad by the gate where the carts waited, and the horses stood drenched and dejected.

Mirrin winced as her sodden sleeves sawed into her chafed and bleeding wrists. She had clapped a poultice of mud on a wound on the palm of her hand and covered it with a mitten. Even so, it impeded the rhythm of the task so much that she had fallen behind the line and had to scramble to make up ground along the drill. Tossing the neeps hurriedly into the sack, she missed sometimes and was cursed for carelessness, cursed with a vituperative foulness that would have made the coarsest collier flush. Tom had been right. How could she ever have thought that travellin' folk carried an aura of romance? "You only need t'look at their faces to see how tough it is being a tinker," Tom had said. Now she believed him.

The rawness of her wrists and the throbbing ache in her back compelled her to ease and stretch.

Old Mag's voice flayed her. "Keep it up, Stalker. This's no easy pit drag. Ye've no time t'coddle yoursel'. Bend yer back t'it. We want them neeps all carted afore dark."

Mirrin clenched her teeth. Gathering a load of muddy turnips, she staggered to the sack. Awkward still, she held the mouth of the sack with hand and knees and toppled the vegetables into it, spilling more than she filled. Mag snarled at her again. Into the ragged hedges the scarecrow figures merged, stooping and straightening. Crows craked and cawed as if jeering the labourers. Mirrin was cold, sore and bored. God, she was no better off here than she would have been at the troughs in Blacklaw. There at least she had mastered the simple rhythm of the work and had no cantankerous old bitch to slave-dirve her on. She was hungry too. Breakfast had been meagre, a puddle of gruel and a stale end of bread, not even tea. The girl-child in charge of the pot had let the fire go out, and had been beaten for her carelessness.

She shouldered the lumpy sack and plodded fifty yards with it to the cart. She hoisted it up the front of her body, for the board of the slope-sided cart was high. A farmhand took it, swung it, expertly scattered the neeps on to the growing pile then, without a word, flung the sack back at her. As she returned to the line of bruised-blue turnips, the rain began again.

The last hour of the afternoon's field-finishing was an almost unendurable agony of wet skirts, stiffening muscles and skinned flesh. There was no banter among the tinks, no songs, no jokes. They worked soundlessly, mindlessly, toiling along the clay drills in the steady grey rain. Then it was over and dusk congealed in the cloud over the mountains, thickening too, like slate dust paste, sending rooks and crows to roost noisily in distant trees.

The camp was on the far side of the farm. On a patch of stony ground by the river the tents had been slung up in the half-dark two days ago to see them through a couple of nights, no more. Tomorrow or the next day, the clan would divide and fork back over the border into Scotland, some strays heading for a good site near Annan and others, Mag's special tribe, veering away into Galloway to brazen out the winter on a cold and isolated shore.

The tinks herded behind the swaying cart like cattle.

The near-side wheel of the cart jarred on the ridges causing the turnips to shift in a landslide that brought shouts of warning from the farmhand, as vegetables dislodged and fell to the ground.

"Keep the bloody wheels to the sides," a tink yelled. "Look out, or the lot's awa'."

As Mirrin stepped back from the rumble of turnips which cascaded over the backboard she was pushed violently from behind.

"Give it room, me Mam says," rapped Colly Marshall imperiously. "You, Stalker, get out the bliddy way."

Colly pushed her again, her forearm striking Mirrin across the breast. Colly's ugliness was accentuated by a peevish, dictatorial expression and ratstails of red hair. "Out t'way: out t'way, me Mam says."

She had no call to single out Mirrin for abuse. It was malicious, trivial and maddening. When Colly shoved her again, driving her from the track into the tall splashing grasses, Mirrin caught her by the wrist, dragged her out of balance and swung her vigorously into the verge. Behind them, the parade stopped abruptly. Still dribbling neeps the cart lurched on.

Mirrin drew back from the sprawling girl.

"Sorry, Colly," she said, with a degree of sarcasm

that even the dim-witted tink could not fail to recognise.

Colly pushed herself up, face scarlet with temper and humiliation. She had no desire to tackle the collier's daughter there and then, however.

"Mam?"

Mirrin turned to follow the cart.

"You."

Mag Marshall stepped out from the tinker's ranks.

"What?" Mirrin refused to flinch from the old woman's fierce authority.

Reaching, Mag dragged a sack from a woman's head, whipping it away with sufficient force to cause the woman to cry out and stumble. Mag hurled the sack at Mirrin. "You, pick up the spillin's."

Mirrin hesitated. It was a punishment: she knew that. The tinks had already begun to gather the fallen neeps, one or two to each. Now she had been told to sack and lug them all. She looked up the track at the retreating cart, at the twenty or thirty turnips scattered like huge seeds in its wake. The farm buildings were a good quarter of a mile off. It was a hard and tiring task that Mag had allotted her, especially at the end of such a gruelling day. Mirrin's cheeks flushed. She was tempted to pick up one of the neeps there and then and bounce it off the old hag's skull. Instead, aware of the eyes trained on her, Mirrin tossed her head and scooping up the front of her skirt to tuck into her waist-belt, said, "Right! If you lot are too lazy t'finish the job, I'll do it. Now get on, if you will, please, before you all sink int' the mud."

Colly struggled out of the verge. Perhaps she expected her mother to attack Mirrin physically, to thrash the girl for such obvious defiance. But the matriarch was too crafty. She had issued an order which the collier's bitch had accepted. The fact that the girl had agreed with cheerful willingness drew the sting out of the punishment.

Whistling, Mirrin was already scooping up the vegetables and popping them into the sack. The cart was out of sight over the hill by now but, as far as she could judge, the neeps had settled and no more tumbled to the ground.

"On wi' ye, then," Mag Marshall shouted.

The tinks shifted, splitting round the fallen turnips, trudging on, faster now down the sides of the track. Still whistling loudly, with an ebullience she did not feel, Mirrin bent to her picking. It would cost her two trips to the farm and back. Needless labour. Glancing up briefly, she saw Tom striding back down the track towards her. Behind him, Colly and Mag Marshall stopped, watching. As he reached her, already grabbing for the sack, Mirrin said, "Don't get involved, Tom. Mag won't approve."

"To hell with her," Tom retorted. "I do as I please."

Mirrin snorted. "Then sing."

"What?"

"You heard me, Tom Dandy. Let's hear your lovely voice in song."

Strong in volume, but tuneful, Mirrin struck into 'My Lad's a Canny Lad'. Her solo was augmented, after a pause, by Armstrong's tenor.

The song helped. Songs always helped.

Throughout that last dismal hour of the October afternoon, the couple wended their way through a whole repertoire of familiar melodies. It was after dark before they tramped into Mag Marshall's camp by the flooded stream, still hoarsely blending their voices in 'The Bold Irish Navvy'.

"It'll not do t'lose your temper again, Mirrin," Tom warned. "She'll not stand for it."

"Then let her whistle," Mirrin retorted. "I'll not be chased out."

"God, but you're stubborn."

"If I'm right, though, *you're* ready t'leave."

"Near enough," Tom admitted.

They were seated on a coconut mat under the eaves of the tent back, a tiny private canvas sanctuary where Tom made his bed away from the stink of the communal hut where the rest of the men and boys slept, those who hadn't women or wives to bundle in their blankets. The women's tent crouched low and black in the flicker of light from the cooking fires. The smell of stew rose with the belching smoke from the rusty canister that served as a chimney. It was hardly a homely place, squalid and unstable like many of the tinks and their relationships. She could hear squabbling within the tents, a man and his mistress slanging each other with a shrillness that indicated hatred. Over by the bushes, two small boys were pummelling a third and making him howl, while four or five dogs snuffled curiously around or barked at the fray.

"Are you comin'?" Tom asked.

"What are you offering me now, Tom Dandy?"

"We'll find something."

'We're better off here."

"I won't ask again, Mirrin," Tom said. "It's now or never."

"Now or never," said Mirrin. "I didn't imagine that word 'never' had a place in your vocabulary. Where's your fight, Tom? Are you all jingle, like the medals on your hat?"

"Maybe you've more of the tink in you, Mirrin Stalker, than I have. If your length in a stinkin' tent and a scoop of greasy stew is as much as you want, then you're welcome to it. It won't do me much longer."

"I'm lookin' for something, Tom," Mirrin said, more seriously than before.

"What, for instance?"

"I don't know m'self, to tell the truth," Mirrin answered. "A point, a purpose, I suppose."

"You've been with the tribe long enough t'know that you'll not find it on the road."

"The road's all I have at the moment," Mirrin said.

"Go back home."

"That I'll not do."

"Then come with me: I'll help you find what you're lookin' for."

"Even if it's security?"

"I'm in no mood t'argue, Mirrin."

"Don't argue, then, Tom, just talk."

"I've done enough talkin'."

"Aye, I have too."

"Goodnight t'ye, then," Tom said.

"Tom?"

"Goodnight."

He rolled away from her and slid through the flap of his tent. She heard the scuff of knuckles on canvas as he tied up the ropes which kept out the worst of the wind. He lit no light. She sensed somehow she had insulted him again.

What was it he'd said: she was more of a tink than he was. She could understand the treadmill slavery of the tinkers' round now. It was true: she would not find what she sought in a brawling gypsy encampment. Now that she thought of it, she hardly knew the others. She had clung to Tom, lumping the rest of the tribe, with one or two exceptions, into an anonymous cluster of faces, classed by age and sex, but without other identification. They had no names, no real identities; not like the colliers of Blacklaw, all of whom were stamped with an individuality that made them unique even in the closed world of the pithead village.

Tom was right. The travelling folk—at least this tribe of them—were devoid of romance or glamour. Their pride was personified in the selfish bigotry of Mag Marshall, their self-appointed queen.

She hesitated. She could call on him now. She felt sure he would gladly admit her to his tent. It would be a good time to seal the bargain. Though she was attracted to him, however, she was still filled with the memories of the winter past and of the meaning of giving herself to a man, in love not out of whim.

Shifting quietly, she rose and walked round to the hut. It was silent now, the families gathered on the grass under a draped awning where the men had lit themselves a fire and there was food and a bottle or two of ale to swill it down. Pots cooked in the fire in the women's hut had been taken out. The entire tribe gathered like shadows, animate and somehow pathetically sly in their huddle under the belly of the primitive shelter.

Stooping, Mirrin went into the hut to unearth her 'coggle', the tin bowl into which her portion of the meal would be splashed. She must hurry or the ravenous youngsters would scrape the pots before she got there.

On hands and knees in the low smoke-wreathed interior she groped for her bedroll. She was all tink at that instant, her mind empty of everything but anticipation of the warmth the stew would bring to her stomach and the laziness that would accompany digestion in the stuffy hut, a passivity which would blot out all inclination to trouble her mind with tomorrow.

As she straightened, bowl and spoon in her hand, the steel pin, whetted needle sharp, touched her jugular vein.

Instinct warned Mirrin not to flinch. She moved nothing but her eyes. The sensation of the pin, though she could not see it, brought up the image of Mag's favourite weapon, a horned brooch which stuck out of her withered red braids like the bone in a cannibal's nose.

Mag Marshall's voice, as thin and dangerous as the eight-inch pin, hissed venomously in Mirrin's right ear.

Mirrin said softly, "Is it yourself, lady?"

The challenge of daring to speak at all was not lost on the tinker mother. The point of the pin wormed into Mirrin's flesh, extracting a drop of blood. The old woman's dexterity was a sure indication of her expertise with the weapon. Mirrin was afraid.

"Just a wee word t'the wise," Mag whispered. "Ye can go or ye can stay as you've a mind, me lass. I'm not the one to hive off a good worker, an' that ye are, I will admit. But shy clear o' Tom Armstrong. He's not for you nor the likes o'you. He's for my Colly, the love. She'd have had him for sure this summer but for you interferin'. Let the man bed ye an' be done with it, if ye must. I know how the blood simmers in that feller for a fresh thing like yersel'. But when that's done, he'll come back t'me an' my Colly. I'm tired of waitin' while you string him along with your prissy ways."

"And if I don't?"

"I'll prick out yer eyes," Mag said.

"And the law will take you?"

"Law? What law is there but me? Accidents can happen t'anyone, an' I have a dozen witnesses t'back me story up."

"Has Tom no say at all?"

"Tom Dandy's a daft feller, idle enough t'be trapped."

Before she could resist, Mirrin was caught by the throat and swung round. She peered into the old woman's evil face, at the sharp steel needle which hovered in front of her eyes, ruby light from the dying fire like blood smeared down its length. Mag's claw-like hands held her, though she would not have dared to resist.

"He'll court, bed an' wed my Colly," the old tink said. "That'll be the way o'it, with you out o'the way. Bear it in mind, Stalker."

Mag Marshall released her and slithered backwards out of the hut before Mirrin could break the spell that the pin's proximity had cast on her, a mesmerism born less out of fear of the old woman's threats than from the inherent dread of being condemned to a life of total darkness by her unwitting involvement in a mean and trivial plot to find a mate for her ugly daughter.

Raucous laughter floated in from the campfire. She touched her neck with her fingertips and looked at the tiny bloodstains. She was afraid; not racked by terror, though. The woman was not mad. She had been given a choice. Provided she did exactly as Mag Marshall commanded she would come to no real harm. But *would* she do what the tink wished? Her obstinate pride was every bit as intractable as the woman's. She realised that she had played a game with Tom, a game as destructively flighty as her sister Betsy's cruel teasing of Dalzells' clerks, but in a circle where such silliness could turn back against her. Even so, she would not capitulate to threats.

Lifting bowl and spoon Mirrin backed out of the hut into the damp night air. Walking straight and light as if she had no cares in the world, she headed for the awning, the pots, and the bosom of the tinker family.

Defiance was all she had left. And Tom Armstrong's protection.

The group taking the air between lectures in the university quadrangle was larger than usual and Drew Stalker was able to insinuate himself into it without being rebuffed by imperious stares and cutting remarks. Drew longed to be accepted by the McAlmond côterie, that premier 'club' whose members displayed all the privileges of wealth, status and fine breeding.

Fraser McAlmond, linch-pin of the circle, was a natural leader of the young bucks. Reputed to be richer than any other student, he certainly had the aloof, handsome bearing of a fellow born to the manor. The truth was that the McAlmonds' first land in Perthshire had been purchased with cash earned by prudent investment in railway stock and, through a bachelor uncle, heavily subsidised by the profits of brewing cheap beer. Fraser's sire, Archibald, had been sufficiently perspicacious to hive off direct connections with 'crude trade' and as soon as practical had married into the aristocracy as an additional means to his end. Isabel Harriet, youngest daughter of Sir Gilbert Oakley, had dutifully supplied Archibald with three sons. She had also raised his station from that of brewery-rich speculator to 'laird' of the policies of Pearsehill, a miniature baronial estate which just happened to adjoin the few hundred acres of hill pasture and mixed forest that Archibald had bought a couple of years before the marriage. There were many other McAlmond holdings and investments, all snug and secure, tinkling out the baw-bees to plough into those fine Perthshire fields, to spend lavishly on the ornamentation of Pearsehill House and the consolidation of a position of inviolate respectability.

Ronald McAlmond, Fraser's elder brother, had been earmarked for the lairdship since birth. It was felt, however, that it would do no harm to actually have a lawyer in the family, to take the business away from Gow Havershaw. For that simple reason Fraser had been directed to qualify as a solicitor and, eventually, have himself called to the bar. His success as a star pupil of Fettes College had largely depended on personal magnetism and prowess with bats and balls of various shapes and sizes. Now, however, Fraser Mc-

Almond was in process of discovering that money and influence carried little weight in the Faculty of Law. Pater could not purchsase answers to the learned professors' questions or influence the marking of the term class papers. Besides, Fraser had always been far more interested in girls, gaming and carousing than in books. It had just begun to occur to him that failure was possible, indeed virtually assured, without a high degree of application to scholastic rather than sensual pursuits.

Little of his uncertainty showed on the surface. Outwardly Fraser was as swaggeringly assured as ever, lording it over his cronies, including Hector Mellish and the foppish twins, Balfour and Innes Sprott.

That dinner hour Balfour Sprott was recounting in graphic detail his amorous adventure with his aunt's second parlour maid, an exploit which, though not crowned with ultimate success, had paved the route for final conquest next time he spent the weekend in the lady's house in Cupar. The others in the group endeavoured—by 'haw-hawing', by winks and nudges —to convey the impression that they too had gobbled up many a young parlour maid in their time.

Drew Stalker could also have joined the bragging. But it was no part of his plan to try to cap the roués. He cared little enough for the approval of Mellish and the Sprotts. It was McAlmond's friendship he coveted. Consequently during the boasting it was McAlmond's eye he sought. If Fraser appeared bored, so did Drew. If Fraser composed a witticism, Drew smiled appreciatively. If Fraser cracked a joke, Drew laughed.

Initially Drew thought that it was all to no account, that the blond young man was wrapped up in himself to the exclusion of all else; but, as the boys' invention flagged on the subject of women and the conversation turned to argument on points of law, Drew saw his chance. He was too cautious to enter the lists, for he could have slain any or all of the lordlings in debate. Instead, when McAlmond made a hit, Drew chuckled and nodded in agreement as if the banal comment had been a masterpiece of profundity. Fraser's glance brushed over the scruffy upstart and, for the first time, he graced Stalker with a speculative smile. Drew was careful not to press his advantage at once. McAlmond was no fool. He would not entertain toadies. He had enough of those already. Comradeship was what Drew Stalker sought. On that early winter's day, he received his first hint that he might soon achieve his aim.

Life in the capital had brightened considerably. Kate had sent on the six shillings, together with a crabbit wee note to the effect that Mam and Betsy wished him well. Betsy had also written to him, separately, pleading for news of Edinburgh and of 'his progress'. He would send her a card on November 1st, when his next quarter's grant fell due. He did not intend to alienate his pretty twin sister, not now that he had an idea as to how she might be of use to him. As for Kate—he did not care whether she approved of him or not. He was finished with Blacklaw. He could not imagine himself ever returning to that black hole—unless, of course, Houston Lamont sent for him. So far he had had no personal contact all with his patron, an arrangement that suited Drew well enough under the circumstances.

Of all the favourable developments that the late autumn brought, however, his discovery of Heather Campbell and his enjoyment of her was by far the most important—at least for the first half dozen nights.

As he had suspected the girl was so stupid that she gave herself to him almost at first asking. Though he had not been suave as he would have wished, he had turned his awkwardness into a plea for pity, a ruse which worked spectacularly well. Out of sympathy for his loneliness, the highlander had allowed herself to be coaxed to the truckle bed and, after some hugging, kissing and similar demonstrations of affection, she had surrendered to the urgency of sexual desire, an emotion that seemed to possess the girl almost as much as it did Drew.

At its raging height, that phase lasted only a fortnight. By then, Heather had spent nine nights in Drew's bed. She left for the *Cockerel* at the same time as he left for first class, the pair of them sneaking down the winding open stair, past the sentry-box doorway of the apartment where the lodging-house keeper lived and out of which she spied upon her tenants. That Drew had so far avoided conflict with this harridan, a Mrs. Sankey, spoke well of the fortune that favours young lovers. He had, of course, several glib lies prepared to placate the old dragon if ever she should challenge him with morally degrading her pension.

So Heather Campbell came and went freely enough. Her companions in the billet at the nether end of Geddes Wynd thought nothing of her night-long absences. They tweaked and chivvied her bawdily about them, giving her more respect now that she had shed her virtue and sunk a little closer to their level.

Once he had tasted fulfilment, however, Drew Stalker found the highland girl irritating. He had no patience with her meek requests for loving attentions. As a buffer against her dependence on him—and the possibility of his own weakening—Drew perpetrated all sorts of humiliations upon her. He criticised her lack of education, her modesty, her accent, her acceptance of her lowly station, twisting and turning his remarks cunningly so that the girl remained almost constantly confused and pliant. Perhaps—he thought later—he had tried to drive her from him, had sought to give her strength enough to walk out and never associate with him again. If so, he had misjudged her need of him. Not until long after, did it occur to Drew Stalker that he was all the girl had had in the world.

Six

ANGRY SHOUTING WAKENED Mirrin. She wallowed into the swaddle of old coats that kept out the damp of the October morning. She could tell by the light under the edge of the tent that it was barely dawn yet and that the day, like yesterday, was wet. She listened to the outraged sounds, indifferent to their meaning. Some tink lad had perhaps been found with a girl of the tribe, or an act of petty theft discovered by an early riser. Dogs yapped. The noises came closer, then, before she was properly awake, she felt the whole tent shake. Clawing hands stripped the blankets from her and dragged her by the ankle from the mattress.

Struggling, Mirrin saw Mag Marshall bent over her. The woman's features were contorted by fury, her eyes livid with hatred. Behind the matriarch Colly's moon-face was swollen with tears.

"*Slut! Penny whore. Get out o'me camp, d'y'hear?*" Mag shouted.

Wriggling, Mirrin reached and broke the woman's vice-like grip and plunged forward out of the tent on to the wet grass. She was still bewildered, afraid of the threat of steel pin, but her anger was also roused. Whatever her crime, Mag did not intend to keep it secret. The rest of the tribe were crawling from their beds to observe the proceedings with interest.

"*Brazen bitch!*" Colly wailed. "*She done it, the sow.*"

"What have I done, then?" Mirrin leapt to her feet as the old gyspy rushed from the tent.

"Tom's gone," Colly snivelled.

"Aye, an' it would be you that arranged it," Mag said. "Arranged it between ye, like as not, since ye knew he was for Colly."

"Gone?" said Mirrin. "Tom's gone where?"

"Dinna act the innocent wi' me," Mag yelled. Fumbling at her bodice she unclipped the pin which held the brooch to her bosom. Her hair was unbraided, tousled, bristle-stiff around her head like a reddish grey mane. "Ye devised it between ye."

"How can you b'sure he's gone?"

"See, see for yersel'."

Glancing to her left Mirrin saw that Tom's small tent had vanished. There was no sign of it, save a yellowish patch of grass, a broken peg and some chicken bones on the ground. Fear and a sudden sense of loss shook Mirrin for an instant. She was almost caught off guard by the old woman's savage attack.

As the brooch pin jabbed at her face, Mirrin ducked. She reached out and, as she had learned to do in scraps with colliers' daughters back in Dominie Guthrei's schoolyard, caught handfuls of Mag Marshall's skirts, tugged and furled them until purchase permitted her one good solid yank which dragged the tink off her feet and planted her square on her buttocks on the ground.

Mirrin stepped in at once. She pinioned Mag's wrist and, snapping it backwards, broke the woman's grip on the brooch. Mirrin kicked the weapon away then swung round, expecting Colly to rush to her mother's aid. But the ugly girl was a coward. Shocked by the thoroughness of Mirrin's counter-attack and her mother's tumble, Colly only howled louder, her bellowing sobs waking the farm dogs to set up an uproar in the distance.

"So Tom is gone," said Mirrin. "He's left you before now, every November, in fact, if what he told me's true. But this year, you want t'blame *me* for it. You're *mad,* old woman, you're bloody *ravin'* mad. Tom's *never* goin' t'wed that horse-faced daughter o'yours, an the sooner you realise it the better."

Mirrin punched the words at Mag Marshall, their noses almost touching, eyes glaring.

The tinker's voice was hoarse. "Clear out o'this camp, an' never come back t'it. You'll find no welcome in any gatherin' o'the travellin' folk from this day on, Stalker. No, nor yer fancy Tom Dandy neither. He's out, finished, wi' his own kind. When ye bed wi' him t'night, tell him that. Now, *get!*"

"I'm goin'."

Mirrin did not have to dive back into the hut to retrieve her dunnage. Some thoughtful tinker had already flung her bedroll and sack of clothing out on to the mud.

Fortunately she had slept dressed, except for bloomers and overskirt. She snatched up her bundles together with the coat that, in Blacklaw, had been her Sunday best black but which was shabby and soiled now. The tinkers moved aside as Mirrin collected her chattels. Donning the overskirt and coat, she stuffed

the rest into the blanket and bound it with a length
of rope. She hoisted the pack, looping the rope with a
twist round her wrist. Later she would adjust the
burden and fasten it tightly, high on her shoulders, the
way Tom had taught her to do.

Tom! She could hardly blame him for sneaking off
in the night. Perhaps he thought he was doing her a
kindness by drifting casually out of her life. Perhaps!
But she doubted it! Though she regretted his disappearance, she did not grieve over it. She had too much
on her mind. She was possessed by a relief so vast that
she realised at once how sick she had become of the
tawdy tinkers' encampment and the furrows that the
proud, mean folk ploughed round and round the seasonal fields. Why had she ever fallen for Tom's persuasive lies? He had only wanted a companion for the
summer, that was all. Selfishly he had led her into the
tinker camps, into the dank backwater of casual
agricultural labour, simply as a buffer against loneliness
and as a safeguard against Mag Marshall's insinuating
demands.

Mirrin did not understand Tom's motives. She had
no interest in them now. He had shucked her off, like
a sack of millet off a cart, dropped her by the wayside,
to go his own way to the sea or to some pick-and-
scrape croft, perhaps. She questioned if she would ever
see him again.

It took her ten to fifteen seconds to secure her load,
then, without a moment's hesitation, she pivoted on
her heel and headed off down the length of the field
towards the footbridge and the clump of blackthorns
which shielded the track to the turnpike.

Behind her the tinkers were silent, relieved, perhaps, to be shot of such a fierce *gorgio*. Mirrin flattered
herself that there might be one or two of the men who
would be sorry to see her go now that Tom had left
her defenceless and vulnerable to wheedling induce-
ments.

Barefoot she walked, skirts swinging, feet swishing
in the wet grasses. She crossed the wooden foot-bridge
and, for a second, turned her head and stared back
at the encampment, at the huddle of figures surrounding

Mag and her daughter, at the miserable huts slick with the fine mist which coated the flanks of the dales and gathered in the sump of the valley. Nobody waved, of course. She in turn gave no signal of ill-will or defiant farewell. The tinks had been part of her life for a season and yet had hardly affected her. Only Tom Armstrong had done that. At the bridge end, she turned south along the stony track out of sight of the camp, then paused and glanced round, half-expecting to see Tom seated on a tussock of grass, arms folded, pack by his feet, waiting for her, ready to mock her swift exit from Mag's clan.

But there was no sign of the man. As she put the miles behind her, Mirrin gave up looking for the tinker, and slipped into thinking about the past.

She supposed she could go home again, home to Blacklaw.

It would not take her long if she was lucky; the broad highways which crossed the border carried much traffic. Two days, three days, a week at worst, and she could be right back home in grubby, gritty, friendly Lanarkshire.

But no, she would not choose that simple solution to her problems. Her quest had not bogged down yet. She had plenty of energy left, and, as the morning extended, plenty of curiosity about the towns, villages and big manufacturing cities of England. Blacklaw *wasn't* the hub of the world.

At a little after ten, Mirrin reached the first marked crossroad, eight miles out from the bowl of the mountains, into broader fields that spread along the coastal plain. She craned her neck to read the signpost's pointing arms. Metal brackets and wooden arrows were freshly painted by the coaching company, very bright and not yet weathered, matching her new mood. North? South? Manchester, Carlisle, Glasgow, Edinburgh, Leeds? Through the mediumship of the signs, she might make her choice.

Setting her pack on the grass at the base of the post she seated herself, back against the upright. She had not eaten yet that day. There was nothing edible in her pack, but the money belt around her waist pressed comfortably into her stomach. There was a little left of her harvest earnings, probably enough for a dozen hot meals and five or six nights dry lodgings.

So, she thought ruefully, I'm wealthier than I would be in Blacklaw, dropping all my coppers into the family jar to feed and fatten Drew. At least what I have is mine, to keep or spend as my mood and necessity dictate. Huh! Maybe the man only wanted to marry me for my money.

She hummed a snatch of 'My Lad's a Canny Lad' but then, because it increased her loneliness, ceased. She put her head back against the post and dozed. In sleep, however light, she forgot her hunger, though the memory of Tom Armstrong lingered in her mind— Tom Armstrong now, not Houston Lamont.

The fire in the boardroom grate smouldered sullenly that damp October morning. It flickered into life only an hour after the meeting began, close to the moment when tension and ill-feeling first flared into anger. Of the three men seated at the long deal table, Houston Lamont was the least involved. He was, however, no longer quite so indifferent to matters of business as he had been of late. Since Sydney Thrush had been appointed assistant manager and had ventured into policy-making areas, Houston's interest had reawakened.

The room lay left of the mansion's front door. It had been neglected for many years until Mirrin Stalker had reclaimed it and given it a modicum of comfort. Lamont was glad she had done so. Round the pithead offices were too many eavesdroppers anxious to spy on managerial meetings. The boardroom, it seemed, was coming back into its own again, thanks to Sydney Thrush's persuasive insistence on a regular weekly congress between management and owner.

The three men were separated by seven empty yew-backed chairs, symbols of alienation abetted by the ledgers and files which spread along the table top. In the large room, the men's voices rang hollowly, like those of actors on a rehearsal stage.

Leaning on his elbows, Lamont addressed Thrush,

showing no trace of his dislike or distrust. "I take it that you have figures to substantiate your opinion?"

"Naturally, sir."

Sydney Thrush's lips slithered into a smile. It was the most humourless smile that Lamont had ever seen, vulpine—if one could imagine an almost hairless wolf —and self-confident, as neat and precise as an engineer's drawing, inked with a steel nib across Thrush's cartridge-paper complexion. Files were squared on the table before him, memoranda and agenda, models of neatness too, carefully annotated, each point struck off as it was raised, discussed and accepted.

Though there was little difference in their ages, Donald Wyld looked the elder, slightly tousled and harassed in contrast to Thrush's glasspaper smoothness.

"Let's hear them, then, *Mister* Thrush," Wyld glared across the table.

"Donald." The coalmaster's raised hand restrained Wyld. "The figures, please, Thrush."

Thrush lifted a sheaf of foolscap. "Recent export figures, incorporating all areas of industry, except shipping, are of interest. In 1837 the total gross value of Britain's exports was put at £255 million. In 1874, gross value dropped to £240 million. In '75 the drop continues: £233, and . . ."

"Is this relevant?" Wyld interrupted. "We aren't concerned with industry as a whole, only mining, *coal*. I can produce figures to show that we've hewn out thirty per cent more this year than we were doing eight years ago."

"The American figure is higher than thirty per cent: the German higher still," Thrush declared.

Clean-shaven, balding, the silky black flanges of hair that still adhered to the region of his ears clipped and brushed, his eyebrows thin crescents that might have been applied to naked flesh with a signwriter's brush dipped in Indian ink, lips of strangely dark coloration too: if Lamont had entertained any suspicions that Edith might find Sydney Thrush physically attractive, he discarded them. Not even Edith for all her perversity could be attracted to this smooth, black-and-white Delft-porcelain person, not sexually at any rate. Both

Thrushes seemed genderless, Anna no less so than her brother. Even so, Edith held the couple in high esteem and, this past hour, Houston was beginning to appreciate his wife's sagacity.

"Coalmaster?" The fellow was reproving *him* for inattention.

"It's obvious that you have thoroughly researched the market, Thrush," Lamont said. "However, I am inclined to agree with Donald on the accommodating nature of figures. If this discussion is to be productive, might I suggest that we leave other branches of industry to fend for themselves and concentrate on the crisis in the pits."

"How does Mr. Wyld suggest we counter our crisis?" Thrush asked.

"Firstly, we must cut wages," Wyld said. "Colliers are no fools. They realise that *any* work is better than no work at all. Redundancies are inevitable. Apart from what we can save on the face shifts, we can certainly slice the pithead and clerical staff."

"Trifles, sir," Thrush said.

"You have a more . . . more concrete proposal, *sir?*" Wyld demanded. "I mean, theory's all very well, Thrush. But damn' me to hell, what *practical* proposals have you put forward since you came here."

"Coalmaster," said Thrush, "may I be given the chance to speak, please?"

"Donald," Lamont said, "let's hear what he has to say."

"Thank you, coalmaster."

The use of his title instead of his name was archaic; the implied subservience annoyed Lamont. He said nothing, however, nodding to Thrush to continue.

"In *addition* to Mr. Wyld's sensible, if minor, exigencies," Thrush said, "I have drafted a three-fold proposal. The intention behind my proposal may be summarised in a single word—expand."

"Expand?" Wyld burst out. "Jesus, the man's a ravin' lunatic, Mr. Lamont."

Lamont waved down Wyld's appeal. Thrush might be iconoclastic but he wasn't stupid.

Lamont said, "Your suggestions, Thrush?"

"First, we breach a whole new section in Pit Two." He extended forefinger and thumb. "Second, we explore the feasibility of employing mechanical cutters."

"The cost, Thrush!" Wyld exclaimed. "Consider the cost."

"Third, we curtail the use of checkweighmen at once."

Lamont studied his new employee carefully. Edith had not been mistaken. Though unscrupulous and cunning, Sydney Thrush was an owner's man right down the line. There were several in colliery circles but Lamont had never trusted them. He suspected the motives behind Thrush's profit-making drive. The man's ultimate loyalty would be to himself.

Practical and down-to-earth, Donald Wyld never wholly divorced himself from the cause of the miners. Like Lamont, Wyld had a streak of humanitarianism that, in times of grave crises, made the task of balancing profits against social hardship very difficult indeed. Thrush was hindered by no such scruples.

"We'll *never* get those measures through!" said Wyld.

"I don't see why not, Wyld," said Thrush. "Who's to prevent us?"

"The men of Blacklaw," Wyld answered.

Lamont felt like a bone gnawed by two terriers. He was weary of wrangling. Probing, he said, "I agree with Wyld."

"Are you *afraid* of your work-force, sir?" Thrush asked.

"I am . . . respectful of them," said Lamont.

"No doubt they will whine and complain and threaten strike action," said Thrush. "But if they are reminded of the unemployment and short wages prevailing in other pits not ten miles from here, they'll see sense rapidly enough."

"An' find a new way of breathin' too, maybe?" put in Wyld. "For your information, *Mister* Thrush, there's a foul air in the vicinity of Number Two Pit: if you took a wee trip down in the cage sometime instead of . . ."

"I am aware of the ventilation problem," Thrush interrupted.

"Then how in God's name can we breach new tunnels?"

"With mechanical cutters."

Lamont said, "In many English pits the cutters failed."

Thrush said, "In England, yes, but the seams of most Scottish pits—Blacklaw included—are thin and steep. Ideal for the use of machinery. It's more economic than man power."

"I assume these machines don't operate themselves?" said Wyld.

Thrush raised crescent ink-black brows, as if he had failed to remark the heavy sarcasm in Wyld's tone. "They are operated by specially trained men, of course."

"Specially trained to exist on carbon monoxide gas?"

Thrush sighed. "Ventilation need not be a *bête noire*, Wyld. Yorkshire and Lancashire have successfully used steam-driven fans for several years now."

"The cost of installation is astronomical," said Wyld.

"You're carping," said Thrush. "The initial outlay of capital is certainly high. According to my figures, however, we would recoup the expenditure out of profits in a single year, allowing for a down market."

Wyld grunted. He did not trust Thrush's figures but was not prepared, at that point, to argue against them. The sheet of foolscap that the assistant manager slid down the table was impressively itemised.

Wyld changed tack. "You'll never get away with terminating the use of checkweighmen. I don't give a damn what's happening in Wales and Yorkshire. In Blacklaw, the checkweighmen must stay."

"Must?" said Thrush.

"*Must*—unless you've invented a machine for coping with a bloody riot," said Wyld.

Thrush grinned, as if to indicate that just such a machine did exist.

The position of checkweighmen was peculiar to the mining industry. Colliers were paid according to their output, wages computed at the pithead by means of tallies attached by each miner to every basket filled. If left exclusively to employers' representatives to weigh and account the daily totals and subsequent wage, the possibilities of unfair treatment were legion. For many years now it had been part of the process for a representative of the colliers to make on-the-spot checks on the employers' calculations. The system, though, remained open to abuses, in spite of amendments and clauses in the Mines Regulation Act. The problem was that checkweighmen were also employees of the owner; they could be dismissed on the slightest excuse by an unscrupulous owner.

Lamont said, "I take it you've absorbed the changes in the Mines Regulation Act, Thrush?"

"I have, coalmaster. The clauses are no more than recommendations. You know how long reinstatement can take once a checkweighman's been dismissed: eighteen months, two years—even when they have the courts' support."

Wyld made a sound of disgust. "It's bloody dishonest. I won't condone falsifying a man's tally."

The manager looked challengingly at the coalmaster. Lamont made no immediate reply. He was thinking of Mirrin. She would have been vociferously against this manoeuvre. Perhaps she would even have persuaded him to dismiss Thrush for suggesting it. Mirrin could be very persuasive: her conscience had touched the roots of his own honesty. But Mirrin was no longer part of his household, of his life.

Cautiously, Lamont said, "Do you have figures to indicate where the money will come from to effect these innovations, Thrush?"

"Yes, coalmaster, I do have a paper."

In three weeks, Thrush had done more accounting work than the whole staff of the pit had turned in during the past year.

"I have also discussed it with Mrs. Lamont," Thrush said.

"Have you indeed?" Lamont murmured.

"There are two sources of acquiring the capital needed for a programme of expansion—bank loans and private monies."

"Private monies?" said Lamont.

"From small investors," said Thrush. "My sister and I, for example, would be only too pleased to make our small savings available. Also, Mrs. Lamont assures me that she could drum . . . I mean, encourage certain ladies and gentlemen with a little spare cash to invest it in mining."

It was exactly the kind of gesture that would appeal to Edith's new mood of competence. She had always been too energetic simply to swan about the drawing rooms of the rich and semi-rich indulging in casual chit-chat. Thinking of it now, hazily, Lamont realised that his wife had made excellent contacts in Glasgow's commercial houses. The cleverness of turning her de-merit as a leader of society—that is, the source of her capital—into an advantage gave Lamont a fresh respect for his wife's ingenuity. If she could not push Blacklaw into the background, then she would frankly bring it to the fore, utilise it as a means of enhancing her reputation in Glasgow society. Edith would not admit the possibility of failure, of dragging her 'friends' into loss and bankruptcy.

For an instant Lamont envisaged the scheme as the flowering of a New Jerusalem, a venture bold enough to make him, and his investors, very rich indeed.

But what would it matter in the long run? He had no children, no blood kin to inherit his fortune.

"I see." Enthusiasm waned again into a cold appraisal of Thrush's projections. If the period of deflation continued, Blacklaw colliery, almost alone among the Lanarkshire pits, might ride out the storm. "I would be grateful if you would prepare your documents for my further scrutiny, Thrush."

"But, Mr. Lamont . . ." Wyld began.

The manager's protestations were interrupted by a knock upon the boardroom door.

"Come," Lamont shouted.

One of the daily maids, quivering with nervousness, stood in the doorway.

"Well, girl?" said Lamont.

"B . . . be .'. beggin' your pardon, sir, but there's a doctor here, from Glasgow."

Lamont rose to his feet at once. "I must leave you, gentlemen."

"But nothing's been decided," Wyld said.

"I suggest, Donald, that you apply yourself to studying Mr. Thrush's proposals in detail."

"Mr. Lamont, you're surely not considerin' . . . ?"

"At this precise moment," Lamont said, "I must attend my sister. I'll return shortly."

Donald Wyld had enough sense to put up no further argument. He had every sympathy for the coalmaster's sister. In that department there was no place for an adviser, other than medical specialists.

Thrush rose too and, with an oddly formal bow, said, "I trust that Miss Lamont will benefit from the doctor's ministrations."

The gesture was nicely timed.

Lamont paused at the door. "Thank you, Thrush," he said and favoured Edith's protégé with a faint smile, acknowledging for the first time Sydney Thrush's place in Blacklaw's scheme of things.

Dorothy Lamont's room was on the first floor, in the opposite wing of the house to those rooms full of memories both sad and sweet—the nursery in which his son Gordon had lived and died, the bedroom in which he and Mirrin had made love, the master bedroom, more appropriately the bedroom of the mistress of the house, a frilly, perfumed boudoir in which her husband's clothes and small personal possessions were kept discreetly out of sight in a large closet. Dorothy's room was simply furnished; flower prints on the walls, china ornaments on the overmantel and little occasional tables. The sofa was positioned in such a way that it gave a view of the trees bordering the drive and, unfortunately, of the top of the colliery winding towers, an uninspiring prospect on this drab winter's day when the sad rags of the oak leaves hung limply from the branches. The grid which squared the window was not discreet, though side curtains hid the massive bolts which secured it to the outside frame. It was with regret—remembering the room in the institution from which he had brought his sister—that Lamont had agreed to Edith's demand that the woman's suite be made secure.

Anna Thrush had relieved Doctor Minto of his hat and overcoat, an act of courtesy that should have been performed by the downstairs maid—another example of the slip-shod service that his wife got from her servants. He shook Minto's hand: a dry palm, strong fingers, square and clean, like the rest of the man.

"You may leave us, Miss Thrush." Lamont gestured peremptorily to the housekeeper.

"Sir," Anna Thrush said, "I've attended to the fire and secured the guard."

"Thank you," said Lamont, without so much as glancing at the woman.

A moment later the door closed.

Minto had already made his way to the canopied bed, a piece of furniture that stood midway along the gable wall and which, in design and ornamentation, reminded Lamont of a cross between a nursery cradle and a high-kirk altar.

"Ah, Miss Lamont," Minto was saying. "How delightful your room is. I see you share my fondness for floral prints. I've quite a collection myself, though not so fine as those which decorate your walls here."

Time-honoured medical small talk; Minto was erecting a screen of affability from behind which he could study his patient. The Glasgow doctor did it well, Lamont noted, though the pleasantries elicited no response from Dorothy. Months ago the woman had retreated so far from reality that only intimate knowledge of her history could equip one to follow the intricacies of her thoughts, a tapsalteerie puzzle of childhood allusions and memories, jumbled like the glitter in a kaleidoscope. To a lesser extent it had always been so but, until recently, there had invariably been some connection with reality, some means of entrance, of contact. Mirrin had manged to bring his sister out of herself a little, to make her laugh, to keep her amused. That period of responsiveness had gone now. Dorothy responded to nobody except himself, blanking out Anna Thrush, Edith, the servants, even the affable and expert Doctor Minto, as if they did not exist.

Staring out of round, dead eyes, out of a gaunt plastercast mask of a face, propped on her long and wrinkled neck, Dorothy Lamont addressed her brother.

"You did not come?"

"I did, my love, but you were sleeping."

"I was sleeping?"

"Yes."

Transformed by pity, dread and love, Lamont sank to his knees by the side of the bed and took her withering stick-like fingers into his hand. It was like touching some ancient thing, a crone in her eighties: Dorothy was younger than he was by a couple of years. She was fading before his eyes, a fraction more each day, a gramme less of her. Even her hair was thinning; 'moulting' Edith called the process of degeneration.

"Pretending," Dorothy said.

Minto watched, alert, not smiling now. He would observe her responses in relation to her brother.

"Mirrin pretends," Dorothy said. "I pretend."

Lamont nodded. He could not trust himself to speak.

No words lay in Dorothy's mouth. The connection seemed suddenly to have been broken between her and the world. Her expression was totally vacant, her body perfectly motionless.

Quietly Minto said, "Is she commonly like this?"

"More common of late," murmured Lamont. "Is it a dangerous condition?"

"Wait," Minto said. So far he had not touched the woman, examined her, yet Lamont trusted the observation. He was paying Minto for vast experience in treating the demented and disturbed.

Dorothy's vacancy was subtly replaced by agitation. The process took almost three minutes to accomplish. Using Houston's shoulder, she pulled herself up on the pillows and, gripping her brother's neck, broke into a high, chattering gabble that fluctuated between terror and wistful longing.

"Don't. Oh, don't. Should not go. Go there. No. Too small: too little small. My flowers. Mirrin. Mirrin."

Sweat beaded Lamont's forehead. He strove vainly to remain detached.

The child's voice in the woman's mouth flayed him. He understood.

"I see smoke. I see green. I see water. I see mouses. Mirrin. I see. See. There, water. No, oh, no. Yes: all gone Houston?"

"Yes, my love?"

"Houston? Houston?"

"Yes, Dorothy. I'm here."

She was gone from him, too, the tenuous strand snapped by the load of fearful memories that crushed her and would, perhaps soon, destroy her. She shook her head wildly, thrashing her body from the waist. Still Minto made no move to calm her. Confused, Lamont did not intervene to prevent the frantic and outlandish motions. He held her wrist, forcing her hand to remain against his neck and cheek, as if that contact must stand for more rational communication. Then, in a split second, Dorothy's contortions ceased. She became rigidly immobile, head slightly cocked, expression girlish and wistfully tender.

In a fragile soprano, plaintively, waveringly, she sang, *"Song bird in the sky, sing for me. Flowers that bloom nearbye, bloom for . . ."*

Mirrin had taught her the song. Patiently Mirrin had sung the words to and with his sister, coaxing her into learning something new, a diversion that did not lie in the rotting marshland of the distant past. How much could have been accomplished if Mirrin had remained?

Repetitively, Dorothy sang: *"Song bird in the sky, sing for me. Flowers that bloom nearbye, bloom for me. Song bird . . ."*

Lamont felt Minto's sympathetic grasp drawing him away from the bed. He rose. Dorothy's fingers slid from his cheek, slid down his shoulder, slid, lax, to the quilt.

The coalmaster crossed to the window and peered into the colourless landscape. Everything he could see from this window belonged to him. Even the smoke that tainted the sky was his smoke. He did not weep. He was long past weeping. He would never weep again.

"There's nothing we can do to break down the walls,

is there?" He had put that question to Mirrin on the hilltop, that last day. He had known how she would reply. "Not together, Houston: only apart." And she had left him. And he had lost her. And now, he was losing Dorothy.

"Mr. Lamont?"

He turned to the doctor by his side.

Dorothy was silent now, like some huge mechanical doll tucked into the bed, a clockwork puppet with spring wound down, which nobody had the gumption to rewind. Broken.

Minto indicated the door. The men moved stealthily towards it out into the corridor at whose end Anna Thrush and Edith loitered, spectral against the gelid reflection of the big window. Deliberately Lamont steered Minto away from the women, down the cul-de-sac of the west wing to the second window. For a moment the men looked down on the lawn. A squirrel, big and bushy, was scurrying across the faded grass, pausing now and again to wash his face and scout around for food, and enemies. Not until the vital little animal had vanished into the trees did Minto speak.

"I can offer little hope of a recovery, Mr. Lamont."

"A . . . recovery?"

"Miss Lamont is akin to a spent candle. Mentally and physically, it is only a matter of time until she flickers out."

"I . . . I appreciate your honesty, doctor," Houston said. "How long?"

"Who can say? She has good nursing here, I expect."

"Yes."

"This person she talks of—Mirrin? Is she from the past?" Minto asked.

"Yes."

"I got the impression that she had nursed your sister, in childhood, perhaps?"

"No, last winter."

"Ah!" Minto had probably heard details of the tragedy from Doctor McKay. He did not press the subject.

Lamont said, "If . . . if Dorothy were removed from

here . . . into your care in a hospital ward, say, would that . . . ?"

Minto shook his head. "There's nothing that medicine can do. She's better here."

"Ah, God!"

"If you wish to consult another specialist . . ."

"No," Lamont said. "I accept your diagnosis, Doctor Minto."

"Doctor McKay will continue in attendance to administer sedative draughts when necessary, though I do not recommend over-usage of the opiates."

The doctor's tone was professional again.

Lamont accompanied Minto down into the hall below. Edith and Anna Thrush were gone. The housekeeper would be with Dorothy now, like as not, seated on the bedside chair like some smooth-feathered raven.

The doctor's overcoat and hat had been negligently left on a chair by the front door. Lamont helped the Glaswegian into the coat then shook his hand.

"I am grateful for your honesty, Doctor Minto."

"I will call again, if I may, in a month."

"Doctor Minto, is my sister dangerous?"

"Dangerous? Lord, Mr. Lamont, does she look dangerous? No, no, your sister is not dangerous. In fact, she is even past the stage of being a danger to herself."

"Thank you, Doctor Minto."

Lamont closed the front door and wandered aimlessly into the centre of the hall. From the boardroom came raised voices, Wyld's didactic baritone, Thrush's mild laconic falsetto, womanish but not shrill. His managers were at each other's throats.

They needed his strength: the colliery, the whole of Blacklaw needed his strength, his power of decision.

In mental turmoil he condemned the folk of Blacklaw as guilty parties in reducing Dorothy to this pass. She had always been childlike and fey. Not until her traumatic involvement with the death of the Sinclair child, however, had wasting sickness bloomed in her brain like a weed. Edith's arrant selfishness and the behaviour of certain village hotheads had cost Dorothy

Mirrin Stalker's companionship, and swiftly, lethally, her sanity. His teeth clenched. *They* had done it: out of ignorance and malice and spite. Their black begrimed fingers had poked out her innocence and destroyed the last potential vestiges of happiness. Poor bemused Dorothy!

Seized by an anger that swamped his grief at Minto's verdict, Lamont strode to the boardroom and flung open the door.

Wyld and Thrush were both on their feet, snarling like dogs through a fence.

"Hold your tongues, both of you," the coalmaster shouted. He walked down the length of the table, kicked out the tall-backed chair, placed his foot on the seat and braced his hand on his knee, scowling at the managers who, sheepishly, returned to their places.

"I've made my decision," Lamont told them. "Thrush, I cannot accept your hypothesis that an improvement in the fortunes of the coal trade is imminent. Wyld, you have always been a workingman's manager. While I have supported your equable policies so far, I see ruin in what you have had to say today, in the degree and direction of your advice to me."

"Mr. Lamont . . ." Wyld blustered.

Lamont stared him into silence. "My decision is that opening a new section and investing in mechanical cutters and ventilation equipment would be improvident at this particular time. Expansion must wait."

Wyld looked astonished, then nodded smugly, smirking at Thrush.

Lamont went on, "Considerable savings must be made at all levels of the working: management, administration, cutting, sorting, transport, the whole range. We will discontinue the use of checkweighmen in Blacklaw pit as from the first of next month."

Thrush remained impassive.

"Tallies will be made, as usual, by representatives of the manager's office. Thrush, you will be responsible for that."

"Yes, coalmaster."

"I also intend to cut the basic wage rate."

"By how much?" demanded Wyld, livid with anger.

"I will determine the new rate when I have gone over the figures in detail," Lamont replied. "I will also reduce the work force."

"Pay-off!" Wyld cried. "Cut wages *and* pay-off?"

"I am not a charitable institution," Lamont said. "I am a coalmaster. I must have my profit."

Wyld was on his feet. "Never, sir, never have I heard you say that before. What's taken hold of you, Mr. Lamont? Is it this . . . this . . . work-glutton that's persuaded you?"

"Profit," Lamont repeated. "I've had enough of loss."

"Very well, sir," said Wyld grimly, gathering his papers. "If that's the way you intend to run Blacklaw, you may do so without my help. I'll be no part of a slave-pit."

"That," Lamont said, "is your choice, Donald."

"If I might advise," Thrush said, as Wyld hurried past him, "I would think it over very carefully, Mr. Wyld. Work is hard to come by, even for managers."

Donald Wyld did not deign to reply. He slammed the boardroom door behind him. For a moment, Lamont felt a pang of regret at his harshness. They had been together and worked well in tandem for several years, Donald and he. Hardening himself, he shrugged, kicked the chair out further and seated himself.

Beckoning with his forefinger, he summoned the new assistant to him. "Bring your wages and rating tallies, Thrush."

"Certainly, coalmaster. And the redundancy programme I took the liberty of drafting—for your approval, of course?"

Lamont hesitated, appalled at the cunning and gall of the man who would soon be manager of Blacklaw: then he snorted. "Aye, Thrush," he said. "If you've sharpened the damned axe for me, I may as well use it."

"Very wise, coalmaster," Sydney Thrush said. "Very wise indeed."

Packed with furniture, the vehicle was cumbersome. Tables, chairs and wicker baskets within which crockery rattled and chattered swayed as the wagon, drawn by one sturdy horse, ground towards the crossroads. The name *Matthew Brummidge* was stencilled in gilt on the side of the cart and under it, *Carter and Hauler* in plain red paint. Hopefully Mirrin rose and, lifting her bundle, hugged it to her arms as the cart halted at the signpost. She stepped forward and smiled at the thin-faced man on the driving-box. He was well into his sixties, with pale eyes and a thin pink nose. Silvery hair feathered his hat brim. A huge woollen scarf was wound round his neck and draped fore and aft of his body like an anchor chain.

"Good morning to you, sir," Mirrin called. "Damp t'day, is it not?"

"Seasonable: seasonable." The carrier glanced up and down the empty highway. "Are you walkin'?"

Mirrin grinned. "Just gatherin' my strength for another few miles, sir."

A movement among the furniture at the rear caught her attention. An awning had been rigged across the breadth of the cart. From the canvas flap a woman appeared. She picked her way through the obstacles to make a seat beside the man.

The carter said, "This is my wife—Mrs. Brummidge. An' who might you be, girl?"

"Mirrin Stalker's my name."

"Where are you bound for?"

"I'm in search of work."

The old man and old woman pursed their lips and, in unison, shook their heads.

"Precious little of that in any part o'the country," the man said, dolorously.

Mrs. Brummidge craned forward to squint at Mirrin. Perched on the seat, the pair seemed more like sister and brother than a married couple. Calmly Mirrin returned the wife's scrutiny.

"You look decent enough, child," the woman decided. "Church going?"

"All my life," Mirrin answered. "Never miss a Sunday."

Two pairs of eyes met, heads nodded. The husband jerked his thumb towards the awning at the rear of the piled cart. "We're lading furnishings south for a gentleman. Heading Leeds way, lass. Unless you've a hankerin' to wait for a ride into Scotland you're welcome to come with us. I'm thinking that if it's work you're after, you'll fare better in the Midlands than the north."

"Find your own food an' pay a share of the horse's fodder, though, since we're not wealthy enough t'dispense charity," the woman added. "The Almighty provides just sufficient for our needs."

"With my help here an' there," put in Mr. Brummidge.

Hesitating, Mirrin bit her lip.

South? North?

God knows, the situation in Scotland had not been easy for a casual hand back in the spring. If Mr. Brummidge was correct, then it must be near impossible by now. Work, just follow the work, like Tom Dandy said.

Mirrin said, "I've money. An' a notion to try the Midlands. Thank you kindly, I'll travel with you."

The carter informed her that she would find a chair under the canvas and could make herself comfortable on it provided she was careful not to soil or tear the upholstery. Mrs. Brummidge said that they would stop soon for a bite of dinner.

Mirrin climbed into the cart, found the armchair and carefully settled herself.

"Are y' set then, lass?" Brummidge called.

"I am."

"Off we go."

The cart luched forward, at no great pace. The crossroads signpost dropped gradually out of sight.

Mirrin watched the landscape drift patiently past, showing no discernible change from mile to mile, yet never quite the same.

South? Why not? Nobody was waiting for her in Scotland. South was as good as north any day of the week, she supposed. She would be sure to find work in the Midlands where mills and factories were always crying out for hands. Wages, so she'd heard, were good. Perhaps she'd earn enough to buy a few clothes. She could badly do with smartening herself up.

Ahead of her, a reedy female voice broke into song:

"Speed Thy servants, Saviour, speed them;
Thou art Lord of winds and waves:
They were bound, but Thou has freed them . . ."

Mirrin smiled to herself and burrowed deeper into the chair.

She hoped that Mrs. Brummidge's choice of hymn might prove an appropriate omen for the days that lay ahead.

Seven

ANGUS SALMON LL.B., member of the faculty of Advocates and Curators and lecturer in Roman Law, was known to all and sundry, including most of the Scottish bench, as 'Fish'. By a life-long process of transmogrification, Fish had assumed an astonishing likeness to that creature of the river and sea. Fish was prone to rise to bait and, with a stupidity that would have shamed any cock salmon, never seemed to realise when he had been hooked, gaffed and landed. Fish, therefore, provided the perfect subject for Drew Stalker's exhibitions of mordant wit. During the course of Salmon's lectures interminable duologues somehow developed between tutor and student and poor Fish was lured into intricate discussions on matters totally immaterial to Roman Law. Given line, inched in, spooled a wee, slacked and fetched round by the nose, the tutor could gradually be angled into flatly contradicting his initial hypothesis and taking a stand against himself. No other student dared intervene. Fish was Stalker's prize. The beauty of the jest was that Fish considered Stalker no end of a fine fellow, the only serious-minded seeker after knowledge in a roomful of sniggering vulgarians.

One afternoon in early November, Drew proved himself beyond doubt the most adroit haranguer in the freshman year. For an hour he skillfully steered Salmon towards defending Thomas Carlyle's philosophy of Titanism, though the lecturer, an avowed Christian and supporter of democratic liberalism, was known to detest Carlyle. At the end of the performance, as Fish paused in bewilderment at his own utterances, the class rose and applauded, leaving Fish puzzled but gratified by the suspicion that he had at last touched a collective nerve through the brilliance of his repartee.

Andrew Stalker knew better, of course.

As Drew gathered his books at the lecture's end, he was aware of the scrutiny of his fellow students, especially of the 'inner circle', the McAlmond set. Outwardly Drew remained nonchalant, but he sensed that on that afternoon he had shed anonimity for ever.

In the crowded corridor between the lecture halls and the main portico, Fraser McAlmond caught up with him.

"Well played, young Stalker," he said, in a cultured drawl. "I say, you really had our old Fish on toast—on toast, hm?"

Drew laughed, as he was expected to do.

Mellish and the Sprotts had caught up with them.

"Worth a case of claret to see the Fish hooked and gaffed so expertly," Mellish declared. "Like the cut of your jib, young Stalker."

"Case of claret, did you say, Hector?" McAlmond enquired. "A fair price; your contribution, what?"

"Stick us for the meat, Fraser," Innes Sprott said.

"Much your province," McAlmond said. "Meat, I mean."

Drew laughed again. He was confident enough now to acknowledge the Sprotts' carnal foibles.

Fraser McAlmond said, "And young Stalker will provide the *bon mots,* will he not?"

"Who better," Mellish said.

"Tonight at eight, Stalker, if convenient," McAlmond said. "Discreet quintet, good food, good wine, good talk. We'd be pleased if you'd join us; in the *Barn*."

"Know it?" Balfour Sprott asked.

"Union Place," Drew said.

"The very same," Mellish said. "Our guest, of course."

"Kind of you, gentlemen," Drew said. "I'd be delighted."

"Good chap."

Good chap in a suit that would not have passed muster on one of the McAlmond bailiffs: Fraser's cigar-cutter, Innes Sprott's tiepin or Balfour's silver-knobbled malacca cane, pawned in the Vennel, would have supplied him with ten suits better than the one he possessed.

As he walked into the brittle November sunshine, Drew experienced a moment's dismay at the steepness of the pyramid he had chosen to climb; then, rationalising, rejected for ever that particular qualm. He was riding to town on his intellect not his elegance. The McAlmond crew knew it. It would please them to adopt him, not as a lapdog but as an unpredictable mongrel. They might patronise him, but they would always be wary of his power. He savoured that thought as he hurried back to Shannon's Close to unpack the almost-new shirt with the Shakespeare collar and the octagon necktie that he had preserved for just such an occasion.

Tonight, the Campbell girl would tap on his door in vain.

It had been a grand night, a night to remember, dish following dish, game birds succeeded by rare crown of beef, blancmanges by strawberry-flavoured ices, and, of course, one vintage poured on top of another until by the end of the dinner, none of the participants had been in a fit state to pass opinion on anything. Drew had eaten hugely and drunk meagrely. He had no intention of losing control of himself in that company. It had been his lot, at an hour close to two o'clock, to troll Abbotsford Park and Bruce Place in search of a hackney and, when the conveyance was found, to load Fraser, Hector, Innes and Balfour into it like so many sides of pork, and, yelling farewells, pack them off to their Morningside apartments: a woolly enough introduction to spendthrift circles where money was scattered about like gravel off a shovel.

In the period before the wine took hold Drew had made a striking impression on his new companions. He could drop hints with the best of them, he discovered, and had a delicate touch with innuendo, forging a bond with the Sprotts by his dissertation on the sexual peccadillos of the working class. Early in the evening he had also planted an invention about his parentage. To his surprise, he had gained sympathy from Mellish who, as it happened, had inherited stock in a Fifeshire colliery, though he had never so much as cast eyes on the place.

As the hackney clopped away, the strains of a ribald ditty trailing in its wake, Drew gave way to a small celebration of his own, an impromptu jig upon the pavement, stirred by wine and the gleeful realisation that his background and lack of cash would not be obstacles after all. Nothing could hold him back. He could read the chaps of the McAlmond set like cheap novels, play them like penny whistles and crank patronage from them like washing from a mangle. Using them as models he would soon refine his speaking voice and manners, thus substantiating his claim to be the son of a member of the middle class—or damned near it—stumbled on hard times.

Shannon's Close was dark when he reached it. The stench seemed more foetid tonight. A stirring in the shadows made him stiffen. He paused, waiting: a savage dog in the area, a marauding stray, had already attacked a woman and two children. Drew did not care for dogs at the best of times. Broken heads and stolen wallets were also ten-a-penny in the environs of High Street.

When the movement occurred once more, realisation dawned upon Drew. A slight figure materialised in the scant light of the gas-mantel at the close mouth.

"Did you not have the damned sense to go home?" Drew hissed, glancing up apprehensively at the door of the lodge where the Sankey woman lived. "How long've you been here?"

"An . . . an hour. More. I don't rightly know, Drew."

She was shivering. Her cheeks were streaked with tears. She made to move against him the way a feral cat might do when it seeks to coax a tidbit from a stranger.

"I had t'talk to you, Drew."

"It could've waited until tomorrow."

"Can we go inside?"

"It's late, too late, Heather. Besides, I'm tired."

Drew stepped to the railing and put his hand upon it, waving at her with the other. "Off home with you. Your friends'll let you in."

The girl's voice was shrill and loud. "No, please, Drew."

Drew glanced again at the windows overhead. Faint light in one of them. With ill-concealed anger, he stepped into the courtyard again and, hauling Heather by the elbow, pulled her across the cobbles to the area at the back of the midden.

"I don't want you t'come here any . . ." he began. She was sobbing even before he spoke.

"I'm with child."

"What child?" Drew demanded. "What the devil are you talkin' about?"

"With child: my child: I'm havin' a baby."

"What? Now?"

"No, but . . . Please, Drew, listen."

Drew felt nothing. The claret glow waned and his irritation with it. He peered at the girl cowering back against the brickwork as if she was no more than a chalk drawing, a sketch. After a split-second's hesitation, he said, drily, "An' whose child is it, Heather?"

"Yours, Drew."

"First, may I establish that you are, in fact, pregnant."

"I am: I am."

"Who told you?"

"Betty Keegan."

"How does she know?"

"She's had two babies herself."

"An' this woman, this Keegan, has she examined you?"

"Aye."

"How far into your pregnancy are you?"

"Six weeks."

"I've barely known you that length of time."

"It's yours, Drew. It *must* be yours."

"Second, then, let's consider your claim that I'm the father."

"You are: you are."

"Quiet, Heather: d'you want to wake the whole neighbourhood?" Drew told her. "You say you've not been with any man except me?"

"You *know* I haven't. Drew what's . . . why d'you question me? It's the truth I'm tellin' you."

"Very well, Heather." He hesitated again then, awkwardly, shifted towards her, put his arm about her shoulders and escorted her sedately across the well-like court towards the closemouth. "Very well, my . . . my love. We'll discuss it tomorrow. I'll tell you what t'do tomorrow."

"You won't . . . Drew, you won't . . ."

"Won't what?"

"Make me get rid of it."

"Not unless that's your wish."

"I couldn't. I mean, I couldn't stand it."

"No, well, we'll see," Drew said.

On the spire of St. Giles and on the tattered awnings of the ragman's warehouse, frost sparkled in gibbous moonlight. The cobbles were sugared with it, too. Tomorrow the horses would skid and stumble on their pull up from the Grass Market.

He kissed her on the mouth, let her cling to him, not sobbing now, for several agonising minutes. He did not know how long he could remain manly and steadfast. He did not dare push her away. Murmuring, he said, "You must go now, Heather. Go home. I'll . . . I'll think of something."

"Tomorrow, Drew?"

"Aye."

"Here? You will be here tomorrow night?"

"Aye."

"I'm sorry: I'm sorry, Drew. I'm . . ."

"Goodnight, dearest."

"Oh, God, I don't know what I'd do without you."

"Goodnight, Heather, my love."

A knife, a pillow, the hank of rope with which he tied up his travelling case, the leather strap that bound his library borrowings: any one of them might become a tool in effecting release from the bondage of the orphan bitch whose hysterical claims would wreck all that he had slaved and sacrificed for. The Sprotts would chortle when news of his foolishness leaked out. To be saddled with a skinny serving wench from the *Cockerel* tavern, to father a bastard on her: the sordidness of it, the waste, was sickening. Lamont's sponsorship would be withdrawn. Havershaw would see to that. It was probable that Mam would not accept him back in the household. He was only seventeen years old. It had not occurred to him that, in years if not in intellect, he was still a youth. Untrained youths were a drug on the labour market. What could he do?

He could kill her.

As he performed ritualistic chores about the attic, lighting the fire, boiling water in a pan, brewing coffee from a packet of grounds, undressing, donning his robe, Drew veered between panic and a cruelty shared with the worst of a long line of Scottish murderers. Homicidal fantasies kept him from disintegrating, from flying back home to hide his face in Mam's apron and sob out his tale of woe.

Mam would make him marry the girl. He would be found work, if he was lucky, in one of the pits, probably as a clerk. He would spend his days under a pall of coaldust and his nights imprisoned with an illiterate highland sow and her importunate farrow in a small tied cottage. The golden aura of McAlmond's world faded.

De Quincey had considered murder as one of the

fine arts. Aye, murder could be that all right, and more. It could be a necessity, justifiable as an act of self-defence.

Sipping coffee to clear his head and sucking slowly on a black cheroot, Drew travelled down from the ultimate means of redressing the tenor of his life through more realistic methods to bottom in despair. In that trough he wallowed in the callow terrors of boyish guilt and the anguish of realising that he had been naïve. He leapt to the top again. Murder was a better philosopher's stone than responsibility.

Heather Campbell would not be missed. Her ignorant cronies would assume that her man had taken her away. If by chance she'd let his name slip to any of the tavern whores, they would hardly be likely to remember it. *Corpus delictae:* without that, no prosecution, not even discovery. Where? The Pentlands. How would he get her there? A day in the country. He would need to carry a spade. Difficult. How else? Drowning? Much more promising. A fall from a high place? A distinct possibility. If he mocked up a suicide, the authorities would surely not probe too deeply into circumstances. On the other hand, the sow was pregnant. Reason enough to prompt a self-inflicted death fall. But it might—and here luck entered the picture—*might* lead to an investigation. He could not be sure. Successful murderers did not have casebooks written on their crimes. In trial reports he had perused, Drew recognised the vagaries of pure, blind chance. He did not intend to stake his future, his very neck on such a gaming table.

Suddenly Drew knew what he must do.

If his judgment of Heather Campbell's character was any way accurate, then his plan would not fail. Indeed, it would hasten his upward progress.

He had less than twenty-four hours to act.

Gow Havershaw returned from taking his dinner at the *Curling Stone* tavern, sober haunt of lawyers, merchants and brokers and as unlike the dens of the lower reaches of the Mile as could be imagined. He had eaten spare ribs and a baked potato and drunk a single glass of port with his cheese. He had smoked a pipe of Birdseye Shag and conversed with a fellow solicitor on the state of the nation for a peaceful half hour in the coffee room, toasting his shanks at one of the room's two fires. Thus rested and refreshed he returned, puffing a little on the hill and taking the stairs by cautious degrees, to his chambers to apply himself to preparing a brief in the case of Regina vs. The City of Edinburgh Brickworks, an involved claim by the Crown Lands Commission over infringement of building supplies and materials by the borough-owned company.

The door of the inner sanctum was, of course, locked. But Havershaw's clerk, a wizened male virago by the name of Daniel Horn, supposedly took his midday meal on the premises and was instructed not to turn business away. The business that Horn had not turned away that dinner hour took the form of young Drew Stalker who, as Havershaw entered, rose from the clients' bench, closed the volume of murder trial proceedings in which he had been immersed, and boldly requested an interview.

"What is it now, Stalker?" said Havershaw, unlocking the door of his office and walking on in. "Come in, come in."

Havershaw hung his Ulster on the peg behind the door and, brushing a few crumbs from his waistcoat, drew an appropriate file on Crown Lands from his shelf and set it importantly on his desk, indicating that he was unwilling to grant Stalker more than a couple of minutes of his precious time.

"I'll come to the point, sir," Stalker said. "I wish to change my lodgings."

Havershaw stroked his lip and seated himself in the wooden throne. "Have you been, ah, asked to quit?"

"No."

"Reason?"

"A personal friend wishes me to take up lodgings in his apartments."

"Personal friend, Stalker? What, ah, will this companionable exchange cost you in terms of increased rental: or, aha, does your personal friend happen to reside in one of our, ah, less salubrious areas?"

"My friend lodges in Planetree Gardens, Morningside."

"Lord, Stalker, you are ascending, aren't you: hm?"

"An apartment there isn't yet available but will be at the end of the Christmas term. In the interim I intend to lodge in Marlborough Street, which is close enough."

"Are, ah, you asking for money?"

"No, sir," said Stalker. "I am informing you of my intention to change my lodgings."

"You still haven't given a satisfactory reason."

"My friend wishes me to tutor him in certain subjects on the curriculum."

"You?"

"Yes, Mr. Havershaw."

"Tutor?"

"Yes."

"Well, aha! Hmm! If that's what your, ah, friend wishes, I suppose it's up to him. Will he pay?"

"I will receive the bounty of his table, thus saving considerable expenditure."

Havershaw frowned and, leaning forward in his chair, enquired, "Who is this generous, ah, friend, Stalker?"

"His name is Fraser McAlmond."

Havershaw sat back. "McAlmond?"

"From you, sir, I wish to acquire a letter to Mrs. Sankey, manager of my present lodging, requesting the return of the major portion of the advance quarter's rent, less two weeks, which Mr. Horn paid over in cash today week, past."

"Return of the unused rent to, ah, whom?"

"To myself, Mr. Havershaw. I will transfer the sum, in cash, to a lodging house in Marlborough Street, where there is a vacancy, and return the balance into your hands."

Brooding, Havershaw strove to find the key to the trick. Instinct told him that Stalker was up to something. But if he had indeed made a friend of McAlmond's son then the matter could not be casually dismissed. Havershaw did not doubt that Stalker was quite capable of infiltrating that august group of students which, so he'd heard, formed this year's university clique. By all accounts, young McAlmond was a dunderhead, and an idler to boot. The path to riches lay through such juvenile contacts. Swiftly, Havershaw reached a decision which involved a radical change of attitude on his part.

Climbing from the chair, he rounded the desk and administered an avuncular arm to Stalker's shoulder, though the contact almost made him flinch. "Progress, Stalker: ah, progress! I'm pleased that you have made friends in our city."

"And the letter, sir?"

"Horn will draft it and I will sign it. You may handle the transaction. The balance of rental need not be returned. Call it, ah, countenance money."

"Thank you, sir."

"Good, ah, luck, Stalker."

Stalker nodded, curtly. He did not need luck.

"By the way, when do you, ah, intend to exchange your place of residence?" asked Gow Havershaw.

"This afternoon," young Andrew Stalker said.

"May I walk with you, Fraser?"

"By all means, young Stalker. Not much of an afternoon for a perambulation, though."

"I'm going in your direction."

"Are you, indeed? Found a little doxy in my part of town, have you?"

"I'm lodging in Marlborough Street."

"I say, that's handy."

"Hm?" said Drew.

"You can pop round for a spot of supper," McAlmond said. "Not more than a step or two from my chambers, y'know."

"Not really!" said Drew. "Ah, yes, of course, Morningside, isn't it?"

The young men walked twenty yards in silence, the grey, mist-fettered afternoon opening to a vista of the Salisbury Crags, the hillock of Arthur's Seat like a faded silhouette behind motionless veils of smoke.

Even the wheels of the street carts seemed muffled by thick felt.

"Class examinations soon," Drew said.

"Hum," said McAlmond. "Hum-hum-hum!"

"Shouldn't be too bad, takin' it all in all."

"Not for you, perhaps."

"I'm sure you'll do well, Fraser."

"I'm *not* so sure."

"Torts are the problem, are they not?"

"I really cannot hold everything in my mind at once, Stalker: a facility you seem to have developed."

"Perhaps because you do not understand the function of the various parts of law."

"I do not understand Torts, if that's what you mean. The Lord knows, I've tried."

"Once you grasp the principle," said Drew, "the mental retention of relative facts becomes much easier. The law, in that respect, is like mathematics, a science of cause and effect, with, admittedly, a liberal sprinkling of anomalies."

"Perhaps it's the sprinkling of anomalies that throws me off my stride."

"Pardon my bluntness, Fraser," Drew said. "But Hector suggested that it will not go well with you—parentally, that is—if your results are less than favourable."

"Mellish told you that, did he?"

"He happened to hint at it," Drew said, cautiously.

"What's it to you, in any case?"

"I consider you enough of a friend to speak frankly," Drew said. "Perhaps it's a little presumptuous of me, but I feel that you have much talent and that it merely needs . . . encouragement to blossom forth."

McAlmond had long nursed similar sentiments. Eagerly he said, "I say, that's deuced perceptive of you, young Stalker."

"First year, second term," said Drew.

"Hm? What?"

"If I might suggest it, Fraser, it's best to keep ahead of the landslide."

"What landslide?"

"First year, third term," Drew said.

McAlmond halted. They were half way down hill towards the sheep meadows around which the gigs and phaetons of the very rich clicked neatly.

"Do please explain yourself, Stalker?"

"Cram *now*, Fraser, or you *will* go under."

"You whippersnapper!" McAlmond said, without venom. "Are you implying that I don't know how to conduct my career as a student?"

"Yes."

"Well, I'll be damned!" McAlmond extended his short, military-style cane and poked Drew in the chest with it. "I may not know much about Torts, but I can recognise a proposition when I hear one. Out with it."

"I will act as your crammer, now and in future. I will furnish you with cribs, and . . ."

"Cribs, you say! Cribs are dangerous."

"Do you want to fail?"

"Go on, go on."

"I will explain everything that comes down to us and provide full lecture notes."

"*And* sit my examinations, I suppose."

"That's not possible, nor necessary," said Drew. "To be blunt about it, I'm offering you a valuable service."

McAlmond swung the stick and laid it across Drew's shoulder, cocking his handsome head to study the boy quizzically.

"What if I feel that I do not need the help of a fellow student? I can *hire* a crammer, you know: the very best crammer in the city."

"He will force you to study."

"And you won't?"

"One hour of your undivided attention per evening, that's all I'll require of you," Drew said, confidently. "And, before the finals in the last term, two weeks of cloistered study."

"What do you ask in exchange? A fee?"

"Please," said Drew, as if the idea of taking money from a university fellow offended him. "I'm not qualified to receive payment. I'll do it, Fraser, out of friendship."

McAlmond swung the cane away and, turning, strode off down the hill, saying, "Come along, Stalker."

It was a ruse, of course. Drew recognised it immediately. McAlmond was taunting him, endeavouring to force him to plead, to array his 'terms' for the services offered. He wouldn't rise to that bait, though. He caught up with the elegant young man and fell into step beside him, waiting, saying nothing.

Fifty yards further on, McAlmond stopped again. He shouldered the cane and stuck his gloved hand into his topcoat pocket. "Just what *do* you want?"

"Accommodation."

"Ah!" said McAlmond, relieved. "Why?"

"So that I may take my patron's quarterly grant and spend it in a more useful manner, on clothes, for instance, and on a little self-indulgence. To be honest, Fraser, I'm not cut out for a 'stinking garret' sort of existence."

"You're a shrewd little jackanapes, Stalker."

"You have a double parlour in the basement of your house. Your man-servant uses only one room of it."

"How the devil?"

"Balfour Sprott told me. Why waste the space?"

"Why, indeed!" said McAlmond, shrugging. "A free comfortable lodging for you, and a crammer on the premises for me."

"In short, yes."

"I think," said McAlmond, twisting the cane over his shoulders to rest both hands upon it like a barbell, "I really do think that I had *best* do you this favour, Stalker."

"There is no obligation—other than friendship."

"And my need to do well in class?"

"Is it agreed?" said Drew.

"My hand on it."

Inwardly Drew sighed with relief as he shook Fraser McAlmond's hand. He was clear at last of the unpleasant entanglements of the Old Town's wynds, of Heather Campbell and her alleged pregnancy.

The lesson would be well learned. He would not fall into that self-indulgent trap again. Indeed, he had come out of it well, magnificently well. Within a week he would be rooming with the famous Fraser McAlmond, and within a term, he promised himself, he would have the influential young dandy eating out of his hand.

In a region of ugly, smoke-spewing towns Grossby, twenty miles out of Leeds, was by any standards, the ugliest. Barricaded on one flank by the desolate range of Limewell Rise and on the other by a canal, its narrow streets, back-to-back hovels and massive cotton mills were crushed into an area so confined that no glimmer of sunlight ever penetrated there. Throughout the county the township was known as the Dark Parish.

Mirrin's high hopes of finding lucrative employment vanished within a couple of days of her arrival in Grossby. Red-cheeked and strong after her months in the fields, she was, however, signed on in the picking shed of Truesdales' Mill at a wage of eight shillings a week. Over half of this sum was immediately transferred back into the mill owner's coffers in return for 'provender and lodging', both of which, on meanest terms, the benefactor provided whether his employees wished it or not. The food was swill, the lodgings nothing but a palliasse on the floor of a 'dormitory' cellar at the rear of the mill, under that oppressive retaining red-brick wall.

The Brummidges had advised Mirrin to travel further south. "Easier to get into a mill town than to get out of it," Mr. Brummidge had informed her.

But she had almost run out of cash on the slow journey south and was afraid that she would wind up penniless and jobless. No, she had told the kindly carters, Grossby would have to do.

She should have heeded the Brummidges. The miserable dwellings, built on a slope like goblin-holes, faced on to streets and alleys that were hardly more than sewers. Squadrons of children played among the ordure, chasing rats and cats and skeletal mongrels, or fighting over some crushed piece of fruit or vegetable husk that had miraculously appeared in the barren waste.

Truesdales' Mill swallowed Mirrin Stalker alive. The process of ingestion was rapid. Four days as a sweeper, then shifted to the picking frames, Mirrin found herself sucked into a treadmill of dust, dirt, stink and noise that, within a single week, deadened not only her nerves but her will. The most pitiless aspect of Blacklaw had been paradise compared to the slavery of Grossby's insatiable looms.

The cotton frame, result of the American Civil War, had brought benefits to the workers in many mill towns, improved conditions in manufactories vying for trade. The Truesdale 'family,' however, had cannily ignored both famine and progress, maintaining their equipment at minimum cost, until the premises degenerated into a relic of the worst type of 'liddle mill', unchanged for half a century.

Mirrin's partner at the picking frame was Faye Ashcroft, thirty-year-old wife of an unemployed weaver. Faye had three young children and a fourth, as she put it, 'in the oven'. Lifting of heavy wads of cotton from the slashed bales cost her much effort now, whips of pain beneath which even her indomitable stoicism wilted.

Mirrin brandished the heavy flexible picking sticks, three feet in length, and, in spite of her own fatigue, said, "Let me do the pluckin', just for a couple of days. I need t'learn, you know."

"I'm capable."

"Do me the favour," said Mirrin.

The woman seemed about to argue then, annoyed by her own understandable debility, nodded. "Just for today then, lass."

A warning hiss from down the length of the frames indicated that an overlooker was on the warpath. Mirrin had already had her knuckles cracked for blethering. She clenched her teeth and concentrated on her task.

Raw cotton was broken down by draping hanks on a slatted wood frame, battening them by stretched cords, and thrashing them until the fibres loosened and seeds, leaves and other detritus shook through into ground-level trays. In principle a simple enough job:

in practice the thickly matted cotton resisted all but the beater's most strenuous efforts.

"Solid rock," Mirrin declared, pounding furiously.

"Give it here," Faye Ashcroft said, resignedly. "If the bleedin' stuff won't split an' shred then you've got t'rake it with your fingers. See, like this."

Mirrin watched as the Ashcroft woman tore at the wadding mounded between the cords. She waited until Faye had roughened the smooth, implacable surface of the stuff, then fell to flogging it again with the pliant sticks. She had no sense of rhythm. It was more exhausting than picking neeps in a farmer's field, more monotonous than sorting at a colliery trough.

Faye said, "The overlooker's got his eye on you, Mirrin. Speed it up."

By the end of her third day's labour, Mirrin's nails were broken to the quick and her arms ached so much that every small gesture, even the scrape of her spoon in her dinner bowl, sent pain shooting through her shoulders into the base of her skull.

At night she dozed fitfully, too exhausted to sleep. She remembered how Mam had taken her hands after the first day-shift at the pithead troughs and had bathed the bleeding knuckles and soothed and smoothed the skin with an ointment and comforted her, saying, "It'll get better, Mirrin. You'll see, it'll get better." But it had not improved. Her hands had roughened, not her heart.

By the end of a week, Mirrin had developed a cough, stimulated by the filigree particles of lint which floated like a haze in the atmosphere of the crowded ill-ventilated shed. That fibrous vapour, seeded with tiny itching granules, seemed to coat her skin, her hair and infiltrate deep into her chest and lungs. She could taste nothing but oily cotton. It was not merely uncomfortable: it was lethal, a slow route to the grave.

On Thursday afternoon, that first week in November, the thud of a falling body disturbed the clattering, battering flails and brought women running to a frame midway up the row.

The slumped girl was hardly older than herself, Mirrin noted, though an empurpled complexion and the strangled writhings of her limbs made it difficult to assess her age.

"What's wrong with her?" Mirrin asked.

Two older women bent over their companion. They ignored Mirrin's naïve question, working busily but without panic.

"Head back: push her head back."

"Can yet get at it?"

"Eee! Lookee there."

"What is it?" Mirrin asked again.

Then she saw.

The recumbent girl's jaw was yanked open. Two hooked fingers were thrust to the roots of her tongue and, after much groping on the nurse's part and much gagging and retching on the part of the patient, a long slimy strand of teased cotton waste was extracted from her gullet.

Nausea gripped Mirrin. She doubled over, wrapping her arms around her stomach. The taste of the lint in her own mouth frightened her. She choked on it. The older women chuckled and one crone laughed. With horror, Mirrin looked into the old woman's mouth and saw that the membranes were ingrained with that greyish speckling.

The crone gaped, pointing a stump-like finger into her mouth, then said, gleefully, "Never see'd that afore, 'ave ye, luv? Never see'd none o'them bouncin' an' jumpin' 'til they choked on cotton, eh? Plugs big as yor fist I see'd cut out o'them. When I war yor age I'ad me throat slit wi' a gully-knife t'pull the plug out an' save me life."

Mirrin reeled back to her frame and slumped against it. Her mouth was arid, her throat constricted. The shed swam before her eyes. Overlookers were scolding the women back to work. Even the girl, the victim who had been on the point of suffocation a few moments before, was being roughly dragged to her feet.

"God! God!" Mirrin sought to gulp air but the realisation of what she would inhale with it prevented her. Her throat spasmed.

Faye Ashcroft patted her solicitously. "Don't think

about it, luv. First sight's the worst. Got the plug out, didn't they? Do the same for you."

Mirrin bowed her head, pressed her tongue to the roof of her mouth and tried to breathe only through her nostrils. It was easy enough at rest but with the exertions of flailing she knew that she would have to suck in the foul, mote-filled, killing air of the shed.

An image of the past rose, ironically, in her mind. One Christmas, when she was young, the minister had treated faithful Sunday School attenders to a soirée in Northrigg hall. Kate had been there, and James; even wee Dougie. They had eaten raisins and oranges, listened to recitations and sang songs to a melodeon accompaniment. But what she recalled most vividly was a conjurer who, having caused a roll of bright silk ribbon to vanish into his fist, magicked its reappearance from his mouth, unfurling it yard by yard from the back of his throat. Nobody had cheered more loudly than Mirrin. It had been years before she realised that the trick had been done by sleight-of-hand. Now it might be done in reality, by any one of the hundred women in the shed—or by herself.

"Stop it, lass," Faye Ashcroft advised. "Stop thinkin' about it. Here, lift them flails an' get on with yer work."

Don't think: work! That was all she could now do, Mirrin told herself. Work: don't think! Don't dare think! A feverish energy possessed her and, snatching up both sticks, she hammered and thrashed at the stripped cotton on its bond frame until sweat beaded her brow and dripped down her nose and her breath rasped in her throat and the oily taste of lint was salted down and the thought of rest, of death, late or soon and by any means at all, was no longer to be feared but welcomed.

Mirrin soon lost all track of time. Hours dripped into days, days, for all she could tell, accumulated into weeks. There was nothing to life but the mill and the flailing of rods on the frames. Work at Blacklaw's chutes or in the tinkers' lines had never been so stultifying or so physically damaging as the labour extracted by Truesdales' overlookers. Mill-hands assured her that there were worse occupations. Mirrin could not imagine them. Even her few brief hours of sleep huddled each night under an overcoat in the damp, verminous dormitory, were racked by spasms of coughing and dreams of the picking shed so lurid that the girl jerked and thrashed upon the mattress and obtained no rest for her tortured muscles. If it had been possible to save even a few shillings she would have walked out and taken her chances on the road again. But, so invidious was the tariff system, that Mirrin could save not so much as a farthing and, frightened beyond reason by tales of illness and starvation, fell deeper into bondage, sick in soul as well as body.

The Scotch lass was only one of many suffering illness. Fevers and dysentery were encouraged by bad food, foul water and lack of proper sanitation. Women reeled about the shed like walking skeletons, sagging over the frames in states nearer to death than exhaustion. The overlookers were merciless, protecting their own jobs, jealous of their power and few extra 'bits o' brass'. They yelled and jabbered and poked the culprits with their billy-sticks and paid off a dozen hands each day, casting them into the outer darkness of penury and probable death.

If she had been stronger, the rebellious streak in Mirrin would have come to her rescue. She could have displayed her former political fervour in such an overt manner that she would have been run out of Truesdales' as a militant radical. But Mirrin did not have the strength to fight a battle of principles. Even her obstinacy had been reduced to a shuffling thing that moved her no further towards mutiny than tight-lipped silence whenever the billy rapped her knuckles or shoulders. In her debilitated state she imagined that her protection of Faye Ashcroft was an act of retaliation against the system, instead of responsive kindness towards a person in even more desperate straits than she was herself.

Though her baby was not due for seven or eight weeks, Faye Ashcroft's stomach was gigantically swollen. Mirrin, who had never seen such malformation before, was appalled at the condition and at the fear which drove the woman to continue her exertions at the picking frames. The positions she contrived to give the flails clearance and, Mirrin suspected, to ease her internal pains, were grotesque. Each night this woman returned to a house no bigger than a closet, to three demanding children and the tender mercies of a husband whose only thought now was for the money that would be lost to him, and by extension to the local publicans, when his wife's time of deliverance arrived. Time of deliverance? There was no such thing. It was a myth as distant and remote as heaven. Even if the babe should, somehow, be born into this world alive, its chances of survival would be infinitesimal. It might even be 'helped' back to join the cherubim some dark night by its father's drunken antics.

"Here, Faye, lean on me."

"Nay, nay, lass."

"Rest up a while. They won't see."

"They'll see. They see all."

Did they see, Mirrin wondered, the flushed cheeks and dry skin, scalding lungs and feeble limbs? Aye, the overlookers saw all right and, she imagined, sniggered at the changes that the weeks had made, chalking her off already as one too weak to last the pace, another 'failure', a score for the system. How long could she go on like this, burned by fever, drained by the deep lung-wrenching cough, sapped of all volition?

When Faye Ashcroft fell, Mirrin dropped the sticks and endeavoured to support her, but the woman slumped heavily against her, pushing Mirrin down on to the coarse bed of greasy raw cotton, pinning her. They balanced there like drunks sprawled on a sagging fence, arms entwined, cheeks touching, Faye's mouth wide open. She might have been laughing, but the sound was more subtle, a sifting throttle, very deep and soft and furtive as if her unborn child had whimpered discontentedly in her womb, once before dying and, in dying, had selfishly summoned his mother to the grave for company. The grey encrustations round her lips were stained with blood. Mirrin knew at once that Faye Ashcroft was dead.

The billy was wielded by a hard-faced sow of a woman, the longest-serving overlooker on the company's books. She had survived and endured. Latterly she had learned to enjoy the privileges of her rank, developing the streak of meanness that had hallmarked her as a born plenipotentiary, part of the force that protected the owners from the workers.

The first blow struck Faye Ashcroft across the small of the back. Already dead, Faye was beyond the reach of pain. Mirrin did not react impulsively as she would have done six weeks or even a month before. She needed now to think it out, to choose between negative descent into selfishness—a heartlessness of which she was, perhaps, capable and which would have stood her in good stead—and the avowal that, even in the lowest depths there is a point at which the human animal must stand for dignity.

"She's dead, miss," Mirrin said.

"Ay, I've heard that tale before."

"She is: look: she's dead."

The overlooker scowled and prodded the billy-stick between Mirrin and the pregnant woman's chest, prizing them apart. Levering, she altered the balance of the corpse and dispassionately watched Faye Ashcroft's body slide to the floor at the base of the picking frame. She touched the body with her boot, flopping it over.

"Ay, she's dead, right enough."

Mirrin lay back on the frame, thinking, at that moment, of nothing but the relief of rest, sharing vicariously the peace that Faye enjoyed, beyond the reach of fear and care and pain.

The billy thudded on her breast.

"You," the overlooker said. "Back t'yer work. The bosses don't pay ye t'mourn."

The sow would bear the scar for the rest of her life. Another inch and Mirrin might have killed her. As it was, sudden horror increased her energy, focussed it on the one object, and shaped her action.

Ripping the billy from the overlooker's hand, Mirrin struck with it, snapping it down across the bridge of the woman's nose. Blood spurted and flowed, an effusion that by its warmth and brightness, melted Mirrin's indifference to the callousness of Faye Ashcroft's passing.

Shouting, Mirrin raised the stick again. If she struck even one more blow, however, she would condemn herself for ever to the sort of viciousness that enabled Truesdales' mills to clack on at full volume. In disgust, she tossed the billy away and, hands clasped to her head, ran unimpeded down the length of the shed, out through the haze which clouded the doorway and into the oily daylight beyond.

The side door led to a lane. The lane was empty. No hue and cry of overlookers, foremen or owners' managers trailed her, though Mirrin, haunted by the enormity of her crime, was obsessed by the feeling that she was the object of Truesdales' collective vengeance. She tottered down the lane between soaring walls of weathered red brick towards another wall above which the symbols of the mill town lofted into the grey sky; chimney stacks, Grossby's equivalent of Blacklaw's winding towers.

Reeling, she fled as fast as her legs would carry her through the brick maze, suffocated by heat for a yard or two then shaken by cold. Her shoulders and arms ached. She shook her head in an effort to concentrate, to reach decisions, find direction. Her coat and skirt and few personal belongings were still in the dormitory. She could think of no course of action which would allow her to retrieve them without running foul of authority and risk being arrested for having dared strike an overlooker.

Halting, she groped in panic at her waist, found her money roll and, weeping with relief, sank against the wall and fumbled out the little sack. Squatting, she spilled the meagre collection of coins on the ground and, head bent, sweat pouring from her brow, concentrated on counting them.

Eleven pence was all that she owned in the world. She blinked stupidly. How much could she do with that? Buy a ticket out of Grossby—a ticket to another town, another stinking city. She was owed four days' wages. Could she somehow collect them? Remembering the gush of blood from the pig-faced woman's nose, she discarded any hope of acquiring her dues. The wages were gone, gone like everything else. I must *walk* to another town, she told herself, rising. I *must* find work. I can't do *anything* without work. I *must* earn money to keep myself alive. She looked down the lane at the chimneys' plumes of smoke, haphazardly choosing that direction at the lane's end.

Nothing seemed real, solid. Even the ground beneath her feet shifted and trembled as if it was the crust of a quaking lava bed.

She knew she was ill. Acknowledgement of that most obvious of facts steadied her a little and gave her an objective. She could do nothing until she cured herself, broke the fever which raged in her veins. The eleven pence must be spent on medicinal powders to clear her head and ease her distress, to buy a remedy and find a fourpenny lodging to lie up in until she recovered sufficiently to get out of Grossby and back on the road. Elevenpence would not go far. Worry roared back into her mind, enlarged by fever into yammering fear.

Every moment was precious. She must begin at once to be rid of the illness, to start on the road to recovery, the road to health and strength, the road to another picking shed, or a loom, or a coalpit chute.

She must find a pharmacy. She veered right at the lane's end and emerged from the mill area into the top of the town.

It was coming on towards dusk now, though the clock in the chapel tower said it was not yet four. Gas lamps had been lighted and whatever sun there had been had sunk behind the crags of Limewell rise. The canal was like a trench of dross below her, the mean tiers of houses drenched in the same brown hue. She felt light now, indifferent to direction. She would find what she sought in time. All her urgency had been left behind in the red-brick maze.

Hamilton was a nice town. She could be home in half an hour. Betsy worked in Hamilton. Betsy would take her home. Mam would tuck her up in bed in the back room with a hot lemon drink and a piggie at her feet. When she was better, Kate would bring her gruel

and coddled eggs and soup, sit on the edge of the bed
and feed her with a spoon. And Da would come in and
see her when he got off the shift. And she would hear
James and Dougie laughing and Mam telling them to
shush. And maybe Rob would come too. She liked
Rob. He would cheer her up almost as much as James
and Dougie. She would be safe with her family and
friends, snug out of the cold streets in her own bed in
the back room of the narrow house. Where was it now?
Where was the road home, the road back, into the
happy past?

Not Hamilton! Grossby, England.

The lamps were brighter, the last of the daylight
fading fast. She moved aimlessly, floating like lint, on
down the narrow cobbled street towards the crowded
square where the pharmacy would be, if there was a
pharmacy.

Folk approached her, then sheered away, noticing
her flushed cheeks and dazed, shining eyes. Typhoid
and influenza were starting up in towns not thirty miles
away. Couldn't be too careful.

Houston would come in his carriage, rattling out of
that lane by the town hall. He would rein to a halt
and leap from the seat and gather her in his arms and
take her into the warm, leather-smelling interior of the
coach and hold her while the coach rocked, and rocked
her all the way home, home in Houston's arms.

The cobbler's shop she recognised by the rap of the
hammers, the draper's by the *ping* of the bell above
the door. The lights of the windows shone brilliantly,
blindingly, making her head and eyes ache. Next was
the butcher's, the nauseating stench of raw meat, pig
and mutton and skeins of ox-tripe draped like Turkish
towels across the entrance. Sickness rose in her gorge.
She thrust her hands to her mouth, turning modestly
away from the women at the shop doormouth to cough
phlegm into the gutter.

As she stooped, the pavement tilted and formed a
coil, the people on it poked out like spokes on a broken
wheel. She was the axis, the cobbled street the rim,
trundling, spinning, faster and faster, rolling with a
deafening, lurching, cracking sound. It was all Mirrin

could do to reel to the inside of the pavement again
and grab at the heavy iron staves which mounted
guard between the shops and the first of the brown
brick houses. Hooking her elbow around the post, she
clung there, upright now only by sheer effort of will.

Though her eyes were wide open and contemplated
the street, her brain played cruel tricks. Her vision
was blurred by the image of a huge green field
in which stood effigies of her past, motionless, wooden,
dead: her Da, poor Loonie Lachie who had lived in
Blacklaw and been happy there once, and Houston,
Rob, Callum Ewing, even Tom Armstrong.

Were they all dead now? Oh, God! How many more
had died? Tilting her head, squinting to find reality in
her waking nightmare, she caught sight of James in the
bizarre Aunt Sally crowd. As a cloud moved silently
and smoothly across the green field and darkened it to
dun, she saw her elder brother walk from the row of
wooden figures, then run, diminishing in stature as he
approached. The field was gone. The street restored
itself, and the figures were the figures of inhospitable
strangers: all except one. James was still there, small,
child-like, staring at her out of his piercing blue eyes,
not smiling. That one fragment of her hallucination refused to vanish like the rest. Of them all, she *knew*
that James was dead, dead and buried and at rest.

But even he did not recognise her? Had she fallen
so far in grace that not even her dear brother would
acknowledge her and welcome her to the realms of the
hereafter?

"James?" she said.

He ran on, the boy that she had mistaken for her
brother scampered on. But she could not relinquish
him, her last ray of hope.

Reaching out, she cried piteously, *"Jaaaaamm-
mmmesssss."*

The small boy stopped abruptly and turned to stare
back at her, uncertain and half afraid.

"Edward, come here." The voice was not peevish
but firm and maternal.

Lifting her head Mirrin struggled to focus on the
woman who had summoned the child and who, two or

three yards from her now, had also become wooden, trapped too in that distorted world of the past.

"Oh, my God! It's our Mirrin!"

Amazement did not veil the warmth and pity in the woman's tone, nor disguise its comforting familiarity. Suddenly Mirrin recognised the features of Lily Dawson Stalker, her brother James's widow, and the small, serious face of Edward.

"Mam, Mam, who is it?"

"Mirrin Stalker, son: your Auntie Mirrin," Lily answered. "Edward, run back int' the house there and fetch your Grandpa. *Quick.*"

Sighing, Mirrin pitched forward into Lily's arms.

Eight

MIRRIN'S RETURN TO consciousness was gradual. For a long time before she opened her eyes, she travelled a road that was dark and twisting, past fields and hedges and cottages peopled with half-forgotten faces. She seemed to see a child perched on a stool beside her. But even as she attempted to focus on him and relate the little boy to the dark places, he pulled away and she was left wandering in the clouds that piled around her, shadows that canalised into ditches full of brown smoke that, softly now, raised themselves up into the likeness of chimney stacks and tilted winding towers.

Several times she attempted to struggle awake. Once she thought she heard voices, felt hands upon her shoulders. For most of that period, however, everything remained vague, and she was content to allow herself to be borne along, knowing that no positive action was demanded of her.

Finally when she became curious enough to open

her eyes she viewed her surroundings with a surprising lucidity. Daylight fell in geometric shapes through a skylight set in a steeply sloping ceiling. The angle of rake immediately informed her that she had not somehow been miraculously transported home again.

No house she'd ever been in had a roof plane like that. It was a small room, furnished with a rather ornate bed. Brass knobs at head and foot reminded her of Russian palaces. A corner chiffonier looked to be walnut but turned out later to be best quality *papier mâché* imitation. The narrow upright bed-table had a chintz frill round it and the room's one chair, a comfortable miniature recliner, was covered with identical material. Along the base of the sloping ceiling the wall had been papered in a floral-cape design. Pleased with her visual exploration, Mirrin closed her eyes again and dozed.

The chime of a spoon on a dish wakened her. She eased herself on to her elbow. She had no difficulty now in separating fact from feverish fantasy. She identified the young woman and the little boy at once.

"Lily! I thought I was dreamin'."

"So did I, I can tell you, luv," Lily replied. "I mean, what way was that t'come visitin' relatives, on your back in the public highway."

"But, Lily . . ."

"Hup, Mirrin: not a word, not 'til you've tucked away all this soup. It's what the doctor ordered; plenty liquids."

"How long've I been here?"

"Not so long, really. Couple of days."

"Two days!"

"Don't excite yourself, luv. We're not chargin' you by the night," Lily said. "Here, drink."

Hoisting her into a sitting position, Lily spooned the warm liquid between Mirrin's parched lips. To Mirrin's surprise Lily kept up a stream of inconsequential chatter, saying how much the butcher charged for bones compared with Scotland, and how hard it was to get wee Edward to take his nourishment, and look at Auntie Mirrin wasn't she good to eat all her soup and not a word of complaint. Edward, who had presumably gazed his fill on Mirrin and already formed his opinion of this surprising 'auntie', got down on the floor to amuse himself by playing with a to-bacco tin full of odd buttons.

When the soup was finished and Lily had wiped Mirrin's hands and face with a cool wash-cloth, Mirrin flatly rejected her sister-in-law's suggestion that she cuddle down for another nap.

"I feel as if I'd been asleep for a month, Lily. Tell me, where am I?"

"Grossby," Lily said. "This is m'father's place, a boardinghouse."

"I thought your Da worked in the mills?"

"He decided he didn't want t'die before his time. Packed it in."

"But the money?"

"To buy this place, y'mean? He borrowed it. He'd some saved up, an' took out a note on the United Bank for the balance. He wagered on hard work payin' off. It has too."

Mirrin shook her head in bewilderment. "Business on his own. That's what a man should do."

"It was a real shock t'see you lyin' there, Mirrin. I near died."

"That makes two of us."

"Folk round here are shy of strangers: aye, an' wary of anythin' that even resembles typhoid."

"What was the diagnosis?"

"Influenza," said Lily. "Compounded by malnutri-tion, the doctor said. God, I never thought I'd see the day a Stalker would suffer from that."

"I've been workin' in Truesdales'."

"We guessed that by the state you were in. The pickin' sheds can destroy a buddy faster than any col-liery job. I take it they flung you out when you got too sick t'work?"

Mirrin nodded: she could not be bothered with ex-planations just yet.

In the crowded months since she'd left Blacklaw in the wake of James's death and the stillbirth of her second child, Lily had changed. She was more ma-ture, though less pretty than she had been when

James brought her proudly home to Blacklaw after his one and only foray out of Scotland in search of fame and fortune, a year's gut-empty, footsore tramp round the black spots of England that had stilled disenchantment with Blacklaw for ever.

"I'll be up an' away in a day or so," said Mirrin.

"You'll be up when the doctor gives you the word, an'not an hour before."

"Lily, I can't impose on . . ."

"Hark't her!" Lily exclaimed. Edward peeped hopefully over the end of the bed to see what his eccentric aunt was up to now. "Impose! The Stalkers pulled me through when things was at their blackest for me. Oh, God, aye! I'll admit I was bitter at the time, but not towards the family, only at Lamont an' his damned pit."

If James had been present in that room he would not have approved of Lily's language, especially within the boy's earshot. It was part and parcel of Lily's changed personality, a bluffness that often came after great loss and suffering. Mirrin could appreciate it now. She wondered, languidly, how much change the people back home would notice in her when she returned. She would have to return now. As soon as she could get herself back on her feet, she would make a beeline for the Scottish border and Blacklaw. Even thinking about home brought tears to her eyes.

"This bed's big enough for both of us, 'til the house gets busy nearer Christmas," said Lily. "You're goin' nowhere for a month at least."

"Lily, I . . ." Mirrin sniffed.

Edward watched, uncertainly.

"Ah, Lily," Mirrin sobbed. "You're so kind t'me. I could've died there in the street, a strange, foreign street. It's good t'see a friendly face."

"How long've you been on the road?"

"Six months, near seven."

"Did you run away?"

"No, not really. What makes you think that?"

Lily grinned. "This chap you kept bletherin' about."

Mirrin's eyes creased with apprehension. "What . . . what chap?"

"Tom Armstrong, y'called him," said Lily. "I thought maybe you'd run off with him, like."

Mirrin laughed, wheezy still, at the ridiculousness of Lily's conjecture. "Tom Armstrong's a tink."

"Tink or not, he's still a man," Lily said. "Is he nice?"

"Nice enough. But he was never mine."

"Tink?" said Edward from the brass cage at the bed-end. "Tink?"

"A gypsy," said Mirrin. "Don't y'know about gypsies, Edward?"

"Noooooaaaaah."

Mirrin winked. "I'll tell you some grand tales about the tinkers, when I'm stronger."

"Tonight?"

"Maybe tomorrow," Mirrin said. "We'll have a right old chin-wag, you an' me, Edward."

Edward giggled. "Chin-wag," he said, giggling louder. "Chin-wag."

"Right you, m'lad," Lily said, firmly but not severely. "Out. Auntie Mirrin wants t'sleep."

"Auntie Mirrin sleeps?"

"Aye, son," Mirrin said. " 'Til tomorrow."

The boy was reluctant to leave, until, by the only means at his disposal, he had given the woman a sign of his acceptance. Coming up the side of the bed he held out his hand and, solemnly, dropped a shiny red object into Mirrin's palm.

"Have a button, Auntie Mirrin." He was a little puzzled when his new-found aunt wept again.

Ernest Dawson was shovelling potatoes from a bunker set in a corner of the clean, cluttered kitchen when his daughter returned from attending the invalid. He scowled at her, his smooth flabby cheeks flushed with irritation and his brows, grey as badgers' brushes, knitted together over his fleshy nose.

"It's about time you got down here, Lily." An avalanche of small spuds rattled into the wooden bucket. "Vegetables to be prepared, custard to make."

"It'll be done, father," said Lily, patiently.

"Can't do everything m'self, while you're dancin' attendance on that one, up there."

"She's asleep now."

Dawson grunted, levelled the potatoes with his shovel and gestured to Lily to carry the load. "She's not stayin' here, mind you. Each and every room in this here house has to pay its way, like. I don't have no charity beds for vagrants."

Anger glittered in Lily's eyes. Before she could move to Mirrin's defense—not for the first time—her mother entered the kitchen from the door that led out to the cavernous laundry rooms, holding a cotton bolster case before her like a flag of truce.

"Doesn't want it," Hilda Dawson said.

"What's wrong with it, like?" her husband demanded.

"Brought her own silks," Hilda said. "Ideas about bein' better than she is, that Mrs. Teape. Claims she's an admiral's widow, an' the silk cases come all the way from India."

Dawson smirked, his annoyance at Lily forgotten. "An admiral's wife! Jolly-hoh! A bargee's tart, more like. Are her cases *real* silk, dearest?"

Hilda nodded, folding the cotton case carefully to return to the airing cupboards which flanked the corridor of the drying room.

"Airs and graces. Her nether garments is patched like rags."

"I thought as much."

Hilda Dawson was a severe woman, pinched and angular. She matched her husband's asperity snipe for snipe, though comparative prosperity in recent years had caused him to grow bloated as she grew more rigidly skinny. They lived in harmony, however, sharing the same aspirations, the same sustaining snobbishness and bigotry. Having escaped from the ranks of the working class, the Dawsons held it now in awe and contempt and considered every parliamentary concession to the improvement of the common man's lot as 'mollycoddling'. They believed firmly in the gospel of Samuel Smiles. *Self-Help* was their Bible, the boarding-house and all its accoutrement, plus a safe little nest-egg in the Grossby Bank, living proof that only by their own efforts could persons raise and improve their lot.

Ernest Dawson continued his attack on Mirrin as Lily filled the bucket from the tap above the sink and, with the bristle broom kept for that purpose, chafed at the spuds to remove the outer layer of peel. In the corner under the zinc washing sink, Edward had been given a potato and four spent matches to play with, a regular part of the pre-dinner ritual.

"I don't see what you have against Mirrin," Lily said at length.

"She's a vagrant."

"She's my relative," Lily said.

"What will the other boarders say?"

"They've hardly noticed."

"We pride ourselves on keepin' our standards of the highest."

"An' the proof of that is we have seven rooms out of ten let this week," Hilda said. "An' the Fowlers down at Number Twenty have only three."

"When she's on her feet again, out she goes," Dawson said.

"You can't mean that, father," Lily protested. "The Stalkers were good to me when I needed help."

"Good to you when you carried a Stalker child, y'mean," Ernest Dawson said. "You wouldn't have had to suffer at all if you'd wed Charles Probert, now would you?"

"Charles Probert never had any interest in me."

"Not true: not true. With a little bit of encouragement."

"Anyway, I don't like him: never did. He'd have married Claire Grantham, anyway, no matter what I did."

"Look at him, a fine handsome man," Hilda said. "A property owner in a big way. He rides with the Brambledale pack, y'know."

"I've seen him," Lily said. "Fat as a pig in his daft red coat."

"I suppose your collier was better?"

"Aye, he was: far better."

"Better now he's gone."

"Ernest!" warned Hilda, who knew when her husband was overstepping himself.

Lily sighed. The arguments were too familiar to hurt her much now. Matter-of-factly, she declared. "Well, if you put Mirrin out before she's ready to go, I leave with her—an' Edward, too, o'course."

"I'll need the room," Ernest Dawson said. "It's the busy season. The Talboys are comin'. We're fully booked."

"She can sleep with me," said Lily.

"Will she do a turn in the kitchen or at table?" Hilda asked.

"I expect so," said Lily. "When she's stronger."

Hilda and Ernest exchanged another glance, the woman encouraging the man's capitulation. Lily knew that her threat to leave, to remove Edward, upon whom her parents poured the affection that they had withheld from her, had been taken seriously.

"I'll look after her," said Lily. "I feel I'm payin' back some of what I owe. You can understand *that*, father, can't you?"

"Well, all right. But only 'til she's recovered, like. An' she's not t'show her nose out of her room. Hear? If that commercial gentleman in number six even caught sight of her . . ." Dawson shuddered at the contemplation of such a contingency.

Edward gave a short demanding cry, pouting for attention. Putting down the brush, Lily scooped up her son and planted a kiss on his soft warm cheek.

"Auntie Mirrin stayin'?" the child asked.

"Aye, Auntie Mirrin's stayin'," said Lily, firmly.

Drew Stalker and Daniel Horn had much in common. It had become quite a habit for the gentlemen to eat dinner in the cellar of the *Kenmore,* a short step from the High Street. The timing of the excursion was exact, of course, taking in only that period during which Gow Havershaw engaged in the partaking of luncheon, minus one half hour. Drew and Daniel Horn fed on cheese pie and ale. The younger man paid for the meal.

"So," Horn said, "it's McAlmond you're after."

"Not so," Drew replied. "I merely said that as I had received an invitation to Pearsehill over the Christmas vacation it would do no harm to be briefed beforehand."

"Who else will be there?" asked Horn.

"Hector Mellish."

"Mellish, aye: we have a record on his family."

"And the McAlmonds?"

"Not much, I fear. Just orthodox business."

The pair had no need to talk quietly, for the eating house was a rabble of voices, the conversations of clerks of all varieties rising like a plaint of crows under the square beams of the *Kenmore's* ceiling.

Horn was a man deceptively aged by his vices, dried out like a mandrake root. He lived in a two-room apartment in the Canongate Road with two young women, and managed them as more lofty fellows might manage a pair of race horses, entering them only for select and high-paying events. Horn was forty-seven. He had served a short term as a garrison sergeant in the Queen's Own Foot back in the forties—or so he said—and had fought against the Sikhs in India. The sun had dried out his skin then and it had never recovered its proper tone, hanging on the bones of his face like charred parchment. He had entered the law, in the position of clerk, to escape the army, hiding out in Edinburgh in preference to his native Dumfries—or so he said. Drew did not believe a word of it.

Scooping the last wedge of his cheese pie into his mouth, Drew said, "Can you find out?"

"Find out what?" said Daniel Horn, who had finished victualling minutes before and was doing justice to a second mug of ale.

"Anything."

"Be precise, young Stalker."

"Come now, Daniel, you know the sort of thing I want."

"Ask your friend Fraser."

"He hardly knows how to wipe his nose," Drew said. "He is, believe me, incredibly stupid."

"You wish to impress the old man."

"I wish to be well thought of, yes."

"Then avoid brewing as a topic of conversation."

Drew laughed. "What do you suggest?"

"Cattle, crops."

"Cases?"

Horn sucked his teeth. "Agricultural Holdings Act: Land Transfer Act: Artisans' Dwelling Act. Archie probably won't understand those, and his sort are always impressed by what they don't comprehend."

"All well and good," Drew said.

"Luscombe and French handle the investments for the McAlmond estates. The bankers are the Capital Merchants."

"What about the wife?"

"She's connected to the Oakley fortune."

"Anything I should mull over?"

"Ancestral oddments. She's proud of the family."

"Political persuasions?"

"Die-hard Tory, o'course."

Drew nodded.

Horn wiped his lean chops with his knuckle. "Does Havershaw know you're invading Pearsehill?"

"Not yet."

"He who looks rich, gets rich," Horn said.

"Meaning?"

"Tap the boss."

"He won't open his purse."

"He might, for a larger share of the McAlmond pie."

"That," said Drew, "will take years t'slice."

"The boss can wait: patience is one thing he's learned."

"Will you drop a word?"

"Simple." Horn tapped his nose with his forefinger.

"And the information?"

"Also simple."

"May I leave it to you, Daniel?"

"Trust me, young Stalker."

"That," Drew said, "I'll never do."

"But when you open chambers of your own, you will take me on, won't you?"

"That goes without saying," Drew told the clerk. "*If* I ever manage to achieve that august status."

"You will, you will," Daniel Horn assured him.

"And if I don't?"

"We can go into partnership in a knocking shop."

"Quite!" Drew Stalker said, and winced.

The 'Admiral's Widow' had packed up and left before Mirrin Stalker recovered sufficient strength to interest herself in the affairs of the House of Dawson. The Dawsons were not sorry to see the widow woman go. They had been flummoxed by her rank and could not quite fathom into what category she should be placed. It made no matter in the long run, for the lady upped one morning, paid her bill and was gone in a hired fly no less, before Mirrin had come downstairs. The widow was replaced within the day by a travelling gent from Suffolk who bought and sold agricultural machinery. Edward did not take at all to the salesman, who had a squint in one eye and a curved calabash pipe that looked as if it had grown on to his jaw.

In addition to Mr. Quayle, 'the implementarian' as he styled himself, four other gentlemen of more or less 'commercial' bent were in temporary residence, plus a couple of ladies who had a six months' lease on the second-floor back. These ladies paid in advance and did business in the buying of musical instruments for their father and brothers down London way. More discreet prying, necessitated by the fear that the couple would lug pianos into their bedroom by cover of night, unearthed the fact that they had leased a store in Wolfram Street to keep their items in prior to shipping them south.

It was almost a fortnight after her first emergence from her room before Mirrin had much contact with the guests. The moment her feet touched the floor of the skylight room, Ernest Dawson made his appearance like a pantomime demon insisting with bald civility that she remove her belongings—referred to with a pointed sniff—to Lily's room and that she did not use the water-closet at the corridor's end after ten at night as the plumbing was not exactly silent and decent folk liked to sleep undisturbed.

Mirrin was glad enough to shift in with Lily and Edward. The room, quite large enough to accommodate all three, was already furnished with a double bed and a cot for the boy.

As Mirrin's energy increased, so did her gratitude to Lily and her willingness to draw the Dawsons' sting by working for her keep. Cheerfulness and her capacity for ordered labour and, perhaps, wee Edward's adoration, won over Ernest and Hilda in a short space of time.

In Mirrin, unexpectedly, they found the servant they had always sought, capable, uncomplaining and—probably—trustworthy. With her housekeeping experience, Mirrin soon made unobtrusive improvements upon the lodging-house economy. Most of all, however, the Dawsons warmed towards Mirrin because she so obviously 'knew her place'. For the first time in many months she was secure, comfortable and loved. She had no wish to endanger the sanctuary.

It was Edward who added the quality of love. The child transformed the prim boarding-house into a place full of warmth and laughter and united the diverse characters of his grandparents, his mother and his aunt in a kind of worship. He even distracted his grandpa, from time to time, from thoughts of money and advancement. Mirrin made Edward happy and kept him constantly amused. Thus, unwittingly, she softened the Dawsons' distrust of the collier's daughter, sister of the man who had lured their one-and-only away from a first-class marriage and all the status that went with it.

They did not even object when Mirrin filled the little boy's head with tales of gypsies and miners and refreshed his tender memory with questions and answers about his very early life in Blacklaw.

"What d'you remember most, son?"

"Grannie, an' Auntie Kate; an' Auntie Betsy givin' me sweets."

"What else?"

"Luggie."

"Who?"

"Luggie: Luggie."

"Who's Luggie?"

"The cat with the big ginger tail."

"Mrs. McPhail's cat. I'd forgotten."

"Luggie liked milk. I liked Luggie."

"Remember the picnics?"

"The eggs with faces."

"Easter Monday. It was rainin'. We all went into the washhouse an' had our dinner in there."

"Rolled eggs down the board, an' mine's broke."

"I remember."

"Me too," said Edward proudly.

But as to the dirt and the lung-disease, the horror of disaster sirens screaming out over Main Street, of poverty and many deaths, Mirrin did not enlighten her nephew. She could never quite screw up her nerve to ask if he recalled his father. The boy never mentioned his father nor his Stalker grandfather, though he had worshipped them both in his babyhood and copied them in his childish way. Mirrin wondered if he had somehow blanked out the loss and the bewilderment it must have caused in his little heart.

Sometimes when she talked with Edward she was beset by homesickness. Dormant recollections stole into her mind and lingered long after Edward had been packed off to bed and she was sewing cloths by the stove in the quietness of the winter evening.

She thought then of the girls of Blacklaw, the Sunday afternoon promenade up and down Main Street, faces scrubbed, hair brushed and ribboned, boots polished. Linked arm to arm, a troll net for suitors, they swung along, giggling at secret jokes, playing haughty for the benefit of the lads perched on the *Lantern*'s wall, flirting their eyes and their hips to draw jeers and cheers and the first adolescent growls of sexual hunger. Not long ago: yet an eternity. She was young still; yet her youth was gone, her girlhood at any rate.

Since those dim days she had been rebel, lover, bread-winner and tinker. Now she was an Auntie, Edward's one and only available Auntie, a role she enjoyed.

"Mirrin, he won't go to sleep 'til you kiss him good-night."

"Right."

She climbed the stairs, entered the room and seated herself on the foot of the big comfortable bed that overlooked the cot. She put the candle safe on the dresser where it would not shine in his eyes.

"Sing me a song, Auntie Mirrin."

She sang the first thing that came into her head, soft and sweet, the lively tune mellowed by a wistful irony that was mercifully lost on the little boy. His eyes peered sleepily up at her from above the hem of the patchwork quilt. The candlelight made his hair and lashes golden.

> *"Here we go the jingo-ring,*
> *The jingo-ring, the jingo-ring,*
> *Here we go the jingo-ring,*
> *About the merry-ma-tanzie."*

Edward opened his eyes wide, fighting sleep. "Merry-ma-tanzie? What's that?"

"Shush now," Mirrin said. "I'll tell you tomorrow."

"Auntie?"

"What?"

"Sing more."

> *"Guess ye wha's the young goodman,*
> *The young goodman, the young goodman,*
> *Guess ye wha's the young goodman,*
> *About the merry-ma-tanzie."*

"More."

Mirrin smiled, stroking her nephew's hair. She leaned forward, face close to his, her lips hardly moving, the game-song teased into a breathy, crooning lullaby, the way her Da had sung it to her when she was small.

> *"Honey is sweet, and so is he,*
> *So is he, so is he;*
> *Honey is sweet, and so is he,*
> *About the merry-ma-tanzie."*

"More."

But she sang no more words, stroking, humming gently in her throat, until the song was no song but just the assurance of her presence, and Edward drifted swiftly down into sleep.

"Mirrin?"

Startled, she looked round.

Lily stood by the door.

"Why did you sing that?" Lily asked.

"I . . ."

"Don't you remember?"

Then she remembered—the day of the wedding; all the long line of Stalkers, with the Ewings and the Pritchards and the Ormonds, even old misery McNeillage, a whole sprauckle of lassies and lads spilling out into the street from the Stalkers' house, joining hands and dancing and singing up hill. Ahead of them had been her brother James and his brand-new wife, Lily Dawson, a Stalker now. They had sung all the way up to the fresh-painted cottage that James had tithed. James and Lily, flushed and nervous, had played their part and skipped ahead. When the chain of wedding guests reached the cottage, James had lifted Lily in his arms and carried her in through the open door. The door was new-painted too, red as a rose, and shiny. He had turned with her, her arms about his strong neck and her head shyly hidden against his chest. He had grinned at his mates and winked at his Da and turned again and kicked the door with his heel, closing it tight. Then, Mirrin remembered, they all gathered in a circle out on the street, the crowd swelled by neighbours and acquaintances until it seemed that the whole town was there, and they sang.

> *"Now they're married, we wish them joy,*
> *We wish them joy, we wish them joy;*
> *Now they're married, we wish them joy,*
> *About the merry-ma-tanzie."*

And then the crowd had gone, laughing and gossiping, into the gloaming and the lamps of the town were lit. Mirrin had loitered curiously in front of the new cottage, wondering at the drawn curtains and the oil lamp burning, blurred behind the flowered cotton. Then Kate had come back to fetch her and take her home to share the succulent dumpling that Mam had made and to join in the general celebrations that rattled on far into the Saturday night.

"Aye, Lily, I remember," Mirrin said.

"I miss him, Mirrin: I miss him still."

"Aye, Lily," Mirrin said, and, taking her sister-in-law in her arms, consoled her while they recalled the happiness of a past that was dead and gone.

Nine

❧

CHRISTMAS WAS NOT a season that brought much joy to Ernest Dawson's heart. While his guests, resident and temporary, were satisfied with plain, wholesome vittles throughout the year, the Yuletide brought a fit of gastronomic madness which drove all thought of economy from their minds. Grumbles rolled like thunder from the dining room down into the kitchen where Ernest's ears flared red as boiled beetroot at the slights cast upon his best culinary endeavours. What did they expect: turtle soup and fillet of veal, filberts and lark pie and flamin' French plums, all for a guinea a week? He did not grudge them a special little something on Christmas Day, but he could not be expected to feed them like fighting cocks from December first through to Twelfth Night. In reparation for the lack of variety, and as a fillip to the promise of a Grand Xmas Dinner, he was obliged to camouflage the customary run of mutton and veg with sauces and to provide, on alternate evenings, blancmange or jelly, or some similar colourful frippery. It was at this stage that Mirrin Stalker made the transition from skivvy to *maître d'hôtel*.

Five fowls, as tough and battered as a team of fairground pugilists, were purchased early by Ernest Dawson, before the price of birds soared sky-high. He hung them in the wood-shed, as if they were pheasants and not mere barn-door hens, while he debated what, in a week's time, he would do with them and how he would perform the miracle of feeding a score of hungry folk from such a scrawny flock. Of course, he would pad out with pies and tartlets and steamed currant pud, but the main course worried him so much that he lay awake at night fretting in case his miserliness be considered mean. Fowler, at number twenty, was splurging on a goose but Dawson baulked at such needless expense and, though he surveyed the plump-breasted specimens in the poulterer's window, he could not summon up the nerve needed to put down hard cash for one. In any case, he had already paid for five boiling fowls.

Giggling, Lily told Mirrin of her father's dilemma, quite an annual circumstance as it happened. Mirrin chuckled too before she remembered, in a flood, the tricks that Mrs. Burns, Lamont's cook, had practised to pare down the budget.

Casually, the following morning, Mirrin raised the subject over the hurried breakfast that the family took together after all their guests had departed and greasy plates stood stacked for washing upon the trolley in the dining room.

She led Ernest into the subject easily. "Fine chickens you bought, Mr. Dawson."

"D'you think so, then?"

"I do," said Mirrin. "You'll be cookin' them in salad oil."

"Salad oil? Will I?"

"With some cuts of rabbit to add up to a fine plateful of pieces, disguised with mushrooms and a wine sauce."

"Wine?"

"Any old sort of wine," said Mirrin, "makes all the difference."

"I . . . er, not sure about the wine," said Ernest Dawson, as he dipped bread into the puddle of ham fat in the pan and chewed thoughtfully. "I . . . er, hadn't considered what t'do with the fowls, like, but that recipe sounds . . . possible."

"It'll look good on the menu."

"What menu?"

"You'll need a menu," said Mirrin. "Put a fancy French name on somethin' and it tastes better at once."

"I'm not much up on fancy French names."

"*Poulet à la Marengo*," said Mirrin. "A great big steamin' salver of chicken pieces interspersed with rabbit; the whole heap draped wi' a rich white wine sauce."

Ernest studied the girl. "How much would it cost?"

"You could do enough for twenty on a pound, plus the birds."

"Get away?"

Mirrin nodded.

"You've . . . made this dish before?" asked Ernest.

Mirrin nodded again, stretching the truth a little.

"Where?" said Hilda Dawson. "Not on a miner's stove, I'll be bound."

Lily joined in. "Mirrin was housekeeper t'a coalmaster for quite a while."

"Never!" said Hilda Dawson, exchanging glances with her husband.

So interested was he in the conversation that Ernest had almost swabbed the pan clean of fat. "You mean a maid?"

"A housekeeper," said Lily. "In charge."

"You never told us that, Mirrin," said Hilda.

"You never asked," said Mirrin.

"What other recipes do ye have, then?" said Ernest,

trying to appear only faintly interested. "Ones suitable for the modest scale of our establishment?"

"Apple Snow," said Mirrin. "Tipsy cake, Hunters' Beef Stew—guaranteed to taste like venison. *Cod à l'Italienne.* None of them expensive."

"I'm not quite up to those," Ernest admitted.

"I could give you a hand," said Mirrin. "Write out the recipes, if y'like."

"Much obliged," said Ernest Dawson.

"By Gum, Dad!" said Lily, grinning. "The Talboys will wonder if they've strayed into the Cosmopolitan by mistake if you flash such a menu."

"Wilf's a man who'll appreciate *continentale,*" said Ernest, almost hugging himself at the prospect. "Now, Mirrin, you know our budget; what sort of show can we make?"

"A fair one," said Mirrin, carrying plates from table to sink and fastening on the canvas apron that was her working outfit.

She had just lifted a scouring cloth and reached for the kettle of hot water on the hob when Ernest Dawson said, impatiently, "Leave that: leave it to our Lily. You an' me had better go t'the market, don't ye think? An' see what we'll need t'make a splash. *Poulet à la Marengo* sounds just the ticket."

Mirrin hestitated. "Now?"

"Why not now?" Dawson said, buttoning his cuffs. "Early means cheap."

As Lily passed Mirrin on her way to the sink, she murmured, "You're well in now, Mirrin. He'll be adoptin' you next if this works out well."

"God forbid," Mirrin said, and handed her sister-in-law the apron.

It was later that evening. Spices, cloves of garlic, jugs of salad oil and cask wine and other small purchases that Mirrin had persuaded Dawson to make had been neatly put away on the shelves of the larder. The evening meal, a humble macaroni pie, was being contemplated, when Edward, seated on the table while Mirrin laid out the dishes, said suddenly, "Somebody's upstairs, Auntie Mirrin. D'you hear his loud voice? It might be Father Christmas come early."

Mirrin explained that Father Christmas was too good a time-keeper to arrive a week before Christmas but, pausing, listened to the jovial laughter that echoed down from the front hallway.

Lily hurried into the kitchen, tucking straggles of hair into her pins. "What a commotion. It's the Talboys."

"Just who are the Talboys?" asked Mirrin.

"Friends of my father. Come on up, Mirrin. You come too, Edward, but be a good boy and stay close t'me."

Discarding her apron Mirrin followed Lily upstairs.

The hallway was crammed with people and luggage. Long leather wallets, hatboxes, creased valises and scuffed carpetbags were piled willy-nilly on the waxcloth strip. The door gaped open, showing a haze of frost against the gaslight. Through it, toiling from a railway handcart borrowed from the Manchester line, came Wilfrid Talboys. His womenfolk had already crushed into the hall, three of them, wrapped in jackets and travelling wraps trimmed with various kinds of fur, wearing double skirt dresses and hats in the Rubens or Capote style dolled up with extravagant amounts of trimming. Ernest was helping Talboys unload the carts, the men shouting to each other, Ernest with highly uncharacteristic glee, until the last box had been removed and an urchin paid twopence to trundle the cart back to the station on the other side of town.

Talboys clambered over the wall of luggage. He swung his valise on to the rocking hatstand and, as Ernest edged past him, stretched out his arm and expansively declared, "My dear friends, Ernest, Hilda and Lily, we bid you welcome and a thousand blessings appropriate to the season. It is *so* good to see you again."

Approaching sixty, Wilfrid Talboys had a round face and bright brown eyes, flourishing gestures and a booming well-modulated voice that seemed to come from the depths of his patent-leather boots. He wore a long overcoat trimmed with astrakhan, and a shiny chimney-pot topper with a wrinkled black satin ribbon. Two of the women were about the same age as Wilfrid. From the strong similarity between them Mirrin took them to be sisters. The younger woman was undoubtedly Talboys' daughter, her features thick, her complexion rubicund. The smile sat stiffly on her lips, however, and Mirrin decided that young Blanche, in her twenties, was either naturally bad-tempered or excessively fatigued by her journey.

Ernest poured out effusive welcomes, adopting the same oratorial style as Talboys until the formalities had all been observed and only Mirrin and Edward, standing back by the newel post of the stairs, remained unaccounted for and, as it were, unblessed by either of the colliding parties.

"Allow me," Talboys cried, twitching his brows. Sweeping off his topper, stepping over the luggage, he made a bow so deep that, for an instant, he was peeping up at Edward instead of down. In that crouched position he paused and, grinning, produced in his left hand a grubby card—which Mirrin took— and a small furled flag. "For you, young nipper."

Tentatively Edward accepted the flag which shook out from its stick into a streamer of coloured pictures of sundry parts of the Empire.

Edward gasped, then chuckled and wagged the flag so wildly that Talboys' topper went skidding to the floor. Everybody, including the victim, laughed uproariously.

Mirrin glanced at the card: *Wilfrid Talboys and the Cropley Sisters: Premiere Variety Act: Songs : Choruses: Dances: Dramatic Dialogues: The Family Show Personified.*

Theatricals; she had heard of the profusion of touring troupes in England. In one of the towns she'd passed through with the Brummidges a theatre bill had her attention. But Mrs. Brummidge had railed against the immorality of 'the halls', full of loose women and rude men, laughing like jackasses at vulgar jokes and songs.

"Mirrin, Lily, please assist our friends to their rooms."

The Talboys had been allotted the two best 'doubles' on the first floor. Hilda Dawson shepherded the women up the staircase, leaving her daughter, husband and Mirrin to haul up the luggage.

"Dinner at seven o'clock, on the stroke of the gong," called Ernest. "You'll find a little glass of something in your room, though, to fortify you after your railway ordeal, or you may have tea if you prefer it."

"Not for me, Ernest," said Wilfrid Talboys. "Not a moment to lose. Must distribute the handbills." He rummaged, found and lifted a heavy carpetbag. "Two weeks in the Grossby Civic Hall still ain't to be sneezed at. It seems we went down real well last year."

"Not surprised: not in the least surprised," said Ernest from under his load of portmanteaux. "Off you trot then, Wilf, an' do the needful. Let the good folk of the town know what a treat's in store for them."

Wilfrid Talboys opened the outside door. Hunching his shoulders he inhaled the stale cold air of the Midland manufacturing township as if it was a draught of nectar. "Nine years: nine Christmas seasons: and here we are again. It makes you think, don't it, Ernest?"

"How time flies," Ernest agreed. "It does, indeed."

Then, with a faint eager whoop, the carpetbag tucked under his arm, Wilfrid Talboys was gone.

Lily and Mirrin trailed Ernest upstairs, carrying the heavy luggage which, Mirrin assumed, not only contained personal belongings but the costumes and other appurtenances that the Talboys used in their acts. She was glad that Wilfrid wasn't a strongman. To judge by the weight of his trunks, however, perhaps he dabbled in that too.

In the room, Mirrin had an opportunity to study the women more closely. In Wilfrid's presence they seemed overwhelmed, certainly overshadowed by his uproariousness. Ada, Wilf's wife, had been a fine-looking woman in her day. Her eyes were still large and warm, showing great tolerance and humour. There was a quietness in her manner that Mirrin recognised as stoical patience. She wondered what possible events in such a varied and scintillating existence might require patience as an attribute.

"That one belongs to my sister," Ada said. She raised her voice to carry through the open door to the adjoining room. "Pru, luv, your cosmeticals are in here."

"Shall I take it to her?" asked Mirrin.

"Thanks, luv," said Ada, sinking wearily onto the bed and beginning to unlace her boots. "I'm quite wore out what with the early start and the train ride."

"Where did you come from today?"

"Marlingford."

"Where's that?"

"I'm not surprised you never heard of it. On the east coast, a nondescript little place with a theatre about as big as a pigeon-loft, and not much cleaner. Are you Scotch?"

"Aye."

"How did you come here?"

"Lily's my sister-in-law."

Picking at the tight laces with her finger-nails, Ada asked, "Your brother warn't the one that was killed, was he?"

"Aye, he was. My brother James: Lily's husband."

"We don't know we're born, some of us," Ada sighed. "Poor skimpy lassie, a widow at twenty, an' with a kiddie too."

Mirrin lifted the small box of cosmetical preparations and would have gone out then, if she had not been blocked by the abrupt appearance of Wilfrid and Ada's daughter. Blanche flounced into her mother's room already launched on a peevish tirade. "Why is it, mother, that I always land without a mirror? Even the dressing-table's plain. I can't posssibly be expected to attend to my coiffeur sharin' Pru's skinkie little hand mirror. You know how long she takes to primp, anyhow."

From the resigned expression on Ada's face, Mirrin guessed that the young woman was prone to such petty outbursts.

"If you like, miss," Mirrin intervened, "I can fetch you a mirror; a large one."

"You?" said Blanche.

Mirrin was taken aback.

"Aye: me."

"I shall complain to Mr. Dawson, in person. He shall fetch me a mirror of suitable proportions," Blanche announced. "As the owner of this establishment he should be responsible for the welfare of his guests. The Lord knows, my father shells out enough in lodgin' money."

Mirrin bit her lip. "Very well, miss," she said. "An' will Mr. Dawson also serve your tea?"

"Tea?" said Blanche. "I don't quite take your meaning."

"I thought a cup o'tea might be welcome, as suggested by the owner of this establishment," Mirrin said.

Ada said, "You can bring me tea, please, Mirrin. I take it Mr. Dawson's busy with the dinner."

"That's right, ma'am," said Mirrin. "Very busy."

Blanche was too gauche to appreciate the slight. "Of course, you may bring me tea," she said. "What do you mean?"

"Nothing, Blanche," Ada said gently. Mirrin realised now just why the elder woman had been obliged to learn patience to survive. "A pot of tea would suit us fine, Mirrin."

As she went out of the bedroom to brew tea for Ada Talboys, Mirrin encountered Lily bringing the essential mirror upstairs. Apparently Blanche had raged at her too.

"What d'you think of them, then?" Lily whispered.

"The youngest's a right tartar," said Mirrin. "But I like them fine. It's excitin' havin' theatrical folk on the premises. I've never met any of that trade before. Will we have the chance to attend the theatre an' see them perform?"

"We don't have t'visit the theatre for that," said Lily. "Wilf and Blanche perform all the time, everywhere."

"I can well believe that."

"What's wrong with you?" Lily murmured. "Is it the fever again?"

"Fever? No, I feel fine."

"Must be the excitement," said Lily with a shrug. "Funny how the Talboys affect some folk: my Daddy —an' now you."

"Don't blether," said Mirrin. "It's just the change that I find stimulatin'. In this past year I've grown t'like changes."

Changes there were in plenty during the remainder of that week. Meals had to be fitted round rehearsals. The long kitchen table was as frequently spread with dresses and costumes for mending and ironing as with pots and pans. The Talboys had the run of the house. Only Mr. Gudgeon, a cantankerous boot salesman on the upper floor, complained about them—and he was due to leave on Christmas Eve in any case.

Playbills, extolling the versatile talents of the troupe, appeared on walls and in shop windows throughout the town. The interest aroused by them reflected the need in the millhands for diverting entertainment, especially at the Christmas season.

For Talboys and his women, Grossby was just one more stop, one more booking, in a professional life that had carried them up and down the north of England, from one provincial theatre to another until each dressing room, every individual fly and curtain, was as familiar as the wallpaper in a stay-at-home's living room.

Wilfrid and Ada had a close relationship. Both cherished a high regard for the third member of the act, Pru Cropley, Ada's quiet-spoken, uncomplaining sister. Seasoned veterans of the road, they had tried in vain to instil into the fourth and youngest the sterling qualities of dedication and perseverance. But Blanche, so Pru later confided in Mirrin, had been spoiled as a child, fussed over and flattered until her head had been turned. She had never learned the difference between arrogance and conceit. Now, encountering the harsher realities of the performers' life, Blanche sulked and moaned and vented her bad temper on her aunt and parents without the least regard for their feelings.

"She reminds me a bit of our Betsy," Mirrin said to

Lily, as they laid the foundations of the Grand Xmas Dinner.

"She's not near as pretty."

"But just as spoiled. Did you hear her this morning? All that fuss and uproar about a hair-bow. There's somethin' about people like Blanche Talboys, aye, an' our Betsy too, that puts my back up. They consider themselves as the centre o'the world."

"Don't we all?"

"I hope I don't," said Mirrin. "At least not t'that extent."

"I wouldn't mind bein' spoiled for a while."

"Is that all y'want, Lily? To be made a fuss of."

"In the first year, James spoiled me," the girl said. "I enjoyed it."

"That's a wife's privilege," said Mirrin.

"What would you know about it?"

"I've had my share of . . ." Mirrin bit off the sentence.

"From Rob Ewing?"

"No, not him."

"Tom Armstrong, then?"

"Certainly not the bold Tom Dandy," said Mirrin, laughing. "I meant, when I was wee. Daddy and the boys, James and Dougie, they fussed over me."

"An' who else, since?"

"It would be nice," said Mirrin, changing tack. "Aye, now I think of it, it *would* be nice t'be spoiled. But not for nothin'."

"Mirrin! What do y'mean?"

"Oh, not that!" said Mirrin promptly. "I mean, it would be grand to *earn* respect, to be popular—like the Talboys."

"Nobody cares about them."

"I don't believe that."

"A few strays, maybe: people like my father. But he's known Wilfrid since the days when Ada and Pru worked in the Dunsford Mill an' sang in the Chapel choir on Sundays an' in the gallery o'the *Goose and Gander* every other night of the week."

"Is that how they met?"

"So I've heard."

The conversation was interrupted by Hilda Dawson who sharply advised the girls to concentrate on their work and do a little less gossiping.

Christmas, thanks to Mirrin's influence on Ernest, was to be celebrated in style after all. The theatricals were overjoyed.

"I can't remember when we last had a real sit-down Christmas dinner. It must be ten . . .no, fifteen . . . nearer twenty years. When Blanche was a baby." Pru gave up her attempt to count the passage of the years and bestowed on everyone a happy trembling smile. Wilf bellowed with laughter and insisted that she put on her bonnet and jacket and toddle out to help Edward and himself select a Christmas tree, the first that had ever decorated the Dawson household.

"With a star on top," said Lily, almost in a whisper, the memory of another tree, in another town, rising into her mind.

With the Talboys' show due to open on Boxing Day and the unfortunate necessity of conducting a full dress rehearsal on the evening of Christmas Day, it was decided that, tradition notwithstanding, dinner would be a mid-day affair. Only Blanche, by her manner, seemed to indicate that the arrangements did not suit her, though she gave no reasons for her disapproval and offered no alternative suggestions.

By dusk on Christmas Eve, it seemed to Mirrin that she had been on her feet for a week. Returning with the tree, Talboys had also contributed great bunches of shiny red-berried holly which had been set to sprout behind the pictures and under the gas brackets in the public rooms and stairs. He, Ernest and Edward, like three children, decorated the tree and planted it in a pot in the dining room.

All day there had been a coming and going of guests, swift, excited arrivals from last minute bits of business and equally swift departures for trains and coaches to outlying towns and villages where the solitaries who lodged with Dawson sought, after all their complaints, hospitality with friends, relatives and generous acquaintances. Mr. Quayle remained, resolutely determined to enjoy dinner *en famille*. Mrs. Perkin and her daughter Sue, the musical instrument dealers, could, in the end, find nowhere to go on that day of days and, with resignation, donated two bottles of wine to the proceedings they would be forced to enjoy, plus the gift of an elaborate and noisy 'one-man band' for Edward.

By seven o'clock the fowls and the rabbit had been united in an uneasy alliance in the tenderiser, the pieces garnished with garlic, cayenne, a liberality of wine and some other herbs which Mirrin supposed would do no harm to the flavour. The ingredients of the sauce were laid out in bowls under cheesecloth and the mushrooms, bought only that morning, were steeping on one measured inch of sherry. The tipsy cake was settling in its huge cut-glass dish, ready only to be roofed with cream. The soup stock, labelled as *Prince of Wales's Delight* and consisting largely of turnips, stood passively in its black cauldron on the cool of the stove. Pies, tarts and sweetmeats, baked by Mirrin and Lily and aided by Ernest's 'advice', were stacked away in the larder's mouseproof shelves, though Wilfrid Talboys was heard to ask pointedly if the larder was 'guestproof' as well. Plates and dishes, table-cloths and glasses were brought from hiding, scrutinised by Hilda's scrupulous eye, approved, washed, dried, buffed and laid out in the dining room upstairs. At last cleaning began: general parlour, stairs and hall for a start. Like an army weaponed with buckets and brooms the women went to work. The 'worst rough' had been done inch by inch and tile by tile during the preceding week but that final 'rederound' took the best part of the evening, before kitchen chores again called to the girls.

Propped against the table, rolling out breadcrumbs, Mirrin followed Lily's pointing finger. Set to polish apples for the dish on the sideboard, Edward had nodded off and, cloth still in hand, slept with his nose resting on his wrist, one large pippin still in his grasp.

"I know how he feels," said Mirrin. "I'm about ready to drop myself."

Lily coaxed the sleeping child into her arms. Mirrin held the kitchen door open. "Supper shouldn't be long an' then we can all go to bed," Lily said. "I think everybody's tired."

Everybody, it transpired, but Blanche.

Since the arrival of the Talboys' menage, a light supper had been dispensed, with some little formality, in the Dawsons' private parlour, during the course of which Hilda and Ada reminisced about old times, and Ernest extracted as much 'green-room gossip' as Wilfrid was able to invent. It was not usual for Mirrin and Lily to be invited to join the parlour group, but, on that evening, because of the season and the impression that Mirrin had lately begun to make on Ernest Dawson, the young women were graciously permitted to stay.

Wilf had spent the morning with the leasing agent of the Civic Hall and had returned well pleased with the early returns on bookable seats to announce that all the 'reserveds' had gone for Boxing Day, both houses, and for Saturday as well. He beamed round the parlour, and patted his wife's knee.

"Tomorrow we must rehearse as never before," he said. "All that new material has to be shined up, you know."

"It's not bad as it is, Wilf," Ada remarked.

"Not bad isn't good enough," said Wilf, amiably. "I've laid on the orchestra for six o'clock, splittin' the cost with the manager, Mr. Ockram, and . . ."

"No."

Blanche's normally rubicund cheeks were ashen. Her eyes glared defiance. "I will *not* rehearse on Christmas Day. I see no reason why we should rehearse at all. We're quite proficient enough for the ignorant audience we're liable to attract in this dismal backwater."

With a quick, startled glance round the assembly, Wilf said, "Come now, my dear, that isn't polite to our hosts. Besides, Grossby has always been good to us, and we must reward them with our very best efforts."

"Most of the songs and dances I can do in my sleep."

"Oh, nonsense, Blanche!" said Ada. "What about

that delightful new ditty your father had specially commissioned for you. It has never been performed before
the public."

"Delightful! It's tuneless and silly, and set too high
for me. Commissioned, indeed! Father bought it for
a shilling from a drunken sot in a public house
in Sutton last year and hasn't had the temerity to
foist it on the public before."

"Now, now, Blanche," chided Pru, mildly.

"Don't *you* talk to me. You're just hoping I'll crack
on the top notes and make a fool of myself, so *your*
stupid solo will sound better."

Pru's injured gasp was followed by an embarrassed
shuffling of feet and a sudden urgent rush on the part
of Hilda and Ernest Dawson to press tea and arrowroot biscuits on everyone.

Ada, however, was used to dealing with such crises.
Drawing herself up, she fixed her daughter and said,
"You are tired, Blanche. I suggest you retire at once
to bed. You'll feel better in the morning, and then you
may apologise to Pru."

"I will not feel better in the morning."

"Christmas Day, dearest," put in Wilfrid.

"And I have no intention of apologising to *her.*"

"Blanche, Blanche!" Wilf murmured, sorrowfully.

"I will, however, retire to my bedroom. I will thank
you all not to make too much noise."

Blanche made a theatrical exit, sweeping out like
some haughty princess who has just spurned the proposal of a prince because she didn't like the colour of
his stockings.

"Ahem: ahem!" Hilda, it seemed, had developed a
cough. Solicitously, Lily hurried to pour her mother
a fresh cup of tea, while Mirrin made another hospitable round with the arrowroot biscuits.

Ada sighed, "Blanche hasn't got over what happened in Marlington, I'm afraid. It upset her deeply."

There was a pause. Nobody seemed anxious to press
for details, though Ada's statement invited them.

At length Pru said, "Blanche's vocal performance
was rather coolly received in Marlingford."

Wilf made a soft roaring sound in the back of his

throat and, with a gesture of indifference to such niceties of expression, seated himself on the sofa and, with
the tea cup in his hand, said bluntly, "The truth is
Blanche was howled off the stage. Admittedly, the
audience were, in part, a shade worse for drink,
though they took to the rest of us warmly enough."

Mirrin said, "Why not to Blanche, then?"

"She resents them," Wilf explained. "They sense
it, you know. You've got to love your audience, even
when they're givin' you the gooseberry. You've got to
put out to them and ignore what comes back."

"Tell the whole truth, now you've started," said Ada.
"We're all friends here."

Wilf sighed heavily. "Blanche deserved it. She was
unrehearsed an' careless. Two false starts to the song,
then she forgot the words. Can you credit it, a daughter of mine, forgettin' the words!"

"That was quite bad enough, but . . ." said Ada,
then handed the narration back to her husband, like
the good trouper she was.

"One lout threw a pear. It didn't touch Blanche,
mark you, but it skidded across the stage, and . . .
and . . ."

"At times," said Ada, "Blanche behaves quite . . ."

"Irrationally," said Pru, curtly. She got to her feet.
"I for one don't feel like discussin' Blanche's failings
at this hour on Christmas Eve. If you'll excuse me,
all."

Smiling politely, the woman turned and left the
parlour and, shortly thereafter, the supper party dis-
banded in unusual gloom.

Later, in bed, Lily turned her head on the pillow
and through half-closed lids inspected her sister-in-law.
Mirrin's eyes were wide open, fixed on the ceiling, a
smile on her lips.

"What's the matter with you, Mirrin? I thought you
were dyin' with sleep an hour ago?"

Mirrin's smile widened. "I am," she said. "But I
was thinkin' about Blanche Talboys and her encounter
with that pear. D'you know what I'd have done, I'd
have thrown it right back at the ruffian."

"Would you?" said Lily. "That's just what Miss

Talboys *did*. An' she hit him too, right on the bokoo."

Mirrin lifted herself on her elbow.

"You don't mean it?"

"I had it from Ada," said Lily. "Mushed the lout right on the bokoo, I'm tellin' you. There was such a riot the manager had to drop the curtain and the Talboys had to run for it."

"Fancy!" said Mirrin.

Lily laughed drowsily. "Right on the bokoo. She must throw better'n she sings."

Chuckling, Mirrin lay back, hands behind her head.

"Well, I wouldn't run," Mirrin said at length. "I'd square up to them, that's what I'd do. I'd love my audience, like Mr. Talboys says. Lily, d'you think . . .?"

But Lily had fallen asleep.

Snow lay on the rolling hills of Perthshire and, in waving sunlight, gleamed on the higher mountains to the west. It was that hour before sunset when the McAlmonds' young guests had come in from their riding and the women had gone upstairs to prepare for dinner, to dress themselves like pheasants in trimmings of lace and velvet. The library windows of Pearsehill Castle looked north-east across the valley of the Froud, a broad winding river noted for its salmon pools and its picturesque highland beauty. The air now was clear and very cold. Pine logs blazing in the arched stone hearth were a welcome sight to Fraser and Drew who, though young, had thinned their blood a bit of late with indiscriminate feeding and an excess of ale. Hector Mellish had enough style not to follow fashion if it didn't suit him. He had spent the afternoon sprawled in a deep moquette sofa whose back and sides were tied together with hawsers of silk. Hector was drinking Madeira wine, nibbling brazils and laconically conversing with Sir Archibald McAlmond.

McAlmond Pater stood with his back to the fire. He was dressed in casual tweeds so thick that—as Fraser remarked—he resembled a ferret peering out of a sack. Sir Archibald's features were weak, but not febrile, his bearing shaped by practising upright postures and emulating the autocratic down-the-snoot stare of his wife's ancestors all of whom surveyed the mansion from heavy gilt frames, their portraits crowding hallways, stairs and the walls of all public rooms like permanently materialised phantoms, reminding the good gentleman that he was not *quite* the true blue-blood that he pretended to be.

Dinner the previous evening had been small and comparatively informal. Drew had said very little, answering only such questions as were addressed to him, mainly by Lady Isobel, a personage whose warmth was strained and whose innate shyness, had Drew only known it, almost matched his own. Lady Isobel McAlmond, of the Oakley stock, fished for information about her son. She was probably anxious in case Fraser had taken up with low company and that his guest, Drew Stalker, was an emissary of that underworld of artisans whose influence would eventually bring down not only Fraser but, in time to come, the whole feudal establishment of a class-structured society.

At first Fraser's mother, an imposingly handsome woman, threw Drew into a state of almost dumbfounded awe. The young man acquitted himself well enough, however, parrying her questions with lies and neat evasions about the habits of students living in Edinburgh, discoursing, when pressed, about the fascination of Law in such a way that Fraser too was incorporated into the conversation and seemed to shine more brilliantly than his humble companion. By the meal's end, the dear lady was impressed, less by her guest than by her son's serious attitude to his profession.

But that had been yesterday. This evening, Drew knew, the sundry guests who had been skidding in all day long for the formal dinner and Christmas entertainment would show up his origins, typified by his cheap new suit and unpolished manners. He would be more obviously what he really was, a bit of an upstart who had fallen under Fraser's spell and whom the McAlmond lad had cultivated as a curiosity. Still, he had done well to reach this point in so short a time and the Pearsehill vacation was a valuable introduction to the world he eventually hoped to conquer.

Though Drew was unaware of it, Sir Archibald was not so diffident as he appeared to be. Prior to the couple's arrival, he had been pumping Mellish about the young fellow with whom his son seemed so taken up. Hector had developed enough respect for Stalker over the past month to manfully support the youngster and sing his virtues. It was in that pre-prandial hour in the library, before Sir Archibald's more important guests demanded all his attention, that the head of the Perthshire McAlmonds and the collier's son met with a view to establishing a fuller knowledge each of the other. Sir Archibald poured Drew a glass of wine and offered him a cigar, which he refused. Drew was still awkward in his movements, his confidence all vocal. In this special particular he differed completely from Sir Archibald who had learned grace early in his life but had never mastered the art of quick thinking and articulate phrasing so that his conversations, casual and serious alike, had a limping quality as if the legs of his sentences were bowed and stunted.

In the ten minutes it took the winter sun to sink over the hills and the lamps in the library to gain yellow strength, the young man and the laird succeeded in establishing a relationship which would carry Drew through the stiff rituals of a grand-scale dinner party without blowing the gaff on his background. He gained Sir Archibald's respect not by flattery, not by agreeing with the half-baked opinions which the gentleman put out to probe the boy's worth. He did it by firmly sticking up for his own beliefs and by defending them with calm logic. It seemed like honesty, an impromptu acknowledgment of their relative positions, sophisticated to a degree far beyond his years.

After some preliminary introduction, Sir Archibald said, "You will, of course, be in favour of trade unionism?"

Drew said, "In its present form, certainly."

Sir Archibald stuck his tongue in his cheek. "You support the present wave of reforms?"

The blanketing of all reforms suited Drew. He said, "I support those which allow men opportunity."

"Opportunity for . . . what?" said Sir Archibald.

"Advancement."

"Strikes and pickets?"

"Is it your belief, Sir Archibald, that preliminary reform will bring equality?"

"That is the avowed aim of certain factions in our . . . midst."

"No, sir," said Drew. "It's not possible to accept the bounty of the government, legislatively, and remain true to original causes. I have seen rabble-rousers, listened to strike leaders. There's little or no sense in what they say. I would let them have all that a Troy democracy promises. The party system is catchpenny, the working classes easily swayed by minor circumstances. The Licensing Act, for instance, lost more Liberal supporters than the Ballot or the Artisans' Dwelling Act ever gained."

Drew paused. He was treading carefully. His own knowledge of political subjects was makeshift, mostly learned by rote, with understanding but no conviction. He was counting on Daniel Horn's assurance that McAlmond did not keep himself abreast of such complicated affairs.

Sir Archibald hummed for a moment then, reluctantly, admitted that he did not quite follow the argument.

Drew said, "The distinction made between skilled and unskilled workers in the trades creates yet another division in our society, sir."

This thought had obviously not occurred to the laird, or if it had he had not understood its implications. He nodded, inviting Drew to expand.

"The skilled labourer, threatened with extinction by industrial machinery, wishes to obtain power to protect his special station. The Conservatives have backed him. The Liberals, Gladstone, apparently made men free to help themselves. In effect, however, the working classes do not wish to be free. They are, sir, I assure you, slaves at heart. Divisionism within their ranks will create an expansion of the middle class, a proper respect for power in the ballot box and aspirations towards the stabilisation of society as it is now. For example, the majority do not appreciate that by legalising 'peaceful picketing' at strikes the parliamentary government has cheated them of the right to show their discontent by aggressive behaviour. The government has ensured that workers' leaders, the skilled and the educated among them, will file meekly to a committee room where compromises can be reached, compromises designed to ensure greater output at minimal outlay to the owners or manufacturers."

Drew was rapidly reaching the limits of his knowledge of political science. He had prepared his brief from editorials in the Radical Press, sugared with negative summations culled from established journals.

Sir Archibald seemed anxious to press for more information but he could not, in the face of such an erudite onslaught, find a means to phrase his question.

Mellish came to his rescue. "Tell me, Drew, do you regard this as a deliberate plot of Westminster?"

"Of course not, Hector. Altruism has always been the snare to catch the unwary, whether Whig or Tory. It arises from a gross misunderstanding of the lower classes," Drew replied.

McAlmond Pater understood that pointed statement well enough. He grunted an approval, and cocked his eyebrow at his son as if to applaud Fraser's selection of friends.

Drew said, "The majority of reforms are not radical but humanitarian. Certainly tyrannical and stupid masters will suffer. But in the end most social reforms will benefit trade, and healthy trade means healthy profits. The welfare and fitness of the labouring classes is essential to progress."

The contradiction puzzled Sir Archibald. "But . . . ?"

Drew said, "Confine resentment, where it exists, channel it into internecine struggles." He had borrowed that entire phrase intact from Peter French's inflammatory tract and had merely shifted the emphasis. "And you will find that the gentlemen of this country no longer have to soil their hands or waste their valuable time on suppressing riots and unruly mobs."

"Very clever, Stalker," Fraser said, almost as if he was congratulating Drew for having so arranged the social geology. "You see, father, we are in no danger of being beseiged by the tenants and stormed like the Bastille, as Mama fears."

"I doubt, Sir Archibald," said Drew, "that *you* will ever have anything but the loyalty of your workers."

"I have always avoided coalmines," said Sir Archibald, apropos of nothing except a strange apprehension that by tampering with that dismal trade he would become a target for radical wrath and be smoked out of his comfortable ignorance.

Mellish said, "Will you become a leader of men, Stalker, old fellow? Will you put your degree to the service of your class?"

"I will put my degree to the service of the Law, Hector," said Drew with a hint of reprimand. "The Law is not a dray-horse to be packed with ideals and driven down a main street like a bread cart dispensing charity. I will be—hope to be—a servant of justice. No more, no less."

"I'm sure you will be, Stalker," said Sir Archibald. "A brave speech, and . . . and . . ."

"Admirable sentiments," Fraser added.

Sir Archibald nodded and, as the clock struck five, said, "Come, we must dress for dinner. I hope we'll have an opportunity to talk again, Andrew. If not on this visit, on your next."

As the three young men followed the laird out of the library, Fraser patted Drew on the shoulder and said, "It seems that father likes you."

"How could he fail to?" said Hector drily. But Drew, at that moment, was too pleased with himself to detect a warning in Mellish's tone.

Ten

❧

IN THE DAWSON household, that Christmas morning, breakfast was a scrappy affair. Everyone was preoccupied with final preparations for one o'clock dinner. Delicious smells issuing from the kitchen, however, kept the guests warm with anticipation of good things to come later in the day. Father Christmas had, of course, called on Edward. The boy's wonder at the magical advent of the whiskered philanthropist from the North Pole had given way to wild excitement, an energy which manifested itself in a non-stop careering up and down stairs, in and out of all the rooms, his head enveloped in a cocked hat, legs clasped over a brightly painted hobby-horse and a fiendishly shrill trumpet clenched in his teeth. The young hussar realised that as amnesty had been declared on noise, he could kick up as much din as he would without fear of reprimand. More presents were piled under the tree in the dining room including the small items that Mirrin had been able to afford; lavender bags for the women, watch gloves for the men, though she had stretched to a muffler for Lily and a large box of paints for her nephew.

Blanche Talboys' disposition had not been improved by her night's sleep or by the significance of the day. Even Mirrin had felt the sharp edge of the young theatrical's tongue in lieu of a seasonal greeting. As on the previous evening, the thorn in Blanche's side was her father's insistence that they should rehearse. It was part of Wilf's perfectionism, a penalty for the fact that he preferred to present a family show intact rather than seek a booking in one of the newer halls and submerge his act in a whole variety bill. Wilf,

158

Ada confided to Mirrin, could no longer abide to have his songs, dances and monologues topped by ladies sporting with crocodiles, prancing puppies, somnambulists, dancing Zulus, wire-walkers and fat girls who allowed themselves to be shot from cannons. It was all very well to subordinate one's talents to such curious freaks in a really grand house like the Crystal Palace or the Argyll, but the provincial theatre's strength lay in the versatility of its troupers or, as Wilf put it, in the multifaceted skills of its terpsichoreans and warblers. That was what the humble folk of Grossby wanted and, by Gad, that was what they were a-goin' to get for their money.

"I'm not going near that place today," Blanche shouted.

"I say you are, Blanche."

"We are as good as we need be for Grossby."

"Put your shoulder to the wheel, Blanche, please."

"For what? To be pelted with over-ripe fruit again."

"It's Christmas, luv."

"I *know* it's Christmas."

"Blanche, dearest, please."

"Leave me alone."

The fact that Blanche was skulking in her room was enough to cast a faint gloom over the other occupants of the house. But some time in mid-morning when snow began to sift out of the leaden sky and the Salvationists' Band could be heard playing carols softly and sweetly over in the town square, the joyful expectancy of Christmas gradually reasserted itself, and the bustle of eager activity increased.

Fires were lit in all the rooms, plates set to warm on the stove racks, the glass gauge on the stove peered at constantly as if it was an oracle which augured the future. Ernest Dawson made punch to his own frugal recipe. Hilda painstakingly sliced up *glacé* cherries to ornament cakes. Wilf, Ada and Pru, listing a little without the fourth member of their quartet, attended church, then went on to the Civic Hall for a half hour to practise extra verses, written for the occasion by Wilfrid Talboys in person, of 'Slap, Bang, Here We Are Again'. They were back in a couple of hours and it seemed, to Mirrin, that they had hardly been gone at all.

"All that fuss," she remarked to Lily. "Blanche could have been with them easy enough."

"It goes deeper than idleness, I think," said Lily. "It's worse than I've ever seen it between them four."

"It's all that spoiled cow's fault," said Mirrin.

"I'm not so sure," Lily said. "Well, at least she'll be down for her dinner. Blanche isn't one to miss a treat just to prove her point."

"I hope she doesn't make it miserable for everybody else," said Mirrin.

"We won't let her," Lily said.

All further conversation was obliterated by the advent of Edward leading a charge through the kitchen out into the echoing laundry rooms and on still, like Napoleon, into the wild white wastes of the yard where a quarter inch of fluffy snow already quilted the cobbles.

Blanche did not have to be persuaded to appear promptly for dinner, summoned, as were all the guests, by a prolonged call on Edward's trumpet which, so loud and enthusiastic was it, might have brought in the hungry from the neighbouring county. They were all saluted by Edward as they entered the dining room and all solemnly presented with cardboard chapeaux which everyone, even Blanche, donned before they found their allotted places at the dining-room table. The Talboys and Pru, Mr. Quayle, Mrs. Perkins and her daughter Sue; Ernest had the top and Hilda the bottom, Edward cushioned up by his grandma's side, while Mirrin and Lily took places nearest the door to pop conveniently in and out of the servery.

The dinner was a huge success, the *Poulet à la Marengo* declared superior to greasy old goose or stringy turkey any day of the week, the Tipsy Cake Trifle, in huge quantities, slipping down better than stodgy plum pudding. There was a tiny plum pudding too, of course, as a sop to tradition, and mince pies and iced cakes with cherries and punch and wine and, courtesy of Mr. Quayle, a quart bottle of fiery liquid which the label touted as Best French Brandy without actually incriminating the importer by name.

By three o'clock the dinner was over. Mellowed by it all, the guests napped for fifteen or twenty minutes in sundry casual positions in the parlour before games and singing got underway, led by Wilf and Ernest. For this one afternoon Ernest came into his own as a comic songster, a star lost to the halls by circumstances. In a topper of spangled cardboard, a monocle glued to his eye, Ernest Dawson put dignity aside and rendered a medley of the popular London songs of the day, half the Leybourne repertoire from 'Champagne Charlie' through to 'Zazel, Zazel', without once wavering in the verses or straying from the tune. Much to everybody's surprise he was beautifully accompanied by Sue Perkins and her mother on ocarinas produced from their reticules which, as Wilf quipped, were not quite deep enough to hide a brace of euphoniums, thank the Lord.

Even to Lily it was a revelation of her parents' interest in the vulgar glamour of the theatre, as the couple, Hilda included, crooned and trilled through choruses of songs long forgotten by all but veteran troupers, echoes of the days of the Midlands 'free-and-easies' and Yorkshire stingos, a whole chapter of their youth which had been closed and locked away beneath respectability.

Even Mr. Quayle burst into song during a lull in the proceedings and cutlassed his way to the heart of 'The Chickaleary Cove' before he had to be flanked and supported by Wilf and Ada and carried, dazed but courageous, to the end where a medicinal glass of French waited to cure his wheeze.

Blanche would not deign to accept a polite invitation to render 'Dark Girl in Blue'. But Mirrin, in a clear perfectly-pitched voice, sang 'Lochinvar' so movingly that even Ernest shed a tear and all the ladies present had to be revived with punch and ginger candy.

It was at that moment, though Mirrin had no means of knowing it, that her career in the theatre began.

On Boxing Day after an early lunch—plain fare again —Ada, Wilf and Pru left for the Civic Hall. The lethargy which prevailed in the Dawsons' house was not confined to the girls, who had been up late the previous night washing dishes and generally clearing up. Mr. Quayle slept through breakfast. Mrs. Perkins and her daughter went off to Leeds to attend a concert and Wilf kept an anxious eye on the weather which was cold and still. Even Edward, who had been allowed to stay up long past his usual bedtime, was content to amuse himself quietly with his paints and modelling clay and the other gifts that had been found for him under the Christmas tree before supper the day before.

Mirrin sustained a feeling of contentment only faintly tinged with the nostalgia that was an essential part of Christmas. It had been a good Christmas, the best she could remember for years. But there had hardly been a minute of it, while she was involved with her new friends, that she'd forgotten the old. There had been a letter from Kate and another from Mam, thanking her for the money she'd sent them and expressing their delight that she had met up with Lily once more. Betsy had recorded her greetings on a scented card and, of the family, only Drew had failed to make a seasonal gesture of affection and friendship —not that Mirrin cared. She thought of them all, of Houston too, and Tom and even of Rob Ewing as she napped in the wooden kitchen chair after the mid-day meal on Boxing Day. But, as her sleep deepened, she was abruptly tormented by images of the witch-like Mag shouting 'Plugs as big as your fist. Cut 'em out. Cut 'em out', and then of Colly riding on a turnip cart, the turnips falling, pouring down on her. She struggled and moaned but the weight of the vegetables seemed to crush her.

"Mirrin! Mirrin! For pity's sake, wake up."

Blinking, Mirrin was relieved to be dragged out of her troubled slumber and to look up into Lily's startled face.

"I . . . I was dreaming," she said. "Comes of too much plum duff, I suppose."

"Aye, it's affected more than you," said Lily, urgently. "Blanche is still in her room."

"I thought she'd gone t'rehearsals with the others."

"She was supposed t'follow on in an hour," said Lily. "But she's locked herself in and I can't get a sensible word out of her."

"Let her stew."

"There's a lad here from the Hall sayin' that her father wants her round there right away."

"For rehearsals?" said Mirrin. "What time is it?"

"After three."

Mirrin pushed herself up. "We'd better howk her out of there. To my mind, her Da's had about all he'll take."

On the upstairs landing they encountered Hilda Dawson, flushed and fierce, picking over keys on a circular wire.

"Most of these haven't been used for years," said Hilda. "Lily, try this one. If that . . . that . . . girl hasn't left the key in the lock or pushed the bolt then we'll find one to open the door eventually."

Stooping Lily peered through the keyhole. "I can see through, mother," she said.

"What's she doing?"

"She's . . . she's in bed."

"Is she ill? What could it be? Not typhus? Oh God, not . . ."

"Calm yourself, Mrs. Dawson," said Mirrin. "Now, if you go downstairs and make a cup of tea, I think Lily an' me can effect an entry an' waken young Miss Blanche."

"She *must* be ill."

"I don't think so, mother," said Lily, firmly. "Now, please, make some tea."

By the time Hilda Dawson had reached the ground floor corridor and bustled out of earshot, Lily had fitted the correct key into the lock and had pushed into Blanche's room.

It was immediately apparent that a stronger draught than tea would be required to put Blanche on her feet and restore her senses.

Speechless, Mirrin gaped down at the dishevelled

figure sprawled across the patchwork counterpane. The young woman's cheeks were scarlet, her mouth gaped and she breathed stentorously over a posy of withered violets in her hands. Tied with silver thread, the nosegay was pressed against her bosom, the blooms as brown and weightless now as gull's feathers. Also on the bed was a sepia photograph in a stiff grey cardboard frame. It showed Blanche in a white dress and huge summery hat leaning against an iron railing beyond which was the sea. She was laughing up into the face of a lumpy young man dressed in a coarse herringbone suit, a soft felt hat stuck raffishly on his head.

Mirrin understood at once. She also understood that the gin bottle on the floor, which had probably begun the day as full, was now empty.

"She's . . . she's *blotto!*" Mirrin exclaimed.

"Thank Heavens my Da's gone out to the market," said Lily. "Listen, we've first got to fetch her out of her stupor, Mirrin. We've got to get her to the Hall."

"Wring out a washcloth in cold water, an' I'll sit her up," said Mirrin. Slipping an arm under the girl's shoulder she endeavoured to hoist her from the counterpane. "Hup y'come, Blanche."

Blanche flapped weakly at the intruder and went completely dead-weight so that Mirrin could do no more than hoist the girl's head from the pillow. Lily returned with a sopping cloth from the ewer on the dresser and plastered it against Blanche's flushed cheeks. The girl blubbered and shook her head but did not rise or show much sign that her nervous system was responding to the deluge. Mouth against Blanche's ear, Lily snapped, "You're wanted at the theatre, Blanche. Blanche, d'you hear me? Open your eyes."

"She's guzzled the whole flamin' bottle," said Mirrin. "She won't come round this side of tomorrow."

Hilda Dawson entered the bedroom bearing a tray of tea things.

Forestalling her mother's enquiries and outraged responses, Lily said, "She's been drinkin', Mam, an' she's absolutely pie-eyed."

"But . . ."

"I know; she's wanted at the theatre."

"Civic Hall," Hilda corrected, automatically. She put down the tray on the dresser, poured herself a cup of tea and drank it, while Mirrin and Lily shook and cajoled the prostrate girl, all to no effect.

Hilda said, "The lad's still downstairs, the lad from the Hall. What'll we tell Wilf?"

Mirrin said, "I'll tell him, shall I?"

Hilda said, "Tell him his daughter's drunk?"

Mirrin said, "No, I'll tell him she's . . . unwell."

Hilda said, "I certainly didn't expect *this* sort of behaviour from our friends' daughter, I assure you. An' we were *so* lookin' forward to seein' the show tonight, Ernest and I."

Lily said, "If we work on her, Mam, maybe she'll come round in time."

Hilda sniffed. "Out of that stupor? In less than four hours?"

Lily shook her head disconsolately. "You're right, Mam."

Hilda said, "Wilf and the ladies will just have to improvise, that's all."

"So, I'll tell him the truth?"

"Best do that, Mirrin."

The front awning of painted wood was ornamented with a gaudy paper streamer which announced that the *Grand Family Show* would begin at eight that evening. Other bills pasted to boards flanking the doors touted the *Family Act Supreme: Totally Eclipsing All Similar Concert Parties*. They seemed highly inappropriate considering that the youngest member of the Talboys' troupe was, at that moment, giving a fine performance of drunken stupor.

The snow had stopped. On the main thoroughfare it had churned into a brown soup under the wheels of traffic which seemed to have converged from all over the county on that Boxing Day afternoon. Mirrin knew, of course, that the Civic Hall was not the primary attraction in Grossby, that most of the traffic had to do with seasonal visitation and the dozen or so taverns and public houses that thrived in the streets of the mill town. Even so, it was not difficult to imagine the chagrin of the crowd in the packed hall when the Grand Family Act turned out to be a trio, not even a quartet.

The prop boy led Mirrin down an alley and opened a side door, impolitely preceding her into an almost pitch dark corridor which smelled of beer and cats. She was led on now less by the boy than by the sound of a piano repetitiously hammering out a phrase from 'Slap, Bang', and by Ada's faded voice endeavouring to fit lyrics to it. The smell of cats gave way to the earthy odour of limewash and paint, sharpened by turpentine. The four 'flats' that the Talboys used as backdrops were hung like drying sheets across the rear of the Civic's stage, roped to pulleys which in turn were guyed to the crankshaft of a device that looked like a mangle. The gloom was alleviated by a filter of light from under the flats. The racket of the piano and voice became very loud indeed, amplified by the deep box-like construction of the stage.

The Civic Hall, Mirrin had been informed, was used for all sorts of events, from Flower and Vegetable Shows and Cotton Workers' Meetings through to Choral Society Concerts and the inevitable cycle of Educational Lectures and Lantern Slides, covering every subject under the sun. Bills, all wrinkled and scrawled, still decorated the outer corridors touting for performances long since over and forgotten.

The boy led Mirrin round a threadbare curtain to the side of the narrow stage. She peered out across the empty benches, up to the curve of the gallery and the 'gods', then her eye travelled wonderingly round the crouch of the tiers back to the island of gaslight left of centre in which Wilf Talboys and his women stood like castaways.

Boots clumping, the prop boy, who was the son of a Borough employee and slept on the premises, stalked across the stage and held out his hand. He might have been offering himself for the part of Oliver Twist, though he was much less timid than Dickens' urchin as he cupped both palms as if in expectation of a shower of coins.

"Where is she?" Talboys asked.

"Ain't come. Sent 'er friend."

Wilf peered past his sister-in-law, who was standing in front of an open Castilioni pianoforte, and called out, "Is that you, Hilda?"

"It's Mirrin Stalker, Mr. Talboys."

"Time's money, Wilf," the youngster said.

Wilf fished in his vest pocket and produced a single coin which he dropped absently into the small grubby hands which closed on it with a derisively triumphant gesture, as if extracting copper from a theatrical was a great feat indeed. The boy, known as Ling for short, tramped back past Mirrin and vanished behind the wing curtain, leaving the scornful phrase, "Trouble now, Wilfred, ol' cove" hanging in the air like fake ectoplasm.

"Where is she, then?" boomed from the 'gods'.

"I don't know yet, do I?" Wilf retorted, pitching his voice to reach through the musty darkness to the lone spectator in the centre of the uppermost tier of seats.

"You conned me into acceptin' the four of you, 'stead of a full bill. Now you got down to three. I'll 'ave a solo artiste 'stead of a variety hackt on me hands 'fore the week's up."

Mirrin could just make out the tall figure in the 'gods' leaning on the iron rail which kept the rowdies from flinging themselves into the stalls under the influence of alcohol, enthusiasm or violent disapproval.

"Booked you for four," the manager shouted. "I ain't seen the filly but once since you got 'ere, Talboys, an', by Gum, even that treat were hardly worth the waitin' for."

With an extravagant gesture of dismissal, Wilf advanced on Mirrin, murmuring, "Where is Blanche?"

"She's . . . she's . . . unwell."

"What's wrong wi' her?" asked Ada.

"She seemed well enough this mornin'," said Pru.

"She's . . . " Mirrin began.

Wilf put his hand on her shoulder and steered her back into the folds of the curtain. It might have been a performance now of *Murder by Night*.

"Is she incapacitated by liquor?" asked Wilf.

"Aye."

"Damn the girl: damn her!" He stared into Mirrin's

eyes like a mesmerist. "Can we bring her round enough to do the third act, d'you think?"

"I doubt it," said Mirrin. "I'm sorry, Mr. Talboys."

"Not your fault, luv," said Ada, who had come up on them now. "She's been mooning for the last three months."

"It's that rascal in Hatherton, that's who . . ."

"Hush, now, Wilf," said Ada. "How much has she imbibed?"

"One full bottle, I think: gin."

Ada nodded. "Like the night in Bradford."

"But that wasn't just *us:* we were only a spot on the bill then, could fill in," said Wilf. "He'll hang me. Ockram will hang me. And I wouldn't blame him."

"Ockram'll hang you sure as eggs," said Ockram who, having descended on silent wings from the gallery, appeared now from the steps at the top of the orchestra trough.

Later Mirrin learned that Ockram was the representative of a Leeds-based agent whose profession was the outlaying of the deposit necessary to secure a lease of halls and small theatres all across the North and Midlands, and the booking of a conglomeration of acts and performers to fill those engagements for the public's delight and his own profit. Ockram's master seldom lost out on the transaction. A printed iron-clad contract made the artistes responsible for loss of revenue and insured him against having to dip into his own pocket in the event of a flop. In exchange for his capital investment, the agent, Mr. Harrison Colcutt, cleared all his expenses and sliced off fifty per cent of the box-office haul, leaving the residue to be divided among the performers. It suited Ockram, and Colcutt, to book a single act into the small-capacity hall in Grossby. The Talboys had proved popular enough in the past to warrant the minimal risk of a riot and a subsequent boycott by the good folk of the little cotton town.

At the time, however, Mirrin had no knowledge of such financial machinations. Her pity was directed towards Wilf, Ada and Pru to whom Ockram's acid comments seemed to mean so much.

Ockram was younger than his world-weary voice suggested. Very tall and gaunt with blond hair, almost white-blond brows and eyes the colour of dried rose-leaves; he wore a well-cut, expensive dress coat and a white cambric tie, which gave him the look of a clergyman. A life-long dislike of towering above his fellows, or the need to accommodate his height to incompatible surroundings, had given him a permanent stoop, like a joiner's ruler about to fold into pocket dimensions.

"What's 'appened, Talboys? Where's the filly, then? I thought you sent Ling along for her?"

"Blanche is unwell."

"Oh, right! Yes, right!" said Ockram. "One jumpin' monkey an' two crows can carry an hackt, I suppose? What sort of show's that, without a ankle, without a well-filled bodice t'keep their minds off your caterwaulin'."

"Oh, right!" said Ockram.

"I assure you, sir, that the ladies and I are perfectly capable . . ."

"Perfectly capable of bein' stuck with the bill for damages."

"You wouldn't do that."

"Wouldn't I?"

"Mr. Colcutt and I have known each other over these many years."

"Oh, right!" said Ockram. "Many years. So you knows how he'll view this breach o'contract. Four pounds the night, Ling an' props hextra."

"We're booked stiff tonight and tomorrow," said Wilf plaintively.

"The bigger the crowd, the bigger the disappointment."

"Yes," said Wilf, who probably subscribed to that adage too. "But we *won't* disappoint . . . disappoint them, Mr. Ockram."

"We can pull it through," said Ada, without conviction.

"Too risky. No ankles: no show."

"But . . . ?"

"Get 'er 'ere: on crutches, if you must, but get 'er 'ere."

"She can't sing."

"Then she can show them 'er knees."

"*Mister* Ockram," exclaimed Ada, "that's my daughter you're talkin' about."

Ockram wagged his finger. "Harrison Colcutt won't care if she's the flamin' Princess Royal. He'll have yer, Talboys, an' you knows it. I should never have booked a solo family hackt."

"Mr. Talboys," Mirrin said, "we might just be able to bring Blanche round in . . ."

"Who the 'ell's she?"

Ockram inspected Mirrin with surprise and, even then, with instant calculation.

"A friend," said Ada.

"A trouper?"

"No, not me," said Mirrin, uneasily.

Ockram walked slowly round her, bashing the soft curtain aside with his elbow. It was degrading, yet, strangely, flattering. The coldness of his inspection seemed unrelated to any human consideration and divorced from the admiration which the man expressed by way of a low whistle.

"'Andsome creature, ain't yer?" he said, still looking at Mirrin's figure. "Open the coat."

"Why?"

"Is that yerself, or a muffler?"

"If you mean what I think . . ."

Flushing with mounting anger and embarrassment, Mirrin glanced up at Wilf Talboys. He too had a faint, if suppressed, glint of calculation in his eyes.

"She can sing a bit, too," said Pru. "We've heard her."

"An' juggle with plates and mesmerise helephunts," said Ockram. "Open the flamin' coat, gel."

Mirrin drew in a deep stiff breath and let indignation hiss out of her. Staring straight into Ockram's petal pale eyes, she flicked open the buttons of the overcoat and, like some regal personage divesting herself of a cloak, flung it apart.

"Does it look like a muffler now?" she demanded.

Ockram grinned.

Grimly, Mirrin reached to her knees and lifted up

her brown skirts and cotton petticoat. The boot laces were tight about her ankles and the boots were muddy. She hitched the skirts high enough to show him her calves in black servants' stockings.

"See," she said. "A pair of legs: not teak either. An' they both reach the ground at the same time."

"Spunky, ain't she!" said Ockram. "For a Scotch lass."

"She can sing 'Lochinvar'," said Pru. "Make the tears start t'yer eyes."

"Wait," Mirrin protested.

"If she's got a voice, hany kind of voice," Ockram said, "she's on. Like hit or lump hit, Talboys. She's with you, or you're howt."

"Mirrin, please?" Ada Talboys said. "Try it, please."

"I do know some Scottish songs," said Mirrin. "But what about rehearsal, music, the orchestra?"

"Hardly a man among them can read the notes of the scale," said Wilf, shrugging. "Five old stagers buskin' it by ear that's all they are."

Mirrin looked wildly round. Ockram had hopped down into the orchestra trough again and, vaulting the rail, had begun to stalk up the central aisle towards the single gas lamp which lit the entrance door.

"Sing," he shouted. "Sing loud enough t'let me 'ear, back 'ere, an' you're on for the run, gel."

"I'll kill that wee . . ." Mirrin said. Her threat was obliterated by notes on the piano. Hastily, Pru struck a selection of chords. The sound went out into the empty hall, echoing, yet merry, giving dimension to the dust and vacant musty spaces.

Mirrin remembered the barrackers at the political rallies at which she'd spoken when she was young and ardent and all for the cause of the working man. She remembered Christy Moran, the agitator, who looked at her sometimes just the way Ockram had that evening and how Christy, the cunning wee devil, had gently persuaded her to wear a white cotton blouse which showed off her figure and how some of the men, many of them in fact, had paused not to hear the preaching of radicalism or the sound common sense of militant policies but just to get a free eyeful of fe-male contours.

What difference was there? It was part of the male nature. Aye, and if she was honest with herself, part of her nature too.

"*Sing!*" Ockram shouted. He lit a pipe. She could see the match flame in the gloom. "Chant. Anythin', gel."

"Please, Mirrin," said Ada, touching her arm. "Help us!"

Was this worse than a tentful of tinkers stinking in the ferment of a week-long rain? Was this worse than a tongue webbed with cotton lint, the pulsation of the threshing flails on the frames? Was this worse, even, than Blacklaw's dreich coal chutes vomiting out their filth shift after shift. There was at least a light out there, the wavering flame of a match, and the jangle of a pianoforte, and some gaiety, however spurious, tint-ing the shabbiness and fashioning a kind of cheer.

There was excitement in her, an instinctive response to the challenge of oppression, fertilised perhaps by her dislike of Ockram, another extension of the slave-master, the demanding voice of capitalist authority. She fixed her eyes on the warped boards of the stage and came forward.

"Look't the show-off," Mam had said when she was strunting about the kitchen to catch her Da's attention. "Look't that lassie. Someday we'll hire a hall an' put her in it."

Now there was a hall, though Mam wasn't doing the hiring. Mirrin concentrated, running over the tunes and the verses of all the songs she had ever learned, her mouth dry, her throat beginning to tighten. She knew where she was. She had a sense of that, though she stood only on the pallid outer ring of the pool of gas-light. Before her were the cowled footlights, the tissue stuff of the reflectors.

"Come on, come on, gel. I 'aven't got all night."

Deliberately she put her hands on her hips, cocking out her elbows, her head still hanging so that her face could not be seen, then, even as Wilf and Ada began to coax her again she lifted up her head and launched into the first verse of Rabbie Burns' most beautiful song, that one which, wherever or whenever it was sung back home in Scotland, brought tears to the eyes with its sadness and romance.

> *"O my love is like the red red rose, that's*
> *newly sprung in June,*
> *O my love is like a melody that's sweetly*
> *played in tune."*

Behind her, the piano accompaniment stopped. Mirrin's voice strengthened. She could not halt herself now. Her gaze was fixed on the front row of the 'gods'. She thought of her mother there holding her father's hand, thought of nobody else, nothing else of which she was consciously aware. Yet the song and the singing of it, the resonances in her throat, drew a passion of wistful longing from her soul and made her, for those few minutes, oblivious to the place and the circumstances of her performance. She would have sung no less feelingly had she been alone upon a heather hillside far above Blacklaw. It was an instinctive release, a commitment to the power of melody within her.

> *"But fare thee well, my only love, and*
> *fare thee well a while,*
> *And I will come again, my love, tho'*
> *'twere ten thousand mile."*

She let her voice drop and fall away into the silence of the empty auditorium. Her hands slipped down from her sides. She felt ungainly and awkward, yet uncaring. She had sung for one reason and, through the song, had discovered quite another.

After a long pause, she shouted, "Well, Mr. Ockram?"

After an even longer pause, the laconic answer came back, "You'll do."

She was not afraid of them. That, Wilf declared, was the truly amazing thing about young Miss Stalker. She did not appear to be intimidated by the animate faces that crammed the rows below her and piled up tier on tier to the 'gods'. When she first stepped on to the stage of the Civic that Boxing Day night at fourteen minutes past eight o'clock it seemed that the tusks of the footlights were her only protection against a wall of men, women and children, a wall that might topple down and crush her at any moment. Some halls, Pru confided, imposed that scary illusion on performers. The trick was not to let the first impression scatter your wits and make you go all taut and sandy in the throat.

The waiting period might have been worse than the step on to the stage. But there was so much to be done, so much advice to absorb that she had no time to brood, carried along by Wilf's professionalism and Ada's soothing reassurance that the folk would take to her, consoled by the fact that Pru could adapt the 'twiddly-bits' to suit Mirrin's occasionally wayward tempo during songs. As Wilf said, the five-man orchestra was hardly more than a collection of public-house buskers. Even uniform black cotton jackets and 'spring-onion' ties could not disguise their cheery, beery countenances or cause the cornet to quite harmonise with the fiddle or the percussive gentleman to restrain himself in the choruses.

But it was the costumes that brought Mirrin to a full realisation that she was about to become a public performer. The costumes gave her confidence by removing her identity. It would not be Alex Stalker's daughter who would skip out there in to the vast open expanse of the stage and show herself off to three or four hundred strangers, but another girl entirely. The costumes were nothing special, a makeshift, pinned-in dress or two from Blanche's hamper, a tartan apron and matching plaid that Pru had preserved from days of yore and a bright tartan cap, a 'tammy', that persisted in slipping over Mirrin's nose when she danced, and which amused the audience so much that it became quite a featured prop.

It was typically generous of the Talboys to allow the four acts of their family show to be taken over by a stranger, an amateur at that. They were flexible enough to alter and adapt the structure of rehearsed scenes and sketches to include as much as possible of Mirrin Stalker who, from her first appearance, had the audience on her side and, by the second intermission, could have led them barefoot over the Rocky Mountains. After a while Mirrin made no bones about it that she was a novice. She played up the impromptu nature of her stage-craft, gaining sufficient confidence to call out to the spectators and invite their participation, to draw them into the fun and games and to exercise her caustic wit with a quickness that stemmed from her days as a pithead orator.

She stunned them at the end of the first act with her rendition of 'The Red, Red Rose', left them rollicking at the end of the second with 'My Name is Annie Campbell', and took a trick on her one and only appearance in Act Three by strolling across the stage with a bottle of porter in one hand and a wedge of cheese in the other while poor Wilf was endeavouring to sing 'Hark, the Goddess Diana' in duet with Pru.

"I'm sorry, Mr. Talboys. I shouldn't have done that."

"Think nothing of it, young lady. What other ditties do you know?"

Eyes shining, cheeks flushed, Mirrin answered. "Hundreds."

"You lead the singing, then."

"But . . ."

"Go on with you, lassie," Ada said.

"Can you play 'Serenading Sara' on your banjo, Wilf?" Mirrin asked.

"That's it: that's the one."

"Ling, find me a cloth cap."

"Yus," Ling said.

She longed to go on again: she wanted the evening to continue for ever. She felt that she was loved by them and was lifted by her desire to please them, to draw them out of their miseries for a while and prolong their pleasure in the show. Just by singing, she could make them sad; by singing she could make them uproariously happy. It was not her talent as a song-bird or her skill as a tapper but the fundamental fact that she was one of them, a big, tall handsome girl who could blend sentiment and sauce at a pitch they could understand and appreciate. She had no pretensions, only a verve that most of the audience had had dinned out of them by the oppressive conditions of life in the mill town, and a waggish energy that reminded older folk of how it had been to be young and brimful of enthusiasm for life.

Ling's own cloth cap upon her head, thumbs stuck into a make-believe waistcoat, Mirrin adopted the long stride and exaggerated swagger of a man and, with a knowing tilt to her head, rolled out on to the stage, followed by Wilf armed like a troubador with his banjo.

> " 'Twas late at night to see her
> By love's passion I was led,
> I was so disappointed
> When I found they'd gone to bed."

She began to mime, a technique that Ada had to perfection and which, Mirrin thought, was one well worth emulating. She sang loudly, the rapt audience beginning to giggle already at the *doubles entendres*. Below her, the five cheery buskers were grinning widely, resting their instruments to look up at her. She strutted and wagged her head in time to the melody and let Wilf run a little to catch up with her. She made Wilf pause, the audience wait for each of the funny lines, breaking the song up, as she had heard it done once at a kirk concert by Bray Donaldson who had tippled too much and was severely rebuked in public by the minister the following Sunday.

> "The window rose, her mother
> Emptied something on my head.
> I was wringing wet through
> Serenading Sara.
> Just Serenading Sara
> Serenading Sara after dark."

With gathering motions of her arms, standing alone in the front centre of the stage, the fumes from the footlamps coming up over her, Mirrin invited the audience to join in that saucy, catchy and very well-known song. And they did, one great shouting, swaying sort of voice swelling up from the once-shabby interior of the Grossby Civic Hall, through 'Sara', and 'Bubbles' and 'The Flying Trapeze' and others led by Wilf and Ada, to finish with the ultimate in working-class camaraderie, 'Paddle your Own Canoe.' It was Mirrin's choice, a remembered classic from the miners' rallies on the green field outside Hamilton.

> *"Then love your neighbour as yourself*
> *As the world you go travelling through,*
> *And never sit down with a tear or a frown,*
> *But paddle your own canoe."*

When it was over, the curtain lowered, the audience howling for more, Mirrin took a bow herself. She received not only a standing ovation but also a party of boarders who, far from wishing her harm, flung coppers on to the stage in token of their gratitude. The full troupe took the second curtain call, then the threadbare drape descended for the last time and Mirrin staggered back from it as if she had wakened from a trance.

Wilfrid Talboys hugged her. Ada and Pru hugged her and, within minutes, Hilda and Ernest Dawson arrived from the stalls to hug her too. The two men carried her away between them in an impromptu jig up and down the creaking stage.

"Our Mirrin showing off," Mam Stalker would have said.

The thought did not sober Mirrin now, nor reduce her gaiety one iota. She was home at last.

Because Edward was asleep, they were not able to light the lamp. They pulled their chairs close to the sloping window where the pale gleam of the snow which had fallen that afternoon gave them sufficient light to consume the supper of pork pies and bottled stout that Ernest had sent up to the room.

The Grossby engagement was over. It had been the

most successful series of performances that Wilfrid Talboys and the Cropley Sisters had ever given. The house had been choked for every show and Ockram would have signed them on for another month if he could have wangled the lease of the hall. As it was he booked them in at the Bridlington Variety theatre for three weeks, risking his neck with Harrison Colcutt and braving the dim January season which was notoriously unfavourable for touring troupers. But Bridlington Theatre was new and bright and trimmed with gilt and, importantly, not too large to lose the Talboys' rapport with their audience between footlights and stalls.

Each morning now Mirrin rehearsed with Wilf, each afternoon with Ada, Pru and Blanche. Sensing the power of the usurper, Blanche had returned chastened to the fold and, though she sulked and would hardly address herself to Mirrin, she had drawn closer to her father as if she feared that he would cast her aside. Nothing was said about her behaviour on Boxing Day, no reference was ever made to it or to the withered posy or sepia photograph.

"Are you sure this is right for you, Mirrin?" Lily asked. "Is it really what you want?"

"I can't explain it," Mirrin said quietly. "I can't explain it even to myself. But standing up on a stage, even at rehearsals when the hall's empty and bleak, it's . . . it's as if it was where I belong."

"My father says it's where you belong," said Lily.

"It's the Talboys, too. I like them so much. They give me so much."

"They get enough in return," said Lily. "An' this is only the beginnin', Mirrin. You could go a long way."

Mirrin shrugged. She was not vain, would not, she hoped, develop that kind of vanity. "I want t'learn, Lily. I want t'learn how t'dance properly, how t'sing in all the keys. Most of all I want t'learn how t'walk on a stage an' act the way Ada does when she sets her mind to it."

"But in a year, Mirrin, will it not pall?"

"Maybe—but I doubt it." Mirrin smiled. "A new audience every night, as Wilf says: a new challenge."

"An' when the challenges are met, what then?"

"The theatre's all challenge, I think," said Mirrin. "I've heard the bad side, too, from Pru and Ada. Oh, no, they don't intend me to cherish my illusions for too long."

"Wilf wants a London billing. More than anything else in this world he wants top billing in a decent theatre in London. I've heard him talkin' with father, talkin' of the Islington Palace, the Holborn Empire, Gatti's, even the Gaiety. It's you, Mirrin. You've given Wilf fresh hope."

"I've still a lot to learn," said Mirrin. "Besides, I'm not sure I've got anythin' to offer London. It's all very well, Lily, when I sing an' dance to folk like my own folk, labourers and cotton workers and factory hands, but I'm not the grand lady sort."

"Maybe you could learn to be that, too, Mirrin."

Mirrin sighed. "I'll tak it all as it comes. I can hardly believe that a couple of months have changed me so completely."

"Paddle your own canoe, luv," said Lily. "As long as you're sure you're doin' the right thing in plungin' into that sort of life."

"Aye, I'm sure. But you know me, Lily, I'm *always* sure I'm doing the right thing."

Lily laughed softly. "Maybe that's what makes you do so much with your life, Mirrin."

"Aye, but it's folk like you that come to the rescue when owt goes wrong," Mirrin said. Suddenly, she reached out and embraced her sister-in-law. "Without you, Lily, I would have died in that gutter."

"I doubt it," Lily said. "Anyhow, Mirrin, you'll be back in Grossby soon like as not."

"I wouldn't be surprised," Mirrin said. "It's the way it goes—round an' round, like the Merry-Ma-Tanzie."

Disturbed by their voices Edward stirred in his sleep. Mirrin crossed the little room to look down at her nephew. How like her brother he was; how like her father too in some ways. She quelled nostalgia, thinking instead of Blacklaw's dirt and despair. She was well out of it; this wee lad too was well out of it. He wouldn't die young in a sweating seam or be scarred by fire damp or choked by gas or fumes. He would never be a hunched-up prisoner of the pit like his father or his grandfather. He was well shot of that fate, thank God.

Dropping to her knees beside the cot, her hand went out to the sleeping child and she brushed his fair hair lightly with her forefinger, crooning the beginning of 'Merry-Ma-Tanzie.'

"No, Mirrin, not that one," murmured Lily.

"I'm sorry, luv," Mirrin said. "How about this for an old auntie's lullaby, then?"

Very softly, very sweetly, Mirrin sang,

"*Five white ponies up on a hill,*
 Now they dance: now they stand still,
 And they wait for the lad to creep out of the
   mill,
 Then they prance away with the dawning,
 They dance away with the dawning."

"Like you, Mirrin," Lily said.
"Aye, like me."

PART TWO

Butterfly Summer

One

❧

MAY CAME IN clear, bright and warm. The grass on the Bruntsfield Links and the slopes of the Salisbury Crags reminded Drew of fine nap velvet, and the sea in the far distance was like polished silver plate. Daffodils burgeoned in the gardens and many new green leaves clung to the grey stone walls of the University's academic walks. Outwith the gates, the ladies of the town had shaken out their light ensembles to show an inch or two more of white throats and gently curving bosoms. This display was greatly appreciated by the McAlmond set, including its 'tame intellectual' Andrew Stalker, who had transformed himself over the past months from a meek hanger-on into an opinion-maker of the first magnitude, holding the same august, if mysterious, position in the hierarchy as a druid to a Pictish king.

The period between Christmas and spring had been vital to Andrew Stalker's development. He had gained a confident suavity through regular contact with Fraser, Mellish and the Sprotts. He had impressed his tutors by his questing mind and had made his mark on the class by subtle irreverence towards the very tutors who lauded him. Most important of all, however, he had laid the foundations of a social career that, when crowned with a degree in Law and a post in a legal firm, would stand him in excellent stead. He had also buried the hatchet with Gow Havershaw—a gentleman too cautious to antagonise an intimate of the McAlmonds—and he had gleaned much sound information on the inner workings of 'the back-scratching businessmen of Edinburgh' from his friend and confidant Daniel Horn. Planetree Gardens, Morningside, had become his home, and William Blair, a douce Aberdonian, valet to Fraser, had, by proxy, become Stalker's erstwhile servant too, cleaning and ironing his wardrobe and seeing to it that the daily maids kept Andrew's small basement room in new-pin condition along with the young master's suite.

Fraser responded well to having Law explained to him in words of one syllable and being bullied into boning up the big, simple foolscap notes that Drew tacked on the wall of the study parlour where, fortified by tobacco and strong coffee, the collier's son earned his keep by honest, conscientious academic toil. The results were gratifying. Fraser had outstripped the Sprotts in curriculum placement and had even been praised in class by Angus Salmon, no less.

Easter had been spent at Pearsehill. The five young friends had braved the sleet showers to ride over the policies during the day and had spent the evenings eating and drinking moderately and being 'awfully civilised' to Lady Isobel, talking literature and philosophy and doling out discreet city gossip which had come their way during term.

By the beginning of April, Drew felt secure. His veneer of refinement became more polished with each passing week. In a year or so he would be completely indistinguishable from the high-toned fellows with whom he associated. That fierce, precocious intelligence which had set him apart from his generation back in Blacklaw kept him ahead of the Edinburgh pack.

They strolled, that May afternoon, through the gate of the College courtyard in their familiar 'fighting wedge', three and two, inner arms linked, canes whirling, arrogant chins lifted to survey the changes in the busy scene that the passage of the short academic day had brought but, most of all, to appraise the ladies' springtime fripperies and consequent 'revelations.'

In fact the McAlmond set had just paused to comment on the amplitude of one young heifer, who was very well aware of the students' attention, when an old woman shuffled from a niche behind the granite horsepost by the flank of the arch and laid her gnarled and filthy hand on Drew's elbow.

Startled, he flinched away from her.

The beggar was between sixty and seventy, her bony body draped in a faded dress, held together, so it seemed, by a heavy shawl pinned with brass brooches. Her skin was pallid and grimy, her hair lank. When she spoke her lips caved over toothless gums and her breath was foul with gin, though she was not drunk.

"Get back to your sewer, you old cow," Balfour Sprott exploded, pushing the woman from behind. Drew stayed him, making a barrier with his cane. The gesture was inexplicable. Perhaps he recognised the seriousness in her beady eyes, the direct attention she gave him.

"Beggar bitch!" said Fraser. "Strike her off, Andrew."

"Wait," Drew said. "I wish to have a word with this person."

"Oh-ho!" Innes Sprott said. "Undoubtedly she's a lady in charge of a soup kitchen."

Drew said, "Then I will bring you a bowl, Innes: cold leftovers."

The young men left, all except Mellish who loitered curiously within earshot.

Drew said, "Hector, will you apologise to the fellows for me. I will catch you up shortly."

"Who is she?"

Drew forced an evil grin. The woman waited impassively, confirming his instinctive judgment that she had come for him and that whatever message she carried, from Blacklaw perhaps, would best be heard in privacy.

Drew said, "I will explain in a day or two, Hector; in detail, if you wish."

Mellish did not take the bait, the hint that some delicious piece of sinfulness was simmering on the stove. He knew only too well that that was not Stalker's style. But he appeared to accept the suggestive wink that Drew gave him and, nodding, turned on his heel and walked on to join the others at the corner of the bridge.

"That was wise," the woman said. "Did y'tak' me for your mammy, then?"

"What do you want with me?"

"Ach, Mr. Fancy-Dan, you've come a fair bit since y'used t'slip int' the *Cockerel* for free tuck."

Sweat started on Drew's brow.

"I'll give you no money, you old beggar. I'm not ashamed of my past."

"The lass's sick."

"What lass?" He knew what lass. He fought against the impulse to glance behind him at the corner.

"The Campbell lass. Her time's come early. She's sick, verra sick."

"What's it to me?"

"I'll tell ye, son, what it is t'you. She's dyin' in my property an' if she dies, delivers, or baith, I'll have the polis sniffin' round like dugs."

"How did you find me?"

"She telt me where."

"She's lying."

"Phizz!" the woman said. "I'm no' carin' i she's lyin' like a lord. The girl's dyin' an' that's the truth o'it. So it's your peck o'trouble, sonnie, or it's me for a word wi' the college authorities. An' where'll that leave you?"

Drew smiled. "The girl is a conniving little whore," he said, pleasantly. "But I want no trouble by implication; so I'll come."

"Implickaton? That's a braw way o'puttin' it," the woman said. "Any roads, it was yoursel' that implickated her, an' I'm the one as knows it."

"Where is she?"

"Not a half mile awa'," the woman said. "In the 'dykes."

"Give me the address an' I'll come this evening."

The woman's lips crinkled and her brown gums showed in a fleeting grimace. "B'tonight your bonnie wee bedmate may be in Heaven."

"Very well," Drew said. "Will you take me there now?"

"That's what I cam' for, sonnie. It's your peck o'trouble, remember, no' mines."

The area lay by the South Backs at the bottom of Canongate's crosslink with Cowgate, a region that Drew, even in his most exploratory mood, had always avoided because of its foetid squalor. Of all the blocks and vennels in the fair city of Edinburgh, this acre was the most foul, a haunt of alcoholics and disease-ridden prostitutes who lived like rats round close-packed middens that had once been tavern yards and the workplaces of small disreputable traders.

Some evidence of jobbing still pertained here and there. The rectangle of the 'dykes where the old woman had her 'property' was rented to a tanner and skinner as a slaughter shed, the enterprise owned and operated by two elderly relatives of the crone. The stench was gut-churning. The spectacle of rotting, bloated animal carcases hung up to await the axe, great pyramids of meaty bones and ill-cured hides and fleeces draped over chaps and rails was like a vision of hell. An ancient horse, hardly less raddled than the cadavers on its cart, slumped in the shafts while crows and gulls and other carrion eaters perched on its insensitive spine and yacked defiance at the intruders. Over this scene the mid-afternoon sunlight smiled anomalously, spring-like and serene.

A handkerchief to his face, Drew followed the old woman through the yard, up a gallows-like wooden staircase and along a canted balcony to a door sunk into the joints of the building, a door down which rain and gutter muck had poured for countless years from the slatey nostrils of the roof. Slick black mud oozed in under the rotted door and half across the room in which Heather Campbell had spent the last week of her confinement.

There was no table, no chair, only a flagstone hearth and, close to it, a broken bedstead. As soon as Drew saw Heather he knew that the old woman had not exaggerated. A finger of sunlight, diminished in strength by the state of the tiny protruding window, lay upon the coverlet, upon the grotesquely humped mound of Heather's stomach, a massive contrast to the emaciation of her face and arms. The mattress was verminous. Mice skittered in the corners of the room, too numerous and bold to start away at the young man's entrance.

"How . . . how much does she pay you for this?"

"Florin a week," the crone said. "An' what's mair, she's fower weeks'n arrears. You'll b'payin' me that, like as not?"

Heather lifted her head an inch from the mattress and squinted out of eyes that were like slivers of tarnished tin. "D . . . Drew?"

The old woman cackled. She pushed Drew in the small of the back. "Hear how she's cryin' out for'r man."

Drew swallowed. He said, "When is the . . . the infant due?"

"No' for three weeks yet. But it seems he canny wait t'shove his way int' the warld."

"Drew?"

"G'on, she'll no' bite you."

As he moved closer to the end of the bed, he realised that the girl had sensed rather than seen him. The lead-rimmed eyes opened. He watched in horror as her lips parted, sticky with mucus and a smile started into the flesh of her cheeks, a smile that was at once contorted into an agony that brought her rearing up towards him, screaming in anguish.

He did not, could not, touch her. He would have backed away and fled the place if the owner had not thoughtfully planted herself in the doorway.

"Fine work, y'done, Fancy-Dan," the old woman said. "A grand night's implickaton."

Revulsion and fear gripped Drew. "What . . . what d'you expect me to do for her now?"

The old woman squinted. "There's a midwife'll cam' along sine I tell'r—but it'll cost you."

"I'll pay."

"An' when it's over, you'll be takin' what's left out o'my lodgin'."

Take her: that was an irony. Take her where? Besides, there would be nothing to take. Inexpert as he was, even he could tell that Heather Campbell was too far gone to stand much chance of recovery. And if she died . . . ? Damn her: he should have had the

courage to murder her as he had planned back before
Christmas.

"All right," said Drew. "I'll take all the responsibility. Now, I want you to stay with her for a couple of
hours."

"I'll b'doin' no such thing."

"I need to fetch money, don't I? I will pay you what's
owin' then."

"If y'don't come back," the crone threatened, "I'll
b'up at yon university again t'morrow."

Drew shuddered. He would have enough explaining
to do as it was. He would need to invent some plausi-
ble lie to cover his disappearance for the night. Suddenly, he realised that such niceties might be rendered
irrelevant. By tomorrow he might be stuck with a
bastard child and expelled, if not from the faculty, at
least from Fraser's company. His only hope now was
that they both might die, and die soon, before this
hideous crisis threw him too deeply into debt. Under
the circumstances he could not borrow from Fraser.
Daniel Horn was the fellow to shell out a pound or
two, no questions asked. Daniel and he understood
each other. He would go from here to Havershaw's,
tap Daniel for a personal loan. He had some savings
in his apartment in Morningside, too; ten or twelve
shillings.

First, however, he must send for Kate. He glanced
at the cheap watch he had bought to ornament his
vest pocket. It was not yet four o'clock. With luck Kate
would be here before midnight; train services direct
from Hamilton had been much improved of late. There
were so many things to be done, not for Heather
Campbell but for himself.

"Drew?"

Her eyes were closed. She formed his name without,
it seemed, opening her lips at all now. Her skin was
translucent. She lay so still that he thought for a moment that she might already be dead. Only a teardrop
sliding from one lash contradicted the corpse-like im-
mobility.

Coldly, he told the woman, "I'll be back here by

six o'clock without fail. Send out for the midwife immediately."

"Aye, master; anythin' you say."

She was enjoying the situation. Despair engulfed him. This hag was an extension of the Blacklaw women who had sneered at him for trying to pull himself out of the muck. It gave her enormous satisfaction to see him hauled from his lofty perch. How could he explain that he had achieved that status by his own efforts, that he deserved what he got and what he would get, this crisis notwithstanding?

"Never fear, you'll get your damned cash," he said.

"I will that."

Turning, Drew reached past the woman and dragged open the door. Even the sunlight had turned to the colour of blood. The stench of the slaughter yard came up forcibly to meet him.

"Hoy?" the woman said, catching his arm as he endeavoured to brush past her. "Sonnie?"

"What?"

"Y'never gave her a kiss."

With an expression of disgust, Drew thrust himself on to the balcony and hurried along it to the steps which would carry him away from that place and all its significances. But before he reached the street, the tortured screaming of the girl had started up again and seemed to ring in his head all the way uphill to Havershaw's.

Kate crouched on the front step of the narrow house. The main street tonight was full of life. The children were not yet in bed, played peever, hoops and cuddie-loup-the-dyke in the sun. Two little girls had brought flowers from the meadow behind the Poulter's burn and were threading them into posies on the bench outside Mrs. Grimmond's across the way. Kate was stiff from the hard day's shift at the sorting troughs but felt more cheerful than she had done for months now, responding to the fine spring evening like everybody else. Mam was indoors preparing supper. Betsy would be home at any minute, jaunting down the street from the horse-bus terminus by the *Lantern*.

In her hand Kate held a small battered axe. She was chopping lengths of kindling for tomorrow's fire. Chapping with the axe, she broke the plug into finger-length splits, breathing in the sharp resinous smell, so clean and stimulating. Strange to think that the amber wood was the constituent of coal, that gritty black substance that hid itself away underground.

There was an odd silence in the street. Kate looked up from the kindling block. The games had temporarily stopped. A hoop trundled aimlessly away and skittered to a halt, falling on its side. The wee flower girls were looking round-eyed across the street to the Stalkers' side of the pavement. From her kneeling position, Kate stared uphill.

The young man walked with a steady loping stride. He wore a dark brown pea-jacket and light brown trousers and had a crimson hat on his head, like a bandsman. But he was no bandsman. Even Kate knew who he was and what he represented.

The young man came on, inexorably approaching the Main Street's end, the last house. Heart thudding with anxiety, Kate scrambled to her feet.

"Stalker," the uniform said. "I'm lookin' for Stalker."

"I'm Kate Stalker."

"That's you then. Special delivery; Herrick's Cross-country Messenger Service."

"Where . . . where from?"

"Edinburgh."

It could only be Drew. He had met with an accident. Kate drew the young man closer to the wall so that Mam could not see from the kitchen window.

Unbuttoning a deep pocket inside his jacket the messenger extracted a long buff-coloured envelope and a flat canvas-backed book. He opened the book, pulled a pencil stump from his cuff, licked the point and handed envelope, pencil and book to Kate Stalker.

"Can you write?"

"Aye."

Laboriously Kate pencilled her name on the line provided. Against the blank, in firm brisk copperplate, was the name of the sender: *Andrew Stalker*. It had cost Drew one guinea, the price was there too.

Kate held the letter in her hand, hardly daring to open it.

If Drew had actually sent the message, then he could not be badly injured or sick or dead; at least it did not seem likely. But he had paid a guinea, a small fortune, to reach her with all haste. She looked helplessly at the uniform.

"Read it, Miss," he advised. "A reply might be needed."

Kate tore open the envelope.

The buff-tinted paper was covered in Drew's own writing.

Kate: come at once to Skinner's Courtyard, Carlindykes Road, Edinburgh. I am not ill but I am in grave straits and have urgent need of you here. Please come alone. It is no place for mother. I enclose a banknote for one pound to assist in your travelling expenses. I want you to come immediately, that is, tonight. Andrew. Postscript: if you are unable to come personally, return a message by the Herrick Service, which will cost the one pound only. I need you here. Drew.

The young messenger watched Kate closely. He had had to catch swooners before now, for he was often the bearer of bad tidings.

"How . . . how quick can I get t'Edinburgh?" Kate asked him.

"How soon can you leave, Miss?"

"Ten minutes."

"Come wi' me, then. I've got the train connections all worked out for me. I'll be home, in Edinburgh that is, by half past eleven."

"I'd . . . I'd offer y'a cup of tea . . ."

"I understand," the young man said.

Hurrying now, Kate burst into the kitchen. She explained to Mam what had occurred and, a little to her surprise, did not have to squander precious minutes in consoling her mother.

"It's idle t'speculate, Kate," Mam said, frowning. "We can't tell what it's like for our Drew there, or what he's been up to."

"Mam, I'm scared."

Flora Stalker looked at the letter once more. She read slowly.

"It's just you he wants, Kate: not me. He makes that clear."

"Mam, what'll I do?"

"Do? You'll change your dress, put on your bonnet and overcoat, an' take the money from the jar . . ."

"The money?"

"A safeguard," Mam said. "If our Drew's in hot water, it'll have somethin' t'do with money, sure as fate."

"But he sent a pound: I don't understand."

"Change, Kate, an' just get there as fast as y'can."

"Aye, Mam," Kate said, and hurried on into the back bedroom to pull her best Sunday dress from the wardrobe.

Drew pressed his shoulders into the flaking plaster in the corner by the cold hearth. Now that the sun had gone down behind the Castle Rock the room was chill. He shivered and huddled inside the Ulster he had the foresight to fetch from his room in Planetree Gardens. Mercifully, Fraser had not been at home. Drew had left a cryptic message with the valet informing Fraser that he had been called away on urgent business and would not be back that night.

Morningside had been his last port of call. He had already slunk into Havershaw's chambers and borrowed five guineas from Daniel Horn. Drew could not be sure if the guineas came from Horn's private fund or from Havershaw's box. He had no time to fret over the source. Herrick's office, at the top of the Mound, had been his final stop before he swung out into the suburbs. He took a cab back from Morningside to Skinner's Courtyard and reached the room above the slaughter sheds only a short while after the midwife's arrival.

The woman's name was Lumsden. She was even

more ugly than Mrs. Nimmo, the owner of the premises. She had a hunched shoulder and a scooped-out
face, pocked with the scars of childhood disease.
Though her experience in coaxing infants into the
world might be considerable, Drew suspected that her
main business was terminating unwanted pregnancies
among the whores who plied their trade in taverns
like the *Cockerel*. Mrs. Lumsden seemed totally unconcerned at the condition of her patient. For all the
effect they had on her, Heather's screams and wrench-
ing groans might have been the crooning of a highland
lullaby.

Taking in a shuddering breath, Drew washed his
hands over his face and peered blearily across the
room at the bed, pushed into the centre of the room
under a smokey lamp which hung from a wire hook
in the ceiling.

The Nimmo woman had gone long ago. For three
hours now he had been alone with Mrs. Lumsden
and the creature on the bed. The shrieking remnant
of the girl he had known once as Heather Campbell
seemed, in the trauma of sickness and delivery, to
have relinquished her identity, even her humanity.

From time to time in her ministrations, Mrs.
Lumsden would turn, hawk and spit on the floor, wiping her lips on her naked forearm. She used no instruments at all. The full range of her equipment came
in a burlap sack—swaddles of boiled rags, lengths of
hemp rope and a pickle jar full of goose grease: no
pans of boiling water or soft blankets such as Drew
had seen in Blacklaw when the mysterious act of birth
was taking place in one of Main Street's cottages and
his Mam or Kate had been called in to assist the
motherly village midwife, Alice Lorne. He wished that
Alice Lorne was here now instead of this gross, dis-
gusting female.

At first he had wandered anxiously about the room,
steering well clear of the bed. But at length fatigue
had forced him down on to the floor. In the corner
among mouse dirt and the scattered cinders of old
fires, he had tried, in vain, to shut out the noises,
smells and sights of that place.

Night had brought the Skinners' yard to life. For a busy couple of hours, carts rumbled in and out with the cadavers that the Nimmos had bought that day. Drew could hear the fleshy chop of axes, the rasp of saws, the hoarse bellowing of men below. He had tried to blot that out too, spinning his mind like a humming top, lashing it to make it stand on points of logic and balance there long enough to permit him to connive. But it was useless. His senses were raped by the impressions of that place, by the magnitude of the event that was happening not ten feet away.

After a time, when the courtyard had quietened again, he found himself watching the midwife's horrifying manoeuvres, the knotting of hemp lengths about Heather's ankles and shoulders, the splaying of her knees, the arching thrusts of her back and hips as she sought, by instinct now, to expel from her ravaged body the child that engorged her womb.

Birth was not wondrous, not even decently dignified. In his wildest imaginings he had never thought it to be so agonising. Six children his mother had borne. Six times she had gone through this rending struggle. It had been bad, he had heard, with himself and Betsy; twins were never easy. Bad: the word was inadequate to cover the tortures of birth. How could any woman put up with it? How could any woman allow a man to lie upon her and enter her knowing that the moments of pleasure or dutiful passivity would lead eventually to this jagged peak of pain?

What had such agony to do with the libertine sports that Fraser and the Sprotts chortled over in their cups? What had it to do with the flirtatious enticements of the young girls of Blacklaw, Hamilton, Edinburgh? Why were they so feverishly keen to thrust on towards this summit? Men, of course, had no reason to care. It did not hurt them. They demanded only selfish gratification and naturally had no thought of consequence. In future, however, he vowed that he would never allow his blood to become hot with longing for a woman. In days to come, he could recall this May night, remember it with vivid clarity as the final link in a chain of cause and effect.

Heather's screams had quieted. She hardly uttered a sound now, only thin high whistling like air escaping from a toy balloon. Drew longed for a sip of wine, for water even. But he did not move. It was part of his penance to sit in that corner, see and hear the most inttmate secrets of birth, of death, and be exposed in full to their ugliness.

Knees hunched, forearms resting, cheek on his wrists, he dozed for a few minutes. The precise moment when his son entered the world and his lover passed out of it went unrecorded.

Fractious whimpering rose to a wail. Drew opened his eyes and pushed himself stiffly to his feet. Even in his ignorance he knew what that sound meant. The baby had been born. No more pain. What would happen now to Heather? Would she sleep?

The midwife turned. Blood made a vast dark stain on her apron. Her bulk cast a deformed shadow across the bed but Drew could see the baby plain enough, laid on a piece of grey cloth, wrinkled, moist and discoloured like a skinned hare.

"The girl's gone, poor lassie," the woman said.

"Gone?"

"Dead. Nothin' I could b'doin' t'save her. God help this wee mite, though. He's only got you t'look after him."

"Me?"

"Tak' him. He's your son after all."

Drew stepped back against the flaking plaster. "What . . . what the devil d'you mean? What can I do with . . . with a thing like that? I . . . I don't want it."

The woman sneered. "Dare say y'don't. But there's no use denyin' he's yours. The widow Nimmo telt me the story."

"Put . . . put it down," Drew said. "Put it . . . beside its . . . his mother."

"Beside the dead?" said Mrs. Lumsden. "I'll do no sicca thing."

"All right," said Drew. "Put it on the floor then."

Shaking her head, the midwife laid the infant, swad-

dled in the soiled grey sheet, across the bottom of the
bed. She gestured Drew to approach. He inched himself out of the neuk by the empty hearth and peered at
the girl's wasted shape under the blanket. She looked
serene now, as if she had found peace in a long, deep
sleep. Stress had smoothed from her features. They
were youthful again, unblemished, save for the darkness around her eye sockets. Her hair had a sheen to
it and the midwife, for some reason, had run a comb
through it to make it neat. The infant whimpered
weakly.

"What . . . what about the . . . baby? Will it live?"

"Aye: he had a hard enough time gettin' here. He'll
be fine when he's been fed."

"How . . . how do I feed him?"

"Employ a wet nurse."

"How much will that cost?"

"A shilling or two."

"Can you find me one?"

"Aye," said the midwife. "There's enough o'them
about."

"I . . . I want one that's clean."

"I'll see to it—once I've been paid."

Drew extracted his purse and took out two crowns.
"How much?"

"That'll about cover it."

"All right," Drew said. "What else?"

"What d'ye mean?"

"What about . . . her?"

"Och, aye, the plot an' the ceremony an' the flowers."

"The death certificate."

"For a consideration I can attend t'that, too.
Where'll y'put her t'rest?"

"Wherever I can."

Mrs. Lumsden cocked her head, squinting. "You're
no' meanin' a pauper's grave?"

"My funds are limited," Drew had no need to jus-
tify himself to this person. "It'll make no difference to
her, will it?"

"Poor hapless wee lass."

"How much for a death certificate, a legal one, and for the nurse: all inclusive?"

"Another guinea."

"That's robbery."

"Bribin' a doctor's no' cheap."

Biting his lip, Drew extracted another guinea from his purse and placed it in the woman's palm. He said, "My sister will take charge of . . . of the infant. I want the nurse here within the hour an' the certificate of death before morning. Is that clear?"

"Clear as crystal," the midwife said scathingly, and, hurriedly bundling her ropes and clothes into the burlap sack, left the young monster to his own devices.

The transaction calmed the rebellion of Drew's senses and smothered the dangerous sentiments which had risen in him when he looked down upon that lifeless thing, so pretty and pale now. The infant seemed well enough, stirring a little and vocally active, wrapped tightly in the swaddling sheet. It did not delight him. Indeed he felt a positive distaste for the snuffling creature. A tab of skin on its upper lip reminded him of a trout. The eyes were large and roving but without sight or knowledge of the world. It did not, however, seem to be in any distress in spite of its fretfulness. He did not lift or touch it, leaving it where the Lumsden woman had laid it in a fold of the blanket by its mother's feet.

He had seen death before. He had seen his father's burned body stiff with death, and, fleetingly, the doll-like corpse of his sister-in-law Lily's stillborn baby. Betsy and he had tested themselves against death; neither of them had been much affected by it, except as its circumstances affected them. But the pale, smooth features of Heather Campbell had an unexpected effect upon him. She bore no real resemblance to the girl he had held in his arms that night last autumn in the attic in Shannon's Close. She was closer now to the idealised image of a lover formed in his daydreams, still and alabaster pale and strangely refined. He could not remember her as warm and soft.

What had she said to him that last night of all? "I

love you so much, Drew. If you ever want me, call my name an' I'll come."

It had seemed naïve then; now it seemed sinister.

He swallowed, murmuring, "Heather."

The sound sent him leaping back from the bed, hair bristling on his nape. The door opened and a young slattern entered—the wet nurse.

Sweating, shaking, Drew said, "Have . . . have you been paid?"

"Aye, sir."

"Then there's the baby."

Paying no attention to the corpse, the slattern smiled and lifted the baby, cradling it in her arms, neatly folding down the hems of the sheet from its face. She was a big untidy country girl. Her heavy jaw and opaque blue eyes suggested simplicity. She said nothing as she unbuttoned her ragged jacket and blouse. Drew caught a brief glimpse of her milk-swollen breasts, then turned away to look from the window across the yard. He could hear the nuzzling of the infant in the silence, the nurse's faint, pleasurable crooning.

Still trembling, Drew went out on to the gallery over the yard. He could see the gate from there. There was no barrier across it but in a slanted hut close by one of the wooden uprights a watchman had been posted. He leaned over a brazier filled with glowing coke, smoking a clay pipe, a very old man, patient as Job. Absently, Drew supposed a watchman was necessary to keep the poor from raiding the flensed carcases, stealing the fleeces and untanned hides. An owl swooped from the ridge of the sheds. Rats squeaked down by the inner wall. He watched the cobbles just outside the gate. It was after ten now. He prayed that Kate had got his message, and would arrive soon. He did not doubt that she would come. Laughter and raised voices. A fiddle scraped shrilly. Somebody, a woman, yawped out a few bars of a song. Foolishly, he wondered who was flitting between the tables of the *Cockerel* tavern now, in Heather Campbell's place. Those few free suppers had cost him very dear in the end.

Exhaustion made it all unreal.

When the nurse had finished she left, promising to return first thing in the morning, before dawn. She would be 'hurting' again, she told him, and the babby'd be hungry. Now the infant slept, as motionless as his mother.

At ten minutes to eleven, Mrs. Lumsden returned. He saw her from the window. She did not enter the yard, however, to deliver the signed certificate of death personally. Drew waited on the balcony as the watchman toiled up the steps and handed him the folded document.

"I expect my sister here shortly," Drew said, giving the old man a shilling. "Will you show her up?"

The phrase had such an aristocratic ring that the irony of the situation brought a sudden welling of sorrow. It grieved him that Kate should find him in this place. He should have greeted her at his home in Planetree Gardens. She should have met his friends the McAlmonds, Archibald and Lady Isobel in particular. *That* was his milieu, the measure of his achievement, not this squalid garret, this millstone incident which made him appear to be a lecher and wastrel, worse than the worst of the Williams' tribe who lived in a fortress of battered tin shacks in the shadow of the Clayburn coups back in Blacklaw.

Sobbing, Drew crouched down in the corner to wait.

"Drew. Waken up, Drew."

It was a year since last they had met. That twelve months had not been kind to his sister. She looked weary and old, he thought, in that first instant impression when he opened his eyes and struggled to his feet.

"Kate," he said. "I'm grateful to you for coming so quickly."

"The girl?" Kate said. "Is . . . that what's wrong?"

"Yes."

"My God!"

"The girl," said Drew. "And the . . . the child: more particularly the child."

"Who was she?"

"A girl," said Drew. "Just a girl."

"An' the baby?"

Drew was silent. Kate turned, gripped him by the collar of the Ulster and yanked him towards her. She too was emotionally keyed up. It had not occurred to Drew that Kate of all people might have a temper, might have been strained by the events of the winter and the worry of the Special Delivery message.

"Is it yours, Drew? Is that baby yours?" she demanded. *"Tell me the truth."*

"I . . . I wish I could be sure," Drew said.

"An' the girl: who is she?"

"Heather Campbell. She threw herself at me," Drew said. "I was a fool, Kate. I realise that now. I encountered her in a tavern, the place where I ate my meals. I was lonely, an' . . . an' she . . ."

"You married her?"

"What?" Drew almost laughed. "Lord, no. I'm not that daft!"

"But you . . . you did . . . ?"

"Yes."

"Why?"

"I told you, she threw herself at me, on my . . . my mercy, y'might say. I was lonely, Kate, an' she came t'my rooms one night with some story about how she'd been flung out of her lodgin'. She asked if she could stay with me for a while. I gave in. I couldn't help myself. I gave in to her."

"How long did she live with you?"

"Not long: a few nights, that's all. I knew it was dangerous t'associate with a girl like that. I insisted that she find another lodgin'."

"You're lying."

"I'm nothing of the kind. I saw her for another month, now an' again. She was persistent, though I admit I enjoyed her . . . her company."

"You slept with her?"

"Yes, yes: I admit it."

"An' then?"

"I told her not t'come back. The fact is she'd found

somebody else anyhow. She . . . she was that kind of girl."

Kate gestured to the bed. "That wee lass was . . . was . . ."

Drew shrugged. "She was older than she looks."

The baby whimpered; Kate lost the thread of her questioning for a while. As she stooped and lifted the infant, Drew noticed with relief that the anger in her softened. There was kindness, love even, in her eyes again. She seemed transformed into the old Kate for an instant, the patient, gentle elder sister that he had remembered with a certain fondness. At that moment, he had the feeling that all would be well, that she would do exactly as he had planned. The whining quality went out of his tone. He sensed what he must say and do now.

Rocking the baby gently, Kate said, "When was he fed?"

"A couple of hours ago. I hired a wet nurse. She'll be back early tomorrow morning."

"You've learned a lot in Edinburgh," Kate said. "I can see that."

"No need to be sarcastic, Kate," Drew said. "I had a brief liaison with this girl; that was foolish and stupid. But when she came t'me claiming that the child was mine, when I *knew* that she had had many other . . ."

"It's your baby, Drew, isn't it?" Kate said, then shouted, *"Isn't it?"*

"Yes, it may well be my child."

"Why didn't you marry her, take her t'live with you?"

"Firstly," said Drew, prepared for this line of questioning, "I didn't even know what had become of her. I didn't clap an eye on the bit . . . on her since a while before Christmas. I didn't *know* she was with child. She never approached me. Not a solitary word did I hear from her 'til this afternoon. She sent a woman for me."

"What woman? A relative?"

"No, she has no relatives: none at all. She sent the landlady of this property."

"An' these men she was supposed t'have taken up with in the interim?"

Drew shrugged. "Abandoned her, I suppose."

"But not you? You didn't abandon her?"

"I tell you, Kate, I didn't . . ."

"Where did you get the money t'send special messages?"

"I borrowed it."

"How much?"

"Five guineas, from Havershaw's clerk."

"An' how will you pay him back?"

"I have a job," said Drew. "I'm . . . I'm tutoring a fellow student, Fraser McAlmond. He gives me board and lodgin' free. I save most of my quarterly patronage."

"An' that fine, expensive coat?"

"A gift from Fraser."

"What are y'doin', Drew Stalker? What's happenin' t'you?"

He lost his temper. "I'll tell you what's happenin' t'me. I'm makin' my own way in the world. I'm nobody's charity boy now, Kate. I don't need handouts from bloody Houston Lamont; no nor from any other bastard who happens t'fancy my sister. I'm doin' what I promised my father. I'm doin' what he wanted. I'm climbin' up t'the top of the pyramid, Kate. I'm takin' the opportunity offered t'me. This is a city where I can flourish. An' that's what I've been doin'. I have friends now. Friends who *like* me. Friends who *appreciate* me. Ay, an' friends who'll be useful t'me in future years."

"Drew, I didn't mean . . ."

"Five guineas!" the young man stormed. "When did you ever see five guineas, Kate? Who did you ever know, Lamont excepted, who could dip his hand int' his pocket an' lend five guineas? Aye, an' take a handshake on its repayment. Trust: a bond between gentlemen."

"An' her, this poor wee lass . . . ?"

"Poor lass, be damned! She got her hooks in me when I was vulnerable," Drew cried. "It didn't take me long t'see how the bloody wind was blowin'."

"So you threw her over?"

"She left me, I'm tellin' you."

"She also left you a son, Drew."

The young man was suddenly silent. The incontrovertible fact of the new-born infant remained. There were other things still to be done, to be swept under the carpet. But they were paper problems. He could cope with them discreetly enough. He already had the Certificate of Death. With that document he could arrange a burial at the borough's expense, the pauper's grave that held so much terror for superstitious fools, that ultimate symbol of rejection, the end of all hope. What the devil did it matter? To Heather Campbell, not one whit. She had nobody to mourn her, anyway, nobody to be ashamed of a public acknowledgment of poverty. If there were such things as immortal souls, Heather Campbell's had long gone to its celestial abode. But the baby, his son; *that* was the problem, the sole reason why he'd had to send for Kate.

He said, "Take it, Kate, take it out of my sight."

It was not a request. The command took the breath from her, shook her. He knew it would: he had banked on that.

"But . . . but he's . . . he's your bairn."

"Probably," said Drew. "But that makes no difference. I want rid of him. He is, to me, a fatal encumbrance. You have a choice, Kate. You may take him back to Blacklaw, or I will put him into a workhouse orphanage."

Instinctively Kate hugged the infant closer to her breast as if she suspected that her brother would attempt to tear it from her and dash away with it there and then to throw into the cold catacombs of the orphanage.

"That, by the way, is where its mother came from," said Drew, with a casualness that drove Kate into a wild rage. If she had not been burdened with the baby, she would have struck him then. Drew smiled.

He had calculated that far, thrown much weight on his sister's innate love for the weak, the helpless, the rejected. Besides, the bastard was a Stalker in blood and the Stalkers were as obsessed with family name, as bad as any highland laird with his pedigree.

He was so aloof, so distant, that Kate's fury seemed to run out before it reached him, like a huge sea which dwindles to passivity before the horizon. It was hard for his sister to see him for what he was, for what they had helped him become. To her he was just a seventeen-year-old boy. But he knew better. He looked older, he acted much older, and they could say that he was precocious if they wished. He was a man now, on his own two steady feet and, if they wanted their own kind of proof, he had fathered a child. He was no longer Kate and Mirrin's 'wee' brother: he was their superior in all ways.

"I need not have sent for you, Kate," he declared. "I want you to understand that. I could have handled this whole situation myself. I could have put that baby into the parish workhouse just as easily as I obtained a Death Certificate for his mother and will have her buried tomorrow or the next day by the parish. But I thought you might prefer . . ."

"I'm ashamed," Kate said. "*Ashamed* that you're my brother."

"You made me, or helped make me. You gave my father a solemn promise, Kate. You swore t'him that you'd see me through university. I'm no longer obligated t'you to do that. I can see myself through university. But I cannot be burdened with a bastard child. I *refuse* to be saddled with . . . with that."

Kate's eyes were closed. The baby was held high against her chest, her lips almost touching its paper-thin crown and the wisps of hair that plastered the tiny skull.

"For the first time in my life, I thank God m'father died when he did." Her voice was hoarse with emotion. "You're not worth one minute of his pain, or of our sacrifice. No matter how high you climb or what you become, or what you make of your life, from this night on *we're finished*."

"But you will take the child?"

"Aye, fine well you know I'll take the child."

"Good," Drew said. "So that's the arrangement, is it? You'll take responsibility for him instead of me."

"It seems all wrong that the best o'men should've died just so the likes of you might live," Kate said, with brutal softness.

"The best of men . . ." Drew began, then prudently checked himself. "Listen, nobody must know that the child is mine. I have a position here in Edinburgh, and . . ."

"When will the nurse come?" Kate interrupted.

"Early, so she said."

"I'll wait elsewhere, then," said Kate. "I'll leave you t'your own designs."

"But . . . ?"

"I dare say I'll find another nurse in the town."

"Kate, I . . ."

Without another word to her brother, Kate Stalker wrapped the sheet more tightly around the baby and, holding him warm inside her coat, walked out of Drew's life.

From the window he watched her go. The dreadful anxiety had left him now. She had removed it. The rest would be a matter of discreet invention and the handling of the parish officials. Now it was almost over. Soon nothing would remain to connect him with the sordid affair. Hector prided himself on seeing further through a brick wall than most people. He must be careful what tale he told Hector to account for his strange behaviour and his absence from classes that coming morning.

Looking round, he saw that there was nothing in the room to occupy him. He would be as well with a bit of a night's sleep in some local dormitory hotel where at least he would have a bed to lie upon and the opportunity of putting a breakfast of sorts in his belly. Kate had not asked him for money. Presumably she had extracted a few shillings from the stone jar. Listlessly now he wondered what his mother would say about the baby. He wondered what sort of fabrications they would make up to appease the rabid curiosity of Blacklaw's gossipmongers.

Perhaps, he thought, as he turned out the oil lamp,

they would say it was Mirrin's brat. He snorted with
wry amusement. The flame flared brightly for a moment then flickered out and Heather Campbell's serene dead face was swallowed up in the darkness.

Though the train left the capital at the ungodly hour of
six a.m., it carried quite a crowd of working men and
women. The baby was comfortable enough. Kate had
made sure of that. She had thrown herself on the mercy
of the hoteliers of Edinburgh, particularly those situated near the railway station. For payment of certain
small sums she had acquired from George's Temperance Hotel a late supper for herself and a warm
groundfloor room in which she passed the three or
four hours of the night that remained. She was then
shuttled by the hotel clerk to Simons', a truly hospitable
establishment close to the station where, thanks to prior
warning by the porter of the Temperance, a wet nurse
of impeccable cleanliness was on hand to feed the
baby. In Simons', at Kate's request, a selection of
small wear and shawls had been assembled from the
hotel shopping arcade. She purchased sufficient for the
baby's needs, paid her bill and was escorted the three
or four hundred yards to the ticket office in ample
time to board the Daylight Express, as it was jocularly
called by the workers who packed its box-like coaches.
It was not until she changed trains at Bathgate and
settled into the shabby carriage of the Wilsontown,
Morningside and Coltness Special, however, that Kate
had the leisure to consider all that had happened and
to be stunned, for a while, by the magnitude of the
problems that the child would bring.

For all that, with the sun streaming down upon hazy
green fields, and the tiny baby lying asleep in his new
woollen shawl, Kate experienced a wave of sheer happiness that extinguished the miserable defeatism of the
past year.

It was almost exactly a year since Drew had left
for Edinburgh and Mirrin had sallied out of Blacklaw
to make her own way in the world. Now Drew had
broken away completely. Kate meant what she said.
She would hold him, no matter how her mother might

protest, to that bitter contract. She would answer no
more summonses, do no more for him. In fact, she
realised that she had obtained the best of that bargain.
The baby was hers, and would remain hers as long as
she lived. Overnight she had changed her status.
Mirrin might be blossoming in some fancy world of
theatres and variety halls; Betsy might be the belle
of Dalzells' Emporium in Hamilton; Drew, that ruthless blackguard, might be aimed at greatness in the
capital of Scotland. But none of that mattered now to
Kate. She had no need of her sisters and brother, to
live vicariously throuugh their advancements. She had
a baby, a baby that was virtually her own. And that
was all she wanted.

If possible she would have spared her mother the
knowledge of what had happened. The details were
sordid and sorrowful. But, Kate knew, Mam too would
be delighted to have charge of the baby. He was such
a bonny wee thing. She touched back the shawl. The
features were perfect. Dark hair was a Stalker trait,
the straight nose too—if that comical wee button could
be said to be straight. But the mouth was not from the
Stalker kist: it favoured his mother, Kate supposed,
the poor lost highland girl.

For the second time in her life, Kate made a promise. There was nobody around to hear it, however,
only the baby, which was as it should be under the
circumstances, since the promise concerned him.

"Aye, we'll love you as our own, an' bring you up
t'be a real Stalker," Kate murmured. To her surprise,
the infant's eyes opened for a moment almost as if
he'd understood.

Before she had reached Hamilton, she had found
a suitable name for him: Neill Campbell Stalker. It
had a fighting ring to it which seemed just right after
such an entry into the harsh world.

Neill Campbell Stalker; the first of the new generation.

Two

✤

THOUGH WALLACE HADN'T seen the big woman for eight days, her absence did not materially affect his creature comfort. He was willing to forgive her neglect and listen patiently to her explanations. He kept his huge head still, his jaws munching slowly over the currant bun she'd brought him, as he scrutinised the bundle that Flora Stalker held up for his approval. The rapport which had developed between horse and widow had become so keen that Wallace realised the importance of the small thing even if he did not comprehend its exact relationship to his mistress.

"My grandson, Wallace," Flora Stalker declared. "He'll be havin' rides on your back before you're much older."

Wallace thought he might manage to carry a jockey of such reduced proportions without strain. He clopped his tongue over his teeth and shook his harness slightly.

Flora said, "Neill Campbell Stalker, this's Wallace. He's a gey coarse chap but y'get used t'him after a while." She smiled at the baby in her arms. "He'll clump along slow an' easy when he's got you in back of the van. He'll not shoogle your cot. Eh, will you, y'big lump?"

Wallace made an appropriate noise and nuzzled his nose into Flora Stalker's offered hand. Though he did not find sugar there, he enjoyed the contact and the bullying caress she gave him which, now that he thought of it, he had rather missed during the past week.

Sparrows twittered among the stable's rafters, finished with nest building now but still active with the mating and its results. There was a robin, too, left over from Christmas, though where he had hidden his lady neither Flora nor Wallace had been able to discover.

"How about some straw, then, Wallace?" Flora said. "I'm sure y'can spare a puckle o'straw for wee Neill's basket?"

Wallace indicated that he could.

Holding the baby carefully in the crook of her left arm, Flora brought in a wicker hamper, some twenty inches deep, into which had been sewn a quilted felt lining. Still holding the child, the woman teazed straw from a bale in the corner and painstakingly padded the bottom of the hamper. On top of the straw she laid a plaid rug. On top of the rug she laid the cocoon-like shape of the thing called Neill Campbell Stalker which, even Wallace had realised, was the human equivalent of a nestling.

"M'father's name was Neill, y'know," Flora confided as she fussed over the baby. "That's why our Kate picked it, I'm sure. An' Campbell? Well, that seemed fittin', I suppose, under the circumstances. He's not my first grandchild, though, Wallace. I've another one, Edward. But he lives far from here an' I haven't seen him this long while." With a steel pin in her teeth the stallion could not quite make out the words. Flora said, "But Neill's the first that'll grow up here in Blacklaw. He'll be a right Stalker, will Neill. Won't you, son?"

She fitted the pin into the shawl and patted it, testing the lie of the point with her thumb to ascertain that it would not scratch the baby. The infant remained unconcerned. He had not even been polite enough to open his eyes when introductions were made. For all that, staring down his nose at the wee face almost hidden among the clothing, Wallace was impressed by the gesture of faith that the big woman had shown by bringing such a defenceless creature right into his stall.

At that moment the stable door opened and the master, Willie Kellock, keeked round it. He carried the oval leather collar which he'd taken away to soap the previous evening and which was now as clean and bright as a charger's coronet. Willie's sandy-grey thatch was already powdered with flour and a smut of batter on his chin wagged as he spoke.

"Och, it's yourself, Mrs. Stalker."

"I told you I'd be back today, Mr. Kellock."

"Aye, but I didn't expect you so early."

"We're up with the lark for the baby's feed," said Flora. "Young Mrs. Malone's the wet nurse. She comes over from the farm real early."

"Pleasant folk, the Malones," said Willie, a little embarrassed at this aspect of the unexpected turn of events. He cleared his throat. "I'm delighted that y'feel able t'continue in my service, Mrs. Stalker. I wouldn't have found another hand like you in a hurry, of that I'm sure."

"It's kind o'you t'say so, Mr. Kellock. The wee chap'll not keep me off my work, though I'll need an extra half hour at dinner time t'take him t'the Malones t'be fed; just for three or four months, 'til we wean him properly."

"Quite all right! Quite all right, Mrs. Stalker."

"If, ah . . . if the scandal that might result turns int' a bother an' damages the trade, I'll leave, of course."

"Havers, Mrs. Stalker! If scandal bothered me, I'd no' be resident long in this town, I can tell you. So, no more of that daft talk. Here, let's have a look at this young man."

Setting down Wallace's collar, Willie Kellock bent over the hamper and with a stumpy forefinger parted the shawl to inspect the infant's sleeping features.

"My! But he's perfect. Just perfect!"

"He is that."

Discreetly, Willie Kellock slipped a florin into the tuck of the shawl, the silver hansel that tradition demanded. His interest in and fondness for the bairn were not feigned. But not then and not ever did he enquire as to who Neill's parents might be. Pointed questions directed at him over the counter and in the taproom of the *Lantern,* the baker brusquely brushed aside. It was, he declared, none of his concern. The rest of the colliers and their wives were less reticent in offering solutions to the latest mystery.

"Mirrin Stalker's double. They canny deny it."

"He's like her, right enough. But who's the man?"

"Count on your fingers."

"No' Rob Ewing?"

"Never. He's got his hands full wi' that sick wife o'his."

"Besides, the Stalker bitch's been awa' too long for that."

"How old's the wean?"

"Weeks, at the very most."

"Then it canny be Rob."

"Or Lamont?"

"Houston Lamont? Aye, he packed her off in a hurry."

"But a full year since."

"True. True."

"Unless he's met up wi' her again since."

"Now there's a suggestion."

"I heard he's hardly left the house."

"Ach, he could've been awa' t'England an' back for all we know. It *could* be Lamont, right enough."

"She's on the stage, so I heard."

"It's a fact. Jean Anderson's youngest, him that's in York now, he sent his Mam a notice wi' Mirrin Stalker's name printed on it."

"Did he see her, though?"

"Not that I know."

"There's a pity."

"How?"

"Well, she could hardly be struntin' on a public stage wi' her belly stickin' out, could she?"

"But this was months ago."

"Tight lacin' can work wonders, I'm told."

"It'll be some rascal actor, like as not."

"Aye. I've heard they've nae morals at all, them folk. Sleep four an' five t'a bed. Strip down in the same room. It's sma' wonder it happened."

"Maybe she's wed."

"Huh!"

"I thought . . . well, I thought she'd have had more sense."

"Huh!"

"Take a good keek at the bairn next time. You'll see. Mirrin Stalker's spittin' image."

"Aye."

"Mark my words, ladies, she'll turn up here for her bairn sooner or later."

"Acknowledge it, y'mean?"

"She's brazen enough for anythin'."

"Aye, she's all that."

"Unless it's Houston Lamont's?"

"Well, I'll wager it is."

"Then it'll never go hungry."

"Good luck t'it. It's no what I'd want for mine."

"For your what, Georgina?"

"Dirty bitch!"

"It's agreed then it's Mirrin's bairn."

"Aye."

"There's nobody else it could be, is there?"

"The lad?"

"Drew? Yon skinny wee tyke!"

"Maybe . . . ?"

"Never. He's no' man enough t'blow his nose."

"But . . . ?"

"Huh!"

"You're right, ladies. It can only be Mirrin's."

After a time, as the year advanced through summer into autumn, the spate of gossip slackened and young Neill became a favourite of the men and women who patronised Kellock's Good Bread Bakery.

The baby travelled the streets of Blacklaw day in and day out, snug in his hamper on the floor of the van which Wallace had learned to haul with a dedicated patience that would have done a blind pony proud. Speculation, however, never quite died out and the intriguing mystery often provided a topic of conversation in the sly corners of the mining town.

It was a credit to the Stalkers that the identity of Neill's parents remained a close secret and that the smouldering curiosity of certain Blacklaw citizens was never quite extinguished by the truth.

With the opening of a new road and the extended services offered by the Caledonian Railway, the burgh of Hamilton enjoyed a wave of prosperity such as it

had not known since its heyday as a centre of
bobbinette weaving some fifty years before. New villas
and mansions appeared in the straggling suburbs and a
number of brand new stores, adjuncts of those which
graced Glasgow and Edinburgh, blossomed in the High
Street, competing with each other for middle-class accounts by means of startling window displays and other
retail gimcracks. Regarding the interlopers with trepidation, the Dalzell brothers, owners of the largest
emporium in the whole Middle Ward of Lanarkshire,
devised ingenious means of maintaining their premier
position.

Corsets, chemises, petticoats and undergarments
were whisked from the groundfloor rooms. Ladies'
footwear and millinery were similarly dispossessed.
Tantalisingly secret renovations were made to the main
entrance and foyer. Quantities of walnut wood, maho-
gany and bevelled glass were carted behind the screens
each afternoon to be hammered and chiselled and
planed into position during the dark hours of the night.
One hundred square feet of crimson carpeting and
countless strips of moss-green flock paper vanished
behind the joiners' drapes, followed by fine carved
mirrors and delicate display stands. At last, the re-
furbished floor was revealed to the public gaze as a
Silver Hall, an Aladdin's cave of choice pieces of
silverware, from gigantic tureens down to minute salt
spoons. Mr. Gabriel Reeves, an impressively portly
gentleman from the upper-class end of Princess Street,
Edinburgh, was imported as a consultant in charge of
the department and, to nobody's great surprise, Elizabeth Stalker was duly chosen as his assistant.

The promotion was greatly to Betsy's liking. It
brought with it not only status and an additional five
shillings and sixpence per week, but the bonus of a
full rig of expensive, if sombre, clothing, from dainty
black leather shoes to a pleated velvet tiara that made
her look more mature and, if possible, even more beautiful. In addition, the post gave Betsy the opportunity
to encounter a cultured and sophisticated class of

customer, some of whom, inevitably, were wealthy males.

The past couple of years had served Betsy well. She had grown out of the stage of being girlishly pretty. She had a similar build to her sister Mirrin, only more compact and refined. Like her twin brother, she copied the airs, graces and accents of the gentry with whom she came in contact. Mr. Gabriel Reeves would not have chosen her as his assistant if any trace of superficial gaucheness had remained. Betsy—Elizabeth Stalker, as she was now called—was as polished and fine as much of the silver. With her low, confidential voice and dainty, unsullied hands, she could charm even the Duchess herself when that grand dame visited the department to buy an engraved Christening cup for her latest godchild. Winning over a woman, even the Duchess, however, was only professional protocol for Miss Elizabeth Stalker. She had many other little tricks of behaviour up her sober sleeve to apply, when necessary, to less august clients, gentlemen in search of plate for investment purposes or a swanky ornament to prop in their dining rooms to advertise their rising fortunes. In dealing with male customers, Betsy's features seemed to become a little less conservative, to assume a pertness of expression and a cultivated little pout that was both appealing and provocative.

Though he was far too reserved ever to remark it aloud, privately Mr. Gabriel Reeves thought of Betsy as his Pocket Venus. If he had not been happily married these twenty-two years and a pillar of St. Mary's Episcopal, he might have been tempted to steal a kiss from her. Certainly there were many gloomy mornings when the young woman's mere appearance spread a ray of sunshine through the gentleman's wistful heart, when her modest smile was warm enough to make him primp his moustaches and study himself speculatively in the gleaming surface of a scalloped salver. Not even Mr. Gabriel Reeves, though, was observant enough to detect the subtle change in Betsy that occurred early in the May month, nor was he sufficiently *au fait* with lower cloakroom gossip to learn that Betsy's family had been blessed with a new arrival.

If he had, it's possible that he would have been more wary about introducing his assistant into the home of Randolph Newton, director of the Coalbridge Steel Company, devoted husband, father of three, and a lecher of such cunning and discretion that no whisper of his conquests ever blemished his good name in the parish.

Part of the estimable service that Dalzells' offered was a kind of Grand Show of Affluence, a circus without band and clowns. It was the emporium's policy to take goods to the customer if the status of the client warranted and if a sale seemed certain. Harking back to the high days of competitive trading, the Dalzells had equipped a couple of handsome early-century four-wheeled cabriolets in which such honoured commodities as wine, jewelry, gold and silver wares were transported to private residences to be displayed to best advantage in the natural surroundings of the home. The cabriolets were drawn by identical grey stallions, beautifully groomed and harnessed. Driver and guard, like the store's famous eccentric doorman, Sergeant Walters, were accoutred in Prussian-blue worsted, astrakhan hats and streaming silk scarves. Each load of treasure was accompanied by an 'expert', and an assistant who fussed over the cargo, carried in long black-lacquered boxes, like undertakers with a royal cadaver. The wine-tasting formalities were not altogether successful, as M. Duroc had the unfortunate habit of being carried away by the quality of his product during demonstrations and winding up prone on the carpet side by side with his appreciative customer. Mr. Aymer, goldsmith and jewellery expert and, of course, Mr. Reeves and his decorous assistant, saw to it that no such mishaps spoiled their jaunts to the mansions of the rich, and, indeed, reaped such bountiful rewards for the owners that Dalzells had another carriage on order to extend the service into gowns and millinery.

Betsy Stalker enjoyed her forays into the drawing rooms of the county's aristocrats. She was realistic enough, however, to set her sights on the bourgeoisie, in whose smaller establishments the origins of money had not been lost in the kind of heritage that would for ever debar a girl of her class.

In all this, at first, there was a serious element of play. Betsy wanted only one thing out of life at that stage in her career and everything else was but part of her plan to achieve it. She wanted the fulfillment of the promise that Drew had given her that he would send for her soon and introduce her into Edinburgh society. Always, even in the most resplendent of homes, Betsy sustained a faintly derisive attitude as she compared the provincial environment to her gilded vision of society in the capital.

It was the fabric of this daydream that had been ripped and abruptly torn apart by the arrival of Drew's bastard son. She could not believe that her brother would be so stupid as to father a child on a servant wench, some dirty wee orphan who had probably marked him out as an easy target. A corner of her awe in respect of Drew's precocious intelligence was knocked away by Kate's restrained explanation of how the baby came into the narrow house and why it must now be regarded as their responsibility.

For Betsy, Neill Campbell Stalker was a symbol of disillusionment, ever present, undeniable and at times disturbingly voluble. Much of her shock stemmed from a realisation that if Drew had been trapped into indiscretion once it might happen a second time and that, on the next occasion, without Kate's aid he might well find his career in ruins. In addition, Betsy was piqued by the adulation that her Mam and Kate lavished on the infant. Clearly she was no longer capable of winning their attention and her one short outburst of hysterics had gone almost unremarked. At a stroke, the skinny wee thing in the wicker hamper had usurped her as the baby of the family.

Out of necessity she became more self-reliant. Within the narrow house her behaviour was demure and courteous, though she firmly refused to have anything at all to do with her nephew's welfare. Belatedly she began to cultivate the habits that Drew had demonstrated. She spent more time alone in her room, not sulking exactly but mulling over the tide in affairs that

had carried her further from the golden horizon of
Edinburgh. It had become a matter of some urgency
now. She must embark for the capital as soon
as proved practical. Like Drew, she must make circumstances bow to her will, not merely depend on
others, upon a gradual drift towards fulfilment. She
must, as it were, stop daydreaming and begin planning. In a sense, she was ready to meet the challenge.
The answer to her problems was money. And the
answer to the money problem lay in Mr. Randolph
Newton.

She was quite aware what Mr. Randolph Newton
wanted from her and what he would give in return.
There was no question of 'making a catch'. Newton
had been discreetly explicit in his approach.

She remembered that March afternoon, the wind
flittering the leaves, all brown and shrivelled, along
the flagstones of the carriage yard, and how Newton
had come forward out of the kitchen door of the big
house in Bothwell Avenue in the village of Gleddan
in the open farm country south of Hamilton. He was
dark and tall and handsome, like the heroes of the
novels she'd read, but he was also calculating and
ruthless in a manner that was not make-believe. She
sensed the power in him at once, an animal quality
that marked him as different from most of the other
gentlemen she'd encountered where sensuality was disguised with flippancy or foolishness or adulterated by
nervous guilt. There was no check in Newton, no hint
that he would deny himself any pleasure which could
be bought or coaxed from any girl or woman that attracted him. She wondered if he had an instinct for
selecting girls who were not only beautiful but ripe
for the plucking. Grandiosely she thought of herself
in those terms.

Throughout March and April, during and after
Mr. Newton's transactions with Dalzells' silverware department—he purchased four hundred pounds' worth
of beautiful hand-made silver work and left Mr.
Reeves with a commission to scout for early Georgian
authentics—Betsy gave no more than token encouragement to the rake. She acknowledged that he was a

rake. In spite of his impeccable reputation and lack of hard gossip about him in the emporium, Betsy was under no illusions as to Newton's purpose with her.

There was nothing clandestine in their meetings. Newton came openly to the magnificent Silver Hall on Dalzells' groundfloor, browsed among the displays of tureens and gravy-holders and tobacco boxes, lifted and inspected and laid down the casters, quaichs and epergnes and conversed with the attendant assistant, Miss Stalker, in muted tones about the items and, between commonplaces, about the possible purchase of her virginity.

Callously regarded, Betsy had to admit that Randolph Newton's frankness was refreshingly honest. Seduction was no boys' game to him. He wanted her for the pleasure it would give him.

Betsy would not have dared to give Newton anything but casual encouragement if it had not been for the unexpected events in Edinburgh and the arrival in Blacklaw of Drew's bastard child. It took Betsy a fortnight to steel herself to proceed. Naturally, she was afraid of Newton, of having any man enter her body. On the other hand she realised that logically no harm would accrue from such an action, provided Newton took precautions, which she was sure he would do. She knew also that he would treat her well and, being vain still, imagined that he might even become so infatuated with her that he would throw up home and family and flee with her to Edinburgh or, more probably, London. That last factor was a sop to her dreams, the romantic, silly echo of the girl she'd been back in '75.

The Treasury-type inkstand was laid on a pad of green baize. The lapis-lazuli-coloured pots contrasted beautifully with the smooth polished silver and its plainness, unlike much of the New Art that Gabriel Reeves stocked because fashion demanded it, increased its appeal. Betsy could tell at once that Randolph Newton was interested. He lifted the object carefully and, stooping a little, examined the base, linings and hinges against the gas-light. Though a strong early summer sun shone down through the pebble-glass roof, gas mantels purred all day long in the Silver Hall.

Newton wore a light-weight blue-diagonal business suit which showed the breadth of his chest and torso. His hands, Betsy noticed, were slender, out of kilter with the rest of him, fine, long-fingered hands. She tried to imagine them touching her. The very thought made her shiver a little, not with revulsion but in a kind of dreadful anticipation. Moving only his eyes, Randolph Newton glanced speculatively past the flange of the inkstand. He placed the piece gently on the baize again.

It was quiet in the Silver Hall. Mr. Reeves had gone up to the third floor to take coffee with the other heads of departments. Only in the region of the stair were there signs of activity.

Betsy felt sick with dread, not fear of Newton so much as dread of commitment, anxiety lest she make a fool of herself and seem bold rather than direct, scheming rather than practical.

"A choice item," Newton said. "There are several desirable items in Dalzells'. One cannot have them all, Miss Stalker."

"One can," said Betsy, "if . . . if one is willing to pay the price."

"Price?"

"Oh, yes, everything here has a price label on it."

"But not on show?"

"That would not be discreet."

"Everything, you say?"

"Yes, sir: everything."

A less experienced philanderer would have pushed the conversation to its limit. Newton resisted. Instead he tapped the inkstand with his finger. "I will have this."

"Yes, sir."

"On the account, please."

"Yes, sir. Is that all you wish to have?"

Newton's eyes were particularly hot as he studied the girl. "Is there something else that might interest me on offer?"

"There may be, sir," said Betsy. She knew that she

was beginning to blush. She forced herself to meet his eye.

"It would be better displayed in privacy, sir."

Newton hesitated, then said, "Would it now?"

"I would personally . . . bring . . ."

"Is the night of the day after tomorrow suitable?"

"Yes."

"If you come to College Station on the eight-ten train, I will arrange to meet you: College Station, Glasgow."

"That is . . . convenient, Mr. Newton."

"You will come alone?"

"Of course."

"College Station, Thursday, at a quarter of nine."

"You haven't enquired about the . . . the price, sir?"

"I will pay the price," said Randolph Newton. "Be assured of that."

"Very well. I'll . . . I'll be there."

"Good day to you, Miss Stalker."

"Good day to you, Mr. Newton."

It was not the custom for women to attend the graveside, though colliers were less attached to that tradition than middle-class folk. Edith Lamont was heartily thankful that *she* was not called upon to trail fourteen miles in an open conveyance on that hot June day, dressed in frumpish weeds and perspiring beneath a veil. It was bad enough to have to dredge up vestiges of sentiment, squeeze out sympathetic tears when she really felt like waltzing around the parlour with Anna Thrush, the bearer of the sad tidings.

Decorum, however, and hypocrisy will out, and plump little Edith set up a lamentation which, though it did not penetrate Houston's numb anguish, certainly impressed the servants. The truth was that Edith had disliked Dorothy Lamont to the point of hatred. Her sole cause for regret at the woman's passing was that she would lose an edge over her husband. Dorothy's presence had anchored Houston. She, Edith, was not sure how he might react now that his beloved sister had passed to her Maker.

To Edith's surprise, Houston quickly gathered himself from the depths of grief. He took himself to his sister's room, alone, for half an hour, after doctors and undertakers had done their grisly work, and emerged ravaged but in full control of himself.

There was no reason for Dorothy Lamont to choose that beautiful sun-filled June day on which to die. The gardens were brimming with flowers, the sky placid. The woman couldn't possibly have succumbed to despair. Though she had not been active of late and had slipped ever deeper into her distant introverted state, Dorothy Lamont's health—so Edith had been led to believe—was much more sound than her mind. Nonetheless, Dorothy Lamont had died during the course of that early morning, her head raised upon the pillow, her gaunt face turned towards the barred window, her wide open eyes staring at a spray of new-budded leaves that sprang up from the tree below, and, so Houston had once said, seemed to tap, tap upon the pane as if to lure Dorothy from captivity.

Edith's suggestion, made in the best possible spirit, that Sydney Thrush be permitted to take the burden of the funeral arrangements from Houston's care-stooped shoulders was brushed aside. Her husband was brisk, business-like. Edith wondered if he too experienced more relief than loss at being freed from the burden of a mad relative, even one so cherished as his sister. But Edith did not know her husband well enough to read into his efficiency its proper meaning.

In the house following Dorothy's death and in preparations for interment in the family plot in Glenloch cemetery on the outskirts of Glasgow, Houston was again the strong brother, the man of certain decision that Dorothy had always considered him to be. If he had been a musician, he might have composed a hymn in her memory; if he had been a poet he would have penned an epitaph: but Houston Lamont was a coalmaster and could do no more in his dearest's honor than hold himself together and put her to rest with all the ceremony and decency that society expected.

A March death, in the dumb days before seeding, in the cold scouring hours of the morning; a November death, in the dank brown fogs of the central valley or the hard-baked salt-white frosts of the hills, such seasonal phases would have been more fitting. But Dorothy had slipped out of life in the full blossom of June with summer on the brink of fulfilment. It was as if, at last, her grip on the joy of living had slackened, as if, with merciless clarity, she had viewed her own situation and, in defeat, retreated back into the sleep of childhood, the sound, deep sleep of untarnished innocence.

Houston did it all. He ordered—and paid for—the shell lead coffin, outside case, hearse and four horses, the single coach and pair, with plumes and full equipment of superior description. He ordered—and paid for—a simple polished monument of Aberdeen granite, chose the lettering and form of the inscription and the little addendum which, by the addition of a simple word, seemed to coax a peculiar poignancy from the standard phrase. On completion, it would read *Rest, Rest in Peace*. Cliché had become blessing, the last heartfelt wish of a brother for a sister upon whom he had bestowed so little and from whom he had received so much.

It was not only the memorial that had an element of eccentricity. The funeral, too, though a model of propriety in its trappings, was rendered somehow sinister in its execution. Houston would brook no argument: a short service was held in the dining room of the mansion. Only Houston, Edith and Donald Wyld were present, Anna and Sydney Thrush having received no invitation. The minister, the Reverend William Heath from Hamilton high kirk, was instructed on which hymn to announce, which reading to select and what the tone of his formal eulogy must be. Afterwards Houston and he, quite alone, followed the coffin out to the hearse and took their places side by side in the long padded leather bench of the open landau.

They watched as the coffin was laid on a huge foaming mass of early summer blossoms whose cutting had denuded the garden completely. Then the attenuated procession left, moving with dignity down the driveway towards the gates, the great black horses trained to trot at a suitable pace, dyed black feathers nodding and bobbing, the wheels of the sombre carriage crunching on the gravel. The flowers buoyed up the coffin, cushioning it, a gay untidy mass without a wreath in sight. A petal or two spilled upon the verge as the hearse swayed at the curve.

In the landau Houston Lamont sat erect and silent in black mourning, his tall polished hat upon his knee, his face to the front, looking into the sun over the oak trees and its brassy glitter on the coffin ornaments. The Reverend William Heath had sufficient sense to keep his platitudes to himself. During the long drive down through the oaks and south-west along the ridge route towards Glenloch, he said nothing. He had no comfort to offer.

At noon, under a blazing sun, the interment service was duly read and Dorothy Lamont's mortal body lowered into the sweet earth. Houston crumpled earth on to the satin smooth lid.

Blackbirds were trilling in the hawthorns round the old wall, and chaffinchs flocked excitedly in tangled whins.

The wrought-iron railings would not keep Dorothy in; nor would she seek company, Houston thought, from the other Lamonts who lay around—unless, perhaps, from his son, from Gordon, who had also loved the birds and trees and the fragrance of flowers. If there is companionship in the grave, Houston told himself, then they will be happy together, my sister and my little son here on the hill of Glenloch.

But he feared that death, like life, might be a lonely business and, broken, turned away.

Modesty, Betsy Stalker discovered, could not easily be dispensed with. Vain though she was, she could not for the life of her allow Randolph to gaze upon her unclad body. In the attention he paid to her welfare, in his concern for her comfort was a show of gentleness that the girl found surprising. It was not until their relationship had matured that she realised that Randolph had merely exercised restraint to avoid scaring her off or throwing her into hysterics, disasters which, he ruefully confessed, had happened before.

As to love-making, Betsy found that there was not a very great deal to be said either for or against it. Only the anticipation of pain, humiliation and guilt, which her 'education' had led her to expect, marred the evening. But once she was alone with him in the two-room suite in the big sandstone hotel, the *Alfric*, all was well. Curiosity soon overcame her inhibitions. Randolph did not complain at her initial skittishness or the fact that she wept a little and blushed and generally behaved like a lamb going to the slaughter.

Beforehand Newton provided wine. Afterwards a supper of cold roast beef and chicken breasts appeared as if by magic, together with more wine and spirits. He had even brought her a gift, an expensive oriental robe, a piece of foresight that pleased Betsy enormously. As she ate supper by candlelight in the private room in the posh Glasgow hotel, Betsy felt that she had at last stepped close to her goal, albeit by an outrageous route.

Randolph too wore a robe. It was not unlike the maroon velvet Breakfast Jacket that she had goggled at during her early days in Dalzells' and had imaginatively tried to fill with the form of a 'suitably handsome beau'. Now she knew what sort of a man such a garment was really designed for. But it didn't ruffle her conscience at all that she was involved in an illicit relationship with just such a person. She had little reason to suppose that her liaison would be discovered. She told Mam and Kate that she was going to the Moody and Stanley Evangelical Meeting in the Candleriggs Hall in company with other girls from Dalzells' and would stay overnight with one of them in Hamilton. Mam and Kate were too concerned with feeding and dressing the baby to pay much attention. It would teach them—yes, and that fool Drew—a lesson.

"I must be back in Dalzells' by eight-thirty tomorrow."

"The cab will take you to the seven-forty train," Randolph promised. He forked a slice of beef into his mouth and chewed it with rapacity. "That comfortably leaves us the rest of the night."

Now that her fundamental anxiety had been calmed, she was more curious than ever. It was clear that Randolph Newton intended to have his moneysworth from her, but also that he was no brute and would not hurt her or so far forget himself in passion as to lose patience with a beginner.

"Aren't you tired?" Betsy asked.

"Not in the least," said Randolph.

When he laughed, she noticed, his eyes showed no warmth. For all that, he was handsome. He had a very broad chest, not coarse like that of a collier. After he had risen from her side he had washed himself and put on his robe. Betsy had watched him, peeping from between the sheets. He performed the toilet with remarkable care, rubbing oil into his chest and dressing his hair with an expensive macassar preparation.

Supper had been waiting in the parlour of the suite. So far Betsy had seen and been seen only by the cabby commissioned to pick her up at College Station, and by the hotel clerk who had shown her to *Room Three-Two-Ohah* and who, beyond that monosyllabic utterance, gave every sign of being not only dumb but blind and deaf as well. Obviously Room 320 was frequently reserved for the exclusive use of Mr. Newton, part of his grand strategy for undetected sport involving the seduction of women. Small wonder that Randolph's reputation in the Middle Ward remained unblemished; he went to a great deal of trouble and expense to protect it.

Betsy was not in the least uneasy. In this private chamber, she realised, they were almost equals, or would be as soon as she became a bit less gauche in love-making. Names that might be hurled at her by Blacklaw's pious frumps were invalid. They could not be expected to understand. The commercial nature of the transaction actually protected her. At least she hadn't lost her head and her heart to some grubby collier, deluded by his promises and the urging of the villagers into supposing that life spliced was better than life single.

Seated in that candlelit room with a man who had just become her lover and would soon become her benefactor, Betsy appreciated some of Drew's more sterling qualities and saw herself, at long last, beginning to catch up with her brother.

Betsy drank wine from an elegant glass. The wine was very cold and fizzy and she adored the taste. The last traces of apprehension began to thaw and, shifting her position a little, she allowed the neck of the *orientale* to fall open a little.

"You," said Randolph, "are a born *coquette*. D'you know what that is?"

"Yes, sir," said Betsy, mischievously. "French for a tease."

Randolph leaned his elbows on the table. He studied her for some moments. Betsy did not flinch from his scrutiny. She forced herself to watch him as he devoured her with his gaze.

"God, but you're pretty," Randolph said.

"Thank you."

"You're not even ashamed of yourself, are you?"

"Why . . . why should I be?"

"A young thing of seventeen."

"I've seen girls married and bairned younger than me."

"I'll wager you have," said Randolph. "And thought them stupid, unless I'm mistaken."

"Right," said Betsy. "And thought them stupid."

The man smiled. He inched his chair closer to the table and moved the candlestick to one side so that he could reach out effortlessly and stroke her hair.

"Never," he said, "have I encountered a shop-girl so willing to indulge me."

"An' be indulged," said Betsy. "But don't call me a shop-girl, Randolph. That *is* an insult."

"Oh-ho: pretensions, I see."

"I admit it."

"Is that why you . . . ?" He gestured towards the bed.

"Yes."

"I flattered myself that you were hypnotised by me."
Betsy smiled. "You're not ugly."

"I also think you were a little fortunate," Randolph
said. "If you had chosen another type of man you
might have regretted it."

"But," said Betsy, "I would not have done it then."

"So it *was* me?"

"In a way."

Randolph sat back. "You've a devil of a lot to
learn."

"You'll teach me, I suppose?"

"Oh, yes, Betsy, I'll teach you."

"Other than instruction," said Betsy, "an' free beef
an' wine, what will our arrangement be?"

Randolph winced. "Ouch!" he said. "You *are* a
callous young lady."

"I think that suits, doesn't it?"

"It does: it does," Randolph assured her. "Sentimental entanglements are the bane of my existence. I
question if you'll lose your head."

"How often will you see me?"

"As often as I possibly can."

"Here?"

"Usually."

"I'll need to find some decent excuses for stayin' out
all night," said Betsy. "I'm still living at home."

"I can't help that," the man snapped.

Startled, Betsy took a moment to understand. She
said, "I wasn't hinting or anything, Randolph. It suits
me fine to stay at home for a while longer. I'm not . . .
not demanding special treatment. I've heard about certain clutchin' women an' I'm not inclined to that style,
not in the least."

"I must be cautious," said Randolph.

"In case your wife finds out?"

"I . . . I am not unhappy with my wife, you know."

Betsy shrugged. She had no interest in Randolph
Newton's motives for conducting affairs. She said, "I'll
do what you want, an' what you tell me to, but you
must bear in mind that I'm as anxious as you are to
protect my reputation. I'm not keen to be disgraced."

Randolph threw himself back in the chair once more,

laughing loudly. This time there was warmth in his eyes, a genuine amusement. "How can you talk of disgrace, sitting there in that . . . that silk thing showing off your . . . your breasts?"

"*You* don't think it's disgraceful," Betsy retorted.

"Of course I do. I'm a typical prude, young lady," said Randolph, wiping his eyes with his napkin. "I'll tell you this, if I had freedom and opportunity I would teach you everything. I mean, it would be a pleasure to make the Sunday promenade round the Kibble Palace with you on my arm. To take you into the Argyll Club, or the North Georgian for dinner. It would be fun to dress you and pamper you and . . ."

"It's not possible," said Betsy, shaking her head.

"What *do* you want?"

"Enough to take me to Edinburgh in style."

"Edinburgh: the seat of the mighty!" said Randolph. "You will do well there, Betsy. Is that all you want from me, the means of leaving me?"

"I don't want t'go on living in Lanarkshire. I don't want to marry a clerk and live in Hamilton."

"Even your ambition has a rabidly promiscuous quality," said Randolph. "Why don't you head for London?"

"I have a brother in Edinburgh. I want to join him."

"What does he do?"

"He's in process of becoming a lawyer."

"And, if he's anything like you, he'll probably go to the top of his profession."

"I'm not like him. I wish I was, in a way," said Betsy. "He studied and swotted his way out of Blacklaw. My other sister, she just walked out with the clothes on her back and not much else."

"But that wasn't the way for you?"

"No."

"You intend to be a first-class traveller."

"What's wrong with that?"

"Nothing: it depends how you do it."

"What other means do I have?" Suddenly, oddly, she felt like weeping. Fighting back tears, she said, "I know I'm pretty and that all men all . . . all fancy me, so . . ."

"Now don't cry," said Randolph. "Please, don't cry. I can't abide women who cry. I thought you were strong." . .

"I am. I am."

Without haste or flurry, he rose from his seat, came round the table and put his arms about her, drawing her face down to his chest. She could smell the faint musky odour of the oil he had rubbed into his skin. He did not hurry her, allowing her two or three minutes of comforting contact, during which time her mood changed, and her qualms of self-pity altered into an unfamiliar physical need. His hand stroked her hair and then, sliding down the shoulder of the robe, settled upon her breast. She drew back. But he held her. He held her until the first faint response grew from a nuzzling need for comforting into something quite different and then, drawing her up, he kissed her on the mouth.

It was not as simple now. The arrangement was not without complications. She wanted to cry out, to ask him what was happening to her. But she could not release him or resist his petting. It was, she thought, the most utterly selfish experience of her life.

As he coaxed her gently towards the bed, Randolph Newton said, "Edinburgh it will be, Betsy, I promise you as much."

But at that moment Betsy Stalker did not care.

Three

ALL THREE WERE dressed in dark mourning as befitted friends and relatives of the deceased, though the Thrushes could hardly have been called friends of Dorothy Lamont and Edith, though a relative, had shed no more than a dutiful tear. In fact, Anna and Sydney wore funeral clothing most of the time and of late Edith had taken to selecting black as a suitably fashionable contrast for the orders that went out to Dalzells' every month or so. The heavy-weight suiting was not consistent with the brilliance of the weather, but it did lend a certain gravity to the conversation of the trio who were seated around the hearth-screen sipping tea and nibbling on the pastries that Anna had had baked that morning to appease her dear brother's sweet tooth.

"And how is the coalmaster?" asked Sydney Thrush.

"I have hardly seen him," said Edith.

"Is he drinking?" asked Sydney, forthrightly.

"Heavily," said Anna, whose job it was to replenish the decanters in the study. "Almost a full bottle of spirits each day."

"Slow poison," said Thrush, biting into a custard bun.

"I fear," said Edith, "that it may not be so slow, Sydney."

"I take it, ma'am, that your husband is too bereft to be of sound judgment; I mean, capable of decision."

"Without question."

"I require," said Sydney, "authority."

"You have authority, Sydney," said Edith. "All documents will be signed by me during my husband's . . . indisposition. He cannot complain. After all it was by my efforts that we acquired the capital to begin our programme of expansion."

Anna decanted tea from the silver pot for her brother and her mistress. Edith sighed contentedly. Propped on an embroidery frame close to her left hand were sheaves of Thrush reports, detailed records of the changes that he had made in the organisation and running of the colliery and, more importantly, the resulting figures which showed a gradual increase in monthly profits.

"I do not require signature of a document," said Thrush. "I require guidance on a matter of policy, that is all."

"Where is your report, then, Sydney?" asked Edith.

"I deemed it best not to commit any of this to paper."

"It sounds sinister."

"Not at all sinister, ma'am. But certainly serious."

"Militant action, Sydney, is it not?" said Anna.

"In hot weather tempers come quickly to the boil," Sydney Thrush said. "I have been expecting certain loutish elements to cause trouble. I believe that they will do so this very day."

"My husband *should* be informed," said Edith, dubiously.

"I question if that is necessary," said Sydney. "May I stress, ma'am, that I have not done badly by Mr. Lamont's colliery so far and that, at the risk of seeming immodest, my suggestions and their implementation have pulled us—you—out of the red and firmly into the black."

"But militant action on the part of the miners?" said Edith, who was not in the least perturbed. She revelled in the drawing room dramas that went with being a motivating force in the community. "Is that not dangerous?"

The account books told a very pleasant story, the more so when pits and mines all over Scotland were sinking into bankruptcy and men were being flung into the fields and the whole state of the market was as shaky as a barque on a stormy sea. Lamont's books, however, were in order, sales assured, thanks to Sydney Thrush's original proposals for expansion and mechanisation. It did not matter in the least to Edith that a pall of gloom and misery hung over the streets of the little township or that Sydney Thrush had made himself vastly unpopular by his cracking of the whip. Her privately expressed opinion was that Houston had always been far too soft with his workforce, and had spoiled them almost beyond redemption.

Redundancies had become the order of the day. Men unable to meet the increased demands for a higher daily 'darg' were sacked, along with hotheaded rabble-rousers, militants unwise enough to believe in free speech whose names had been noted in

Thrush's 'wee black book'. Informers and spies were legion in the pit now, Thrush's men, shifty-eyed sycophants who 'cliped' on their mates to ensure their own continued employment. Even at the face-seams men hardly dared open their mouths in case they spilled a natural grouse or two that could be interpreted as rebellion and carried up top by a sneaky Thrushite.

With the sacking of breadwinners, evictions followed. Families who had thought themselves secure found themselves in the gutter, their windows boarded up and the long iron keys being turned in the locks by hands other than their own. Deputations streamed to Donald Wyld. But it was obvious that his power had waned in the months since Christmas and that he could, or would, do nothing. "Go back to your jobs, For your own sakes, I beg you to go quietly back to work."

"For our own sakes!"

"Who the hell is the bloody manager round here: you're Thrush?"

"I am."

"Then do something."

"Blacklaw's still open, isn't it? We're still producing coal. What more do you want?"

"A square deal. More profit for him; more work for us."

"It doesn't work that way, and well you know it."

"We're bein' squeezed."

"Times *are* hard."

"Christ, Wyld, you're as bad as Thrush, gettin'."

"I'll put your case."

"You've said that before, an' nothin' done about it."

"Listen, I . . ."

"An' where's the bonny boy himself: where's Lamont?"

"Mr. Lamont is . . ."

"We know where he is: he's bloody hidin'."

"Control yourselves, for God's sake. Look there, behind you. In the window of the office."

"Thrush!"

"Need I say more?"

"Spying on us."

"I'll do what I can, I promise."

"Bastard!"

"I will: I'll do what I can."

On Friday of that particular week, seven of the fourteen men who had sued Donald Wyld for a hearing were paid off. The remainder, though they raged and ranted in private were prudent enough to make no more 'official' approaches to any member of the staff and kept very quiet indeed about the pit and worked like demons to make amends.

The best of them were gone, the best of the remainder silenced. The incontestable fact was that they could not risk being paid off. Thrush, as more intelligent colliers realised, *had* saved the pit by his ruthlessness.

The Ewings, the Pritchards and the Ormonds had long ago learned to sing dumb. They were good workers and kept their mouths shut. Even in the security of their homes, they did not complain about extra duties and reduced pay. At least they *were* paid, which was more than could be said for their brothers in Fife and Clackmannan who had been locked out altogether for six months. That lock-out had suited the coalmasters just fine. The shipbuilding strike was at its height and the iron furnaces were damped down, and who the hell wanted coal anyway? Thrush might be sleekit and vile but he displayed the same attributes at both ends of the scale. He had wheedled markets for Blacklaw's coal in places that no owner had ever contemplated as possible and, so it was said, had even signed a contract with Africa, though what the blacks wanted with Scottish coal God alone could tell. Out in the wide world, there were bank failures, deductions and closures, 'wee darg' policies so severe that men were willing to break their backs for a mere shilling a day. None of that had really come to Blacklaw yet and there were colliers sane enough, and selfish enough, to realise it. Nor was there a 'truck' system: never had been. But Thrush devised other ways to keep the miners of Blacklaw 'humble' and the hutches full.

Edith Lamont said, "What do you advise, Sydney?"

"I have taken certain precautions on my own account."

"How efficient of you!" said Edith, admiringly. Anna, as if handing out a prize, passed the salver of sticky pastries affectionately to her brother.

Sydney helped himself. He ate without fluster, dabbing jam from his lips with his napkin. He felt quite at home in the mansion drawing room and enjoyed unveiling his strategy to Edith, a lady for whom he had much admiration.

He said, "I have this very afternoon agreed to meet with the colliers in the main yard and to answer their questions."

"Talk with the workers?" said Edith, as if such a suggestion was radical in the extreme. "You'll be permitting them a Union next, Sydney?".

"The Union is disintegrating," said Sydney. "Macdonald and his gang are being ignored, reviled. But it is not the Union that's the problem. Two men died this month in the new breach in Pit No. 2."

"Ah, yes, a sad thing," said Anna. "The price of coal."

"I imagine that will be a focal point of dissension," said Thrush, confidently. "The majority have now accepted termination of the checkweigh system of payment. They have accepted the breaching of the new section under, I admit, difficult conditions, and they have recognised if not openly admitted that reductions and redundancies are unavoidable. But accidents have an odd effect on colliers. They will blame the management."

"And?" said Edith.

"In two weeks' time," said Thrush, "I . . . we . . . will be required to implement the present work force by bringing in experienced miners, forty of them, to operate the new machinery. I cannot afford to risk damaging such expensive equipment, nor can I—we— afford to train men in its use. The pick and shovel brigade will be sure to rebel. They have seen the machinery arrive, have watched some of it being installed. They must be aware what it will mean. Between the accident and the so-called threat of modernisation they will have worked themselves into a dangerous mood."

"We cannot allow the louts to hinder progress, Sydney," Edith said.

"Certainly not, madam."

"What do you propose?"

Thrush paused. He glanced behind him, then leaned a little forward. "With your permission, I propose to start a riot."

"To *start* a riot?" Edith's eyes were round with astonishment, her lips pursed in bemusement.

"Bite the biter," Anna said, "before he bites you."

"Precisely, dearest," Sydney Thrush said.

"I begin to understand," Edith said, frowning now. "My husband would certainly not approve."

"Your husband need never know."

"What a suggestion!" Edith exclaimed.

"It will work, ma'am. I assure you," Anna said, "that Sydney is correct."

"What do you say, Mrs. Lamont?" Sydney asked.

Edith folded her hands on her lap and shifted on to the edge of her chair. It was her tangible demonstration of decision-making. She could barely suppress her smile as the implications of Thrush's proposal dawned on her.

At length she looked round at her housekeeper. "Anna, will you be good enough to take my husband another bottle to refresh him throughout the afternoon."

In the crowd of over a hundred off-shift miners, the eight hirelings from Slamannan went undetected. Two were tall enough to be conspicuous but they kept their faces hidden under peaked caps. The other six were ordinary mortals and merged discreetly into the orderly phalanx of demonstrators who collected in the main yard and, led by a rank of old stagers, tramped doggedly round the gangers' shed, past the tipping shutes, where the women paused to watch, and into the area of sun-baked dirt flanked by the latrines, the hutch-sidings and the managers' offices.

On the office porch, leaning against the wooden

railing like naval officers on a poop deck, the gaffers waited nervously. Inglis and Jock Baird were there, and fat pompous Davy Dunlop who had swiftly shifted his allegiance from Wyld to Thrush when he'd spotted how the wind was blowing. Donald Wyld was there too, of course, standing to the left of Thrush who, of all the managerial staff, viewed the assembling workers not merely impassively but benignly. His thin Indian-ink eyebrows were raised high as if the intrusion into his afternoon's schedule had come as a welcome surprise.

The crowd was curious, not noisy. There was no evidence of simmering violence, no pick-handles, stones, mallets or angle-irons, no visible signs of aggression. The sun, dusty now and entangled in the superstructure of the winding towers, beat down gently on the heads of the men below, making them sweat a little in their heavy pit clothes.

Furtive discussions had singled out four spokesmen, not the most radical among the available hands but articulate, rational men, men who could be dispensed with if that was how Thrush chose to take his revenge; older men and ailing, like Callum Ewing.

At first Callum had refused to take any active part in the demonstration. But he had been pressed into it. He could not deny that he was close to the end of his working life. By November or December he would surely be forced to quit and rely on his son for charity. Rob, to whom a job was all-important, kept far back in the crowd, in the rear rank with young Ormond, the Pritchard brothers and Dave Henderson. Away to their left, the women had moved out from the troughs. The hutch-tippers and the sorters, Kate Stalker among them, stood watching mutely, straining to hear the parley that would affect them all.

The colliers formed a crescent before the office porch, twenty men abreast, Callum Ewing, Abe Fordyce, Gavin Armstrong and Peter McLean in the centre, protected by their brothers. Thrush's smile and the long, long pause he allowed them to settle and fall still before he spoke were ominous.

"Good afternoon, gentlemen."

The politeness of his greeting disconcerted them further. There were a few murmurs of equally polite response, jumbled on the tongues.

Another pause: Thrush smiling: Thrush glancing at Wyld: Wyld sucking in his breath, and Wyld saying, "I take it that you have representation? Spokesmen?"

"Ay' we have that sir," Abe Fordyce answered crisply.

Abe was dying. He would be dead before next spring. He had nothing to lose now to Lamont or his cohorts, nothing to relinquish except his dignity, a quality he had protected through all the dismal humiliation of life in this town and at the coal seams deep underground. His features were wrinkled with the disease that was eating him up. The flesh hung in comical pockets on the bones that had taken such a battering over the past forty years. He was a year short of fifty, Abe Fordyce, but he would have passed muster in a pageant of Methuselahs.

Donald Wyld wiped his forehead with his wrist. "What is it that you want?"

"Answers, Mr. Wyld?" Abe said.

"I can give answers," Wyld said. "Promises, though, are a different matter."

"We had hoped to speak wi' Mr. Lamont in person."

"Mr. Lamont suffered a recent bereavement," Wyld said.

Abe nodded. Everyone in Blacklaw knew that the daftie had died. It was difficult for them to feel any sympathy for Lamont.

Thrush intervened. "Mr. Wyld and I are empowered to speak for Mr. Lamont."

"Aye, but who carries the can?" growled an anonymous voice from the second row of scowling faces.

"Can?" asked Thrush, his sharp ears having picked up the jibe. "There's no 'can' to carry anywhere, gentlemen. We are all at the mercy of the market, as I'm sure Mr. Wyld has explained to you many times in recent months."

"If the market's so damned bad, Mr. Thrush," put

in Peter McLean, "then why is it that Blacklaw's gearin' itself t'produce more coal than ever before?"

"Because," Thrush answered, "we have markets that other colleries don't have: markets that the management have found for you."

"But the wage rate continues to drop," somebody called out.

"The wage rate is related not to production but to the cost of the coal to the buyer," Thrush explained, apparently warming to his theme. "We can sell all the coal we can produce, but only at a low price."

"So *you* say."

"Any man in this pit may check the accounts for himself," Thrush declared. "I mean that sincerely, gentlemen. I will open the monthly trading account to your committee at any time."

Suspicion silenced the colliers for a moment.

Abe Fordyce sensed that they were being side-tracked.

He said, "We appreciate that offer, sir, an' like as not we'll take the opportunity t'read the red ink."

Thrush shouted over the general laughter, *"Black ink: black ink. Blacklaw is not in debt."*

"But," Peter McLean called, "you're askin' us t'accept reductions and redundancies, t'do more for less in fact?"

McLean too had little to lose. He was sixty and had two sons in trade in Falkirk. He intended to retire there soon.

"Yes," Thrush shouted. "Much of our profits is being reinvested in the fabric of the pit, which is, I'm sure you'll agree, to everybody's benefit."

A collier called Roberts exploded at this statement. He had been one of the crew in the breaching of the new section in Pit No. 2 and had lost his nephew and his best pal to carbon monoxide gas.

"Explain that t'Charlie and Willie," he bawled, struggling to make himself seen. "Is it another disaster you're after, then, t'skin the work-force down t'manageable size? Is it another hunner men you're wantin' dead?"

"That's unfair, Roberts," Wyld cried, heatedly.

"Unfair t'dead men an' widows an' orphans?" Roberts yelled.

Turning, Callum Ewing issued a quiet order and Roberts was restrained by his mates around him.

Callum Ewing said. "Will the opening of a new section mean more work, Mr. Wyld?"

Donald Wyld hesitated. "I . . . yes, of course."

"For us?"

"For some of you."

"In the back shed, by the rail yard, you've a wheen of new machinery, sir," said Abe Fordyce. "It is, so I've been reliably informed, cuttin' an' haulin' machinery of advanced design. Is that right?"

"Yes, that's right," said Wyld.

"We were led t'believe that Mr. Lamont was opposed t'advanced mechanisation at this time," said Abe.

"Mr. Lamont changed his mind," said Wyld. "It was necessary to introduce machinery to cope with the thin seams."

"Tell *that* t'Colonel Coco!" Roberts shouted, furiously.

Thrush said, "Machinery means expansion."

Abe Fordyce said, "Tell us, sir, can any pick-and-shovel man operate one o'those contraptions?"

Wyld stepped closer to the railing, but Thrush beat him to it. Pitching his voice to carry to every corner of the yard, he said, "Of course not. Only trained men can operate and maintain such advanced examples of engineering."

"Will that mean more redundancies?" asked Abe.

"Perhaps."

"Give's a straight answer, for God's sake, Thrush."

"Come on, Mr. Thrush: are we losin' the pit t'machines?"

"How soon'll they be installed?"

"How many o'us will b'sent packin'?"

"What about vibrations?"

"The chances o'flash fire must be increased?"

"Give's the truth, Thrush."

Thrush said, "Are you afraid of the machines, gentlemen?"

"Aye."

"New."

"We're afraid o'nothin', Thrush."

"I'm glad to hear it," Thrush called out.

"Quiet, lads! Quiet."

Abe Fordyce said, "Tell us the truth, sir, about owners' policy regardin' machines."

"Mr. Wyld will explain," Thrush said. "He is, after all, the manager."

"You tell us."

Thrush nodded.

The explosion was muffled and fairly distant, a firecracker noise, not underground. As the crowd swayed and pivoted in unison to face towards the railway yard and the line that connected the pit to the shunting engines of the Caledonian, another popping explosion occurred. The roof of a large storage shed rose up on a quilt of blue-black smoke and lazily broke into fragments in the calm summer air.

"Jesus Christ, it's the machine shed!" somebody said, softly yet audibly.

At that instant a barbarous clamour went up from the back of the ranks. *"Up the bloody miners."* An axe-handle spun out of the crowd, whirring in the silence. It cracked against the office railing and, deflected, smashed into Jock Baird's face.

The big night-shift foreman went down like a poleaxed bull, dropping against the wall of the shed. A rock shattered the window just over him and showered his body with glass. The fire hooter wailed. Whistles blew. Another voice bellowed, *"Fair play for the Blacklaw colliers."* Davy Dunlop shot back into the managers' office and slammed the door.

Donald Wyld raised his arms, calling on the men to be calm. A stone struck him on the cheek. He flinched, ducking involuntarily, hands clasped to the wound, then came up again and with blood streaming down his chin, lifted his hands like a prophet and implored the crowd not to panic.

Callum, Abe and the others in the front rank were thrust forward, tripping and stumbling, as confusion in the rear sent their bewildered colleagues surging forward. Sudden uproar developed. Men were pushing and jostling. Henderson, a young, strong collier, jack-knifed abruptly and, clutching his skull, toppled to the dirt.

"Bastards! Murderin' bastards!"

Swimming against the tide, Rob Ewing struggled to reach his father. Even before he had breached half the breadth of the mob, he knew he would be too late.

The whistle shrilled again.

The fire squad's bell clanged along the foot of the hump and the four or five men in the crowd who were members of the hand-cart platoon dutifully fought to break free, to run to their posts. Smoke from the sheds wafted thinly over the yard. The crackle of the burning structure was inaudible.

Once more the whistle shrilled.

Two dozen men ran from the lane behind the latrines. They were plain dressed but armed with batons, left wrists strapped with wooden shields. Some carried short lengths of chain in their right hands as well as polished ashwood truncheons. They were the bully-boys from Glasgow, no secret infiltrators from the heartland of militant strife, but paid toughs, soldiers without the shilling, without leaders or law. All they had was experience, discipline and the assurance that if they did their work well they would be well paid and would work again soon under the pay of some other master. Surprise was on their side and they were armed.

"Clear the yard," Thrush shouted. *"Clear the yard."*

The request came late. The breakers were already at work, flailing at heads and bellies, downing old men and boys indiscriminately, herding the rest of that anxious mob towards the main gate, driving them fiercely but without valour into the cobbled corner at the top of Main Street.

It was no discredit to the miners that they ran. They had no opportunity to nurse fury. Bewildered by the sudden chain of events, cramped into three or four minutes, they harboured a sense of guilt rather than injustice. Precisely what they had done, none could be sure. But the explosion in the machinery store smacked of sabotage and the fact was that every man jack of them had seen Jock Baird felled. So they ran, pausing only to scoop up fallen brothers, to dance around, without stopping, to look back in search of sons and uncles and fathers, but running on like a flock under attack from wolves until the last of the limping, bleeding throng hobbled from the gates and the gates rattled and closed upon them and they were left, expelled, to gasp in horror at the damage that they had somehow brought upon themselves.

Worse, in a way, was soon to come.

Before the colliers could gather their wits and begin to examine causes, the sma' door in the big gate opened and Edna Brown emerged. After her came another woman, and then another, until one by one, all the women and girls from the troughs and tips were ushered from the yard to join the bewildered crowd outside the high slate-grey gates.

By that time other off-shift workers had rushed up from the cottages. Almost two hundred folk gathered on the summit where Main Street bent into the Pit Dyke road. Out of the sma' door now came clerks, gaffers and ponyboys, chippies and freighters, the whole work-force with the exception of firemen, a skeleton safety crew and the cage operators. And, after a half hour or so, before the beehive exodus had time to flag, there emerged the underground shift, brought off early, minstrel-black, blinking and bemused.

One by one, the men stepped over the high sill, telling how they had walked down an avenue of baton-armed bully-boys and how the injured, colliers and management alike, were being attended to by the company doctor who, it seemed, had been on the premises that afternoon. Fractures and gashes, the gaping heads of the expelled demonstrators were patched on the pavement by Doctor McKay who had come at once in his trap. They were bad, a couple of them, but not so bad that they would leave the crowd, virtually the whole populace of the town now, until they found out just what the hell had happened.

By six-ten o'clock that fine June night, the last face-worker had been grubbed out of his hole and conducted to the surface. Willie Green, James McGuire and old Rab McCulloch, the cage-operators, stepped out and the sma' door finally closed. The working of both pits in Blacklaw colliery came to a total halt.

The crowd now spilled along the Pit Dyke road and back down Main Street, clustered into various clans, some angry, some oddly ashamed, a few already endeavouring to deduce exactly what filthy trick had been played upon them by Houston Lamont.

It was six-twenty when both big gates were unbolted and swung wide. The crowd coalesced, bunching for a better view. The bully-boys battalion was not in evidence. Indeed, for almost three minutes, the yard lay empty, then, in procession round the gable of the blacksmith's shop, came the first of the carts. Henderson and Jock Baird shared it, both men bandaged but conscious, propped on sacks, like heroes from a battle front. And then came another cart bearing three more swathed colliers and Davy Dunlop looking as noble as possible with his wrist in a sling to support the injury he had sustained flinging himself indoors out of harm's way. And then a third cart with another aged pony in the shafts and Sydney Thrush standing spread-legged upon the planks, his smooth hair ruffled, his collar undone and the sleeves of his coat sodden with oil or blood. The ponyboys led the three carts out of the yard. The big gates remained open, creating a familiar but dramatically heightened backdrop for the strange parade.

The ambulance carts rolled very slowly through the crowd which parted solicitously, out of habit. The wounded gathered relatives around them as they pulled out of the throng and trundled off down Main Street.

It was very still after that, still enough to hear the town hall clock in Northrigg strike the half hour and the whistle of the Glasgow train as it left the Crooked Halt and headed east. Though none of the colliers knew it, Thrush's team of provocateurs were aboard, headed back to their base in Slamannan, richer by three pounds per head.

Thrush's cart stopped.

The assistant manager got down. Under the grime,

his expression was inscrutible. Reaching into his coat
he brought out a notice inked on a stiff card, a cobbler's hammer and six brass tacks. It was unusual to
witness Thrush engaged in manual work but he did
the job with customary efficiency and the notice, when
tacked to the door, might have been measured off and
squared by draftsmen, so neat was it placing.

Quite unaided, Thrush put his weight on the gates
and tramped against them, heaving until first one and
then the other squatted over its bolt holes in the cobbles. The long iron rods were duly shot from within.
The sma' door opened. Thrush stepped over the sill,
turned and with a key and steel padlock made the
sma' door fast. He stared at the silent crowd for an
instant, implacable, almost bland, then hoisted himself back on to the flat cart and with a wordless gesture
to the ponyboy had himself driven left along the Pit
Dyke and out of sight behind the cottages at the back
of the town.

The crowd surged forward then, pushing and thrust-
ing to study the neatly printed notice that was tacked
to the locked gate. It said:

SABOTAGE AND RIOT.
IN VIEW OF THE ACTION OF MINERS IN
DEFIANCE OF THE LAWS OF SABOTAGE AND
RIOT LEADING TO THE GRIEVOUS WOUNDING
OF OWNERS' REPRESENTATIVES AND SERIOUS
DAMAGE TO OWNERS' PROPERTY, THE
MANAGEMENT HEREBY DECLARES BLACKLAW
COLLIERY CLOSED UNTIL FURTHER
NOTICE.

Signed
Donald Wyld.
MANAGER.

A sighing groan went up, burying the questions and
entreaties of those too far back in the crowd to read
the notice for themselves.

"Out! God, we've been locked out 'til further notice."

"But what for? What happened? What did we do?"

"Sabotage an' riot, so it says."

"Jesus!"

"Will y'look at the signature."

"Thrush?"

"No, it's Donald Wyld's fist."

"Wyld? I can hardly believe it."

"Y'can't trust a soul in this bloody world."

"Where is Wyld, then, the two-faced sneak?"

"Inside, like as not."

"Aye, protected by his gang o' Glasgow toughs."

"Never mind Wyld: What the hell d'we do now?"

"Go home," Callum Ewing advised. "An' wait t'be forgiven."

Forgiveness and retribution came quickly. Sometime during the course of that long anxious night a second notice mysteriously appeared on the pit gate, side by side with the first.

> ALL HANDS TO APPLY FOR RE-INSTATEMENT
> BY PERSONAL INTERVIEW WITH MR. THRUSH.
> SUCH INTERVIEWS AND ATTENDANT
> ENQUIRIES WILL COMMENCE AT 10 O'CLOCK
> THIS MORNING OF THURSDAY 22ND DAY OF
> JUNE, 1877.
> > *Signed*
> > *Sydney Thrush.*
> > MANAGER.

The queue began to form along the Pit Dyke road before seven, word of mouth passing the news swiftly into every houshold in the village. By ten o'clock the file was a half mile long, snaking round the backs and down the lane to the rear of the *Lantern* pub where a roaring trade in mugs of beer was done until a rumor sprang up that Thrush was refusing to admit any man who even smelled of drink. Within minutes the entire population of Blacklaw turned teetotal.

Flora Stalker, in her horse-drawn van, however, continued to sell Mr. Kellock's wares as fast as the wee baker could haul the stuff from the ovens and cart it up to the stationary vehicle. As yet Thrush had

issued no edict against eating, though maybe that
would come soon enough.

It had not passed attention that the official notice
bore Thrush's signature and that he boldly designated
himself Manager. Even Sydney Thrush would not have
the gall to announce his promotion without Lamont's
approval. It seemed that Donald Wyld had been
sacked. Perhaps that last Judas act had done for him,
after all.

There were plenty of topics to keep the throng buzzing with nervous speculation as it crawled to the sma'
door and gained admittance, one by one. Not only
was there the matter of Wyld's expulsion to discuss
but the day's newspapers brought the Full, True Story
of the Blacklaw Riot, most of the reports couched in
a style more appropriate to a description of Balaclava
or, as one wag quietly suggested, an eye-witness account of Flodden.

How the press had come by such a wealth of raw
material was a matter for considerable conjecture. It
hardly mattered, though, for the authority of print
now indelibly stamped the incident of June 21st as a
bloody, barbarous and unprovoked riot in which serious injury had been inflicted on several courageous
members of the management staff. The wanton destruction of several hundred pounds worth of new
machinery had finally necessitated the summoning of
a restraining force to quell the violence and clear the
yard. Mr. Thrush, Pit Manager, had magnanimously
elected to waive a full enquiry. He put the cause of the
riot down to the hot weather and the influence of a
handful of incorrigible agitators upon the honest if
misguided mass. The majority of miners, Mr. Thrush
declared, were in favour of the owners' proposals for
expansion and well aware of the long-term benefits
to the community. The editor of one Tory rag, the
Ward Examiner, took a more jaundiced view of the
proceedings and, while praising the Blacklaw management for its understanding, thundered against the
forces of anarchy who sought, by exploiting greed and
ignorance, to impede progress and disturb the natural
balance of society.

Caps in hands and most unsure of themselves, the miners and their womenfolk trooped singly into the yard and presented themselves humbly at the trestle tables arraigned beneath the port of the pithead shaft.

The manager conducted the interviews in person, the new Manager, Sydney Thrush, surrounded by his clerks and loyal gaffers and defended by a wall of documents, box-files and the tally-sheets on which each worker's drawing was recorded.

In most cases, reinstatement was a formality and took no time at all. The queue was cleared by two o'clock and the night-shift went down at six as usual to the accompaniment of the harsh triumphant song of the winding gear.

In the final count, only twenty-three colliers lost their jobs. Seventeen families were given one week's notice to quit their tied cottages. There was no appeal or redress, only fury and lamentation.

Though there were angry conversations that evening in the sanctuary of the *Lantern* and a secret meeting of some of the sacked hands in a field behind the Poulter's burn, for once the afflicted could drum up no active sympathy among their brethren and, by the week's end, had meekly accepted their fate.

Guilt, bewilderment, suspicion and fear, the malaise of imposed humility, were already taking their toll of the community's spirit, just as Sydney Thrush, Manager, had planned.

Four

THE BRUISE ON Rob Ewing's cheek had spread, purpling the eye socket and pouching his jaw so that the flesh quivered a little when he spoke, as if with suppressed rage.

"So that's the old man paid off," he said, quietly. "Done. Finished."

"What'll your parents do now, Rob?" Kate asked.

"Share what I bring in. It's all they can do. My mother's talkin' about findin' work of some sort now that Eileen can get about the house a wee bit."

"There's precious little work t'be found in these parts," said Kate. "When do they vacate the tied house?"

"Friday," said Rob. "Mercifully there's room enough in our place. We'd counted on havin' children, Kate, so there's the spare room. There'll be no bairns now."

Resentment and embarrassment caused Rob to look furtively away across the placid brown acre of the backs towards the curve of the moor. In his wicker basket on the grass, Neill Stalker slept peacefully. Kate worked the big wooden needles as she spoke, knitting a hank of coarse wool into a blanket for Neill's cot. He would need all the wrapping up he could get come the winter.

Other couples and groups were seated here and there in the gritty grass acres behind the middens, brick lavatories and sloping wash-houses. The gorse was in full yellow bloom, brighter than Kate ever remembered it. Though she felt sorry for Rob Ewing, there was in her now a reservation which protected her from sharing in other folks' problems—even an old and dear friend like Rob. When she glanced at Neill she could not prevent a wisping smile, in spite of the gravity of the conversation.

She said, "Your father wasn't hurt in the riot?"

"Shaken but not injured," said Rob.

"How's your face?"

"It'll heal," said Rob. "It's the state of this bloody pit that worries me more than my gob."

"Has Wyld really gone?"

"Nobody seems t'know for sure."

"Thrush is a devil, Rob. You'll need t'have a care about crossin' him, especially now."

"Thrush! Christ, I could kill that bugger. I mean it, Kate. I used t'think I was a hard chap, tough as pit boots, but I never hated anyone before. But, God, I hate that Sydney Thrush. He's too clever; far more cunning than Lamont ever was."

"What's happened t'Lamont?"

"You should know."

"Me?"

"He's moping for your Mirrin."

Astonished, Kate almost dropped the needles. "Our Mirrin! Away an' don't talk daft, Rob Ewing. Our Mirrin's been gone this year'n'more. Lamont's too responsible to let a girl get under his skin for that length of time."

"But y'admit there was . . . somethin' between them?"

Kate realised that Rob Ewing too had gained in cunning. He had trapped her into the admission. She said, "Somethin', perhaps, but not what everybody thought."

"The death of his sister must've been a blow t'Lamont," Rob said. "I'm not as callous as some round these parts. I think he loved her, his sister, I mean."

"Is it so hard t'credit a coalmaster with the ability t'love?"

"Then there's that precious wife," Rob went on. "She's got her nose in everywhere. Thrush was her choice o'manager. Donald Wyld hinted that t'Jock Baird."

"How is Jock?"

"Laid up wi' a broken jaw. It'll be a while before he tackles meat again wi' that mouthful o'stumps."

"Rob, who started it?"

"None of us."

"Agitators?"

"Maybe."

"In that case . . ."

"Ach, what the hell does it matter?" said Rob. He plucked a leaf of grass and stuck it in his mouth. Kate shooed a fly from the proximity of Neill's cradle. "We all know we've been diddled. We're gettin' used t'it in Blacklaw. I don't give a curse any more, Kate, an' that's the truth. I'll work m'darg an' keep my nose clean an' hope I'm still here a year hence. It *is* worse elsewhere; that's an incontestable fact."

"An' those machines?"

Rob snorted. "The so-called act sabotage was nothin'. I can't say for sure, but there's a rumour that there were no new machines in the fire shed. I heard that Thrush had them moved out the night before the riot. All that went up in the blaze was a pump engine and a mass of cheap ventilation hose."

"But the newspapers . . . ?"

"Thrush fed them the story."

Kate shook her head in mild disbelief.

Rob said, "Ach, it's too fine a night t'waste talkin' about Thrush an' the pit. What are y'knitting?"

"A blanket."

"For him?" Rob nodded at the sleeping baby.

"Aye."

"He's done you a power of good, Kate. You haven't looked this well for months."

"I like him fine. He's a grand wee chap. No bother."

Then Rob was staring at her, straight at her.

"Whose bairn is he?" the collier asked, with almost savage directness.

"He's mine."

"Mirrin's?

"No, mine."

"Kate, y'know what I mean."

"No, Rob, I don't know what you mean?"

"I . . . I *must* know if he's Mirrin's child."

"Must?"

"Because of . . . of what there once was between us."

Gathering her wool, Kate carefully placed the needles and the hank into the wicker basket and got to her feet.

"All that's in the past, Rob," Kate said. "I'm goin' in now. Give my regards t'your father an' mother, an' remember me t'Eileen. If you need a hand with the flittin' just let us know."

"Kate, listen . . ."

He reached out but she evaded him and he did not

have the gall to hold her there against her will. She could have told him the truth, of course. It was tempting to confide in somebody, to save Mirrin's reputation with old friends like the Ewings. But it was imprudent. Mam would not have stood for it. In a way, Flora Stalker enjoyed the mystery. It seemed to make the boy, though only an infant still, different from his generation, to set him that little bit apart. That was the change least evident but most telling in her mother; the growing desire not to be in kilter with the community that had once sheltered her with its respect. It was an attitude that Kate too was coming to understand.

"I'll carry him in for you," Rob said.

"I'll manage."

"I'm sorry, Kate. I had no right t'ask that question. I'll never ask again."

"All right," Kate Stalker said. "Then I'd be grateful for a hand with Neill's basket. But mind you don't drop him."

"As if I would," Rob Ewing said and, for the first time that evening, managed a smile that was not marred by pain and bitterness.

In spite of its vintage, the gig was in perfect condition, with a mint look to it as if it had been painted only that morning. The pony too was plump and sleek and might also have received a coat of clear varnish that very day. Gig and pony belonged to Sydney Thrush, relics of better days when he and Anna lived in a large, if ramshackle, house up in Fife and had struggled to rescue the Barshotten colliery, their shared legacy, from ruin. That the attempt had failed was not the Thrushs' fault. It was due to an irreversible erosion in the fabric of the workings and surface buildings which had eventually led, some ten years before, to a damning report from a vigilant committee of the Inspectors of Mines Commission and the immediate closure of the Thrush death trap.

The experience he had gained as a young man in those hard-bitten days when he was an owner by inheritance, had moulded Sydney Thrush for life, had made him, out of admittedly malleable material, what he was today. He did not think of the loss of Barshotten much now, or dwell on the ignominy that had attended enforced bankruptcy charges, the rout sale of the family mansion and the sullied acres that the Thrush family had claimed as their own for almost a century but through greed and short-sightedness had burned out before Sydney came of age to stage a rescue.

The gig and the elderly little pony were all that now remained of those grinding but exciting days when he and Anna had been obliged to call no man or woman 'sir or mistress' and toady to the influential.

Dusk was an hour off when Thrush steered the gig into the yard at the side of the *Brookhill Frog*, a public house tucked into a cul-de-sac on the eastern outskirts of Hamilton. The establishment was much less exotic than its name suggested, two cottages knocked together and licensed for dispensing beer and spirits to a mixed clientele. It was reputed to be a place of assignation, for the brewing of plots and the meeting of illicit lovers. It was assignation, of a sort, that took Thrush there that evening.

Having tied the pony to the hitching rail, he entered the tiny snug by its back door. A bar no longer than a man's forearm stood in one corner. There were three tables and six chairs. At one table, alone in the low room, sat Donald Wyld, a corked bottle of wine and two glasses upon the table before him.

As Thrush sat down, Wyld opened the wine with a corkscrew and poured out two glasses. Glancing round, Thrush lifted the glass and sipped it speculatively, as if suspecting that it might be poisoned.

"I wish you luck, Sydney," Donald Wyld said.

"Do you, indeed?"

"Why not," Wyld said. "I'm willing to concede defeat. The worst man won, which seems to be the canon law of victory these days."

"I trust, Wyld, that you are not about to ask for your job back?"

"I know better than that." Wyld put down the wine

untouched. "On the other hand, I could have my job back tomorrow if I really wanted it."

"I doubt it," said Thrush. "You resigned verbally to me. I carried your resignation to the owners and they, verbally, accepted it and, under the duress of the lock-out, saw fit to appoint me manager there and then."

"You spoke to Lamont?"

"I . . . yes, I received his sanction."

"He was drunk, was he?"

"Really, old fellow, this is quite immaterial. Why did you request this interview? I would have thought that the situation was perfectly plain. I am the man-ager of Blacklaw colliery. Lamont, sober, has ap-proved my appointment and it will be contracted legally by the weekend. You can't depose me, if that's what's in your mind."

"Tell me, Thrush, old fellow, why are you doing this?"

"I don't understand your question."

"What do you hope to gain from such bullying, from such filthy tricks? Respect? That isn't the way, and you are sharp enough to realise it."

"Respect? From the colliers, you mean? I don't want their respect. Good Lord, Wyld, do you suppose I care what *they* think of me. No, no. I don't care for respect of that order."

"Is it money you want?"

"Money—certainly."

"What else?"

"Power."

"You admit it."

"I'm not ashamed of it. I like power. I will do well for the owners of Blacklaw. I will keep that pit thriving in spite of the disastrous state of industry. I can guar-antee it."

"If Lamont knew how you'd employed agita-tors . . ."

"So that's it, Wyld. You intend to blackmail me into giving you back your job."

"It isn't for you t'say, Thrush. But, no, I don't want work in Blacklaw now. I wouldn't be a damned pony-boy under your management."

"Probably just as well."

"But I do believe that Lamont should know what happened behind his back."

"He does know."

"You told him, I suppose?"

"He knows, for example, that you condoned my employment of armed pickets for the management's protection."

"Does he know that I traded my job for your promise that you wouldn't batter half a dozen stupid colliers t'death?"

"I kept my part of that bargain, Wyld. The most serious injury was to Baird, and he's management."

"All right, Thrush," Wyld said. "But I warn you . . ."

"Warn me?" Thrush tutted: he seemed genuinely irritated. "You are as obsolete as . . . as a flint axe, Wyld. I don't grudge you the tatters of your dignity, but *I* warn *you* not to cross me. You are a sentimentalist, Wyld. What's more you are envious of my success."

"I wouldn't call it success."

"You have seen the figures. Twenty-eight per cent increase in output, allied to a thirty per cent final figure reduction in the work-force. The pit is flourishing."

"For you? For Lamont?"

"I make it flourish."

"Until you push them too far: then they will strike."

"Strike? I doubt it, Wyld."

"You will beat them into submission, won't you? You'll rob them of everything through fear."

"Of course."

"God, but you're evil. Wait'til Houston Lamont learns of this."

"He knows."

"Not him: he's not like you. He'll baulk eventually, Thrush. Then what'll you do: beat *him* half t'death?"

"Ah! So you intend to run to dear Mr. Lamont and tell him all," said Thrush. "Then what? He'll re-instate you, sack me, and all will be rosy again. That is nonsense."

"We'll see," said Wyld, thinly. "You're not the only bloody person who can draft reports."

"Reports on what?"

"Names, payments: the methods you used t'start and stop the mock riot yesterday."

"You have a report?"

"I do."

"And you will present it to Mr. Lamont?"

"I will."

Thrush smiled. "Good."

Wyld leapt to his feet. "We'll see how smug you are tomorrow, Thrush."

"What about this wine: you've hardly touched it."

"You drink it."

"Thank you, Mr. Wyld. I will. I don't believe in waste."

"You're a ruthless bastard, Thrush."

"And you, Wyld, are a foolish idealist."

"Then one of us will have to go."

"Hah! That *is* ridiculous. You, old fellow, have already gone."

Wedges of deep blue shadow still marked the lawns west of the mansion when Wyld and Lamont met in an interview that the coalmaster would have preferred to avoid. Nebulous guilt over Dorothy's death and the loss of that centre of love which his sister had represented gave way, though only briefly, to guilt of another kind. He felt ashamed of the way he had treated his old colleague, Donald Wyld, a man whose loyalty he had never questioned.

"You didn't waste much time being rid of me, Mr. Lamont."

"There was an emergency, Donald."

"What exactly did Thrush tell you?"

Lamont dropped into his chair, shoulders hunched. Deep lines at the corners of his mouth and his hooded eyelids gave him a brooding, introverted appearance. His waistcoat and shirt were not fresh.

"Thrush told me everything," Lamont said.

"Including what's in this report, sir?"

In the early morning stillness, with a ground mist

shrouding the oaks, the Brighouse clock struck six with a sharpness that caused both the coalmaster and his former manager to start slightly. The household was not awake yet, only the poor little scullion who had admitted Wyld at the kitchen door and who had brought the message, in fear and trembling, to Lamont dozing in his study.

Lamont lifted the stiff-backed document and scanned its contents diffidently.

"Most of it, yes," he murmured. "The essence of it, certainly."

Standing before the desk, Wyld said incredulously, *"You knew?"*

Lamont tossed the folio on to the dusty pile of documents which spilled over the wire basket to his left. "What I did not know, I surmised."

"I . . . I find it hard to believe, sir."

"Why, Donald?"

"It's . . . it's not your way, Mr. Lamont."

"What is my way, Donald? I wish I knew myself."

"And my resignation?"

"I'm sorry about that, Donald. I would have preferred you to remain in my employment. But, under the circumstances I had no alternative but to accept your verbal resignation and appoint Thrush immediately to the position."

"Did it not cross your mind that Thrush might have been lying?"

"He had no need to lie. He planned it. The plan worked. You resigned. I even know why."

Wyld said, "So the running of Blacklaw colliery is to be left to Thrush and to your wife?"

"You're well out of it, Donald."

"Mr. Lamont, when will you come t'your senses?"

Lamont said, "I'm more aware of what's going on than you, Thrush or Edith imagines. It's regretful that you'll not be here to assist. But I can't have the management split."

"I see. You accept all that Thrush says and does," Wyld said. "You accept that Thrush rules through fear and the billy-club. Only you can moderate his policies, now, Mr. Lamont. Your miners need you."

Lamont shook his head. "They don't need me. I doubt if they've ever needed me. Besides, I'm tired. I'm out of practice in asserting myself. Sydney Thrush will run a profitable pit."

"For you, not for the colliers."

"Then the colliers may go elsewhere," Lamont snapped.

"I never thought I'd hear the day . . ."

With a sudden blaze of anger, Lamont lunged forward in the chair. "They talk of *their* freedom. 'Make *us* free', they cry. This is the freedom they want, is it not? They have the right to leave my employment, at any time."

"You know that's not possible in most cases."

"Why not?"

"They have wives, families, a tied house . . ."

"Aye, *they* are protected; protected by *me*. *They* take from *me*. But when I ask for something in return, they revile me. What sort of freedom, Wyld, do you suppose I have? They are *my* gaolers."

"The heart's gone out of you, Mr. Lamont, and out of this pit," Wyld said, sadly. "Thrush told me that you knew what was happening and I didn't believe him. But I see now that Blacklaw is a doomed town, a dead town, because of you."

For a long minute, Lamont said nothing, then, his mood changing yet again, he slumped back into the chair. "Where will you go, Donald?"

"I've a younger sister in Shotts. She'll give me board for a while."

"Where will you find work?"

Wyld shrugged. "The Grebe, or the Tar Pit, or maybe in Monksport."

"Hell holes: death traps."

"Where else am I liable to be taken on—an *idealist* like me?"

Lamont reached forward and plucked a long envelope from between the decanters. It was sealed with the old wax stamp that had marked documents many years ago and which Wyld had never seen used before.

"Take it, man," Lamont said.

"I . . . I don't want your handouts, sir. I'm not short of money yet."

"It's a letter of recommendation, that's all," Lamont said. "It should carry some weight, Donald."

"I . . . thank you, Mr. Lamont," Wyld said. "I'm sorry that it ever had to come to this."

"You're an excellent manager, Donald. No coalmaster could wish for better. But you are not right for me or for Blacklaw at this time."

"What changed you, Mr. Lamont?"

"Hard times—and circumstances."

"Circumstances like Alex Stalker's daughter?"

"That's impudence, Wyld. You overstep yourself."

"Aye, but I think it's the truth."

Flushed, Lamont reached for a decanter and poured whisky into a glass. He did not offer Wyld hospitality and the liquor, it seemed was needful to him, to steady him at the very mention of her name.

"You've been kind enough to give me a reference of character, Mr. Lamont," Donald Wyld went on. "May I return that generous gesture by giving you this."

From a notecase in his pocket Wyld extracted a folded newspaper clipping and handed it to the coalmaster. Lamont scowled down at the advertisement.

MIRRIN STALKER, SONG BIRD OF THE
NORTH, APPEARING EXCLUSIVELY WITH
WILFRID TALBOYS AND THE CROPLEY
SISTERS FOR THE SUMMER SEASON AT
THE GRAND PROMENADE THEATRE, BEALE.

"Where did you get this, Donald?"

"It's from a Yorkshire newspaper: a friend of my sister sent it to her. She sent it to me."

"Mirrin Stalker in the theatre," said Lamont. "So that much is true. How old is the advertisement?"

"A week or two at most."

"The Song Bird of the North: how . . . how ridiculous!"

"Beale is a fairly respectable watering place, Mr. Lamont, in spite of its proximity to Blackpool."

Still holding the clipping, Lamont looked up. "The Stalkers are nursing a baby. Could it be Mirrin's child?"

"I've heard it said. But personally I don't believe a word of it, Mr. Lamont."

"Whose, then?"

"Does it matter, sir? She's in the past now, for you. Along with everything else. I think, Mr. Lamont, that you were well shot of the girl."

"Perhaps she is well shot of me," Lamont said. "Why did you give me this information, Donald?"

"Call it a . . . a parting gift, Mr. Lamont."

"Thank you, Donald. I wish you well, wherever you wind up."

"I might say the same to you, sir," Donald Wyld said and, abruptly, turned and let himself out of the airless study and out of Lamont's mansion.

Lamont sipped whisky. The closed door, the faint sound of Wyld's boots on the gravel, rapidly diminishing into soundlessness, left him more alone than ever. It seemed that he had lost, or alienated, all his former friends, the few who had approached close enough to see beneath the stern facade and realise that he was a man as well as a coalmaster. All he had left now were enemies. And yet, by his decisions, by his deliberate refusals to take a hand in the sweep of affairs that threatened to destroy Blacklaw as well as Houston Lamont, he had condoned all that had happened at the pit. He had made himself an ally of Edith and Sydney Thrush, consciously and deliberately endorsing their hard-line policies.

Mirrin Stalker: Summer Season: Beale. On the coast, a burgeoning resort, so he had heard. It had been lampooned in *Punch* not so long since; a town that could not make up its mind. It had a theatre, on the saloon principle. Leech had even drawn it, with little tipsy, ebullient figures clinging to the railings, teacups and champagne glasses in their hands as the wind roared in from the sea.

Mirrin Stalker in the theatre, singing comic songs and dancing: he had always imagined her being miserable, too, as scarred by the short-lived, tragic affair as he was. The little he had heard by way of gossip was true, it seemed.

He supposed he could have utilised his authority, ridden imperiously down to the narrow house in Main Street, as he had once before when Alex Stalker was alive, and demanded explanations as his right. But he could not do that now. It was implicit in the bargain he had made with Mirrin that the family would be left alone. Damnation, he was paying twenty pounds per annum, through that rogue Havershaw, to have her precious brother educated! He had every right to 'annoy' the family if he chose to do so. He could even insist that they inform him who had fathered the child.

No, they were nothing to him. He had relinquished his right to that kind of relationship with any of his colliers, even the Stalkers, when he had given Thrush the opportunity to usurp Wyld, to strike at the spirit of the community. There would be no more singing at the shaft, no more gruff respect now. But that had nothing to do with the events of the past two years. The disaster had ended all that. Like the stability of so many men and women in Blacklaw, his own had been blown asunder that dismal March morning, twenty-seven months ago.

The baby? It *must* be Mirrin's. The Stalkers, proud that they were, would rear no other infant openly as their own.

The thought was like a knife digging into his gut. Mirrin's son. It could have been his son, their son. His shoulders heaved. He pushed the whisky glass away from him, sliding his body forward across the desk. The tide of papers, thrust before him, spread across the carpet.

In his fist the clipping crumpled into a ball.

Edith Lamont twisted the frilled parasol in her white gloved hand and allowed the cupola of watered silk to elevate itself sufficiently to protect Sydney Thrush's head from the rays of the noon sun.

It was not Edith's habit to take the air, particularly at that hour of the day when the weather was hot, but, that very morning, protocol notwithstanding, she had suddenly grown tired of dark mourning and, on whim, had clad herself, with Anna's help, in her lightest and most flattering summer mode. It seemed natural, then, to take a before-luncheon perambulation with her friend, Mr. Thrush, confining her route, of course, to the paths east of the mansion, well away from Houston's spy-hole in the ell of the west wing. Here the flowers were in full, glorious bloom and the rhododendron shrubs provided a little cool shade.

"We have done well, Sydney."

"I would hardly call it a triumph, ma'am."

"Must we be formal?"

"I beg your pardon?"

"Must we be formal?"

"I beg your pardon?"

"I think, when we are alone, Sydney, it would not be amiss for you to call me Edith."

"Very well, Edith."

"And for us to talk quite plainly."

"How plainly?"

"As plainly as you are disposed to do. I refer, of course, to my husband. Houston is not *quite* ready to hand over full control of the colliery. That action will require a deed or bond of transfer, and he is not so removed from reality that he will send for a lawyer and sit himself down and sign. Not *quite* yet."

"Perhaps if you approached him?" Thrush suggested. "I feel that the coalmaster would be relieved to be discharged of all responsibility."

"Indeed, that is my feeling too, Sydney. But there are factors of which you are unaware, private and personal matters that will prevent Houston. He knows that I want control. For that reason alone, if for no other, he will not make Blacklaw over into my charge."

"If the coalmaster continues to drink he will fall ill."

"He has a strong constitution," said Edith.

"Now that Wyld has finally gone," Sydney Thrush said, "many important decisions will have to be made. Let us assume that you—Edith—do not feel competent to make such decisions and Mr. Lamont is persuaded to make them and the results of those decisions turn out very badly . . ."

"Badly?"

"In terms of health and the welfare of the work-force," Thrush explained. "I imagine the Inspector of Mines might be interested in the reasons. I have some sway with the Inspector; a little, not a lot. Enough, however, to make him examine Mr. Lamont's competence more closely."

"Power of attorney," said Edith. "Strangely, I discussed this very subject only last month with Lord Shawcrofts."

"It is difficult to force the court to move against an owner," said Thrush. "Many coalmasters are much more . . . irresponsible than your husband. However, I do believe that you might obtain *effective* governing control, if not the actual purse-strings, by a diligent campaign."

"Unless Houston pulls himself together."

Thrush faltered in his step, the tassel of the parasol brushing his forehead. "Is that liable to happen?"

"Now that Dorothy is dead, I am uncertain as to what he will do."

"Mrs. Lamont—Edith—let us be frank. How far will you go to achieve your aim?"

It was Edith's turn to falter. Long after she had ceased to love Houston, she had reluctantly continued to admire him. Her vanity and selfishness had helped to build the wall between them. But the pit had been at the back of it. The pit was the escape that Houston had used when things had been at their worst. He had done then, after Gordon's death, what she was doing now. He had buried himself in work, in Blacklaw. She could have borne that, found outlets for her own energy in Edinburgh and Glasgow society, in charitable work in the cities. In time, she might even have wheedled a small apartment in town from him. But he had wanted more. The Stalker girl had given him happiness, forcing Edith to realise how hollow her own life had become, how empty of love.

They could have lived well, husband and wife, travelled, entertained. The colliery could have been made to turn out quite enough profit to sustain them in a certain style. That would have drawn them together. It was the kind of life that she had wanted all along. She blamed Houston for denying it to her. How immeasurably sweeter it would have been to be a partner, and not merely a discarded wife, to a man like Houston rather than a sly opportunist like Sydney Thrush.

She shrugged the thought aside.

"I will go as far as I have to," she said.

"Even to suggesting that your husband is mad?"

"I . . . I . . . yes, even to that. His sister was mad. It is in the family, and known to be so."

"Then you must bring him out," Thrush advised.

"Out? Where?"

"Let him be seen," Thrush said. "It is not enough that he has become a recluse. He must also be seen to be publicly irresponsible for his actions."

"I'm not sure that . . ."

"Naturally, Edith, I leave the decision to you."

"How would . . . ?"

"Discreetly," Thrush said. "Society already sympathises with you."

"Does it? What have you heard?"

Thrush brushed that vain question aside. "But once the process has begun there will be no turning back, Edith."

"I do not know that I am strong enough."

"I believe that you are."

"No, Sydney," Edith said. "I . . . I cannot cold-bloodedly undertake to commit my husband . . ."

Edith's refutation of ambition was interrupted.

Ahead of the couple, round the crook of the path from the direction of the kitchens, Anna Thrush made her appearance. She was running. Not even her brother could recall when last Anna had given in to urgency and had cast dignity aside. But she was running now, skirts caught up, thick ankles exposed, the keys on her belt, badges of housekeeper's office, jingling. One lock of hair had come loose too, in her haste, and dangled disreputably over her eye.

Frozen in apprehension, Edith Lamont and Sydney

Thrush waited at the mouth of the path into the shrub-
bery.

Hand to her heaving bosom, Anna said, "He's
gone."

"Who has gone, dear?" asked Sydney.

"Mr. Lamont; the coalmaster."

"Gone where?"

"To . . . to the railway station. He's . . . he's gone.
I asked Archie. He heard the master tell Sandy
Willocks to drive him to Hamilton station. Not only
. . . that . . . but he packed luggage, a very great deal
of luggage."

"Then he has gone for a while," said Sydney
Thrush. "Anna, did Mr. Lamont leave a note for
Edith?"

"I looked carefully in the study and the other
rooms, too, but there's nothing, not the scrape of a
pen."

"Perhaps he's gone for a holiday," Thrush said,
smiling. "How odd!"

"Left me?" said Edith. "Abandoned me? But what
will happen to the house, and the pit?"

"Both," said Sydney Thrush, "will prosper, Edith,
you need have no fear of that."

"But what . . . what if he never returns?"

"Somehow I think he will," said Thrush. "And when
he does, you will be prepared, Edith, will you not?"

Tactfully, Sydney Thrush offered the small woman
his hand. She took it, clung to it, her shock and bewilderment sloughing off rapidly.

"Oh, yes," she said, at length. "I'll be prepared."

"Good," Thrush said. "Now, Anna, you may serve
luncheon in half an hour." Taking Edith's arm, he
escorted her back to the mansion to pry about for
clues as to where the coalmaster had gone.

Five

❧

AT THAT TIME, Beale boasted the longest marine promenade in England, though its neighbour, Blackpool, seemed determined to outstrip it before another season elapsed. Eventually, so Wilf Talboys declared, the two proms would meet in the region of Spearsbridge like runaway locomotives and there would be *the* most almighty crash.

Rivalry between the booming resorts was a surefire source of amusement which Wilf stoked daily with an endless series of sketches along the lines of 'The Gentleman from Beale Meets the Girl from Blackpool', or vice versa. Such quips quickly established camaraderie with an audience all too ready to acknowledge that folk who holidayed in Beale had more 'tone' than those who boarded in the 'infant commonwealth' of Blackpool. For all that, the distinction was not so great that the happy hordes from Bolton, Liverpool or the wilds of Lancashire were made to feel uncomfortable and the robust vulgarity which lay close below the surface of Talboys' acts was carefully preserved.

Heartiness and breezy wit were spiced with songs, dances and an occasional 'tearjerker'. Mirrin could always be counted upon to redden all eyes with a heartfelt rendering of a work-song or a Scottish ballad, though her image was becoming increasingly sophisticated with each passing week. Groomed by Wilf and Ada during the 'tour' in the early part of the year, and encouraged by Harrison Colcutt's expenditure on costumes commensurate with the profits he was now taking, she soon developed a certain stylish elegance.

A month into the season at Beale and Mirrin had gained a reputation that extended up the whole north-west coast, clearly distinguishing the Grand's performers from the ruck of pierrots and minstrels in their flapping tents on beaches and foreshores. Colcutt, that august, ruthless recluse, had no reason to regret his gamble in putting Talboys into the Grand. Even Ockram had been heard to admit that Wilfrid's show was the agent's star attraction these days.

The Grand Promenade Theatre had been constructed at the same time as the pier. In fact, it *was* the pier; the 'shortest pier in England' Wilf Talboys called it, making its lack of size sound like a virtue. The unusual three storey construction of cream stucco, brick, glass and wrought-iron housed tearooms, coffeeshops and two saloons where beer and spirits were served. It also had a red tile roof and four castellated towers which could be seen from miles out to sea. The theatre itself was compact but well equipped, with much expensive gilt and plush in the boxes and circle, and ample ingress from the other parts of the 'Pleasure Palace' and the bracing outdoor decks. But the theatre, Colcutt's investment, was the heart of the palace and Mirrin Stalker, that summer, was the heart of the theatre.

Though they lodged in Nixons, a second-rate hotel in Lucia Street, the Talboys, and Mirrin especially, were respected in the resort and generated considerable interest wherever they went, whether riding on the sands or dining in Blue's Supper Rooms. Mirrin's morning visit to the Bathing Machine brought out a crowd of spectators that stopped all traffic on that part of the front and, so it was said, caused the railing to bulge for a hundred and fifty yards.

Needless to say, Mirrin's attraction was an exploitable quality and Wilf was not above exploiting it for all it was worth, covering the rest of the troupe in its reflected glory.

It was Colcutt, through Ockram, however, who provided the busy comic skit 'Alphabet on the Pier', which involved all the members of the cast through twenty-four short satirical verses and changes of hats, including, under W, a part hand-fashioned for Mirrin: 'I'm a Wicked Beguiling Young Witch'. So much of a show-stopper did that single verse become that Colcutt turned up trumps a week later with a specially-written song with that self-same title, together with a high-waisted and expensive costume and a large, even more expensive hat, from beneath whose shadow Mirrin flirted outrageously with the boys in the boxes and stalls.

By the following Friday, the queue for the last evening performance looped twice round the pier tele-scope. Though the wind was high and the evening gen-erally dull none of the folk seemed to mind in the least. On Sunday, Ockram journeyed into Beale again, bearing in a large package a dress almost identi-cal to the stage costume, which Mirrin was 'instructed' to wear upon her 'constitutionals' with Wilf and Blanche. Scudding before her growing fame like a yacht in the bay, Mirrin hadn't the slightest objection to adding a strain of notoriety to her reputation, though the material used in the show was innocent enough to cause offense only to the most prudish.

At first Blanche Talboys' jealous suspicion of Mirrin had caused much bitterness and repetitions of the Grossby sulks. But Mirrin had more than enough ebul-lience to spread about and was careful, as the sum-mer progressed, to include Blanche in many of her 'escapades', ensuring that the plain young woman was not neglected, on stage or off, and received her fair share of fuss and attention. In another duet, 'Mer-maids', Mirrin chose to play the clown and allow Blanche to show off her voice and her figure and reap the approval of the audience.

The stage was Mirrin's whole life. She carried the manner with her out into the streets of the resort with an easy confidence that, said Pru, was the hallmark of the star. She would laugh and joke with waitresses in the coffee chops, turn aside the suggestive comments of the blades in Blue's, chat to round-eyed youngsters in the shopping arcade and wave to the elderly gentle-men in their chairs along the sea wall. She was out-going without being unduly forward, amusing without being brash, self-mocking without being undignified —and astute enough to acknowledge that, though she was the principal attraction, her success depended on the hard work and experience that the Talboys generously put at her disposal.

During the course of that summer, Mirrin also earned a great deal of money. Ticket receipts from the Grand made pretty reading, running between four and five thousand admissions each week. From that sum, Ockram—who was also Colcutt's roving accountant—extracted the agent's percentage and a cut to recoup the outlay on costumes. The remainder was divided more or less equally between the five performers. In exchange, the troupe spent fourteen hours each day, six days in each week, rehearsing and performing, regularly changing their songs and sketches to coax Beale's summer residents back again and again, to see what the Talboys had come up with now, or to learn, from Mirrin Stalker, some stirring new chorus.

There were children's shows in the morning, and matinées for the more venerable holidaymakers, with the accent on nostalgia and sentiment; an early evening show for the whole family, with much comedy and clowning, and a final two-hour performance for 'the bats and the owls,' when the wit was a little more risqué and the costumes a shade more daring.

As the lanterns flickered in the warm ozone, and the flags snapped in the breezes and the sea lay outside like champagne or porter according to the weather and the state of the tide, Mirrin Stalker thought that the summer would go on for ever, and that the whole world was in Beale and on holiday.

The intrusions that Blacklaw made into this tinsel existence were few. Even Kate's long letter concerning Drew's behaviour and the arrival of the baby angered Mirrin only for a short time. In a postscript Kate implied that the baby was a joy to them—and Mirrin knew enough of her sister to accept that without question. Mam too, said Kate, was blossoming with a grandchild to attend to, and told how the infant travelled in style round the streets of Blacklaw in a basket on the baker's cart. There was much news in that long letter; sad news about Dorothy Lamont's death, bad news about the Ewings and the riot which the new pit manager, Thrush, had put down with such cleverness. During the course of her reading, Mirrin was responsive and interested. But none of Kate's gossip, not even the dramatic parts about Drew, the baby and Dorothy Lamont's death, seemed really capable of touching her now.

When she finished reading the letter, she wrote an immediate reply in tumbling, sprawling, dashing handwriting—she had a show at three o'clock—enclosed a five-pound banknote, sealed the envelope and sent it off at once, via the landlord's eldest, to the post office. That done, she glanced over Kate's letter once more, than folded it and put it away in the bottom of her trunk. Immediately she found herself relieved from homesickness or concern by the need to get around to the Grand. Ada and Blanche were already calling her to hurry.

She paused only for a moment, frowning slightly. She was an aunt again, aunt to a bastard child by the name of Neill Campbell. She could not imagine it. Indeed, she could not, at that time, ever imagine herself entering Blacklaw again. Oddly, the stuff of life in the Lanarkshire coal town, the births and deaths, sickness, danger, hardship, seemed trivial in comparison with the afternoon performance, with the proper rendering of the latest song and the execution of the dance that went with 'Pretty Parasols.'

But Blacklaw, Mirrin was soon to discover, was not so distant after all.

August was approaching, the high point of the English season when gentlemen from manufacturing and trading offices in Lancashire and Yorkshire came to join their little 'wifey-pifeys' for a day or two and the resort would be thronged with visitors all eager to spend their cash. The latest novelty was the Day Excursion, that famous 'breather' offered by the railway companies, which swelled the crowds in Blackpool and even in Beale. Unsettled weather, however, was causing concern to boat hirers and the leasers of chairs, to the donkeymen and the bathing machine operators. But, as Wilf shouted, it was a *very* ill wind that didn't blow somebody good, and the palace's indoor pursuits, including the music hall, benefited from the rain as much as the sellers of umbrellas, yellow sou'westers and rubber galoshes. During a wet spell there was seldom a seat to be had in the Grand, for any of the shows, and Talboys was enough of a trouper to pack in an extra matinée in the wake of afternoon tea. On those occasions, the cast didn't leave the pier at all between breakfast and late supper, snatching meals on trays in the coffin-like dressing rooms which hung below the level of the pier deck and reverberated with the thunder of the big breakers rolling in from the Irish Sea.

The rain was a drizzling haze wafted like fine spray on the wind, tasting of salt and disappointment. It did not daunt some gentlemen, those seekers after health, who strode into it like stalwarts, breathing deeply and wiping the moisture from their whiskers with the flats of their hands. But it did tend to dampen the spirits of ladies and children rather quickly, and Talboys' troupe had to work harder than ever to offer a fair share of jollity for their shillings and pence. Life, for the artistes became one long, exhausting show.

It was a wild night, the worst of the season. The early house had not been quite jam-packed. The sight of mountainous waves lashing pier and promenade persuaded many families to remain indoors to make their own entertainment in their lodgings or retire early to bed after dinner. Venturing into the elements, however, had a quality of daring which young men, and their more reckless female companions, could not resist and the 'Owl House' performance was crammed to capacity. With beer, wine and spirits flowing in the saloons as antidotes to depression, the audience was rowdier than usual and the palace's team of 'pacifiers' kept busy evicting boozy pugilists and strident warblers. As a result there was a certain edgy desperation to the performance that night.

Even Mirrin was aware of an aggressiveness which she had experienced only once or twice before. It came, Pru told her, from fatigue and the thought that the magic which they somehow seemed able to work again and again would fall them on that teeming night.

It took half an hour to settle the audience; another fifteen minutes to warm them up. At Talboys' insistence the intervals were shortened to five minutes, to avoid too much taking on of liquor though the licensees complained and threatened to report him to the directors. The performance trundled on, gathering speed and a nervous brittle energy that communicated itself to the folk in the stalls and made them uneasy.

Wiping her face with a towel then angling it to Pru to powder with a rabbits' foot brush, Mirrin said, "What can we do? Do we carry on as planned?"

"It's in the programme," said Blanche. "The orchestra . . ."

"Damn the orchestra," said Mirrin. "I can't stand this . . . this atmosphere."

"We'll just have to get through it," said Ada. "Somehow."

Pru coughed, turning her head away.

"Are you ill, Pru?" demanded Wilf.

"No, no, I'm all right."

"Then stop that hacking, please."

"Wilf, shouting at Pru won't do any good," Ada snapped.

"I didn't shout."

"Listen," Mirrin interupted. "The music's started. I'm . . . I'm really frightened."

"You'll be all right, Mirrin," said Blanche. "It's me they can't stand the sight of. If one of those ruffians dares throw . . ."

"It's as if they'd seen it all before," said Mirrin. "What's wrong?"

"We're feeling the pace: we're a tiny bit stale, that's all," Wilf explained. "Now, *please,* Mirrin, just do your best. Give them a lot of eyes, y'know. And sing loud."

"I'm hoarse wi' singin' loud."

"There it is. Go on: go on."

She did not feel like a Wicked, Beguiling Young Witch. She felt more like a Withered, Bedraggled Old Hag. She tugged the floppy hat down over her face to hide her ugliness—she was sure she looked haggard that night—and flung herself into the arena of light against the backcloth of a beach with sand and blue sky the like of which had never been seen outside of Africa.

Mirrin sang in a kind of trance. She went through all the actions, playing up, at first, to a beet-faced sergeant of Fusiliers, who glared at her with eyes as glassy as marbles and then, to Mirrin's horror, fashioned an explicitly obscene gesture with his fist. Confused and distraught, she swung away and heard the sergeant, more bibulous than she had imagined, bawling in a barracks' voice what he would do to her if he had her flat on her back. It took two of the Grand's strongest bouncers to eject the sergeant who, mercifully, was not popular enough with his corporals to lead his companions into battle againt Ockram's forces.

Suddenly, it seemed to Mirrin that the entire audience was composed of such grotesques. Through the smoky air, she found her eyes picking out lewd tableaux, couples nuzzling each other in the aisles, fat men in snap-brimmed hats splashing beer and mouthing as they ogled her, young languid seducers verbally stripping her, muttering to each other with effete expertise. What was wrong with them? What was wrong with *her,* that she had become so sensitive all of a sudden? There had been men like that in the house before now and it had never bothered her. She had been on her feet for fourteen hours that day, sixteen the day before; her legs and back ached and her head ached, her eyes were bleary and her throat raw. They didn't care: none of them cared. All they wanted was diversion, titillation.

Sweeping off her hat she walked to the centre of the stage and finished the final chorus, shouting out at them, galloping the seven-man orchestra along. A section of the audience half-heartedly tried to join in the chorus but Mirrin gave them no chance. On the last note, she turned and flicked the fancy hat into the wings where Wilf, Ada, Pru and Blanche had gathered like mourners at a wake. She glanced at them, saw Wilf gesturing her off, then, with a defiant toss of her head, she drew in a deep breath, stuck her hands on her hips and stared hard into the stalls.

The hub-hub died a little. The clash of glasses and mugs in the larger of the saloon bars became quite audible.

Ignoring the cat-calls she made them wait.

When she was ready, she shouted. "What's wrong with you all tonight? Is it the rain? Have you never seen rain before? Don't it rain, then, in Bradford, in Bolton or Huddersfield? You think this is bad? I tell you, where I come from this is fine weather, a gran' day. Aye, listen, where I come from a little puff of wind an' a touch of the wet don't dampen our spirits. But we're the Scots. We're the hardy ones."

She was beginning, just, to catch them. She was angry. She remembered Sabbath afternoons on the corner of Duggan Street in Northrigg, and the square in Eastlagg and the mouth of the yard at the *Lantern* in Blacklaw itself, with Christy Moran egging her on and all the hot tumble of words that had come to her then, the clichés that she had learned from pit-boot politicians, from her father.

"Listen," she shouted. "Hear that rain? Hear it?"

They listened. Even the swillers and swains paused to cock their heads and listen to the batter of the waves on the piles and the rattle of the rain on the seaward gable.

"There's men out there in fishin' smacks, an' brigs an' barges, carryin' food for us, an' pig iron, an' coal. Coal. They call me the song-bird o'the north, but back home where I come from, I'm no song-bird; I'm a duck, a seagull."

Some folk sniggered, but not many.

"I splashed in the mud while I learned my trade. Aye, an' coal was my trade then, not singin' naughty songs," Mirrin cried. *"You work with cotton, you work with lead: you tear your hands on the bobbin an' thread.* Know that one, do you? I'll teach you another one. I'll sing you one now that tells you what it was like for me. Ach, I was not pet canary then, no beguilin' witch. I was a collier's daughter, an' m'Daddy was killed in the mine."

Her voice was harsh and grating. At first, she did not pander to the sentiment in the song. She sang it unaccompanied, as if it was a marching hymn, a rally cry, flat and hard and full of bitterness. She stood on the apron with the gaudy desert backcloth behind her, the lights still blazing down, the expensive dress clinging to her, and she sang them the one song she had never sung before, except softly to herself when she walked to roads across the Border and was full of sad regret.

The extravagant motions which Pru had taught her to augment tearjerkers were neglected. She kept her hands on her hips and her head high, defiant and challenging.

"By the Clyde's bonny banks as I sadly did
*   wander,*
Among the pit heaps as evening drew nigh,
I spied a young woman all dressed in deep
*   mourning,*
Weeping and wailing with many a sigh."

Apart from the singer's voice there was no sound in the hall. The words and the drumming of the rain and the raking of the wind merged and strengthened each other. Mirrin no longer thought of the effect on the customers. Once more, she tapped the deep hurt within herself. It was natural that she should dredge up this song, this real, plaintive cry that would silence an audience made up of men and women who, in one degree or another, had suffered, or had witnessed suffering, too.

If they were in no mood to be entertained, then at least they could be moved by an expression of shared emotions.

She sang:

"The explosion was heard, all the women and
*   children,*
With pale anxious faces made haste to the
*   mine."*

She could almost taste the coal dust in her throat, smell the stink of charred flesh and the thick sulphurous fumes of the choke-damp fire belching up from Lamont's pit.

She sang:

"When the truth was made known, the hills rang with their mourning."

They had brought up her brother Dougie, with his young, innocent face smashed to pulp by exploding chip-rubble; they had brought up her brother James with his hands blasted off and a shear-spike driven through his gut; they had brought up her father, alive, burned like an old pot. And rain had smeared their names on the list on the door of the managers' office and rain had dappled the cobbles and rain had filled the sky.

She sang:

"Shed a tear for the victims who'll never return."

The story was over. She had hardly been aware of the singing of it. When she was finished, there was silence still in the gilt and plush interior of the Grand Promenade, and then applause. Nobody whistled; nobody cheered or shouted. They applauded, and applauded, and many of them wept.

Mirrin looked up through her own tears. In the gloom under the gallery she could see the gaslamp at the entrance to the bar, and the crowd of men there, young men, the most of them, craftsmen and clerks, soldiers and tradesmen, their class putting them a little apart from the men she had sung of, hard-bitten colliers who crawled underground and maybe once in all their lives, if they were lucky, got away from the shadow of the winding towers to glimpse the sea and smell the salt wind clean along the coast.

In the stalls, an old woman wept unashamedly, and hugged her grandson to her. It was no ersatz music-hall heart-rending ditty that she had treated them to but a whiff of the real world, the actuality of Blacklaw and of Grossby and a thousand towns where work was all and masters ruled over men.

She was drained now, not as she'd been at Christmas back in the Civic Hall, but truly drained. She would not do it again; never again. She had used up the source within her. Tomorrow, she must be flighty and gay once more. She hoped that the sun would shine to aid the transition.

They were still applauding.

Mirrin scanned the circle, the sweep of faces, hands pale in the gloaming above the pepperpot lamps.

When she saw him she could not believe her eyes.

He was standing by the scroll at the side of the circle where the aisle swept down to the rectangular rail: *his* face, drawn and shadowed, and *his* manner, that quiet, watchful manner, like the time he had come to her from between the sheds on the day of the tragedy and offered her sympathy. She had rejected him then.

No, Mirrin shouted soundlessly. No. It *can't* be Houston.

I've worked myself into hysteria.

It isn't him.

Then Wilf was by her side. She was confused, disoriented. Wilf had one of her hands and Ada the other. All three were bowing. Wilf was making her take a call as if the whole performance had been planned in advance as part of the Talboys' Surprise Package for Wet Summer Nights in Beale.

"Are you all right?" Wilf whispered out of the corner of his mouth. "You look terrible."

"Aye, I'm . . ."

"Bow, an' get off, luv. Leave it to us now," Wilf said.

"I . . ."

"Take a breather, Mirrin," Ada murmured. "We'll pick them all up again, never fear."

Mirrin staggered back into the wings.

Wilf was making one of his little speeches. She knew that she had left them a difficult task. But, a moment later, Blanche passed her, then Pru, and a little after that as she leaned against the wing post, her heart pounding, she heard the strains of 'Paddle Your Own Canoe' start up from the orchestra trough.

She moved away, drenched in sweat, stifled by the theatre trappings, out of the rear door on to the narrow area of planking reserved for the artistes.

Rain streaked the lamps along the promenade. The crests of the big combers were faintly phosphorescent, huge and surgingly powerful, rolling in from the dark to swarm and seethe against the wrought-iron stanchions and swallow up the shingle.

Quickly the night air's turbulence and the activity of the sea calmed her and brought her down to earth again. Her dress was wet. It would require to be dried, cleaned and ironed before tomorrow evening's show.

Tomorrow's evening show. The thought did not stimulate her. She was beset by the incredible vividness of her vision of Lamont there in the circle. Some man who resembled him, no doubt; a trick that her imagination had played on her, a penalty, perhaps, for opening memories of Blacklaw like a blocked-up seam.

No it could not be Houston. But the rationalisation did not still her longing to be with her coalmaster once more, even to be home in Blacklaw and thole the family's crises as they came.

A house becomes a home when a child is in it: while Flora Stalker whole-heartedly approved of the sentiment, there were times that summer when she suspected that it had been coined by some spinster lady who had never personally experienced the disruption that a baby can cause to domestic routine. Not that wee Neill was not a joy and deserving of every minute devoted to his welfare, but the round of feeding, washing and changing, added to the fact that both his Auntie and his Gran' were working women, took its toll of peace and quiet. It was only in the last hour of the day, long past bedtime, that Flora and Kate were able to snatch a few minutes of relaxation together by the hearth. Even then their hands were not idle.

Neill was a bonny child, his features, though decidedly Stalker, disarmingly softened by fair curling lashes and the bluest of blue eyes. Flora had shown little or no curiosity about his mother, though Kate had told the older woman all that had happened in Edinburgh, quite enough to expose Drew's callousness to the poor highland girl who had died. It was too sore a subject for discussion.

Flora held up the cotton cut which she had scissored from an old sheet to add to Neill's collection of nappies.

"How one wee scrap of a lad can make so much work, I don't know."

"Don't blame the lamb," said Kate. "All your boys were the same; spoiled."

"I'm not spoilin' him, am I?"

"It's hard t'avoid it," said Kate. "I suppose when he's a bit older, it'll be me that has to give him a lick wi' the strap when he needs it."

"He'll not need it," said Flora. "He's an angel, that's what he is."

The wet nurse had made her last visit over an hour ago, and the infant lay sound asleep in the wooden cradle that Alex Stalker had made for his first son almost thirty years ago. It had done Trojan service since then, that strong well-balanced piece of carpentry, and all the Stalkers, save Drew, had slept in it during infancy. Being a twin, Drew had been obliged to grant the use of the cradle to Betsy, and had been bedded in a dressing table drawer instead.

Flora folded the blanket from Neill's sleeping face and returned to the big chair by the hearth to unpick the remains of an ancient knitted petticoat. With the best of the wool ripped out and washed it could be knitted up into socks and a coat for the baby, though it was a pity the colour was so awful. Plum was hardly fitting for a mite only months old.

"Maggie Fox's man's back at work," said Kate, glancing up from her sewing. "His broken head's mendin' fine. They were always a hard-headed bunch the Williamses."

"Have y'heard where Donald Wyld's gone?"

"Not a word," said Kate. "Not even Dunlop seems t'know an' he's usually full o'other folks' business."

"Where's it goin' t'end?" Flora asked. "With this Thrush man in charge."

"Not in closure, that's for sure," said Kate. "Thrush is far too determined ever t'see the Blacklaw colliery shut down."

"It's all Houston Lamont's fault," said Flora.

"Maybe it is." Kate knew better than to be drawn. Flora said, "I've sometimes wondered if he an' Mirrin . . . ?"

"Honestly, Mam, that imagination of yours will bring trouble some day."

"But she . . . she got so much out of him, an' him the coalmaster too."

"She pricked his conscience, that's all."

"I never cared for her working at Lamont's house. Your father would never have approved."

"She did it for Drew, an' for the rest of us."

Flora sighed. "Still, she's well out of it, even if she is mixed up with theatricals now. The Lord knows what'll become of her."

"Mirrin'll always fall on her feet," Kate said. "Is Betsy comin' home tonight?"

"No, she's stayin' over in Hamilton."

"Again!" said Kate. "Who with this time?"

"Margaret-Anne, I think. There's a big prayer meetin' in the Hamilton hall. They're goin' t'that, she said."

"Our Betsy never struck me as the sort t'catch a dose of religion."

"Now, now, Kate," Flora admonished. "It doesn't do t'talk that way. Our Betsy's entitled t'worship as she chooses. Besides, it's better than flirtin' after men, or gettin' caught up with a fast crowd."

"She's changed."

"She's growin' up," said Flora. "It's natural she should want a bit of freedom."

A stinging remark came to Kate's tongue but she resisted the temptation to blurt out her suspicions. She had met Margaret-Anne Potter, another employee of Dalzells', two weeks ago and Margaret-Anne had been decidedly cagey about her friendship with Betsy and their sudden burgeoning interest in religion.

Kate said, "Did y'see the 'beauty hint' Betsy's got pinned t'the mirror in her room?"

"Aye," said Flora, chuckling. "Spread bacon fat on a linen cloth and tie it up your jaws. Can y'imagine any sane woman goin' t'bed of a night in that state. Her man would have a fit."

"Society ladies do it," said Kate. "It's a cure for a double chin."

"Any fat I've got spare will go for fryin' an' not for plasterin' on my face." Flora paused, however, and, setting down the coils of wool, tapped the back of her hand under her throat. "Anyhow, I haven't got a double chin, have I?"

"Well, not much of one, Mam," said Kate.

Frowning anxiously, Flora said, "Have I? Even the start o'one?"

"In a woman of your age, it's . . ."

"*My age?* What d'y'mean, girl? My age, indeed!"

"Well, you're not exactly a spring chicken, Mam."

"I'm not that old."

Kate said, "Well, Willy Kellock seems t'think you're young enough at least."

Flora Stalker busied herself with the petticoat on her lap again, her big thick fingers scrambling at the skeins.

"I'm not daft, Mam," Kate said. "I've known why the wee man drops in here of a night when the last round's done on the van."

"He comes for a cup o'tea, that's all."

"He's got better quality tea in his caddy at home, I'll wager," said Kate. "I think he comes for your company."

"He's . . . he's lonely."

"Aye," said Kate. "An' on the lookout t'do somethin' about it, if I'm not mistaken."

"I will not hear a word against Mr. Kellock. He's been very generous t'me; a woman couldn't wish for a more considerate employer."

"He'll maybe not be your employer for long, Mam."

"I doubt if Mr. Kellock would pay me off. I give him his moneysworth."

"I'm not thinkin' of you bein' paid off."

"Kate, I find this conversation . . . most . . . indelicate."

"Willie fancies you, Mam," Kate said. "He's a perfect gentleman, an' he's kind an' considerate. All that's true. After all, what's the harm in it?"

"What reason have you . . . ?"

"The casual calls; the cups o'tea; the attentions—I'm not blind, Mam."

"No! Well!" muttered Flora. Her embarrassment was acute, and girlish. "Is it . . . wrong, Kate?"

"Never in this world," said Kate, reaching forward to pat Flora's hand reassuringly. "If Mr. Kellock *has* any intentions, I'm quite sure they're most honourable."

"I . . . I wouldn't want you t'think badly of me, Kate."

"I think you're a treat," said Kate. "An' I can't blame the bakerman for gettin' a glint in his eye when he looks at you."

Flora blushed again.

"The point is, d'you like him?" Kate asked.

"Aye, I must confess I like him fine."

"Then there's no need t'blush."

"But it hardly seems right at my age."

"At any age, Mam, a bit of affection is not t'be ignored."

"I wonder if . . ."

"Well," said Kate, "we'll just have t'wait 'till William plucks up his courage, won't we?"

"Oh," said Flora Stalker, shocked. "I would never dare consider that it might come t'that."

"But if it did, would you have him?"

"Aye, I think I would," Flora Stalker said, without the least trace of hesitation.

Six

❦

THE STORM HAD deposited veils of salt on all the windows of the sea-faced saloons, opaque screens behind which the bay glittered green and white in the sunshiny breeze that blew in from Cork and marched the waves in slanting droves up on the Lancashire shore. Wisely, Wilf Talboys defied Ockram's demand for a continuance of the nerve-racking regime of show after show. After that tormented Tuesday night's performance, Wilf cut back to a standard four, allowing his brave little troupe to rest and store energy for the patrons who paid good money to share the artistes' cheerful vitality.

Mirrin's contribution to the morning hour was reduced to a single twenty-minute sketch. The children loved her as much as the adults who accompanied them but, being discriminating customers only to a degree, the boys and girls did not object to a limited appearance; the more so as Mirrin had equipped herself with a variety of interesting props, including a horse on wheels, built by the resident stagehands, which trundled across the stage with its ears and tail flapping, and even appeared to eat peanuts from its owner's hand. She enjoyed the morning appearance, when she was fresh and responsive to the youngsters' unabashed delight at her clownish antics.

By eleven-fifteen her stint on stage was over, the grease wiped from her face, her costume hung away neatly on the rack. Then she would sally into the smaller of the tearooms, drink tea and eat a Paris bun to keep her going until one o'clock luncheon in Nixon's dining room. With the others still in the theatre, Mirrin usually took her morning refreshment alone, or as

alone as her admirers allowed her to be. There were
many men in Beale, not all bachelors either, who
would have intruded on her privacy if she had given
them token encouragement. As it happened, however,
that Thursday a race meeting in Fridswith had drained
Beale of most of its sporting gentlemen and Mirrin was
alone at the marble table in the quietest corner of the
light and airy room.

Off to her left the big brass urns chugged softly,
punctuated by an occasional rattle of cups and sau-
cers or the hiss of a mineral water being opened. A
dozen or so ladies and elderly gentlemen drank tea
and talked, mulled over the latest journals or wrote
their postcards to friends still stuck in humdrum towns
and smokey cities. There was a feeling of ease in the
air, not languid but gently effervescent, mimicking
the mood of the weather.

Mirrin had lifted her second cup of tea, holding it,
ladylike, with finger and thumb of her right hand while
her left palm supported the saucer. She no longer had
to consciously apply such niceties of etiquette. She was
not so far removed from Mirrin Stalker of Blacklaw,
however, that she could resist the sprinkling of soft
yellow crumbs on her plate. Removing her glove she
dabbed them up with her pinkie and licked them.
She lifted the cup once more.

Behind the salt-speckled glass, the figure was bold
in outline, but indistinct in detail. Mirrin made ready
to angle her wickerwork chair and turn a haughty
shoulder to the man who, she suspected, might be another Peeping Tom, one of several who goggled at
her from time to time with all the insensitivity of spectators at a zoo. Out of the corner of her eye she
watched a grey glove rise and rub the glass with a
circular motion. A visible aperture appeared in the
opaqueness, like an Eskimo's fishing hole in ice.
Through that clear space, Mirrin glimpsed Houston
Lamont's face, quite unmistakably, stooped to look in
at her.

She put down her teacup, watching the man walk
along the deck and enter the tall door. He looked
straight at her, not smiling, paused to remove his hat

and gloves, then came on, walking between the tables with a careful, determined tread, until he stood at Mirrin's side.

The spare lines of his features gave him an unexpected hardness. Lowered lids and compressed lips seemed more suited to a person bent on vengeance rather than reconciliation.

"Houston." Mirrin resisted the impulse to rise. She was no longer a servant. She was lady enough to deserve his respect, especially so far from Blacklaw, especially as *he* had sought *her* out. "Houston, this is such a pleasant surprise!"

She offered her hand. He took it, raising it to his lips. The formal affection was at odds with the emotional intimacy of their last meeting. Even at that precise moment of reunion, Mirrin sensed in her heart that the love she had once entertained for this man had altered and, in changing, had diminished in intensity. From the first she was gentle with him, but cautious of the effect of time and the whirlygig of circumstances upon them both.

"I knew that you were in Beale," he said. "I had to see you."

"Do sit down, Houston," Mirrin said, pleasantly. "Would you care for tea?"

"No, thank you."

"At least sit yourself," Mirrin said. "I find it rather dauntin' to have to look up at you."

Stiffly, the coalmaster seated himself. He was tense too, almost trembling.

"You look well," he said.

"I'm in the best of health, thank you," Mirrin said. "How long have you been here?"

"A day or two," Houston said. "I've been travelling, you see."

"Really! Abroad?"

"I spent two weeks in the Low Countries, but this past fortnight I've been visiting mines and pits in Lancashire and Yorkshire."

"You haven't become an Inspector for the Queen, I hope?" said Mirrin, jestingly.

Houston took her seriously. "No, I have no qualification for that post, even if I wished to obtain it," he said. "I have been examining those pits which have adopted the use of advanced machinery, particularly cutters and steam-pump ventilators."

"I gather Blacklaw colliery is weathering the slump, then?"

"As well as can be expected," said Houston. "Are you not in correspondence with your mother and sisters?"

"I've had the occasional line from Kate," said Mirrin. "She told me about your sister. I'm so sorry, Houston. I hope Dorothy suffered no pain."

"She simply drifted away from me," Houston said. "It was a mercy, I suppose. She was virtually a prisoner in that upstairs room. Barred windows, and . . . However, she is well out of it, Mirrin. She asked for you shortly before she died. She always thought of you—as I did."

Mirrin did not reply. There was nothing to say. Houston understood that there had been affection between his sister and herself, that it was not lack of love, or even of respect, that had broken their relationship.

Now, hesitating only for an instant, Houston Lamont said, "I have missed you, Mirrin. In months I've thought of nothing but the brief period we shared together."

The speech was sincere, yet bewildered, as if, now that he was face to face with her once more, Houston could not quite reconcile memory with reality. Indeed, she had changed. She was a fashionable young lady now.

Confirming the feeling, he said, "I can hardly believe that it's you."

"Would you have preferred it, Houston, if I'd been wearing my black serge hand-me-down overcoat?"

"Don't reprimand me, Mirrin, please. I had to come here. Don't you understand? There's nothing for me in Blacklaw."

"There's the pit, the mansion—and your wife, Houston."

"The pit is in the best of hands . . ."

"That's not what I heard."

"Thrush is a clever manager."

"Clever enough to usurp Donald Wyld."

"You can know nothing of this, except by hearsay."

Mirrin nodded. "That's true, Houston. Besides, Blacklaw is far off. Look out there at the sea. Isn't it pretty?"

"The mansion is no longer home to me," Lamont went on relentlessly. "After Dorothy's death, there was nothing left. Nothing."

"And your wife?"

"Pah! Mirrin! Do you expect me to lie? You know the truth on that score better than anyone alive. Edith may have the house, aye, and the damned pit too. All I want is my freedom."

"Freedom is not so easily come by, Houston," Mirrin said. "I've found that out the hard way, believe me."

"Very well: not freedom then. All I want is to be with you again."

Mirrin was even more apprehensive than before. There had been nothing flighty in her love for the coalmaster, no self-seeking. But his emotional intensity had increased and she was afraid of being engulfed in the torrent of feeling that flooded from this man.

"Come with me, Mirrin."

"Come where?"

"Anywhere."

"Walking, do you mean? I have a performance at . . ."

"Damn your performance." The surly fury in his face startled her. *"Come with me."*

"I'm not your servant now, Houston," Mirrin retorted. "I'd ask you to remember that."

He drew himself together. "Yes, Mirrin. I . . . I apologise. It's just that . . . that I have been so . . . so long alone." He managed a smile of sorts: it had no warmth in it, only a wryness that indicated a bitterness so incredibly fixed that Mirrin acknowledged it as an indelible facet of the man. "Will you walk with me? Will you, please, take lunch with me?"

"My . . . my friends are expecting me."

"Mirrin, please: please, my love."

"I'll leave a note for them," she said. "But I must be back at the theatre by half past two, no later."

"My hotel is not far away, at the Cornville end of Beale."

"Which hotel, Houston?"

"The Park."

"Ah, yes," said Mirrin. "The Park."

Houston may pretend to have appeared casually in Beale, though he made no bones about his motive for coming to the resort, but in selecting the Park Hotel up back of the Cornville promenade, he had shown a certain wiliness that was not typical of him. The Park had a reputation. It was luxurious enough, very luxurious, in fact, and expensive; but it was not the sort of place that a single young lady would, or should, go with a gentleman, not even for luncheon. It was a place where 'arrangements' were brought to fruition. The management had perfected discretion disguised as courtesy, so that the most debased harlot in Lancashire could be sure of an unctuous welcome, provided she dressed to the nines, kept her voice down, and sailed in on the arm of wealth.

"How did you come to choose the Park, Houston?" Mirrin asked, as she gathered her handbag and gloves.

"I asked a station porter for his recommendation."

"I see," said Mirrin.

"It seems a very comfortable establishment. The chef is reputed to be French."

"If you have no objection," Mirrin said, taking his arm, "I would prefer to eat in English style, at least at luncheon."

"Where do you suggest?"

"The White Hart is more convenient."

"For the theatre, you mean?"

"Aye, for the theatre."

"Very well."

"I'll leave a message with the stagehand to tell my friends not to expect me for lunch."

"But you do intend to return by half past two, do you?"

"Certainly, Houston," Mirrin said. "That's the time of my next 'shift', you see."

In marriage, Mirrin had noticed, physical passion often burned off quickly, leaving affection and tenderness as a residue and, sometimes, precious little of those honest qualities. In her affair with Houston Lamont, however, it seemed that the love between them had condensed to a raw, almost painful hunger on the coalmaster's part, an appetite for something beyond sexual satisfaction, for a form of communion that could never be grasped, a longing that could not be appeased by love-making.

Mirrin was reminded of the tales Houston had told her of his family, of the pride and the passions that were in them, a kind of possessive madness that had driven some Lamonts to despair before now and had tainted the survivors and inheritors with the stigma of power, and an urge to treat fate like a caged beast, brutally setting out to tame it, and their own pagan natures, in face to face confrontation, time and time again.

It was her task during those preliminary meetings to reduce the overpowering desperation that was in the man, to stabilise his feelings for her into some recognisable facsimile of the love they had once shared, illicitly, in the mansion in the oaks. Had the fillip of deceit been essential to that love, the girl wondered, or had she merely been too immature to uncover the immaturity in him? The authority of his position in Blacklaw as owner, emperor and lord of the little town, had that been the main source of his attraction? No, she could not believe it. The memories were too sweet, too soft, to suit the changes that had taken place in their lives and characters. If, subconsciously, Lamont sought for a doom as thunderous and outright as his ancestors had fashioned for themselves, then she wanted no part of it.

Oddly, now that she was with him again, she loved him less than she had done in parting and during the eventful months of their separation. Perhaps that was a natural transition for a young woman. It did not seem proper in a mature man, though, a man of such authority as the coalmaster of a thriving policy.

Even as she allowed Houston to court her, forced him to restrain his ferocious desire to possess her, Mirrin experienced a faint wistful regret that she had given up the tinker lad, airy Tom Dandy, without sharing his bed. That relationship should have been purged of romance by the sweat and awkwardness of fulfilment, in physical union. If Tom had sought her out here in Beale, she would have been better pleased. Tom was a traveller, moving out of himself in a search not for cure but for happiness. Tom would have fair enjoyed himself in Beale. He would have made a fine escort for a music-hall queen, in that small town. But it was not Tom Armstrong that drifted into Lancashire that summer, it was Houston Lamont. There was no signal drift in him. He had a purpose, a fixed, dogged purpose—and she, at that period, was afraid of purposes.

It was Sunday before she allowed him to take her to luncheon to the snug dining room of the Park Hotel. She made no great show of resistance, nor had she kept Houston's presence secret. She had changed her style hardly at all, going through with her daily routine of walks upon the promenade, tea at the pier, rides upon the sand, an early morning bathe. Though Houston accompanied her, he did not join in. He remained aloof from all her attempts to make him forget himself, to heal the wounds that he seemed to regard as his due, as a soldier invalided out of war must wear his excuses boldly. She introduced Houston to the Talboys and Pru, to Ockram, to the friendly Nixons. She persuaded him to dine with them, early, at the Lucia Street hotel.

In company, Lamont was formal and courteous but reserved and disapproving. Mirrin could understand his priggishness. This pleasurable world was new to him. If only he would allow himself to accept each day as it came. But it was not in him. He thought only of the moment when he would recapture the love that had been. And yet, Mirrin knew, that kind of love had gone and could never be recalled. If only Houston would realise that it must be shaped anew, in another form. But he resisted change, resisted light-heartedness. He even resisted her.

Mirrin sensed that Houston *was* doomed, fated to suffer grievous disappointment. To delay that dreadful moment of disillusionment she held back, until there was no longer a point to it and she too sought for something, *some* echo of the warmth that had been theirs back in Blacklaw, in the winter of '74.

In the afternoon, when the whole town was out and about in the sunshine, Mirrin and Houston Lamont retired to the room on the Park's second floor, a room dominated by a huge brass-knobbed bedstead, a room curtained, shuttered and overly warm, a room designed for a single purpose.

Lamont was not rough with her. He had not so far forgotten himself as to demand a response as fervid as his own. At the last he was in awe of Mirrin's beauty, the warmth which she, in honesty, gave in response to his need. His gauntness made him seem less strong than the man she remembered. For the first time she was conscious of the difference in age between them, the twenty years that, in love, seemed as naught, but on the periphery of love cast certain doubtful shadows.

Houston's release was sudden. It exhausted him. He drew back from her, sliding up the quilt to cover them as if he was ashamed of their nakedness, hers as much as his own. He had not been demanding. She had found no real pleasure in the act, and he was aware of it, as he would have been of failure. It was, she supposed, failure of a sort. Turning, she put her arms around him and drew him close. But he would have none of that, not even at that most intimate moment, the moment he had hungered for and dreamed of for many months.

"Houston," she said. "Is it so different for you?"

"It appears to be for you," he replied.

He did not brush her away, propped on the crushed pillow, arm raised to shield his eyes, though there was no brightness in the room, only the dusty suffusion of

sunlight through the brocade-like curtain. Far, far off
were the sounds of children shrieking in delight at
some piece of play upon the apron of sand under the
wall of the Cornville promenade. He did not respond
to her caress.

"You are . . . are easier now," he said, hoarsely.

Mirrin sat up, the quilt slipping from her shoulder.
"Easier, Houston? What d'you mean?"

"Have you . . . borne a child?" The abrupt question
was shockingly explicit. She pulled away from him.

She had supposed that he had evaded the issue of
the baby out of delicacy. Perhaps he had simply not
cared enough to indulge in the commonest of street
gossip. Though Houston was entitled to know whose
child it was—after all he was still Drew's patron to
the tune of twenty pounds each year—she had judged
his silence wrongly. In an instant it all became clear,
the maliciousness, the resentment and the serpentine
confusions of feeling which that bastard infant had
raised not only in Blacklaw but in the coalmaster.

"You think the baby's mine, do you?"

"It is possible, Mirrin. In fact, it is probable. Come
now, who other than a Stalker would find adoption in
the Stalkers' house?"

"Have you spoken to them, to Kate or my
mother?"

"Of course not."

"Then who told you? Edith, that damned vindictive
wife of yours? Or was it this new man, this Thrush
person? Is he the kind that carries tales?"

"*Is* it your child?"

"Do you *think* it is?"

"I . . . I don't know."

Mirrin swung herself from the bed. She had shed
her night-clothes. Nude, she stood before him, saying,
"Look at me, Houston. Look at my body, at my
breasts and my belly. Have I given birth to a baby?"

He glanced at her slyly, then looked away towards
the curtained window.

Mirrin leaped on to the bed. Taking his chin in her
hands she wrenched his face towards her. "You've

made your inspection, Mr. Lamont: *now, what's your opinion?"*

"I owe you an apology, Mirrin."

"Is that all you can say? Is that how you talk t'me, Houston, as if I was a committee in the managers' office? Though, by God, you'd never apologise t'them, now I think of it. Tell me, tell me in plain guid Scottish tongue—did you think I was wicked enough t'get myself with child only weeks after I left you?"

"I thought . . . I could not be sure that . . ."

"Houston, look at me."

"No, I . . . I *hoped* it might be mine." He reached for her then, even as she sought to slip from him, and hugged her tightly to his chest. "Yes, that's the God's truth of it, my love. I *hoped* that the baby might be yours—and mine."

Mirrin sagged against him. She felt a great pity for him, an overwhelming sympathy such as she would have felt for anyone so deprived of love that he or she would disregard the mainstays of common sense by which the world wagged and by which the social order, in Blacklaw and out, was rudely maintained. In his eagerness to firm the slender bond between them, in his desire to spawn something that was his own, not just an heir but a son upon whom he could lavish love, Houston had plunged down into fantasy.

Softly, now, gently, her mouth against his cheek, Mirrin said, "Did you not know that it couldn't be, Houston? You *must* have known."

"But I continued to hope, Mirrin. Oh, God, how I hoped."

It did not matter to him who had fathered the child. All that had tormented him was the illogical aspiration that he had planted a son in her womb. He could no longer refute reality.

She said, "Houston, I've been with no other man since you."

"But you must . . . must . . ."

"Must have been tempted, d'you mean? Aye, perhaps a little, but not enough. I may be a performer now, Houston, but I'm no slut. It isn't like you think with theatricals."

"*No* other man?"

"None," said Mirrin. "I've known no other man but you."

"Do you love me, Mirrin?"

She could not afford to hesitate. She did not know herself if pity was the beginning of love, or the withered leaf on the tree of her girlhood, a weightless memory of the first spring her heart had ever known.

"Yes, Houston, I love you."

Stirring, he kissed her hair, then her cheek and finally crushed his mouth against her lips. The hunger that had been dormant in her was released, and she shifted, rolling from him to lie on the quilt by his side.

It was then, once, as it had been before. They were truly lovers again in the fleeting and forgetful warmth of that Sabbath afternoon in a trysting hotel in Beale.

It would have been pointless to try to hide the affair from the Talboys. They had seen enough of life not to judge Mirrin harshly. Indeed, Pru and Ada were pleased for her and the acknowledgement that she had a lover dissolved the last barriers between her and Blanche. Once it was clear that it was no overnight infatuation and that Mirrin had no immediate intention of 'running off' with the fellow, even Wilfrid became an unwitting conspirator by ensuring that she had some time to herself.

It was Houston's plan to take a cottage in the area so that he might spend as much time as possible with Mirrin. But no such rental was to be found within ten miles of the resort at the height of the August season. At last a compromise was reached, a programme, as it were, which permitted Mirrin to retain her good name and gave Houston as much of her time away from the theatre as was possible. She continued to lodge with her friends at Nixons', but the Park Hotel saw much of her in its dining room and foyer, for she conducted the relationship with Houston without peripheral deceits. Houston hired a gig for their exclusive use. Mirrin reciprocated by taking the lease of a box for every Owls' House, though she did not feel in the least slighted when Houston missed a performance: the musical hall was not really to his taste and there was in him a certain jealousy of the young woman's popularity.

Four days after their first afternoon of love-making, Houston returned, over lunch in the White Hart, to the subject of the Stalkers' foundling.

"Mirrin, I hesitate to raise the subject, but . . ."

"The baby, d'you mean, Houston?"

"Yes," he said. "Is it of the Stalker blood?"

"Have you heard no talk at all in Blacklaw?"

"It's generally accepted in the village that he is yours."

"I suppose that's to be expected."

"Don't you object to such slander?"

She shrugged a little. "It suits the purpose, I suppose. It doesn't do me any harm."

Houston said, "Is your brother Andrew the father?"

"Yes."

"And the mother?"

"She died in childbed."

"Were they . . . were they married?"

"No," said Mirrin. "I'm not being defensive, Houston. But I have very little information about the affair."

"I didn't think that your brother had it in him."

"Had what in him?" asked Mirrin, raising an eyebrow.

"Come now, Mirrin," Houston said. "I am his patron. I do have a certain interest in the lad."

"It was . . . a certain hot-bloodedness, I suspect," said Mirrin. "If I know Drew he'll have learned his lesson."

Houston said, "He has learned his lesson."

"What do you mean?"

"I wrote to Gow Havershaw enquiring after my protégé's welfare," Houston said. "Setting aside his indiscretion, it seems that your brother is forging ahead on all fronts. He is a prize student—Havershaw even sent me the class marks—and he is also the confrère of a most influential bunch."

"Really!"

"You don't seem greatly interested, Mirrin?"

"I'm not," Mirrin said. "As far as I'm concerned Drew can stew in his own juice."

"Do you regret our bargain?"

"I . . . no, I don't regret it, Houston. I'm only sorry that it was necessary. Drew wasn't the cause of our parting."

"You're free of him now, Mirrin," Houston said. "I'm convinced that your brother is more than capable of looking after himself. He has no need of you."

"He'd have been in a right pickle, though, if Kate hadn't come along and taken the baby off his hands. Does Havershaw not know of it?"

"Difficult to tell," said Houston. "I question if he does. He's the type of person who could hardly resist dropping a sly hint. No, my guess is that Drew's managed to bury the matter completely."

"You could pick a better expression, Houston. He buried the child's mother, you know."

"You are strange, you Stalkers," Lamont said.

"I don't think we're strange at all."

"I meant no offence, Mirrin, but how did you, for example, come to be involved with the music-hall?"

"I've told you that tale already."

"That's not what I meant," said Houston. "I meant, how is it that fate, destiny, call it what you will, doles out such richness for the Stalkers, not for others of that ilk?"

"My father dinned it into us that independence of spirit is the most important thing a man—aye, and a woman—can acquire. Nobody in this life is going to look out for you, Houston. You must look out for yourself. Seize every chance."

"But you, and your sister and your mother, you have so much . . . caring in you for others."

"Do we?"

"You care for me, Mirrin. You cared for Dorothy. You cared so much for Dorothy, in fact, that you jeopardised your own happiness for her sake."

"Aye, an' little good it did the poor woman in the end."

"I'm not at all sure, Mirrin, that the exchange was not worth it; that Dorothy was not the better for those

few brief months of happiness before her illness and
her death."

"But . . . ?"

"I had to come here, Mirrin," Lamont said. "I am
—I was—being destroyed."

"By your wife, d'you mean?"

"By myself."

"And now?"

"I want to stay with you."

"I don't think you really mean that, Houston."

"But I do, my darling: I do."

"You want me to be with you?"

"It's the same thing, is it not?"

"No, it's not. I have . . . commitments here."

"Honour them."

"Houston, I don't want to desert the Talboys."

"Then I'll . . . I'll simply tag along."

"It won't work. You must see that. Really you
want me to come with you. If you don't, you will—
and soon, I fancy."

"There's nothing for me in Blacklaw."

"Aye, but there is," Mirrin said.

"Then come back with me."

"To be installed in a house in Hamilton, or
Glasgow? To be idle all day, to wait for you? I'm not
cut out to be a mistress."

"I'll sell the pit to Edith. We'll marry, you and I."

"It's fine to sit here in Lancashire and say that,
Houston, but you know it would not be possible. In
six months, in a year you would regret your decision."

"I hate Blacklaw and all that it stands for."

"But you must go back. Oh, not tomorrow, or next
week, but eventually you must go back. What about
the new programme, the machinery?"

"Thrush's scheme, not mine," said Lamont, vehe-
mently. "I hate him, too, and all that he stands for."

"I think," said Mirrin quietly, "that maybe you envy
him a wee bit too."

"Envy Thrush? Why?"

"Because he has no heart."

Houston smiled at her, crookedly, but she could tell
that her assessment had struck home.

It was the first of many such discussions, each one more bitter, more anxious than its predecessor. Soon, Mirrin knew, they would be so caught up in the future that all pleasure would go out of the present. Even at that stage in the relationship, she was honest enough to realise that Houston and she must part. In every moment of their communion now, in the bedroom and out of it, that sense of impending loss tinged her attitude and made her defensive. For his good, as well as her own, she would persuade him that for the time being they must follow their own separate courses.

Blanche said, "Do you love him very much, Mirrin?"

"I did."

"But you don't any more?"

"I am fond of him," Mirrin said. It was late and she was too tired to become involved in lengthy confidences with Blanche.

"Will you go away with him?"

"No."

"My Mam thinks you will. But Aunt Pru's wagering you'll stick with us."

"What do you think I should do, Blanche?"

"Go with him."

"At all costs?"

"I gave up *my* fellow, Mirrin. I will regret it all my life."

"Gave him up?"

"It was last summer." Blanche turned from the bedroom mirror, her hair spilling down her back, hairbrush poised. She was aware of herself, but the emotions at the root of her performance were genuine enough. "Last summer was my summer. His name is —was—Henry Essam. I met him in Marlingford. We stole a few brief weeks together. He wanted me to marry him and go to live with him in Birmingham."

"What does he do?"

"Henry's *quite* well off. He's a carpenter in his own right. His own shop. He has another shop in Marlingford; actually it's his brother who operates that one. Henry was down for the summer. He said that if I would marry him I might live in either town."

"But you didn't accept?"

"Father didn't approve."

"So you gave him up?"

"I wanted to run away to Birmingham with him but Henry wouldn't hear of it."

"Why ever not?"

"He said he had too much respect for me; he was afeared I might later regret my impetuosity. He wanted it to be square and above board, with Papa's approval. That's the kind of gentleman my Henry was. I'll never find another like him."

"I'm sure you will, Blanche."

"Sometimes I think he is suffering, too, my Henry, and that he'll come for me, just as your friend did. I look out into the stalls and pray that Henry will be there, come to take me away with him. But I fear he's found another girl to be his wife. It's five months since last I wrote to him and he has given no reply."

"Perhaps . . ."

"Mirrin, does it hurt to be loved?" Blanche asked suddenly.

"Hurt?"

"Does it cause pain?"

"Not much," said Mirrin. "If you truly love the man then it isn't pain at all, Blanche, only pleasure."

"But it's wrong to take pleasure that way, for a woman."

"Who told you that: not your Mam?"

"I love Henry, but I'm . . . I'm afraid of it."

"There's nothing to fear, Blanche, believe me."

Blanche returned to her combing. In the light of the oil lamp on the dressing table she looked pretty, yet faded, older than her years.

Matter-of-factly now, she said, "I think it's because I was afraid of marriage that I gave him up so easily. I should have defied Papa."

"Next time you'll know better, Blanche."

"If there is a next time."

"There will be," said Mirrin. "Believe me, luv, life is packed full of second chances. The trick is in knowing which is the right chance to take and just when to take it."

"Mr. Lamont: is he your second chance?"

"I can't answer that, Blanche."

"Won't you confide in me?"

"The truth is that I don't know myself," Mirrin said.

On the occasion of that particular Sunday night visit, Mr. William Kellock had attired himself in a smart navy pinstripe suit, a grey half-cock hat with a silk ribbon which exactly matched the colour of his new suede gloves. A nubby fold watch-chain curled from his buttonhole to his vest pocket and another, finer, chain draped his stomach, firmly anchoring a cluster of fobs and small tokens, memorabilia which he had acquired over the years. William might have appeared natty and pompous except for his armful of paper bags and white card boxes. Ducking under the lintel of the Stalker kitchen—though it cleared his hat by a good four inches—the baker went through a little juggling act with the assorted items and eventually spilled them on to the table cloth, only just avoiding destruction of the fairy cakes that Flora had slaved over that afternoon just to show Mr. Kellock that he wasn't the only one who could produce featherlight sponge mixture.

Given notice of his visit, Flora too had changed into her best dress and had even dug out an ornate brooch and clasp that had come down to her from her husband's mother and which she had seldom found an excuse to wear.

The fire was built up—though the weather was anything but cold—and the hob swept and the brass trim polished and the best plates taken from the top shelf of the corner dresser and, in general, the whole ceremony gone through with an assiduousness that made Kate wonder if Willie Kellock had been secretly knighted by the Queen for his contributions to the art of the crusty loaf.

In response to her mother's promptings Kate too had spent some time making herself 'decent' for the baker's visit. As she put the last touches to her hair, it did in fact occur to her that some kind of change was very much in the air and that this traditional, if rare, formality was a surefire sign that Willie could wait no longer.

Flora's behaviour confirmed Kate's suspicions, and Willie's tumbling arrival into the narrow house had all the fluster and nervousness of a younger swain about to bend his knee to a stern patriarch.

Composing herself, Kate rescued Mr. Kellock from the slough of embarrassment, by relieving him of his hat, gloves and all the gifts, piling the objects neatly on a vacant chair until such time as Willie saw fit to dispense his bounty. The baker got rid of them at once.

"Just a few trifling oddments," he said, with a stuttering chuckle. "Better than giving them to the horse, eh, Mrs. Stalker?"

"Thank you, Mr. Kellock."

"An' . . . an' a bone-ring for the babby in that box there, an' a wee something for you ladies."

"Most kind of you, Mr. Kellock," said Kate.

She was glad that Betsy was not at home; by this time her youngest sister would have assumed that expression of indulgent disdain which would surely be her reaction to the baker's onslaught on etiquette.

"You'll be about ready for supper, Mr. Kellock?" said Kate, since both Willie and her mother seemed incapable of intelligent utterance at that moment. They were seated now across the hearth from each other as if testing out the domestic position with caution.

Tonight Willie could relax. He stared up at Kate and wrung his hands, saying, "Supper, Miss Stalker?" as if he never heard the word before.

"Just a slice of ham and a wee bit cold mutton," Kate said.

"Oh' Aye! Supper! Please, Miss Stalker."

Kate put the filled kettle on the hob, then noticing Mam's flushed expression, said, "Maybe I'll . . . er, just pop down t'the corner for a breath of fresh air."

"What?" Mam said. "No!"

"Stay, please, Miss Stalker," said the baker with fluttering anxiety.

"Mr. Kellock, I'm not the one t'play gooseberry."

"Gooseberry? But . . . but, it's you I came t'see."

"Me?"

"Och, I didn't mean it t'come out like this." With a heavy sigh Willie resigned himself to brusqueness. "I wanted t'ask for your hand in marriage."

"Me?" said Kate again, utterly dumbfounded.

"Aye. Did y'not guess?"

"I . . . I thought . . ."

"You must've had some inklin', Kate?"

There was silence in the kitchen for a moment. Kate did not dare look at her mother. She groped for the kitchen chair and seated herself upon it. All along Willie's gentle wooing had been directed at her, not at Mam. She couldn't believe it.

Flora was first to recover. She gave no sign at all that she had been slighted. "Well, that's a surprise, Mr. Kellock. Though you're right: Kate hasn't been oblivious . . . t'your intentions. Have you, dear?"

"But Mam?"

Flora's expression was motherly and reassuring. "Let's all sit down at the table."

Willie Kellock's agitation had changed in tone. He cleared his throat. "How's the wee chap, then?"

"Fast asleep in the back room," said Flora. "It was a struggle t'get him down, as usual. He's as full of energy as a basket o'puppies."

"That's healthy for a growing bairn," said Willie, transferring himself from the fireside to the deal table and, out of habit, bending to inspect the fairy cakes with a critical eye. "Aye, these look nice an' light."

"Kate made them," Mam said.

Kate opened her mouth to protest at the lie, then closed it again. She could not be absolutely sure that her mother had not known all along of Willie's real matrimonial target. She busied herself preparing tea, let it infuse only for a moment then poured out cups for everybody. She put the cold meats on the table together with a loaf and fresh butter, then took her own seat, her back to the door. She had regained her composure. Her impulse now was to thank the baker for the compliment of his proposal, then firmly turn him down. It wasn't Kellock's fault that they—she at least—had misconstrued the source of his affections and jumped to the wrong conclusion. So it would be wrong, wrong and cruel, to hurt him. Fully aware that she had not given an answer she tried to appear genial but indecisive.

"As . . . as t'your proposal, Mr. Kellock . . ." she began.

"You'd better call me Willie, Kate."

"Aye, well, Willie, I'll have t'ask for time to consider it."

"Of course: of course." Delight at not being sent packing with a flea in his ear illuminated the baker's rubicund face. "Take all the time y'want, Kate. But . . . but there's somethin' I intended t'say before I got rushed into things." He darted a glance from Flora to Kate. "I have the very highest regard for both you ladies, an' you know how taken I am with the wee boy. If you'll do me the honour of becomin' my wife, Kate, I'll care for all of you and provide amply for all your needs, just as though you were m'own family."

There was no mistaking his sincerity.

Touched, Kate smiled shakily. "I'm . . . I'm grateful an' flattered Mr. Kel . . . Willie. I'll give the matter most serious consideration an' let you have an answer shortly. It's not that . . . that I don't like an' respect you in return, please understand. But . . ."

"No hurry: no hurry at all, lass," Willie assured her. He too seemed relieved that there would be a breathing space, a period of courtship during which he could impress her with his worthiness and enjoy the excitement, mellow though it was, of a second wooing.

Relaxing, the baker quickly steered conversation round to town gossip and chattered on about one safe subject after another. While Flora responded, Kate was much occupied with her own thoughts. It was something new to her to learn that she had attracted the attention, the love, of a man. Even if her suitor was nearly twice her age, it warmed her to realise that she was wanted. It was only the second time in her life that any man had asked her to marry him; the first one, ten years syne, had turned out to be a rogue just out for a bit of fun, who had a wife and bairns salted away in a hovel in Lanark. But there was no such dishonesty about Willie Kellock: he was as kind and honourable a man as she could hope to find in the whole county. After a while, she gave him her attention and joined in the general conversation until it was after midnight and the baker, used to an early bed, took his leave.

Kate saw him to the door. When she returned Mam had already begun to clear the table and wash up the willow pattern plates in the basin in the sink.

Lifting the drying cloth, Kate busied herself too.

"Well," she said at length, "that *was* a surprise."

"Was it not, now?" Flora said, without turning.

"I'm . . . I'm sorry, Mam. I wouldn't have hurt you for worlds. I thought . . . I thought it was you he wanted for his wife."

"I'm not hurt, Kate. Anyway, I should've had more sense at my age, than t'think about another husband. No, the important thing is that you marry that man."

"You *want* me t'marry Willie?"

"He's fond of you, that's apparent."

"But I'm not in love with him."

"You don't even know the meanin' o'that word, Kate."

"Mam, that's unfair."

"A roof over your head, a fire in the grate an' a bite always on the table, those are more important things than love."

"But we have those things already."

"Aye, but for how long?" Flora swung round. "There's no security here, Kate. Aye, Lamont's made over the tenancy t'us, but who's t'say that he'll not take it into his head t'revoke it. Mirrin's not here now: she was always the bargainer, the one who could handle Lamont. Besides, you've heard how radically he's changed, how unreliable he's become this past year, especially since his sister died."

"Security, Mam? Is that a reason t'marry?"

"Reason enough, Kate. If Lamont throws us out, then where would we go, you an' Betsy an' me, not t'mention wee Neill?"

"It's Neill you're really thinkin' of, isn't it?"

"Aye, it is."

Kate sighed. It was too much for her. Once more she was being coaxed into accepting responsibility for the family. Not that she grudged them their share. Neill in particular had brought purpose back into her life. But sacrificing her freedom was quite another matter, the more so as they were struggling along comfortably enough on their own.

"Did you know that Willie Kellock was keen on me?" she asked.

"I . . . I knew he liked you, Kate."

"But you thought he intended you for his wife?"

"I did incline t'the opinion that he would propose t'me, Kate, not t'you."

"Would you have accepted him, Mam?"

"Aye."

"Why?"

"Because I like him."

"T'provide security for the rest of us?"

"That too, lass," Flora said. "It's all I can hope for at my age."

"But if not you—me?" Kate said. "D'you suppose that it's all up with me, too; that only a man like the baker, nice as he is, will have me now?"

"He's not that old," Flora said. "Willie'll make you a good home. He'll leave you comfortably off when he dies, you can be sure of that."

"An' children?"

"Children?"

"Bairns, Mam? Will he give me bairns?"

"Well, that's . . . that's not a decent question t'ask, Kate."

"Do you think I'm too far gone for that too?"

"Child-bearin's more difficult at your age."

"My age? I'm not yet thirty, Mam. I only *seem* old."

"I take it," said Flora Stalker, "that you're goin' t'reject Mr. Kellock's generous offer of marriage?"

"I don't know," said Kate. "Right now, I'm goin' t'my bed."

"Kate?"

"I promise I'll think about it, Mam, but don't badger me. If I decide t'take Willie Kellock for a husband then it'll be because I want to: not for you, nor Betsy, nor even for wee Neill."

"He's a good man, Kate."

"I know that: that's what makes it difficult."

"Would you rather he was wicked?"

"I'd rather he was younger, if you must know."

"Age has nothin' t'do with . . ."

"I'll be a widow at fifty, Mam, like as not, an' I've no hankerin' to spend my old age alone."

"What'll you tell him?"

"I'll give him an answer in my own good time."

Seven

THE GIG SAT high on its steel and leather springs, riding above all other transports except horse-omnibuses and the huge lumbering carts in which sea-food merchants of Deverham and Spearsbridge carried their wares to the railway at Beale for daily distribution into the hinterlands of Lancashire and Yorkshire. The promenade and coastal rides were crowded that fine August afternoon. A breeze had sprung up fresh and warm, chasing away the somnolent haze which had shrouded the wings of the bay since Sunday, imparting to the resort a brisk cheerful summery atmosphere which was much enjoyed by its holiday guests and the excursion intruders.

Mirrin and Houston sat side by side on the padded leather seat, the man with the reins held lightly in his brown hands, the woman with one hand raised to hold on her hat. The pace was hardly brisk now that the gig had entered the main stem of the town coming from Cornville into dense traffic at the pierhead and the picnic lawns where the hotels and boarding houses clustered on the hill among their massy shrubs and white iron railings.

The coalmaster and the music-hall performer had established a relationship as fragile as the sticks of spun sugar sold from the stalls along the front. At that particular moment, however, Mirrin was content to enjoy the ride, the vantage point, the warm breeze smelling of the sea. She had grown used to the attentions of the crowds, the turning of heads, the disapproving stoop of a wife's shoulders, the whispers of old maids and acid widows, the chirruping of the bolder bucks and apprentices in from Preston, or Bolton or Widnes, as she rode openly with her lover along Beale's most public thoroughfare. She waved to the pierrots setting up their benches on the sand. She waved to the juggler who had curtailed his act to catch a bite of dinner from a paper bag. She waved to the many friends she'd made in the town and to the many who waved to her or called out some jovial remark as the gig threaded haltingly through the other vehicles towards the Grand.

Houston, too, she thought, should be happy enough to seize the moment as it came, though the vulgar bustle of the holiday town was not his proper milieu. There were times when Mirrin had caught him with a brooding, almost hostile fire in his eyes as he surveyed the paddlers and the bathers, the picnickers, the canoodlers, the gamesters and the busy cross-section of England that came for a sniff of the briny and to inspect the bosom of the deep. It was clear that privately Houston did not approve. She wondered what his ideal haunt would be? A grouse moor in the Highlands, a boating holiday in Holland—very fashionable she'd heard—or a trek round the art treasures of France or Italy? Perhaps Houston had no taste at all for travel, other than for the purpose of business—or pursuit. His capacity for passive enjoyment of life's pleasures had always been thin; now it was almost non-existent. Only in the sanctuary of the Park's bedroom, with the drapes drawn against the light, did her lover cast off his burden of depression and become, in part, more like the man she remembered. After three weeks of his company, Mirrin sensed that his moodiness concerned her, though she had not the temerity to press him for reasons.

Look at him, even now, on this gay, light-hearted sort of day, his face bronzed, his health apparently restored, driving with a woman whom he professed to love—yet not here, not present, mentally far, far off in some sinister land of his imagination. Was it the past he longed for, a past that he had created out of the dull fragments of reality? Or did he—the thought made Mirrin shiver a little—did he in fact regret that he had ever come to love her, that they had ever met? How could that regret flourish here so far from Blacklaw's grim and reeking slag heaps, from mud and grime, the tar-black winding towers looming over the railway dumps? Was that, after all, Houston Lamont's only true domain? Had he at last proved the fact beyond doubt to himself?

"Come on, luv, give us a smile: just a little one," she said, putting her hand on his shoulder. "It's such a beautiful afternoon, and the luncheon, as always, was excellent."

"Yes."

"Is that all you can say? Yes?"

"I don't want you to go to the theatre this afternoon."

"Ah, so that's what's biting you, Houston. Well, I must."

"Stay with me."

"It's only a couple of hours."

"I would prefer you to be with me."

"And I would prefer to be with you."

"Then send a message; tell them you're unwell. Talboys will understand."

"I'm as fit as a fiddle, and Wilf knows it. He saw me at the morning show."

"I beg you, Mirrin, please stay with me?"

"Houston, I can't," she protested. "Look, if you like I'll see if I can call out of Friday's performance, the matinée. We could drive to the races. Are there races on Friday?"

"Today. I need you today."

"At twenty minutes to curtain: I'm not that callous."

"Only to me."

"If you had even asked me this morning . . ."

"You owe me one afternoon."

"I can't let Wilf and Ada down. It would mean so much bother for them, so much palaver."

"I see," Houston said. "Your loyalty to them supersedes your love for me. I think you are using me, Mirrin."

"How dare you say that?" Anger erupted in her. She flung herself from his side across to the opposite bench so that she could study his profile, seeking in his sour expression some clue as to the reason for this demanding outburst. Under the sun-tan his flesh was ashen, bruised shadows beneath his eyes, the sockets deep. He was, she realised, completely oblivious to Beale, concentrating only on achieving his desire. It was not unexpected. Sooner or later she had anticipated that he would test her feelings. But this method was crude with a cruel quality which swiftly changed her anger into fear. "What is it, dearest? What's wrong? You were so silent at lunch too. Are you ill?"

"This came."

Mirrin took the letter which Houston extracted from his coat pocket and held out to her. The envelope, she noticed, bore a lawyers' seal on the left-hand corner.

"It was forwarded to me from Menzies Paton, my Glasgow solicitor," Houston explained. "Edith does not know my exact whereabouts."

"Do you wish me to read it?"

"Of course."

"Draw in the gig, Houston, there by the side of the square."

The letter was curt in the extreme. It said: *"It may interest you to know, sir, that Mr. Donald Wyld, lately of your employ, was killed outright during a roof fall in the Geddie Glen pit in Fife on Wednesday of last week."*

Carefully Mirrin folded the letter and returned it to the envelope. She offered it to Lamont. The gig was now at rest, the horse passive, out of the mainstream of traffic.

"Donald Wyld—dead!" the woman said softly.

"Do you see where he died?"

"Geddie Glen," said Mirrin. "Aye, I've heard of it. I thought the Inspectors had closed it down."

"A death trap," said Lamont. "He had been there only a week or two, apparently. It could not have been longer. A day or two, for all I know."

"Don't blame yourself, Houston."

"He was a good, loyal employee and my friend. I dismissed him for no reason."

"You told me he had resigned."

"He felt he could not work with Thrush."

"I see," said Mirrin. "Aye, it's a sad thing, right enough. There were few in Blacklaw had a real bad word to say about Wyld. Oh, they cursed him from time to time and blamed him for all the ills of the day, but they respected him nonetheless."

"And I killed him. He must have known how dangerous the Geddie pit was," Lamont said. "But for me, Wyld would still be alive."

"God, Houston, you're talkin' like a collier, not an owner. I've heard that selfsame thing said about you. Aye, many times. I've heard it said that you killed those folk, my own father and brothers among them, in the black March disaster."

"I . . . I was exonerated: from that crime, at least."

"Donald Wyld knew what he was doing," Mirrin told him. "You must exonerate yourself now, Houston."

Seagulls screamed overhead, swooping down from the roof of the Beale Town Hall towards the sea, a sign, so the fishermen said, that the tide had turned at that exact moment. The clock in the squat tower chimed a quarter.

"Death seems to dog my tracks," Lamont said. "I cannot shake it off."

The statement was incongruous, uttered here in the holiday streets in the bright sunlight.

"It's in the nature of things, Houston."

"My son Gordon, then Dorothy, now Donald Wyld."

"Thrush, and Edith are . . ."

"No, I cannot blame them. It's me. I am the factor, the cause. It's my coalpit, my business, my profit and loss account, my mansion; my damned town, come to that."

Mirrin sat quite still. Houston was sinking again into a morass of self-pity and guilt, into a moroseness close to mental illness. Speaking sharply now, she said. "Aye, it's the truth, Houston. You *are* the coalmaster. You can't escape it. At the root of it all you don't want to escape it. You shouldn't be here with me. You should be in Blacklaw. I've heard enough to realise that. As you say, it's *your* damned pit and *your* damned town. Damned or not, *you* must look out for it and not let a pipsqueak an' a dry-hearted woman make a game-board of it, aye, and of folks' lives."

"You wish me to go?"

"No, no, Houston. I'll not reject you. But I can't be in love with half a man."

"You've no right . . ."

"I have every right. I tell you, Houston, you'll not find what you seek with me, not here in Beale, or in Liverpool, or London, or in Timbuctoo."

"Only in Blacklaw, Mirrin: is that what you mean?"

"I . . . I must go to the theatre now."

"You refuse to stay with me this afternoon."

"We'll talk at length tonight."

"*Talk!*" Lamont exploded, viciously. "What's the point in *talking*. It comes down to this, if I return to Blacklaw, will you come with me?"

The clock hands showed ten minutes to three. Wilfrid and the others would be fretting now, already dressed for the opening curtain, daubed and powdered and agitated, perhaps even preparing to make dreaded last-minute changes to the programme.

The seats of the theatre would be filling, though there would be no sell-out today, not with such fine weather to keep people on the sands and the promenade. Even so, there would be some, a hundred perhaps, or even two hundred, in to rest their legs and enjoy the entertainment.

She said, "I was right, Houston. You do not want to be with me: you want me to be with you."

"Will you come home with me, Mirrin?"

"There's no place for me in Blacklaw, with you."

"Even if I . . . I sold the pit?"

"I'm not worth that, Houston. Besides, it would be capitulation, giving in, and that isn't in you. Aye, you might do it, rashly, but it would only sully our relationship ever after."

"Can I have no peace of mind anywhere? With you or without you, Mirrin?"

Mirrin opened the door on the back of the gig, and kicked down the folding steps.

"Only you can answer that question, Houston."

"Where are you going?"

"To the theatre. It's only a minute's walk."

"Mirrin . . . I . . ."

"Will you meet me after the performance, in the tearoom?"

"I . . . yes, damn you! Where else do I have to go?"

The rest was inevitable. But it did not happen abruptly or tempestuously as Mirrin, that afternoon, might have imagined. By four-thirty, when the couple met again in the crowded tearoom, the coalmaster had shaken off his depression, or, for Mirrin's benefit, cleverly pretended that everything was sweet. He did not apologise for his outburst, and Mirrin, used now to following his lead, let the matter lie dormant once more. She felt sadness over Donald Wyld's death, but only distantly, as everything that happened in Blacklaw now seemed as hazy as the August horizon.

On the infrequent occasions when Houston Lamont and Wilf Talboys met, they exchanged no more than polite greetings. Not so Blanche. The coalmaster appeared to hold a fascination for her and she engaged him in conversation whenever possible. Houston was polite but restrained with the young woman, as he was with everyone. It was Blanche's news, however, imparted in secret to Mirrin, that began the gradual dissolution of that particular phase of Mirrin Stalker's life.

"I had a letter: a letter from Henry," Blanche said.
"What does he say?"

"He still loves me. He still wants to marry me.
He's not in Birmingham at all now. He's gone permanent to Marlingford. There's a lot of work there for
carpenters and the like, what with the new building.
It's the coming place, Marlingford. It's warmer on the
east coast, too, don't you think?"

Mirrin said, "Have you told your parents?"

"Told them what?"

"That you've heard from Henry."

"I will, in my own good time."

"Is he coming to see you?"

"As soon as he can get away."

Mirrin was happy for Blanche, and hoped that her
beau would not be too overawed by Wilfrid, or too
canny and cautious in his wooing.

In the meantime, the troupe played to capacity
houses every evening. There were fresh sketches and
songs to learn and rehearse, though memorising and
timing were becoming instinctive processes for Mirrin.
She had had very little opportunity to deepen her relationships with Ada and Pru during that summer run.
Table talk was dominated by Wilf and his grandiose
schemes for the winter. He had been badgering Ockram
fiercely of late, puffing up the value of the troupe to
Harrison Colcutt, appealing for a spot in a London
music hall for the Christmas season.

"But what about Grossby?" Ada asked. "We've
allers gone to Grossby at Christmas."

"We're too big for Grossby now," said Wilf. "Too
. . . too sophisticated. Ain't that right, Mr. Ockram?"

"We'll see," Ockram replied, which was as forth-
coming as the agent's agent ever allowed himself to become during his regular calls at the Grand.

To Mirrin, though, Ada confided, "I hope Mr.
Colcutt puts Wilf right back in his place."

"Why, Ada? A London booking means everything to
him," Mirrin said.

"It's not as though we're young and strugglin' to
build a career for ourselves. We're past all that."

"But three or four seasons hard work, in London

for the winter, in the likes of Beale, or Brighton, for summers, and you would have a fine nest-egg for retirement."

"If Wilf tastes success in London, we'll never retire," said Ada, dolefully. "And as for the nest-egg, we haven't been spendthrift: we've a bit tucked away."

"I'm surprised to hear you talk this way, Ada," said Mirrin.

"You may be right. I'm just weary, that's all. Warm weather allers makes me a bit liverish. No point in fretting about the future. London bookings don't grow on trees, not good ones at any rate. You can bet that if Harrison Colcutt does hire us out to a London manager it'll only be to a penny-whistle house. We're not London style, y'know, dear."

"I thought . . ."

"Thought you were?" said Ada. "You've been listenin' too much to our Wilf. No, London would swallow us hup, even you, luv."

Ada's pessimism, however, had a basis in wishful-thinking, and it was not shared by the enigmatic Ockram nor, it seemed, by the great recluse, Harrison Colcutt.

It was the last night of the month of August, sardine-tin houses at both shows, excursionists laying siege to the resort in defiance of snobbish attempts of Beale's residents to perform the impossible trick of soaking the transient artisans of their hard-earned cash while making them feel less than welcome in a fortress of aspiring middle-class patronage. It was never more apparent that Beale would soon have to make up its mind, like Blackpool, and jump one way or t'other.

Social considerations, however, mattered little to Mirrin and the Talboys' troupe. They altered their material according to the pattern of the audience and, that Saturday, there was nothing much by way of elegance and whimsy in the programme, rather a return to the level of sentimentality, jollity and 'salt', as Wilf called it, on a par with the Grossby prototype.

Though it was expected that Ockram would be in the house—standing at the back with a brandy and seltzer in his hand like as not—nobody could possibly have known that the rear aisle of the Grand was graced by the presence of no less a person than Mr. Harrison Colcutt himself, an 'excursionist' down for a discreet survey of his valuable properties all the way from Leeds.

It was probably as well that Wilf had no inkling that the Great God Colcutt would be present. As it was, the acts were unforced and energetic in response to the enthusiasm of an audience that best suited the efforts of the performers. There was no false straining after sophistication, no attempt at all to 'do' the smart thing. Rapport between Mirrin and the lads and lassies was at its most acute. The young woman rose to the occasion by giving of her very best, moulding their emotions with an innate skill, abetted by her sympathy with their needs. Only a dozen times or so since her entry into musical hall had she been quite so winning, raising her skills and learned talents to a pitch far above her professional experience.

Mirrin's one and only foray into Gaiety elegance and wit was with 'Wicked, Beguiling Young Witch', something of a hallmark on the north-west coast that summer, a song without which no evening performance would be complete. In the style of rendering, however, was an implied comment, a satire on the whole ethos of self-cultivated refinement which seemed to say that Mirrin Stalker was still one of *them,* and had nothing but derision for the mores of the trading class she portrayed. She was less flirtatious than insulting to the Swell—mimed by Wilf—who sought her favours, and in the end refused to go off on his candy-striped arm. Instead she waited for a cloth-capped millhand, a very muffled Blanche disguished by mutton-chop moustaches, who escorted her towards the wings as Mirrin confided over her shoulder—

"Looking back with clearer vision,
And a mind both sound and sane,
I have come to this conclusion—
I won't have none of THEM again."

An exit line which brought the house down along with the third act curtain.

It was after the performance, later than ever because of numerous encores: Mirrin was changing in the cubicle dressing room below the pier. She was in too much of a hurry to meet Houston to notice that Ada, Pru and Blanche were not in their alcoves and was almost through with her toilet before the door opened and Blanche, still in stage costume, breathlessly summoned her to Wilf's dressing room. Mirrin's protests were ignored as Blanche rushed back along the corridor and ascended the steps.

Puzzled, Mirrin followed.

Champagne on a small table was the first thing that Mirrin really noticed in the dressing room, tall blonde glasses of 'bubbly', a couple of magnums in buckets fetched from the saloon bar. The Talboys family formed a horse-shoe around the table and the scuffed plush armchair beside it. Ockram was there, looking less saturnine than usual, dispensing a brimming glass to the man in the armchair.

"Mirrin," Wilf said in his plumiest accent, "I would like to introduce you to Mr. Colcutt, our . . . our benefactor."

She understood then why Colcutt was shy of travelling. He was a small man in his early fifties, with the hunched shoulders and pigeon chest of the chronic asthmatic. He was also incredibly ugly, the skin of his face pitted with a granular disease which looked as if he had been blasted with a blunderbuss full of black pepper. Soft, silky black hair was combed into a series of three waves, perhaps to give him a few extra inches, though there was nothing at all in his plain manner of dress to suggest that he nurtured any vanity about his appearance. He was clean shaven, and had a cautious twinkle in his eye as he screwed his deformed body round in the chair to survey Mirrin.

"Mr. *Harrison* Colcutt, Mirrin," said Ada, prompting the girl to curtsey or give some similar gesture of deference.

"You were a miner, sir, weren't you?" Mirrin asked.

"Might've known you'd say that without beatin'

round the bush," Colcutt told her. "Even those as guess tend to hop and shuffle around the subject."

"I'm . . . I'm sorry, sir," Mirrin said, recovering from her astonishment. "I just didn't . . . didn't expect . . ."

"North Restal colliery, up in Tyneside," Colcutt said, still watching Mirrin carefully. "Long before you were born, lass."

"Closed down, wasn't it?" Mirrin said.

"Blasted right off the face of the earth. Flooded, too. Cost sixty lives, an' maimed a heap more."

"I'm sure Mr. Colcutt didn't grace us with his presence just to discuss coalmining," Wilf said. "He . . . he has news for us. News which he wishes to impart now."

Ignoring Wilfrid Talboys, Colcutt continued his conversation with Mirrin. He spoke easily, pausing only now and again to suck in air, chest heaving under the black waistcoat, his lungs making that faint hissing which Mirrin recognised as black lung, in one of its various forms.

"I'll say this for you, Miss Stalker," Colcutt said, "you don't look much like a coal-shifter now."

"I'll take that as a compliment, Mr. Colcutt."

"When I watched you there tonight, though, there was something about you that reminded me of girls I used to know. When did you turn your back on the coalpits?"

"Couple of years ago."

"Take it, you wouldn't go back?"

"Not if I can help it."

"I doubt if you'll have to lift a riddle again, lass."

Mirrin waited, the champagne glass which Ockram had given her untouched in her hand. She glanced around the circle, noting Wilf's frantic eagerness, Ada's anxiety, Pru's disguised fear. Strange how Colcutt brought these raw emotions to the surface.

The man got to his feet. Ockram did not offer to assist him though the process cost much effort. Independence, toughness of character marked Harrison Colcutt still. He leaned into an ash stick—no malacca silver-knobbed cane for this man—and smiled for the first time.

"Had to come. See for myself. Can't argue with ticket sales, right enough. But I was curious," he said, "to learn your appeal."

It was abundantly clear that Colcutt addressed Mirrin, and Mirrin alone. Nobody dared interrupt.

Mirrin said, "Perhaps you can explain it t'me, then, sir."

Colcutt laughed, wheezily. "Never could. Some make it in this game. Some don't. Better than you have collected a bushel of stinkers every other performance, and wound up warblin' in the gutter."

"There's a lot better than me."

"Aye, but you're bold," said Colcutt.

"I've Wilf, Ada and Pru to thank . . ."

"I know that," Colcutt interrupted. "Tell me, you're not leavin' the troupe, are you?"

"What makes you think that?"

"Friend Ockram tells me you've turned up a beau; a feller not short of a bit o'brass."

"I don't see what that's got to . . ."

"Look ahead, that's my motto."

Mirrin said, "If it's future bookings, you'll have to discuss that with Wilf."

Wilf said, "I'm open to any offer, Mr. Col . . ."

"You're a fast riser, Miss Stalker. But are you a sticker?" Colcutt asked.

"I'll stick—as long as I'm wanted."

"Beale's a soft spot," Colcutt said. "How about Liverpool?"

Blustering disappointed, Wilf said, "Liverpool, but . . . ?"

"Liverpool for ten weeks, then on down to London for Christmas," Colcutt continued.

"London?" said Mirrin.

"London!" Wilf said. "A Christmas show in London!"

Staggered at the enormity of the news, the trouper was revived only be a swig from his champagne glass.

"All of us?" Mirrin said.

"Yes, the full troupe," said Colcutt. "For eight

weeks, through Christmas. I've put you out to Leburn, manager of the Pantheon, in the Marylebone Road. Not the West End but it'll do to blood you. Pantheon's been doing all right."

"A . . . family hackt?"

"Mainstays," said Colcutt. "Others to support you, of course; solo acts. Variety for the metropolis."

"I agree," said Wilfrid, without further argument. "I agree."

"Leburn will provide the material. I take a cut, of course."

"Naturally, naturally," said Wilfrid.

"And," Colcutt went on, "I want a condition from you that you'll play my theatres next summer. No shiving off to Didcot, or some other whale down there."

"Signed, sealed and delivered, sir," Wilfrid assured him.

"Mr. Colcutt is branching out, you see," Ockram put in. "We'll have a little share in Ramsgate or Brighton come next summer, if we're lucky."

"Might I discreetly enquire as to the fee?" said Wilf.

"Forty pounds the act the week," said Ockram.

"Forty: God!" said Wilfrid.

Mirrin said, "Before or after your slice, Mr. Colcutt?"

The agent grinned. "Might have known you'd ask, Miss Stalker. After."

Ockram said, "You're all very lucky that Mr. Colcutt's created this opportunity for you."

"Very lucky: very, very lucky!" Wilfrid agreed. "We won't disappoint."

"Ten weeks in Liverpool first, though," Ockram put in.

"Liverpool," Wilfrid crooned ecstatically. "My favourite city."

"Ten weeks at the old price, Wilfrid," Ockram said. "You're not all covered in fame and flowers just yet, y'know."

"But we will be," Wilf Talboys said. "Never fear, Mr. Colcutt. We will be. All we need is the chance."

"And Mirrin Stalker," Colcutt said.

Outside the Park the afternoon was already waning towards September's early dusk. Their love-making over, the couple in the bed talked softly, intense in the intimacy of the curtained room.

"No, Houston, it's not for ever. London's just another step along the way for me."

"And what of me?"

"I thought you said you would follow me to Hades just to be with me?" Mirrin turned in the bed and put her arm about him. "I'm sorry, Houston. This is too serious a subject for glib remarks."

"I wish I could understand you, my love."

"It isn't me that's hard to understand," Mirrin said. "It's probably the same with all lovers who choose to reach across the gap. God, how limited we are in our choices!"

"You mean, because I am a coalmaster and you a collier's daughter."

"I'm not that now," Mirrin said. "I'm on my way t'becomin' a famous music-hall artiste."

For a moment the man thought that she was wholly serious. He cocked his head on the pillow and squinted at her. The wry grin on her lips told him that she was mocking herself again—not the actor's profession, however: that she would never do.

"Is such a change possible?" Houston asked.

"Of course," said Mirrin. "I've proved it to be possible."

"Yes, for you, because you are young and have no responsibilities."

"Is the past such a dreadful burden, Houston?"

"It seems that I can't escape it. The past is also my present and my future."

Mirrin placed her forefinger against his lips. "Don't try to be a philosopher, Houston. Practicality suits you better."

"The theatre's a sham."

"I can't let you off with that."

"But it's the truth, Mirrin. What do the audience see? A gay, cheerful girl flaunting glamour and a carefree indifference to reality. Ah! It's no more than an image of what they want their own lives to be."

"Is that so bad, Houston?"

"You can't sustain this dream for ever, Mirrin. What will happen when you waken up?"

"I'll have to find another dream, Houston."

"Really, I have no patience with dreamers."

"But you have, luv. You dreamed of finding me again, didn't you? Even now you dream of taking me out of reality, keeping me for yourself."

"Would that not please you?"

"Houston, there's no place where we would both be free of Blacklaw."

"Nonsense."

"Even here, you're troubled by it."

Gently Lamont pushed her away from him. He reached for the wine glass on the bedside table and, hoisting himself on to the pillow, drank down the sweet red liquid.

"Blacklaw!" he said. "Always you reduce it to Blacklaw. You cannot blame Blacklaw for the change in your feelings towards me."

"It's true, Houston, that me feelings have changed."

A flicker of dismay showed in his eyes, as if she had slighted him. "So, it's finished?"

"You should have taken more from this summer," Mirrin said.

"All I wanted was you."

"Aye, here in this bedroom."

"*No.*"

"Please, don't shout."

"What if you . . . if you . . . are with child?"

Startled, Mirrin hesitated before answering. "Then I will do what all sensible waifs an' fallen women do, Houston: I'll come trailing home again."

"To me?"

"I . . . can't answer. Besides, I'm not with child."

"Can you be sure? We've joined so often here this summer."

Mirrin bit her lip. "That's a woman's trick, Houston. Do you wish me to give birth to a bastard, like that poor lass my brother destroyed?"

"It would be quite different for you."

"God! You want an *excuse*," the girl exclaimed, in

disbelief. "You want something positive and dramatic to give you a jolt, a keg of black powder to blast away the rocks and make a new opening."

"All I want, Mirrin, is you."

"No." She shook her head. "There's nothing lasting for us, Houston. I've known from the beginning—aye, from that first night in Blacklaw, in your house—that today would come. So, I think, have you?"

"You are always so damned sure of everything, Mirrin Stalker."

"I am sure of one thing, Houston. I'm sure that you'll take up the reins of your own life again. You'll be the coalmaster again, not just some passive hand that signs the papers your wife puts before you."

"Is that all you wish for me, Mirrin: power, not love?"

"You've had love, Houston. But I'm not sure that you recognised it."

"I love *you*."

"But I'm no longer the Mirrin Stalker you knew, Houston. I've grown up. I've changed."

"I'll tell you this, Mirrin. You may think that you are free of Blacklaw. But it is my turn to make an assertion: you will be back, back home in Blacklaw soon."

"I doubt it."

"The black earth's in you, too. You can't hide behind silks and rouge for ever. Not you, Mirrin; not Alex Stalker's daughter." He dropped the glass to the carpet. It fell without breaking and rolled away out of sight under the trailing coverlet. "I believe that you will come home again. And I'll be there, waiting. Whatever you think of me, however much you suppose my nature has changed—I will wait for you, and hope."

Now that she had brought him to a final decision, she regretted it, washed by a wave of panic and nostalgia. "I . . . . I won't be leaving Beale for another fortnight, Houston. Stay with me that long?"

"I will go home when it suits me, Mirrin. I may not be the master here, but I am my own man to that degree."

"I didn't mean to hurt you, Houston. Please stay a little longer."

"It was necessary to come here. I don't regret it," he said, flatly. "It was a . . . a cure, perhaps. I went a little mad when Dorothy died."

"It's allowed, Houston, when we love somebody."

"The way I love you?"

"Different: different, Houston."

"I won't give up hope, Mirrin. One day you'll learn to love me as I love you. When the day comes that you weary of this play-acting business, when you are hurt and sick at heart, you'll find me in Blacklaw. I promise that I'll be more welcoming than you have been."

Guilt at her inability to love him as deeply as he loved her overwhelmed Mirrin. She was ashamed of her waywardness, her selfish quest for freedom. There was much in what he said. But she had come too far now to struggle with a fresh beginning.

"It is almost time, Mirrin."

"Time?"

"For your performance," he said. "Dress, and be on your way."

"Houston, will you come to the theatre tonight?"

"Yes, of course," the coalmaster answered.

Mirrin sensed that he was merely being kind. It was no surprise to see the private box vacant at both houses or to receive a sealed letter after the curtain rang down on the supper show.

Still dressed in her gaudy frock, Mirrin took the letter out on to the quiet deck propped above the sea. There, by the light of a hanging lamp, she read, *"Dearest, I will wait for you always, and love you always. When your butterfly days are over, I know that you will come home."*

Butterfly days: how accurate that phrase seemed. How oddly poetic of Houston to coin it. Yes, Mirrin thought wistfully, that was the ideal, flitting from flower to flower, colourful and weightless. But, in parting, Houston had made her aware of the brevity of all pleasures, the need to find roots in reality before she fluttered into nothingness. It was ironic that, in losing her, Houston had somehow changed her yet again.

In two weeks and a day she would move on with the Talboys to Liverpool and, though she did not know it then, the butterfly summer would be over and gone, and another cycle of her life destined to begin.

PART THREE

Call Home the Heart

One

For the most part, the Scottish summer had been dull and wet. Towards the middle of September, however, the weather treated the colliers of Blacklaw to a spell of fair, warm days that dried roofs and evaporated puddles and cajoled displays of blankets and tattered rugs onto the backgreen drying ropes, making wigwams for the bairns' short evenings' play between school and bedtime. But the Indian summer was too late in coming, winter too close for comfort. Besides, in many subtle ways the mood of the community had changed. Even Lamont's recent return to harness did not auger well for the miners' wellbeing in the cold months ahead.

There were some who admired Sydney Thrush's ruthlessness; a burly faction that believed in survival of the fittest and banked their hopes of prosperity on strength of muscle. The aging, the sick and the idle, along with most of the dissidents, had been weeded out, leaving a hard, honed and highly competitive work-force that jerked up the weekly tonnage spurred on by a master whose authority was total and, therefore, unquestionable.

Lamont's reappearance, his careful, watchful, tactful tinkering with Thrush's schemes, divided the colliers, though none could decide behind which throne the wife's power lay. Bold bachelor bucks, imported from other tough fields, were all for Thrush and openly despised the cosy family unity of the village. They lived, fifty or more, in rough shacks on the wasteground by the Clayburn coups along with the sprawling, brawling Williams clan, with whom they fought endlessly, viciously, and spent their hard-earned pay on booze and whores. They were Thrush's brigands to a man. They loved machines and dangerous seams and worked them, tamed them, for the extra shillings that the dirty jobs entailed.

Fear was an emotion that colliers learned to mould to their own purposes. It was part and parcel of the initiation of green apprentices; the constant companion of 'wee hoose' workers wedged into the rotting, water-dribbling niches of newly breached sections; the first speckles of blood in a man's spittal, the racking cough that did not ease with Friar's Balsam and the coming of spring. But few of the Blacklaw miners had ever regarded fear as a proper testing ground to separate loyal hands from trouble-makers, or as a regular contest to divide men from boys, irrespective of age. Experience was valueless, caution a coin of no worth, under Thrush.

Daring to the point of suicidal insanity resulted from Thrush's policies. In the course of that summer four men died and fourteen suffered serious injury in the speed and heat of expansion. When Inspectors came sniffing and asking questions, however, silence was the colliers' answer, defence of the regime under which they lived.

Thrush paid well for foolhardiness. His bachelor gang reaped the best profits and thus indoctrinated the town's impressionable sons in their heedless philosophy. It was a cruel, clever method of wresting from the workers maximum effort for a minimum of silver. It galled those who understood it, men like Rob Ewing, bondserf to circumstances that chained him more tightly than ever to the tied house and Lamont's pit, breadwinner for his father and mother as well as his ailing wife.

Callum Ewing did not find it easy to sleep now. The stagnation in his lungs was worse at night and he had taken to sitting up very late, sometimes until dawn, by the kitchen grate in the chair that had been carted up from his own house and crammed into Rob's kitchen. He sat quite still, hardly moving at all during the long quiet hours of darkness, pipe in mouth, eyes on the shifting patterns of the dross banked behind the iron bars. There was more wistfulness than brooding in his eyes, though, and no bitterness. He confessed that an idle life suited him just fine at his time of life, not far short of fifty-one, with all his youth and his prime left down there in the pit like abandoned props or the bones of the ponies who died below.

As Callum waned, Rob seemed to wax. He even put on weight, in spite of the meagreness of the diet. He had become sullen and bullying, one of the players of Sydney Thrush's game, competing with the ruthless men from Slaven and Redburn, Carsehorn and the Geddie Glen, hell holes and death pits where the only difference between those at the face and those in the shanties up top was that the underground shift were a shade nearer to Auld Nick than their pitiful families above.

Rob seemed to need as little sleep as his father. In summer, though, he did not cling by the fire but took himself off to the fields, even in the pitch damp dark, to walk and breathe the air, and, Callum suspected, to stoke his bitterness with dreams of all that might have been if only Mirrin Stalker had taken him in marriage instead of leaving him on the bough for poor Eileen McMasters.

But that September night, though it was pleasant out, Rob stayed home. There was no reason for it, just mood, as it was mood not sympathy that inched him into stilted conversation with his old man.

"Stayin' in?" Callum asked.

"Aye, for a while."

"The rabbits'll miss you."

"I can do without your remarks, Da."

"Sorry, son."

"Can y'not sleep at all?"

"Och, aye, but it seems such a waste o'time, sleepin' when I'm not tired. Sleepin's for workin' men."

"You're well out of it."

"I couldn't keep up that kind o'pace, you mean?"

"Anybody over thirty's hard pushed."

"But not you?"

"I can manage."

"Have you been in the new section, the branch?"

"Aye."

"I thought the wage packet was gey fat."

"Six bob fatter. Anyhow, my wage is none o'your business. It's between me an' Eileen an' nobody else."

"Is it as bad as they say down there?"

"It's . . . bearable. You won't tell them, will you? Mam and Eileen, I mean, about me workin' the thin seam?"

Callum shook his head. "I doubt that many o'the old school would've tackled that job, squeezin' heavy machinery int' a seam hardly thick enough for a man's shoulders."

"It works though: the cutters chew up that sharp coal like toffee."

"I wonder what Alex Stalker would've done?"

"That's a wasted thought, Da."

"He'd have fought them, I'm sure—even Thrush," Callum mused.

"Then he'd have gone the way of the rest—out on his bloody lug."

"The Stalkers seem t'be managin' fine without him."

"On Lamont's charity; the blood-money he pays for havin' bedded Mirrin."

"Now, lad, now!" Callum admonished. "There was never proof o'that."

"What's more, I'll wager he's been with her since. I'm even inclined t'think that the bastard bairn the Stalkers are fostern' is Mirrin's an' that Lamont is the father."

"Havers!"

"They always do all right, those Stalkers, no matter who they trample on. Look't Kate now. I thought she was the only dependable one in the bunch. But, no. She's as self-seekin' as the rest. She's got her claws in yon poor baker. She'll be after his money."

"What money? Kellock's no' exactly makin' his fortune."

"But he's better off than any collier."

"That's maybe true: but the way I heard it, it was him that fancied Kate. In fact, he'd marry her tomorrow, but she's holdin' him off a while," Callum said.

"T'make him all the keener," said Rob.

"Change the subject, son," Callum growled. "I'm not so senile yet that I'll slander m'friends just for entertainment."

"Where *was* Lamont, then?" Rob said. "That's the big topic o'the day. Dunlop let slip that the master was abroad, inspectin' marvels o'modern engineering. God, the whole process from seam t'grate will soon be done by machines, an' there'll be no place for colliers at all."

"There'll be colliers for ever," Callum said.

"But maybe no' here."

"The pit's tighter, but it's still operatin': that's one fact not even the most rabid man can argue with."

"Thrush did that—an' we know how."

"What'll happen now that Lamont's back, though?" Callum said.

"Strife?"

"Strife between manager and owner is never good for the miner," Callum said.

"Nothin's ever good for the poor bloody . . ."

They were interrupted by a sound from the back bedroom. Both men fell at once into nervous silence, listening intently.

"Was that Eileen?" Callum asked.

"I'll see."

"It'll be those pills the doctor gave her yesterday, makin' her dream again."

"Wheesh," Rob said.

Moving stealthily across the kitchen he opened the bedroom door an inch. Seeing the glow of the candle within, he opened the door a little more. Eileen was awake. Propped on the pillow she looked soft and pretty, like a fine lady. Her brown hair was bound in two plaits and she wore a nightgown that showed off her young breasts. Rob entered the room and closed the door behind him.

"Did we wake you, darlin'?" he asked, with great tenderness.

"I heard voices."

"It was only me an' the old man havin' a blether."

"What about?"

"I don't know that I should tell you."

"Och, Rob, why not?"

"All right, then." Rob made a show of capitulation. "We were just sayin' that I should've waited an' found a more beautiful lass than you for a wife . . ."

"There's plenty t'choose from."

". . . but we counted out all the girls in Blacklaw, Eastlagg, Northrigg and even Hamilton, right back as far as Da could recall an' he an' me came t'the conclusion that you were the most beautiful."

"Rob Ewing, you're pullin' my leg."

"Snuggle down, Eileen. You must have your sleep. I'll keep the old devil quiet."

"Rob?"

"Aye?"

"Stay with me a while."

"I . . . Yes, I'll stay. Of course, I'll stay."

"Lie here beside me."

"Eileen . . ."

"Please, Rob."

"I've still got my boots on."

"Take them off."

"I'll . . . look, I'll sit on the side o'the bed. How's that? I'll hold your hand, like this. I'll even sing t'you if you're not good."

The girl chuckled.

It was so unjust. There were no visible signs of the illness that made her useless as a wife. No signs at all that the excitement of love-making would, perhaps, be fatal. If there had been *some* wasting or swelling or obvious distress. But she was more ripe and beautiful than ever, now that she had grown to full womanhood protected from the hardships of life in the town. Even her hands were soft and pale and plump. There were no other hands like that in all Blacklaw. The flush upon her cheeks was a mockery of health, yet it seemed to add a last touch of sensuality.

If ever there was punishment, it was this: punishment for the lust that had caused him to force himself on Mirrin Stalker and, when she rejected him, for the months of longing for Eileen. The longing had been love and was love still, love without demonstration.

Never once had Rob given his wife an inkling that he was consumed with bitterness. Never once, in her presence, had he been less than gentle. It was harder on her than on him. At least he had his health—and a future. He could escape out into the fields or the pit—aye, even the damned pit—where hard physical activity relieved his tensions. He pitied Eileen and cared for her. But he desired her too, achingly and constantly. Self-inflicted and rigorously maintained denials turned his love into a shameful kind of hatred. His servitude to decency and sham might last for years.

Rob stifled a sigh. He held Eileen's hand in his. "Sleep," he said.

"I'll sleep soon."

She meant nothing by it, yet the phrase was plangent with meaning. Try as he might, Rob could not help but speculate what he would do with his life, when he was free once more, free of the need to protect her from the fact that he was too weak to love her without desire and the contact with which marriage should be blessed.

"Aye, love," he said, smiling bleakly.

Very soon she did sleep, drifting down into sleep as swiftly and innocently as a child. Rob held still until he was sure that her sleep was deep and natural. Only then did he disengage his hand and ease himself out of the bedroom, leaving the candle alight.

Callum turned in the canvas chair.

"Is she all right, son?"

Rob hauled his jacket from its hook behind the kitchen door and clacked down the latch with his thumb. "She's fine." He stumbled out into the dark main street.

Veering east he headed for the moor and a howff he had built for himself in the lee of a gorse bush where, on fair nights, he could snatch a few hours' sleep alone in the fresh clean country air, dream of Mirrin Stalker and wonder how the imperfect balance of his life would be affected if ever she dared return.

The courtship of William Kellock and Kate Stalker was worked out with due deliberation. Kate had given

Willie permission to woo her but had warned him that she would not be rushed into making a decision. Marriage was a subject that required commitment and she was not yet willing to commit herself to the necessary degree. Meekly, the baker agreed to the woman's terms, and gave his promise that he would not mention marriage, or even a period of engagement, until Kate gave him the nod.

Wisely, Flora kept off the subject with her daughter. During the weeks that followed Willie's proposal and Kate's guarded acceptance, Flora covertly watched her daughter for signs of weakening. She found none. Even at the age of thirty, Kate, it seemed, still cherished a dream of marriage based on love and not just respect.

It was this turn of events in her sister's life, however, that almost led to Betsy Stalker's downfall. Coincidence had no part in it. Indeed, it was inevitable that, in the closed societies in which they moved, Betsy Stalker and Randolph could not hope to keep their affair secret for ever.

Willie and Kate had gone for an evening visit to Glasgow, catching the train from Hamilton to College Station. It was a dry, brisk night, though cold. The couple were well wrapped up against the wind which, when they alighted in the city, moaned through the girders overhead. Their destination was not far from High Street, a lecture hall in Sorn Street. Here, as Willie had discovered from an advertisement in the *Glasgow Herald,* Mr. Chester Sloane was giving an illustrated talk on his travels in Africa, a show that had taken London by storm. Kate had no objection to learning more of foreign lands and was fired by Willie's enthusiasm for Sloane's achievements as an explorer. It was rather a rush to return from the pit and wash and change. But Willie was thoughtful enough to have a hired fly waiting at the bakery and they had just caught the seven o'clock train from Hamilton.

It was in College Station that the unexpected incident occurred which spoiled Kate's pleasure in Chester Sloane's descriptions of the wild tribes of Africa and took her mind away from the vivid, and hair-raising lantern slides.

The girl was before them, hurrying down the length of the platform towards the ticket gate. The skittish walk, the dress, the bobbing ringlets under the bonnet: unmistakably Betsy. For an instant Kate almost pulled Willie off his feet in her anxiety to catch up with her sister. Sudden embarrassment checked her, however, and she drew Willie on as fast as she could without explaining her reason. As Willie fumbled for the tickets in his waistcoat pocket, Kate stood on tiptoe and looked out towards the archway where her sister had gone.

Betsy emerged from the dispersing crowd and, to Kate's utter astonishment, was picked up by a waiting cab. The cabbie was there: Betsy did not summon him. The man had the door of the cab already open for her. He nodded familiarly as she approached and even assisted her inside. The cab drove off, making a sweep under the gas lamps across the cobbled yard then, as Kate and Willie came down towards the entrance, disappeared through the gates and out into the city.

"What's wrong, Kate, lass?" Willie asked, solicitously.

"Nothin'."

"You look as if you'd seen a ghost."

"It's nothin', Willie: only the cold. I'll be fine when we're in the hall."

"Here, then, hold on t'me and we'll hurry as fast as we can. You'll be hungry. We'll have a bite first."

But there could be no comfort for Kate in the tearoom, no escape from the realisation that Betsy had lied. Fear that the girl, like her twin, was in trouble haunted Kate all the evening and throughout the night. She looked in vain for a sign of her sister on the return journey to Hamilton but had to hold off for another day before the deception was confirmed.

Mam was putting Neill to bed, and Betsy retired, directly after supper, to her room. It was there that Kate found her, seated before the mirror, combing her hair.

She seemed surprised, but not startled, to receive a visit from Kate, who, in the past months, hardly ever entered the back room.

"You're . . . you're lookin' well, Betsy."

"Yes, I feel quite well, thank you, Kate."

The girl was mocking her, of course: that kind of polite communion was a thing of the past with the sisters. It had never really been their style in any case. Kate composed herself for the investigation.

"Where were you last night, Betsy?"

Was there an imperceptible tension in Betsy at the directness of the question? She continued combing her hair, squaring up to her image in the mirror, not meeting Kate's eye.

"In Hamilton, of course, at Margaret-Anne's house."

"Did you go out?"

"Yes, to the Evangelical Choir; just t'listen, though."

"Where?"

"The Cambridge Halls. Why? What makes y'ask, Kate?"

"Willie an' I were thinkin' of goin' t'the concert."

"Yes, that'll be very good," said Betsy, relieved.

"Maybe we'll see you there."

"Probably," said Betsy. "Probably."

Kate left the back room again, closing the door behind her.

With all the coolness of long practice, Betsy had told her a deliberate lie. As far as Kate knew there was no Evangelical concert in the offing in Hamilton. More to the point, Betsy had been in Glasgow, not with Margaret-Anne. Kate's hands trembled as she transferred the supper dishes to the sink and filled the kettle and set it on the hob.

How many nights had Betsy spent away from home in the past months? Dozens. Had she been in Glasgow on all of those occasions? Kate did not know Margaret-Anne Watson well, but it would surely not be difficult to break the accomplice down, to discover the purpose of Betsy's secret visits to the city. Kate shook her head. What was the point? Surely, the purpose must be all too obvious. Betsy was steering a course towards disaster.

Angrily Kate wondered if she would be called upon to bring another bastard baby into the house, to pull Betsy too out of a quagmire of scandal. There was nobody she could discuss the matter with. She certainly could not give any hint to Mam. She must keep it to herself and simply let events take their course.

If only Mirrin was here. Mirrin would know what to do. But Mirrin had left Blacklaw just to avoid such issues, to escape involvement in the problems of her greedy, impetuous and irresponsible family. It was all very well for Mirrin with her face and her figure and her boldness. But she, Kate, she was too plain ever to hope to escape. All she could hope for, it seemed, was a kind wee elderly baker for a husband, and more than her share of trouble.

Two

LIVERPOOL WAS A city of indiscriminate opportunity. Its cosmopolitan population, homegrown industries and flowing commercial wealth created many areas of divergence within its crowded wards. It could not readily agree on an image, being content to remain all things to all men with money on their minds. It epitomised the adventure of investment in its rawest state, a chequerboard of magnificent docks and huge brick warehouses, parks and coal dumps, shipwrights' yards, reeking foundries and chemical repositories, small bilious factories and large brown works, all importing and exporting, processing, refining, storing, packing, boiling, smelting, bottling, brewing and generally dabbling in every conceivable commodity.

The city seemed in a perpetual lather, busy, robust, positive, at odds with Mirrin's mood that smokey, fog-washed autumn. As she sat by the window of her room in the Commercial Hotel in Linnet Street and listened to the bustle of the old sea-orientated town, she felt detached from her future and indifferent to the fortunes which might await her in the south. It was the northern time, the time of migrations, inward and outward. Only born wanderers were free of the harking to be home again before the winter snows.

Mirrin saw herself as just another piece of cargo, shipped in from a foreign port, processed and put in bond in the confines of the Marine Hippodrome, a quaint, beetle-browed music hall tucked between chandlers' and publicans' premises in Ropemakers' Row, near the delta of the Canning, Salthouse and Albert docks. There she sang for sailors and artisans, stitchers, caulkers and pitchers, bricklayers' hogs and shopkeeper's lads, the wharf rats and their sallow women, the wives, daughters and chirpy sons of small traders and craftsmen. She sang to them of things they understood, mocked, loved or feared, including the odd shanty that Wilf had taught her to tickle the bargees, lightermen and deepsea mariners.

But, unexpectedly, Mirrin found that her attitudes were changing. She no longer liked the unruly crowds that packed the gallery or brawled in the stalls. She sang, danced and pattered now without conviction, reacting to applause with the same degree of indifference as she parried randy cat-calls and drunken insults. What was most disturbing to Mirrin perhaps was her ability to deceive. Until this booking she had seldom had to feign vivacity. Verve now had gone out of her, however, though she gave them every ounce of her skill in exchange for their brass. Skill, it seemed, was enough.

Ada and Pru noted the change and told her it was a natural part of the process of maturing. They assured her that she would be the better for it as a trouper. Blanche taught her more of the subtle meanings of cynicism, and only Wilfrid, lambent with rekindled ambition, remained pure in his ideals and ignored his protégée's disillusionment.

Houston's departure had left Mirrin a sediment of guilt over the ending of the affair. During the season in Beale, she had become selfish and self-protective, hardened in her resolve to remain free. But her freedom had found no direction. She was still in retreat from the black days in Blacklaw. London, she realised, was not her true goal. She had acquired that objective from Wilf, fired by vanity and Colcutt's flattering faith. London, the Pantheon, the Christmas engagement were mirages. The resonant solidity of Liverpool, that waystation for all the world, seemed to tell her so. Optimism was such an exploitable commodity, and the city's tabernacles of hope of profit screened the misery of failure, poverty and death, the impermanence of triumphs over the odds.

It was Sunday, a neutral afternoon, overcast, enclosed and damp. Out beyond Wallasey the foghorns lowed and the bum-boats, plying the floats even on the Sabbath, hallooed mysteriously, a medley of melancholy sounds that sifted from the water fog like pagan answers to the sonorous bells of chapels and missions that called their followers to worship at all odd hours of the dusky day.

Mirrin had gone walking alone. She had invited Blanche to join her, but a correspondence with Henry Essam had sparked into activity again and Blanche's spare time was occupied penning endearments to her ardent young beau who was so intent on setting up his shop in Marlingford that his letters invariably yielded a few grains of sawdust or a shaving or two in lieu of a lock of hair. Ada and Pru were resting. Neither of the women had really benefited from the sea air of Beale. The strenuous summer engagement had taken its toll. Pru in particular had been suffering a dry hacking cough for weeks now. Though the local doctor would not commit himself to an exact diagnosis, Mirrin detected in his non-committal answers more than a hint of anxiety about the aging trouper's health.

Where Wilfrid was, that day of rest, was no mystery. He had gone with Ockram to Manchester to meet with a manager and 'have a swatch' at a couple of acts that Colcutt planned on putting into the Pantheon Christmas Box along with the Family. Having been assured of his worth, and with Mirrin Stalker as his trump card, little Wilfrid Talboys had replaced his obsequious eagerness with a mantle of knowing self-assurance in all matters pertaining to 'Variety'. Her Wilf was coming on as strong as a peppermint lozenge, Ada said, and had better watch that Mr. Colcutt didn't just decide to spit him out.

In Liverpool, though she was recognised now and again, Mirrin was no star. The public attitude to the entertainers was practical in that hard-working city. Outside the Hippo they were accorded a nod or a grin or a touch of the cap but no undue familiarity or awe. Mirrin got her fair share of speculative looks from men, old and young, but not much more than any girl would have done and, indeed, there was a reserve in the manner of the artisans that held more disdain, perhaps, than respect.

She was free to explore the city as she wished, to wander the slum quarter round Fontenoy and Sawney Pope or, for variation, up into the posh neighbourhood of All Saints Church where the stucco mansions of the nouveau riche stood back from the Princes Boulevard. Most often, though, Mirrin found herself strolling the waterfront, eyes, ears and nose stimulated by the diversity of impressions that swarmed from the wharves and quays. She meandered from Canada dock to the Pottery Beach and back again, fascinated by the ships. The names emblazoned on the hulls formed a catalogue to whet the appetite of any landlocked wanderer—the *Ranji Princess*, Calcutta; *Northern Star*, Antwerp; *Windwards*, Valparaiso; the *Demeter*, the *Tern*, the *Loch Garry*, the *Seattle Seamaid*, and many more, a changing litany to roll on the tongue and savour in the imagination.

When the sun shone on the Mersey and Mirrin stood in its rusty autumn glow looking from the Landing Piers to the masts and cluttered riggings that webbed the shores of Birkenhead and the Wallasey Pool, it was fine to let her mind rove thoughtfully over distant places. But on that fog-bound, shrouded afternoon the ships' canvasses seemed weighted by sadness, sails folded like the wings of drowned gulls, or hanging slack in the ropes like laundry that would never dry. Then she was Mirrin again, the Stalker lass from Main Street, homesick and lonely, thinking of the shortening days and her Mam filling the big iron stock pot to set by the hob where it would bubble and simmer all winter; thinking of Kate's nose beginning to go red, and her sister's salve for chilblains, the sharp, pleasant smell of it, and Betsy's mock fur muff unearthed from the wardrobe and scrubbed and fluffed up to be ready for the first cold snap. And the smoke rising soft from the wee lums and spreading low across the Sheenan glen in the early twilight.

She was a far cry from Blacklaw now, with time to loiter and watch the world wag, warm and smart in her winter day dress with its corselet of astrakhan cloth and the skirt with the apron-front, and a bag on her arm and seven button real suede gloves and an extravagant velvet Charlotte Corday hat, a shade informal but quite suitable for her station. But the clothes were really a small reward, a labour to pack, and a chore to clean and press and trim correctly. Besides, it mattered hardly at all what she wore, for only the Sabbath shift saw her and the odd seaman, and she knew she looked too rich for their blood.

There was no blink of sun to the west. Twilight was defined only by the lighting of coal-oil lamps and gas fans along the fronts. The big dim warehouses, whose windows had the faint candleshine shapes of cathedrals in mourning, faded into the salt-grey, darkening fog.

He came along the cobbles by the back of the Huskisson, past bollards and tall wedge-posts, the glow behind him from the dockshed lanterns like penny gold. He walked casually, with all the old jaunty swagger, one fist in the pocket of his black peajacket, the other held down, discreetly, so that the spray of late hand-cut roses in their paper cone seemed like a beachcomber's trophy that he had picked up and forgotten to discard. In the throat of his white shirt collar was a blue kerchief. His trousers were thick cream nankeen, not loose but tailor-shaped like those of a naval officer. On his head he wore a clinker-brimmed cap with a tack of braid on it, pushed back so that his curly hair puffed out above his ears. He was browner than ever, varnished by weather, and had trimmed down his waist and the flesh of his face so that he looked very hard and lean and raffish.

She knew it was Tom minutes before the shadowgraph became distinct against the misty light. She knew he had planned it—and was glad.

Stopping a yard away, he studied her, head cocked.

"Well, well now, if it isn't my flower o'the tattie field," he said. "This is a turn up for the book!"

"The back of a dock's not a strange place t'find a sailor," Mirrin said, her heart pounding like mad.

"Ah, so y'were on the scout for a sailor, were you?"

"I heard there was a rascal tink snippin' the blooms up by the Square: I thought it might be you."

"Lost again, then," Tom said. He drew the bouquet from his side and peered at it self-consciously. "I bought these for the lass who's been knockin' out the eyes at the Hippo for the last couple o'weeks."

"Blanche Talboys, d'you mean?"

"I mean Mirrin Stalker."

Mirrin did not accept the bouquet immediately. "Is this a token of apology, by any chance?"

"Apology? For what?"

"Skippin' off last year an' leavin' me to Mag Marshall's not-so-tender mercies."

"You were to blame for me departure."

"That's a lame excuse. You're as casual as the wind, Tom."

"I didn't look for you all over England just t'argue the toss about something that happened long ago."

"Only a year."

"Be that as it may," Tom said, "it's ancient history as far as I'm concerned. I've been round the globe since then—and made a bob or two. By the looks of it, you're not the girl you were then either. My abrupt leave-takin' doesn't seem to have done you any lastin' harm."

"How did you find me?" The question echoed her meeting with Houston in Beale. Being an entertainer was altogether too public a career. Not that she wanted to hide, not from Houston, and not from Tom Armstrong.

"I thought about you a lot out there on the high seas."

"When you were feelin' squeamish?" said Mirrin.

"When I was lonely," Tom said. "And that was too often for comfort, believe me. By God, Mirrin, but you lead me a merry dance."

"I lead you . . ."

"I've been in search of you for the last three weeks," he explained. "Did you suppose it was blind chance that brought me up this quay this particular afternoon?"

"I thought you docked in Liverpool."

"I did," Tom said. "But how was I to know you'd gone theatrical. I've been back t' Galloway, t' Mag Marshall. As you can imagine, my flower, she was precious little help. But one pal in the camp did tell me that he'd seen your name on a playbill in the Manchester area. Just as well or I'd've been off up north t'scour the colliery towns."

"How could you be sure it was my name on that playbill?"

Tom grinned. "It seemed right, somehow. Any roads, I tracked you down, right back t'Liverpool where I'd started from. And here I am."

"What d'you mean—seemed right?"

"I remembered your voice: not bad, an' certainly loud enough t'wake the boozers in the back aisles."

"Thank you very much, Mr. Armstrong. Just for that I'll accept your posy."

"May I take your arm an' walk with you a bit?"

"Why not? I've nothing better t'do with myself today," Mirrin said. "Besides, I think your determination merits a wee reward."

"I've never strolled about with a genuine Song Bird before."

"And I've never taken a promenade with a sailor."

"Former sailor: now retired."

"That impulse didn't last long, Tom."

"I didn't mind the work, but I hated the confinement."

"Where did you sail?"

"One long voyage: ten months: a cargo of shoddy to Quebec, up the St. Lawrence river in Canada; then coastal trading down the American seaboard to Charleston in Carolina, where we picked up cotton in the raw to bring home."

"It sounds exciting."

"Aye, flower, the places an' the nights are etched in my memory. But the seaman gets to see precious little other than wharves and docks. All the time, I wanted back to . . ."

Tom shrugged.

Mirrin tugged his elbow tighter. She could smell the scent of the roses coming sweetly up from the paper cone in her hand. "You: homesick?"

"It surprised me, too." He changed the subject, abruptly. "What of yourself, Mirrin?"

"I left the tinks just after you did the bunk—they kicked me out, to be truthful—an' I worked in Grossby in a mill for a while."

"God, that's no life for a girl like you."

"So I found out."

Mirrin outlined the circumstances that had carried her from Mag Marshall's encampment to the stage of the Marine Hippodrome, Liverpool, and told him of the London engagement. She spoke for almost an hour, talking more freely than she had done to anyone, even Houston, during the last year. Slowing his step, Tom encouraged her to pour out her disillusionment with the music hall, her divided loyalties to the Talboys, and her prevailing mood of restlessness.

Dusk deepened. Fog thickened and became chill as they wandered the cobbled streets that linked into the Liverpool waterfront. They passed warehouses, and the low unyielding frontages of dwellings, elfin windows gold and yellow in the darkness now, the aroma of Sunday dinners strong.

When Mirrin had recounted her 'adventures' to the man, she was suddenly embarrassed by her garrulousness. Tossing her head, she looked around. "Where have you led me, Tom Dandy?"

"Near enough home," he said.

"Home?"

"Your hotel: the Commercial."

"You've been spyin' on me."

"I saw your performance on Thursday night."

"Did you approve?"

"You're different on stage, Mirrin," he said, seriously. "More . . . more brittle: less . . . real, maybe."

The girl did not reply.

Tom said, "I thought of waitin' at the back door, but that didn't seem right for an old friend. So I followed you back to the hotel."

"An' today?"

"Aye: I hoped you might be out an' about today."

"You're still a cunning devil, I see. You didn't lose that on the ocean."

"I didn't lose anythin'," Tom said. "I made some siller."

"On a seaman's wage?"

"An' with a pack o'cards."

"That's more like the truth."

"I've fattened up the nest-egg, Mirrin."

"Have y'now?"

"It's a great pity you're set on London—if you are set on London."

"Oh, I'm for London all right."

Tom nodded. "I'm for home, for Scotland."

"When?"

"As soon as I can."

"Slippin' away in the dawn again?"

"Tomorrow, first thing."

"To do what? Mend pots? Fleece poor lads at the cards? Marry Colly Marshall, maybe?"

"You have changed: it's not just on stage."

Contritely, Mirrin said, "I'm sorry, Tom. I shouldn't have said that. About Colly Marshall."

"D'you really want to know what my plans are?"

"You've listened patiently to my tales of woe, the least I can do is return the favour."

"Come an' have a bite o'supper."

"At your place?"

"I haven't got a place, Mirrin," Tom said. "I've a

shelf in a mission with forty other drifters. No, no, that's not my purpose in lookin' you up."

"I'd like fine to take supper with you, Tom."

They dined in the back parlour of a small, cosy waterfront inn on the corner of Pine Street and Albert Lane, a plump-fronted hostelry that was not, to Mirrin's surprise, either cheap or vulgar. There were captains and mates, some with their ladies, in the booths at the back, and well-dressed gentlemen obviously disobeying the commandment about honouring the Sabbath by doing merchants' business over roast beef and marsala.

Throughout the meal, Mirrin and Tom talked of the events of the year that had separated them from their shared background, those brief months of hardship and bonhomie with the gypsy tribe. Absence it seemed had deepened their friendship. The meeting there in Liverpool, so far from home, marked a strange bond which neither the man nor the girl was willing to dissipate.

When the pudding plates had been cleared and Mirrin had done justice to the sweetmeats from the tray and Tom had lit himself a thin cigarette rolled in liquorice paper and poured out the last of the wine, he said, "I promised t'tell you what I intend t'do with the siller I've earned."

"I'm not obliged t'believe you, though, Tom?"

Gravely, Tom said, "I think you'll take my word for it this time, Mirrin. I've grown so damned tired of buzzin' about like a bumbly bee. It's time t'settle down."

"Your own fireside; your own table t'put your feet under?"

"Aye, it's nearly winter," Tom said. "Winter's the time when one man's hardship becomes another's gain."

"Let me guess."

"Go on."

"Land: you intend to rent land."

"That's it, flower. I'm after a piece of farm. Some cattle, an' enough grazin' to keep them on. It won't be anythin' grand or expensive. I just haven't that much in the purse. But I do have enough now t'make my move. An' that's what I intend t'do."

"Better do it soon," Mirrin said. "Before you get wooed away by somethin' else."

"Not this time. Not now. It's a farm for me. Thirty or forty acres . . ."

"In the highlands?"

"No, not far north. I'm no crofter," Tom said. "I want soil that'll yield t'hard work an' good management."

"I've heard talk that this is a time of depression for farmers, Tom."

"It is that," Armstrong confirmed. "But the smallholder, if he's cautious an' willin' t'adapt, can still earn a good darg."

"How?" said Mirrin. "And how can you do it when so many are failing?"

"Milk."

"Milk?"

"I'm not as daft as I look, Mirrin: no, nor so wayward. I've read about high farmin', an' I've kept abreast of developments. I've listened t'experts in agricultural matters, an' worked a wheen o'farms in my time with the clan. Damn it all, I've got the soil right through me, like most tinkie brats."

"That doesn't answer my question, Tom?"

"You know that they have huge ice-boxes that they can put down in the holds of ships now an' bring food fresh from foreign parts? In five or ten years Britain'll be fed on all sorts of foods grown in Canada or Denmark or Holland—not just cereals, but beef an' mutton, butter too. But the dairy farmer who lives near a railhead that serves a town, a growing town, he'll find himself in clover—if he's clever. Milk's the answer, Mirrin: fresh milk supplied daily to the townies. It fetches good prices an' there's no processing costs involved. Besides, the capital turnover is rapid, an' virtually assured."

"Why has nobody thought of this before?"

"But they have," Tom assured her. "Many farmers are beginnin' to look to milk to save their failing farms. It's never been popular because it's demanding. Anyhow, it's only these last ten years or so that high farming's begun to fall from grace an' transport's reached a point where daily delivery becomes practical. So I would be lookin' for a smallholding to let. I'll put down a year's rent in advance an' have enough left from my capital to take in stock. If dairy's not enough, then I can branch into fruit growin' or poultry."

"In Scotland?"

"Lanarkshire's my target. It's close to the towns, an' grazing's good for the most part."

"And what about labour?"

"That's the rub, Mirrin," Jack said. "I need a wife who'll work shoulder to shoulder with me an' help the place grow prosperous. It's not a farmhand I need, or can afford, it's a wife."

"It'll be no bargain for the woman, God help her."

"No bargain at all."

"Will you advertise?"

"I will not."

"How will you find such a daft woman, then?"

"Ah!" Tom exclaimed. "I hoped you'd see past the work to the satisfaction that can be obtained from it."

"I've heard that tale about the satisfaction of sheer brutal dog-labour before—an' I don't believe it," Mirrin said. "There's no grace in it."

"No grace in love?"

"So you want love thrown in?"

"I want love first."

"How'll you phrase that in your advertisement? Or will you just wait an' see which of the applicants falls for your charm?"

"I'm a damned sight less charmin' than I used t'be," said Tom, candidly. "I have a purpose now, a purpose that's been buildin' up in me for months, years in fact. I've no time for the niceties. I've got t'get at it."

"I admire your determination, Tom. I wish you luck."

"I'm no longer shiftless, Mirrin: not that I ever was, really, though you seemed t'think so. Do you suppose me t'be just another drifting tinker, now?"

Mirrin shook her head. "No, you've changed too,

Tom. It's strange how quickly folk alter. I acknowledge that there's been change in myself, an' not just
in circumstances."

"You're a music-hall star."

"No, I'm not that, not at heart."

"What are you, flower?"

"I . . . I can't be sure."

"A farmer's wife?"

"I . . ."

"My wife?"

"No, Tom, I . . ."

"I'm not just lookin' for a kitchen servant an' a
dairy maid an' a bedmate," Tom said. "I've admired
you since the first day we met. I think I saw you then
as my wife, though there have been a few occasions
since when I could've clipped your lug so angry did
you make me."

Mirrin looked down at the roses which the innkeeper
had thoughtfully put in a glass of water. She was not
dismayed or confused by Tom's offer of marriage. It
was not, she knew, a convenience arrangement, a
proposition drawn up and calculated. All along she
had known that he cared for her. Perhaps she had
been too immature a year ago, after her sad affair with
Houston, to recognise the sincerity of his offer then.
She recognised it now though. It was abrupt, plain,
positive. Ironically, Tom Armstrong impressed her as
a man who had chosen a direction and would go along
it without regrets, straight and honest, to the end of his
days. Farming: the cold fields and the rain. Farming:
the rough, recalcitrant cattle, the unpredictable returns, disease, short crops, high prices. Farming: worry
and work.

"It wouldn't be my place, Mirrin. It would be our
place. It would be our patch of ground, our standpoint.
Whatever happened would be our doing. Aye, we
would have good times as well as bad. God, if my
thinking's right an' my back's as broad as it should be,
then we would soon make it profit, our piece of good
Scottish soil."

"How much do you know about cattle?"

"I can tell a bull from a cow," Tom said, with that

cocky grin of his. "I'm no expert. But I've taken advice. I know what to buy an' how to keep. I can learn."

"Learnin' can be expensive."

"We can both learn."

"You want my answer?"

"Of course I do," Tom said. "Look here, Mirrin. It was luck that led you to Liverpool, right there at the end of the quay, like. Call it fortune, good fortune, if you prefer: an omen. If I hadn't found you in the 'Pool, then I'd have come lookin' for you. Believe it or not, flower, that was my intention all along."

"You might have told me before you left."

"I did—but you wouldn't listen. Besides, you were right. I was bein' daft an' impractical then. Romantic. It's very different now, though. I have capital enough to get me started. I want you t'share it with me. Do you have another feller?"

"I wondered when you'd ask that question, Tom."

"Do you?" Tom insisted, anxiously.

"No."

"Only the theatre?"

"It's as hard a taskmaster as the land."

"Maybe," Tom said. "But is it really for you?"

"I think it might be."

With an impatient gesture, Tom ground out the butt of his cigarette. "I'm not playin' a game with you, Mirrin. I'm not in a position to traipse round the country like a wee lap dog yappin' at your heels."

"You blow in out of the ocean, meet me, half by chance, an' expect me t'agree t'marry you, give up my career—which is satisfying, comfortable an' well paid —for the promise of matrimony an' a lifetime of sweat and tears."

"I'm hopin', Mirrin, that we'll manage more laughter than tears between us," Tom said. "As for the rest, aye, that's what I offer. I don't *expect* anythin'. I'm just puttin' it to you. I won't plead, or patter, or cajole. I won't hound you, or woo you. But I will marry you, just as soon as you wish, here or in Scotland; next week, or next year. I want you, Mirrin, that's the long and the short of it."

"A marriage made in Heaven?"

"Marriage isn't made anywhere but in the home; aye, an' it's a long, long manufacturing process," Tom said. "But it's you I want. I know we're right for each other."

"Give me a day or . . ."

"I'm leavin' tomorrow, Mirrin. I found you much quicker than I thought. I've said my say, an' I'm gettin' out of Liverpool an' up to where my heart is, aye, an' where my future'll be, just as soon as I can get on the train."

"Tomorrow? Oh, Tom, that's ridiculous. I can't possibly . . ."

"If you want me, Mirrin, you'll find me."

"But . . . but . . . where?"

"Lanark Hiring Fair: where we met."

"When?"

"You could give me an answer now."

"No, Tom. It wouldn't be true or honest."

"That's a fair answer, Mirrin."

"Will you look for another wife?"

"That's not for me: I won't look for a wife. There's a Hiring Fair held next January. I'll wait that long. I'll wait because it's you I want, nobody else."

"Well, I'll . . ."

"I'm not sneakin' off this time, Mirrin. I have a place to go, money to take me there, an' a purpose at the end of the journey." He got to his feet. "Now, I think it might be best if I escorted you back t'the Commercial."

With a vain attempt at humour, Mirrin said, "I think you might have t'carry me, Tom Dandy."

"Why?"

"I'm faint with shock," Mirrin said.

"It's better than bein' faint with hunger," Tom said, with a gravity that silenced Mirrin completely.

Mirrin wakened very early that Monday morning. It was still grey and overcast. She had it in mind to go to the railway station and give Tom a final answer, to tell him that she was no fool and would not be swept back into drudgery just because a tink said he loved her. But she did not go. She lay long in bed, awake, listening to the city come alive, trying to convince herself that Armstrong was just a day-dreamer, an opportunist, that once he had bedded her there would be no more talk of farms and Lanarkshire and matrimony, that he would drag her round the camps just like any scruff and, one day, would abandon her as he had done before. She wanted to believe it; but she could not. He had looked so different, still arrogant, to be sure, but leaner, quicker, less indolent and insolent. Long months at sea had somehow steeled him in his nebulous intention. Even Tom, it seemed, had changed.

Throughout that Monday, Mirrin sought his face, peering into the audiences hoping that he would have lingered on in Liverpool after all. She needed more reassurance, more persuasion.

But Monday passed, and Tuesday, Wednesday, and, by the week's end, she realised that he had kept his promise and left the next move to her. She did not for a moment doubt that Tom would find his farm to rent, buy his stock, make a go of it, or that he would attend the January Hiring Fair to give her a chance. She understood, however, that he would not come in search of her again no matter how much he wanted her. The offer would stand, for six months or a year, and then, in time, Tom would find himself another woman to be his wife and slave for him. Another woman, another fool.

No, she was a trouper now, a traveller, with golden opportunities spread out ahead of her like a carpet of pollen. Besides, she couldn't let Colcutt and Wilfrid down. That was her excuse for not obeying her madcap impulse to pack and follow Armstrong there and then.

Three

❧

It happened during rehearsals for the dance which concluded the troupe's rendition of 'Our Uncle Sam'. For weeks now Pru had been pale and listless. Even Wilf had been sufficiently disturbed at her pallor to cut back on her participation in the more strenuous acts. There was no immediate warning of her collapse, however. So undemonstrative was it that a casual onlooker might have supposed it to be a piece of pantomime thrown in for an extra laugh.

Ada was at the piano, thumping out chords, while Blanche, Mirrin and Pru, arms linked, skipped in a rank across the front of the stage. Mirrin felt Pru's release, the gentle slipping of the small woman's arm, and turned, as Wilfrid yelled, in time to see Pru trip into the side curtain and slide down it, slowly, until she was seated with her legs stuck out before her, chin on breast, like a perfectly-mannered female inebriate.

Ada lumbered past before the Scots girl could react. Wilfrid was already advancing from his stance on a box in the orchestra trough. Blanche instantly began to weep.

"What's wrong? What is it?" Mirrin asked.

"Aunty's sick," Blanche sniffled. "It's happened before."

"She's fine: she's all right: she's just out of puff. Fetch a glass of water: brandy: bring some of the good stuff in my closet, Blanche. Fetch it, child." Wilfrid rapped out orders like a French general. He stooped by his wife's side and gingerly lifted Pru's chin with his forefinger, as Blanche hurried off to the dressing room. The hall sounded big, empty and hos-

353

tile now that the gay tune had died; the troupers talked in whispers.

"She'll be all right, won't you, old gal?" said Wilf.

Ada said, "She won't be all right 'til she gets some proper rest."

"I'm . . ." Pru gasped. "I'm . . . sorry."

"Sorry: nothing at all to be sorry for, luv," Ada said.

"That's the ticket," Wilf said. "Have a nice afternoon in bed. You'll be right as rain for the evening."

Ada caught her husband by the lapels of his broadcut jacket and almost hoisted him over her shoulder. "What's got into you, Wilf Talboys? My sister's ill, *really ill,* an' you insist on her appearin' tonight. Are you a monster?"

"No, I . . . yes, yes, of course, Pru. Take a week off; a fortnight. Have a good lie-up. We'll struggle along . . ."

"A fortnight won't do, Wilf," Ada thundered.

"A month then. Stay off 'til we reach London. London'll perk you up, old gal."

Fortunately Blanche arrived at that moment with a tumbler of brandy and water which Ada held to her sister's lips. Pru managed to sip just a little of the liquid. Coughing harshly, she slumped onto her elbows. Ada cuddled the frail little woman while the spasm racked her.

"What'll we do without Pru?" Blanche sniffled. She too had been under strain lately, and was prone to burst into tears at the slightest excuse.

It occurred to Mirrin that in the ten months she had travelled with the troupe they had performed or rehearsed virtually every day, with the exception of an occasional Sunday. Naturally the strain was telling. Even Ada had lost weight and Wilfrid now was as thin and nervous as a starved ferret.

"We'll rearrange the material," Mirrin said.

"An' put my sister in the first rubbish tip we come to, I suppose," Ada snapped.

"I . . . I didn't mean that, Ada," said Mirrin.

"You're as bad as he is. Without you none of this would 'ave 'appened," Ada said.

"Please . . . Ada . . ." Pru's protests and peace-making intentions were cut short by another bout of coughing.

"What have I got to do with it?" Mirrin demanded.

"Fillin' our Wilf's head with daft notions."

"Ada, that's unfair," said Wilf. "Without Mirrin's . . . er, assistance, we'd still be scratching in penny-gaffs up and down the midlands. I mean, here we are . . ."

"Here we are—*killing my poor sister,*" said Ada.

"It's just a cold, I tell you," shouted Wilf.

"I . . . can . . . get up now," said Pru. "I'm all right."

Wilfrid showed his contriteness by solicitude, fussing round the woman, placating his wife by an efficiency which did little to speed Pru from the Hippodrome to the Commercial Hotel.

When a hired cab had at last been dispatched with Ada and Pru inside, the three remaining members of the act stood disconsolately beneath the snout of the theatre, embarrassed by the memory of the truths that had been spoken in the heat of the moment.

"Not your fault, Mirrin: not anybody's fault," Wilf muttered. "Best see what we can do about salvaging the performance, eh? It'll keep our minds off our problems."

Blanche blew her nose loudly on her handkerchief. "Poor Aunty Pru. She's goin' to die. I know it. I heard her tell mother she was goin' to die."

"Stuff an' nonsense, child!" Wilf stormed. "Now get into that hall. Pru will be back with us very shortly. I know her. Stern stuff. The Cropleys are all made of the very best material."

"I don't want to rehearse," Blanche said. "I want to rest, too. I'm sick an' tired of all this, father."

Sighing, Wilf put his arm about his daughter's shoulders and sought to console her. "Yes, my dearest, I do understand how difficult it's been for us all to adjust to our new-found fame. But, believe me, once we get to London . . ."

"I don't want to go to London," said Blanche.

"You're just upset. Believe your Daddy, London's

a wonderful place. Full of handsome, respectable young men."

"I have a young man already."

"Not that . . . that chippie from Brum?" Wilf cried.

"Marlingford. Henry Essam. My Henry."

"Your Henry! If he comes . . . within . . . a mile of . . ."

"Wilfrid," Mirrin warned, taking the trouper's arm. "I think you've said enough for the present."

"Take your hand off me, young woman. You're not the only star in this show. It's my . . . my talent and experience that have . . ."

"Yes, Wilf, I know," said Mirrin. "But we really had better stop squabblin' an' get on with revising the act, don't you think?"

"What? Yes, yes! Quite right! I apologise, Mirrin. Of course, we should. See, Blanche, that's the stuff that real music-hall favourites are made of: never too good, never too tired to polish up the silverware, hm?"

"Come on, Blanche," Mirrin said, with an effort at being cheerful. "We'll both need to sing twice as loud to make up for Pru, won't we?"

Reluctantly, Blanche allowed herself to be led into the hall again and, minutes later, had become involved in the rearranged song-and-dance sequences that Wilf and Mirrin cooked up between them to cover up the absence of Pru Cropley.

By evening Pru's condition had worsened. She was fevered and had difficulty in breathing, though the doctor's prognosis was that the fever was not unduly serious and that she would be up and about again in a week or ten days. It took all Wilf's persuasiveness to drag Ada to the theatre that night and the performance was the worst that the troupe had ever inflicted upon the public.

During the next three days it became apparent that the seams of Wilfrid's dream craft were leaking badly and that Pru's recovery to full health would be long delayed.

Off her own bat, Ada summoned another doctor, a very posh gentleman from Abercromby Square, who came in a magnificent brougham and wore a sleek tile hat and a flowing cape, as if he was off to the opera and not visiting a patient. It cost Ada three guineas for the consultation. But she counted every penny worth it, in spite of Wilf's howling protests that the doctor was nothing but a rich charlatan. Pru Cropley had lung congestion, allied to a slight but perceptible murmur of the heart.

"Rest and care are the remedies," the doctor declared, as he wrote out a sheaf of three prescriptions for the local pharmacist. "The linctus will ease the congestion; the powders will assist the fever to break, and the dark bottle will sympathise with her heart."

Ada and Blanche thanked the medical gentleman profusely. Warming a little to the anxious women, he added the rider that really drove Wilfrid wild: "She's too old for this profession."

"Pru too old? She's younger than I am," Wilf protested.

"Be that as it may. She must not be fatigued or over-excited ever again."

"Ever?" Wilf's voice was shrill as a piccolo.

"I suggest that a quiet and easy life be accorded Miss Cropley from now on, if that is possible," the doctor said, as he swept his tile onto his head and tapped it down. "Unless you want to be in mourning very soon indeed."

The door closed. All the other guests lurking in the parlour and lounges of the Commercial Hotel quailed as Wilf yelled, *"Quack!"* and stamped upstairs to lock himself in the bedroom in a fit of pique that would have done Blanche at her worst quite proud.

On Sunday Ockram came. He heard Wilf's tale of woe with customary implacability and even allowed himself to be edged away from the others into a corner for a private enclave during which Wilf did most of the muttering. As he left, Ockram turned and said, "About that other matter, Wilf?"

"Yes, Ockram?"

"I'll take it up with Mr. Colcutt."

"Ah, yes, fine."

"What other matter?" Ada asked.

Wilf refused to say.

In the early hours of Monday morning Pru's fever broke and the thick congestive phlegm which had choked her lungs was released. Throughout the night, Ada, Mirrin and Blanche attended the patient, bringing hot water and towels and pieces of rag to sponge her sweating skin, then cool water to bathe her brow.

By first house Monday Pru was obviously through the wood for the time being and slept peacefully enough while her companions somehow tottered through two evening performances with as much verve—as Wilf put it—as a trio of Egyptian mummies.

Over the weekend the weather had turned foul. Leaden skies released a continual downpour. Liverpool's sewers were swollen and overflowing, bringing a stench into every nook and cranny of the Hippodrome to add to the misery of damp dressing rooms and dank backstage corridors.

Like the others Mirrin too felt below par and had to hold a rein on her temper with the audiences. Merciless in their condemnation, as they had once been unstinting in their applause, the clients were noisy and impatient, stamping their feet, throwing things, and spoiling many of the songs by roaring the words all jumbled and out of tempo. Even Mirrin could not settle them and catch their interest, though she tried every ruse she had learned. She poured herself at them, twice nightly, with coquettish songs and sentimental ballads and a barrage of repartee which, if she had been less inflamed, might have evoked their good humour and earned their support. But Liverpool was not Grossby and the polish had gone off Talboys' family act. Even the finale, 'Our Glorious Empire', sounded like a funeral dirge.

Wilfrid called his family together and earnestly implored them to put 'more heart' into it. When that failed and the ticket receipts began to reflect a drop in takings, Wilfred retaliated by purchasing, through Ockram, four new song sketches, three of which were tasteless, vulgar and bordering on the indecent. To Mirrin's disgust the audiences loved them and responded to every innuendo, every dirty wink and shake with a babble of obscene comment and gales of laughter. Even so ticket sales did not pick up much. Family parties thinned, making way for sailors and dockhands of the rougher sort who would stand for nothing but broadest comedy and as much ankle as they could persuade the girls to show beneath their dresses.

The month passed in disharmony and bickering. Unsettled feelings between the members of the family came to a climax a fortnight before the end of the booking. The only bright spot in the scene was that Pru's recovery was well advanced now and the 'snob' doctor had braved further insults to make a second and last call upon his frail little patient.

The final breakdown happened in the Hippodrome during a long Sunday afternoon rehearsal by means of which Wilf hoped to ginger his performers into redeeming the Liverpool booking at the last gasp.

"A finale," he raged. "I wouldn't call this a finale. Lord, we'll be lucky to finish at all. You, Mirrin, will you please not wander so far to the left?" He grabbed Mirrin's arm and swung her across the boards, then jerked her back sharply. "Come in there, come in."

"I'm not a bloody sheepdog, Wilf."

"Smile: smile: smile, *please*. Don't let it flag. You, Blanche, out to centre; slower, slower. Ada, come to the steps. Come *on:* come *on:* come . . ."

"NO!"

Paper-white, Ada clasped her hands in front of her breast and stood stock-still in stage centre.

"What did you say?" Wilf asked.

"NO."

"You'll have to."

"I *don't* have to."

"If we can't muster some discipline in Liverpool, how will we fare in London, I ask you?"

"Wilf, it's time to speak my mind," said Ada, with an effort at reasonableness. "I've talked it over with Blanche an' Pru an' WE-DON'T-WANT-TO-GO-TO-LONDON."

Though she spelled the words out loudly to ensure

that her husband would understand, Wilf gawped at her in total disbelief.

"What are you sayin', Ada?"

"I'm sayin' what's been in my mind for half a year. We're not so young as we was, dear, an' it's time we all took a well-earned rest."

"Rest? But Ada . . . ?"

Crossing the stage the woman placed her hands on his arms and with great tenderness, said, "Thanks to you, luv, we've done well an' made a good livin'. We've given a lot of pleasure, too, in our day. But that day's done, Wilf. It's time to bow out, dear, don't you see?"

"Pru put you up to this, didn't she?" hissed Wilf.

"Pru had nothin' to do with it," said Ada. "She wouldn't oppose you; never has. It's my idea."

"But what'll we do? Live on air and old memories?"

"There are so many things we can do, dear. We all like the seaside. We could live there. Open up a tea-shop or a boarding house. Pru will soon be well enough to help out, an' . . ."

"Give up the theatre?" Wilf gasped. "Open a lodging house? I'd . . . I'd be just as bad as Ernest Dawson then."

"There's nothin' bad about bein' secure and happy."

"Ernest's not happy. He's miserable."

"We'd still be servin' the public, Wilf, but in a different way."

Wilf lost his temper. He stamped his foot petulantly and yelled into the empty gods. "I'll not be cheated at this stage in the proceedings. On the eve of goin' to London, you . . . you . . . turn against me. Blanche, you'll come with me, won't you?"

"Father, I . . ."

"London's not like what we've been used to. Fine shops there, comfortable rooms, parks. *Our* name printed large outside the theatre. I've dreamed about a city engagement for years, now you say you don't want to go. We've an obligation to Mr. Colcutt."

"For ten years, Wilf, Harrison Colcutt's never looked near us. We've taken the risks an' the knocks: he's taken the money."

"He came to visit us in Beale, didn't he?"

"Only because he saw an opportunity to exploit us."

"Exploit? He's giving us our big chance. Blanche, what do you say?"

"I'm not goin' to London, father," the girl declared. "I'm goin' to Marlingford to marry Henry Essam."

"You . . . you . . ."

"You can't prevent me."

"Don't you *care* about the theatre, the family act?"

"Not much," said Blanche. "It was your life. I never had no choice in the matter. Now I have. I'm of age to do as I like. No, I'll not be in London, that's a certainty."

Desperately, Wilf ran round the centre of the stage, gesticulating wildly and ranting at the deserted aisles, as if his mutinous family were there instead of by his side. "Good: good: we at least know where we stand. Better now than later. The Christmas Show at the Marylebone Road Pantheon, right in the palm of me hand, an' you scupper me! *You.* Me own *family!* Oh, that it should ever come to this!"

"Wilf, please: control yourself," said Ada.

"I will *not* be denied it. I will not be cheated of my Christmas Show. None of you deserve it. So, creep away to your seaside lodgin' houses an' your snivellin' carpenters. *I'll go myself.*"

Mirrin tried not to smile. The situation had no real humour in it, but she was reminded of her own father and mother, bristling and bawling. She stepped forward to calm the jabbering theatrical. "C'mon, Wilf. Why don't you an' Ada step out for a bit of dinner an' talk this over calmly."

She was startled at the speed with which Wilfrid swung on her. Eyes gleaming, as though possessed by a wonderful vision, he threw out his arms and embraced her. "Mirrin: *yes:* you and I! Of *course!* Colcutt never did want those others. He said so himself. It was your . . . *your* sparkle an' my experience that pulled us out of the gutter. Well, let's make it you an' I? We'll take the Pantheon by storm." He scrawled in thin air with a long forefinger, and intoned, "Wilfrid Talboys and the Songbird of the North."

"No, Wilf Talboys," said Ada, before Mirrin could reply. "Won't you listen t'sense, luv. It's just too late in comin'. You're too old t'start anew. It's allers been a family act. But now Pru's sick: I'm weary, an' Blanche wants a life of her own. It's not the end of us, Wilf. We can settle in Marlingford, to be near Blanche and her husband. It's not the end. We have our nest-egg. We can still have a nice comfortable life."

"Outside the halls?"

"It was good. But it's over, luv."

"No."

Sadly, Ada said, "We're as determined as you are, Wilf. It's your choice now. You can have the loyalty and love of your family, or . . ."

Cheeks purple with rage, his chest heaving, with an inarticulate bellow, Wilf swung round and leapt down over the footlights into the shallow part of the orchestra trough and stalked, still shouting, up the centre aisle towards the doors. He barged through them into the grey twilight and disappeared into the street.

"I'm afraid we've hurt him deeply, luv," Ada said to Blanche.

"It had to be said," Blanche replied, gathering her coat, hat and gloves from the piano top. "He's had his own way too long."

"Should he be left alone?" Mirrin asked.

"Oh, he'll come round," Ada said, blinking back tears. "He's had a shock, that's all."

"What . . . what'll he do?" asked Mirrin.

"Don't you fret. Colcutt will see you right. It's really only you Colcutt wants, lass. I think Wilf senses that, too. The rest of us—including my poor husband—well, we're not much to write about. Not London material. You'll make it alone, Mirrin."

"But I don't want to make it alone."

Ada said, "You'd take Wilf from us?"

"That's up to Wilf," Mirrin said.

"No, luv, it's really up to you."

The ale-house was not respectable. Under normal circumstances Wilfrid Talboys would not have been found dead there, rubbing shoulders with hardened boozers and rowdy bargees. But it was any old port in a storm; he had half expected his family to come flying after him and had sought refuge in the first lighted hostelry he had come to. He hid himself in a corner, wretched, shivering with nervous exhaustion, and the shock of Ada's ultimatum.

Three tankards of strong ale warmed him, but did not ease his depression. He drank dourly, ignoring the other drinkers, hunched over his mug.

It should not have happened now, not with success just within reach. It was wrong and cruel of Ada, Pru and Blanche to desert him. What if Pru *was* a bit poorly. She wasn't essential to the act. She could travel with them, look after the costumes or something undemanding like that. They could afford to carry her for a while. He would never abandon her. Pru was just Ada's excuse.

Then there was Blanche, won away from him by a rabbit-chinned chippie from an east coast spa. What sort of viper had he reared? Was she so spoiled that she would grab a husband even at the peril of her whole family's career? More of the rod might have done the child good. Too late for that now.

He ordered, and drank a fourth tankard.

Mirrin Stalker: she was still on his side. Trust a Scotch lass to be loyal. Not even his flesh and blood. Still, Mirrin was all he needed to make a go of the London booking. The Londoners would adore her. Colcutt would have to make some adjustments, find replacements for Ada, Blanche and Pru. But that wouldn't be difficult. Indeed, it would probably benefit the act to have three younger women. Anger rose in him again. Ada had implied that he was old. By God, if he had her here now he would show her who was old.

Rapping the empty tankard on the table, he signalled to the landlord to bring him another throat-swab and when it duly arrived made swift inroads into it at once.

So what was it they wanted him to do? Him, Wilfrid Talboys, who had braved the wrath of his parents and the scorn of his mates to carve a career for himself on the music-hall stage. And he had almost succeeded. Almost reached the goal. Now they politely indicated that he was too old to enjoy the fruits of a lifetime's work, and had better bow meekly to his years and—of all things—open a teashop in Marlingford. Even a lodging house would be better. His friend Ernest made a tidy living out of a boarding residence; Marlingford was a better location than Grossby any day, especially in the high summer season. It was rumoured in knowledgeable quarters that now that the railway was in and new buildings springing up, Marlingford might become the Blackpool of the east coast. But he didn't believe it: nor did it matter much. He wouldn't be there. Not him. He'd be topping the Pantheon Christmas Show, basking in rapturous applause, taking bow after bow for the sketches with Mirrin. God, a teashop! Pink cakes, paper doylies and a parade of withered women nattering on about how they kept their hubbies under their thumbs—that was no choice.

Unasked, the landlord brought him a sixth tankard of ale. Hurriedly Wilf swallowed the remains of its predecessor.

"Pay the slate, old mate," the landlord suggested.

Fumbling, Wilf skidded his horseshoe purse across the table.

"Take what's due."

The landlord did so. Wilf continued to drink, more slowly now, with a certain effort to the gullet.

By God, what right had Ada to dictate to him? He would go straight back to the Commercial Hotel and have it out with her. Was he not the captain of his own ship? That's what he should have done earlier. No beating about the bush—London. He thumped his fist on the table. If Pru didn't like the idea of being a costume maid, then she could take her share of the savings and go off and bake pies, for all he cared. Good riddance!

Supporting himself on his hands, Wilf drew himself to his feet. The beams and floor of the tavern were all at sixes and sevens, tilted like the list of a ship at sea. Gaslamps were blossoming into fat orange trees dripping with dozens of round ripe fruit. He shook his

head. Not that drunk, Wilf ol' boy. Can't be squiffed
on a mere six tankards. Imbibe that many quarts and
still walk the chalk line any day. He scrabbled for his
purse, lifted it and shook it before him like a leper's
bell. Not a sound. He let the purse yawn open, saw
that it was empty. His forefinger probed into the
depths. Yes, empty.

"Two pounds!" he said, indistinctly. " 'Ad two
pounds."

Lurching to the counter where the landlord, rubbing
his knuckles down the front of his buckram apron,
waited, Wilf wagged the purse and shrilled, *"Robber!
Thief! I 'ad two quid in 'ere."*

"Who the bliddy 'ell be you callin' a thief?"

"Six shillings I owe. You took two pounds."

"Six shillings I took."

"D'you know whom you are addressin'."

"I don't care if you're the ghost o'Prince Albert, you
owed six shillings an' I took six shillings; notter penny
more."

"Fetch me a constable," Wilf shouted.

"Fetch one yourself," the landlord said. "I'll help
y'on your way."

Wilf had the strange sensation of reverting to a previous moment in his life when he had ventured on to
the stage of the Palace in Newcastle as a volunteer
assistant to an aerialist whose partner had fallen sick.
He had flown through the air, like a parrot glued to
its perch, while the woman—strong as an ox she was
—gripped his wrists and hissed at him to keep still.
His flight across the taproom of the Liverpool hostelry
was much shorter and the landing much ruder. He
struck the sawdust, damp and sodden by the door,
and went skidding on out on his rump straight across
the rainy pavement to sprawl headlong into the gutter.

Only his drunkenly relaxed state saved him from
injury. As it was, the knees were torn from his trousers
and his jacket was ripped. He sustained shallow grazes
upon his palms which bled considerably and added an
horrendous touch to the portrait of wrecked humanity
he presented when, some twenty minutes later, he
barged into the dining room of the Commercial Hotel

in Linden Street, wrestling with the manager of the
establishment who had tried to prevent him crossing
the foyer, and bellowed, "ADA."

The diners jumped. The ladies covered their mouths
with their fans and the gentlemen, who were not really
in the white tie class, pretended that they were and
rose, with dignity, to defend their families and companions from the nightmarish intruder.

"Mr. Talboys: Mr. Talboys: really, sir, I must . . ."

"Shurrup! ADA."

"How dare you, you ruffian."

"I want Ada."

"Father!"

"BLANCHE! WHERE'S YOUR MMMMOTHER?"

Daughter and sister-in-law advanced on Wilf from
a corner table to which secluded nook the theatricals
had been gently eased early in their stay.

"Wilf Talboys, you're drunk," Pru stated.

"DRUNK BUT DETERMINED: Y'HEAR ME?"

"Go upstairs, father, this minute."

Even through an alcoholic fog, Wilf knew that he
had overstepped the mark. The expression on his
daughter's face was enough to chill even the hottest
rage. Sobriety rushed upon Wilf Talboys.

Even as Blanche reached for him, he made one last
ale-inspired attempt to rule the roost again, puffing
himself up like a cock pigeon and jutting his chin out.
"Are y'sorry?"

"I . . . I . . ." Blanche was flabbergasted at the
audacity.

"Well, I'll forgive you," Wilf announced. "I'm a
genn'ous man. We'll say n'more about it. I'll even consider lettin' you come t'London wi' Mirrin an' me."

Eloquent gestures of clemency overbalanced him.
Blanche had little alternative but to clasp him in her
arms, just as Ada and Mirrin, who had been delayed
for dinner, arrived in the room.

But Wilf did not notice them. Abruptly he succumbed to the pressures of strong ale and blind rage,
and swooned clean away.

It was all Blanche could do to support him until
Mirrin, Ada and the hotel manager, acting without

much harmony, managed to drag the bedraggled trouper out of the dining room and up two flights of stairs to his bed.

Even the light of a single candle made his eyes throb and his head ache. His mouth was parched, his throat gritty, as if he had eaten handfuls of wet sand.

"Ada?" he croaked. "Aaaaada?"

Mirrin smiled thinly. "Not so chipper now, Wilf, are you?"

"I . . . I want my Ada."

"That won't be so easy. They've left, all three of them."

Wilf sat bolt upright, like Lazarus summoned from the dead. His mouth sagged open, then formed into a long oval of numb pain. He clapped his shaky hands to the crown of his head as if to hold his skull in place.

"Lie down, Wilf," Mirrin said. "You're not recovered yet."

Stiffly Wilf allowed the girl to coax him back against the pillow of the hotel bed.

A small china jug steamed on a ring over the candle. He could smell coffee. The very aroma made him nauseous, as Mirrin tapped off a cup and held it, black and scalding, to his retreating lips.

"Drink it."

"Nooooooo."

"Drink it, or I'll pour it on your head."

Shuddering, Wilf took the liquid into his mouth and allowed it to trickle over his gorge. Remorselessly Mirrin pressed more upon him until the invalid cup was empty.

Wilf groaned. "Really . . . really left?"

"Oh, don't panic: they haven't deserted you. We've all been politely requested to take ourselves off from the Commercial. You did create rather a scene down there in the dining room. Ada, Pru and Blanche didn't feel like brazening it out. I persuaded the manager to allow you to stay until you'd recovered your senses."

"Wah' . . . what time?"

"It's after eleven."

"I don't . . . don't know what came over me." Wilf

shook his head, then clutched it again instantly. "Give me . . . more of that stuff, Mirrin, please."

A second cup of coffee revived him enough to listen intelligently to the girl.

She said, "They're not far away. Just down the road at the George."

"I . . . feel awful."

"I'm not surprised. But I haven't much sympathy, Wilf; not for you. Not only did you give your devoted family a humiliating experience tonight, you've driven them far too hard for far too long."

"You too," Wilf said. "But you don't complain."

"I can take it," Mirrin said. "But I'll tell you this, Wilfrid Talboys, you'd need the constitution of a coal-heaver to survive this theatrical life for long."

"Yes, it's . . . it's hard. But it's rewarding."

"I've made a bit of silver, Wilf, I'm not denyin' it. But money's not what I want."

"I . . . I see."

Mirrin watched him. Sympathy for Pru and Ada was uppermost in her mind, but there was an irritated compassion for Wilf Talboys, too. As Ada said, she had come into their lives too late. So caught up with his ambition was Wilf that he could not discern what Ada saw so clearly, that they had given their youth to the pursuit of fame and glory only as an excuse to do what they really wanted to do. The fame, the glory, these were mere rationalisations to succour them when times were hard. Everyone needed that kind of vindication for waywardness, for risk, for embarking on a search that could never have an ending. In striving, the Talboys had found happiness and love. But it was over. It was time to change the scene, choose a ballad now to sing them out, not a jig.

Aye, Mirrin thought, I have looked down that road myself, not knowing what I really wanted, made blind by half-forgotten fears, daft pride and vanity. She had shut her mind to Tom's sincerity, a year ago, a whole tapsalteerie year ago. It had been a wild, mad, gay ride, but it was time for her to dismount now. Sense and instinct told her where she belonged—not in London, not even in England, but back home, with her own hard-working down-to-earth kind, in Lanarkshire.

Tom had chased away the spectre of the pit. It was the pit she had really hated, its haunted shafts and perpetual filth. He had sold her, without even trying, the vision of green earth, and the enduring quality of that earth, tangibly handed down from generation to generation. He had spoken of sweat and tears—aye there would be plenty of those, for sure—but he had not played on the romantic in her, nor lured her with talk of the land in spring, or the freedom of working for one's own destiny.

She loved that passion in men, a fire of enthusiasm that did not dwindle when the rain of reality fell. Aye, Tom might talk practical, but his promise to her, his demand on her, was seeded still in dreams.

"It's not for Ada's sake, Wilf; no, nor for yours. I'm goin' home," she said, softly, "because I want to."

"When?"

"When this engagement's over."

"How can you turn your back on . . . ?" Wilfrid sighed. "Hah! I'm a fine one to ask that question. All that . . . that fuss tonight, Mirrin, that's *my* way of turnin' my back on London. Ada won't change her mind. She never has. She's stuck by me, indulged me through thick and thin. If the old gal says it's time to hang up the costumes, then it is. I know it too."

"Who'll tell Colcutt?"

"Don't fret about him," said Wilf. "I could never pick when to work for him, but, dash it all, Mirrin, at least I can pick my time to stop."

"Wilf, I'm sorry."

"Is it the love of some man or other that takes you off home?"

"It is."

"Well, I can't say I blame you," Wilf told her. "I suppose it's difficult to settle at your age. Ay, but it would have been grand to see you at the top, lass."

"Maybe I will be yet, Wilf, though not on a stage."

Wilf nodded. "That's true. Spirit will out, whether you choose it or not."

"At least, Wilf, we'll go out with a bang."

"I already have," the trouper said.

But they did not go out with a bang. Audiences in Liverpool were not forgiving. The last shows of the Talboys' career were not brightened by much applause. Ockram accepted Wilf's verbal 'resignation' with surly ill-grace. For days the company lived in a state of dread lest Harrison Colcutt once more dragged himself from his lair, this time to blackmail them into fulfilling the London engagement. It was the dread which indicated, even to Wilf, that the theatre had lost every last ounce of its charm for his family. Truth was thrown into high relief by the removal of the burden of endless shows and rehearsals. Ada was once more jolly, and Blanche showed a loving side to her nature. Both women were particularly attentive to Wilf. By nature Wilf Talboys had always been ebullient. Even before Mirrin's departure for Scotland, the morning after the final curtain, he had thrown himself wholeheartedly into plans for a different kind of future, that of boarding-house keeper.

Money was not a major problem. Blanche and Pru would go on ahead to Marlingford, to reside, for a while, with Henry Essam's family, while Ada and Wilf took themselves back to Grossby, to 'study' under the Dawsons and, Wilf predicted, to spend a very merry Christmas, indeed. At the start of the year, the couple would make for Marlingford in search of a little bit o'property. The sea air would soon make Pru well again, and the marriage between Blanche and her faithful carpenter would keep Ada occupied. And, if the little Palace theatre in the resort did happen ever to need a concert party of some experience and repute, then . . .

Mirrin remembered her theatrical family in tableau as they stood behind the railing in the railway station. It had been a hectic last hour, with Wilf overseeing the stowing of Mirrin's boxes into the guardsvan, and Ada and Pru ascertaining that she had plenty of things to eat during the long journey north. But when that was all done and the engine building steam and carriage doors slamming and porters' whistles shrilling, Mirrin found them strangely still.

"I hate farewells," Ada said. "I've had so many of them, luv. Each one becomes so much harder than the last."

The plump homely woman sniffed and dabbed her eyes with her handkerchief. Pru and Blanche, too, shed tears. Wilf was there to comfort them, to ginger their flagging spirits with a secret jest. He would always be a man for tomorrow, an eternal optimist who would dream his dreams until the day he died.

Mirrin had known many kinds of dreamer, met many travellers in a year that had been full of excitement and emotion. She had learned the hard way that change was the prerogative of everyone, and that a dream could be the root of worthwhile realities. Houston, Wilf, Blanche, and Tom, her Tom. Lord, did Tom Dandy know what he had taken on?

Suddenly she swung away from the barrier and hurried along the platform, pausing at the carriage door to look back. They had gone, all of them, vanished. Surprised and just a little hurt, Mirrin peered through wreaths of steam and smoke until the guard told her to hurry on, and the tall, imperious blast of the engine's whistle made her quickly pick up her skirts and find her seat inside.

That, however, was not quite the last of the Talboys. For there they were again, breathless and flushed, at the very end of the long platform, having hurried round by the shunter's gate. As the train chugged and heaved to gather speed, they stood in line under a handpainted banner, arms linked, singing to the weeping girl who had passed through their lives like a falling star.

Though she could not hear the words, the tune rang in Mirrin's head. Stippled out in blue distemper on the long white canvas prompter, it said,

THEN LOVE YOUR NEIGHBOUR AS YOURSELF
  AS THE WORLD YOU GO TRAVELLING THROUGH,
AND NEVER SIT DOWN WITH A TEAR OR A FROWN,
  BUT PADDLE YOUR OWN CANOE.

GOOD LUCK AND GOD BLESS.

Yes, Mirrin thought, she would paddle her own canoe all right, back home in Scotland. But, come the January Hiring Fair, she would no longer do it alone.

Four

NOVEMBER GROWLED, OLD and irascible, in the community consciousness. Dusk came early. The sky above the town was dim and cold, promising a frosty night. But there was light enough for all to see the sight that set the tongues wagging. The glow of lanterns and lamps that strung the pithead workings was augmented by limelights bushed above the gates through which the sorters hurried from their shift at the shutes and the next batch of underground workers trudged from their warm firesides.

The bold brass neck of the returning prodigal created a stir that was more than a nine days' wonder and passed quickly down into the town's mythology, sustained by the events that Mirrin powered in the weeks following her homecoming.

"What's that?"

"Where?"

"There, at the gate yonder. Is it Edith Lamont spyin' on her hubby?"

"In that hat?"

"My God! It's Mirrin Stalker. Would y'credit it? Look, look at that conveyance. Must have cost a fortune t'hire."

"My, but she's a brazen bitch!"

"She's come back for the bairn. I said all along it was hers."

"Here, I wonder if Kate knows."

"Kate? Kate? See, there's your sister."

"There, Kate, waitin' at the gate for you, like the Queen o'Sheba."

The sleek black four-wheeler had been hired in Hamilton. That, at least, had been deliberate. It did not occur to Mirrin now to seek out some rumble cart to transport her bandboxes and valises from Hamilton station. She had the money and she had the style—and she was mischievous enough not to ignore an opportunity.

She had spent the best part of two days travelling, putting up at a change-hotel, not hurrying. She was damned if she would sneak in at the back door of the narrow house. She was not ashamed of the rewards of her stint in the south, and knew enough of the mores of Blacklaw to be certain that the villagers would have misinterpreted her success. There was, too, the matter of Drew's child, the poor bastard mite that had been wished on to her, to protect her dear brother's good name. Besides, it gave her pleasure to sit high in Hamilton's best hired carriage and watch the countryside go past, nostalgic as any homecoming traveller who had been away for such a time.

The day dress with matching jacket was less expensive than it looked. The velvet Rubens hat and its silken streamers had cost almost as much. The mound of luggage in the carriage boot was tall enough to be roped. Seated behind the driver, watching the gate, Mirrin nodded without undue effusion, to folk she had once called her friends, who now skirted the hackney carriage as if it was a plague cart.

Then Kate came, running, skirts held up. She stopped at the carriage step.

"Mirrin?"

"Aye, it's me, luv."

"You've come home."

"For a while. Here, climb aboard."

"Me? But . . . but I'm all mucky."

"The upholstery'll clean."

"Mirrin, I . . ."

"Get up."

Reluctantly, Kate scrambled up into the carriage

and Mirrin instructed the driver to take them down
Main Street.

"Mirrin, you look so . . . so different."

"Fatter?"

"No, but . . . different."

"How's Mam?"

"She's well enough. I wish . . . I wish you hadn't
met me at the colliery, though."

"Why not?"

"Everybody's starin'."

"Let them stare."

"But . . ." Kate stammered. "There's somethin'
you should know."

"The baby?" Mirrin said. "They think it's mine.
Well, let them think what they like."

Kate's cheeks were scarlet. She cringed into the
corner of the leather seat, especially when Mirrin
waved to acquaintances on the pavement, women and
men who paused and gaped open-mouthed as the
grand carriage rolled on downhill towards the bottom
of the row.

"Stop it, Kate," Mirrin said, softly. "Stop glowerin'
at me. Aren't you pleased I've come home?"

"Oh, Mirrin! I've never been so glad t'see anyone
in my life."

"That's nice t'know," Mirrin said, then added, "but
I suspect it means you've got problems. Who is it this
time? Drew again?"

"It's Betsy."

"Betsy?" Mirrin leaned across the seat to squeeze
Kate's hand. "Never mind. I think *I* can handle that
young lady."

Then the reserve between the sisters vanished and
they hugged each other, glad to be together again, in
spite of the changes that the months had wrought
upon them both and on the township through whose
twilight streets they rode in such awfully public view.

The whole town was buzzing with the news. Callum
Ewing took it upon himself to tell his son, dropping
the information at dinner with a casualness that be-
lied the anxiety the old miner felt.

"So, Rob, she's back."

"Is she now? How did she look?"

"Fine."

"That's good," Rob Ewing said, then, with equal casualness, "Pass me the tatties, Da'."

It was Anna Thrush who told Edith. The housekeeper collared the bustling little mistress of the mansion in the hallway as she, Edith, hastened to keep a dinner engagement in the house of the Reverend Durley, also a coalmaster of sorts and much interested in reform, who lived rather grandly in Glenryan some ten miles to the west.

"I do not really see what that piece of gossip has to do with me," Edith Lamont said to her housekeeper.

"I imagined that you might be interested," Anna said. "She used to work here, I believe."

"All *that* is in the past, Anna."

"My informant tells me that she arrived in an expensive carriage, laden with expensive luggage."

"Perhaps she has snared another fool."

"*Another* fool?" said Anna, pointedly.

"Is my carriage waiting?"

"For the past half hour."

"I may be late in returning, Anna: there is no need to wait up."

"Very good, madam," Anna said.

Edith Lamont paused in the doorway and, without looking round, said, "Where is Mr. Lamont tonight?"

"At a meeting, in Hamilton."

"Alone?"

"Sydney is with him."

"Thank you, Anna."

"Goodnight, Mrs. Lamont."

"Goodnight."

Sydney Thrush learned of Mirrin Stalker's arrival soon after the event became public. He had it from Davy Dunlop who had it from a weasel-like clerk who had been so agog that he had returned to the managers' office specifically to broadcast the amazing fact, though neither man was aware of its significance in respect of their boss. Though he had never clapped eyes on Mirrin Stalker, Sydney Thrush was acquainted, chapter and verse, with much of Lamont's stormy relationship with the girl. Long ago, Thrush had marked the collier's daughter as a wayward factor in governing the coalmaster's behaviour.

After Lamont's return from his long trip to Holland and Yorkshire, Sydney had noted dramatic changes in the man. By probing and prying, he had gathered sufficient data to ascertain that Lamont had spent part of that summer in this Stalker girl's company.

Volatile relationships within the mansion had settled soon after Lamont's return. The coalmaster, though sour and moody, was no longer a recluse, and had almost given up drinking. Indeed, he attacked the business of pit profits with a zeal that Thrush could only admire, the more so as it married well with his own management policies. Since then, throughout the autumn, owner and manager had pulled like matched horses against the vagaries of the market and sullen work-force, gaining ground all round and increasing the monthly profit by dunning the colliers still further into subjection and by meting out harsh justice to radicals, militants and to shirkers.

Nonetheless, Sydney Thrush was apprehensive when he imparted the news of the Stalker girl's return to his superior. He waited until the droning speeches and interminable, fatuous arguments which concluded dinner in the hotel were over and port and the brandy were, by tradition, circulating, before he murmured in Lamont's ear: "By the way, sir, I hear that the girl Stalker came home this afternoon."

The brandy glass paused and, instantly, a slight trembling of the hand slopped the amber liquid in the bowl. Houston Lamont, who, a few minutes before, had been the personification of a powerful and self-assured ruling class, seemed to slacken, as if Thrush had cut a mainstay which held all the parts of his stern personality together.

"Are you . . . are you certain, Thrush?"

"Quite certain, coalmaster," Thrush answered, and went on to explain what he knew of the circumstances of Mirrin Stalker's return. Lamont listened with an avidity that brooked no interruptions, his sad eyes bright again, a strange smile upon his lips.

"She had luggage, you say?"

Thrush nodded. "A great heap of it."

"Then she intends to stay."

"Perhaps she's like your good lady wife, sir," Thrush said, "and travels with more than she needs."

"No, not Mirrin," Lamont said. "She's come home for good."

"Coalmaster, if you'll excuse my impertinence, what are the Stalkers to you?"

"That," said Houston Lamont curtly, "is none of your concern, Thrush."

"You gave them a house."

"They pay for it."

"And there's the lad in Edinburgh, living on your patronage."

"A charitable gesture, that's all."

"There's a rumour that this Mirrin girl is the mother of the child in the Stalkers' house: what truth . . . ?"

"No truth whatsoever, Thrush," Lamont said. "Now, fill my glass if you please."

Thrush poured a fresh brandy for his boss without another word on the subject which, as the coalmaster had just reminded him, was none of his business. It was ironic, however, that he should never have met this woman, this *femme fatale*, who if he played his cards correctly, might help in his plan to acquire effective control of Blacklaw colliery and all the power that went with it.

Mirrin had been home for five days. The villagers were bitterly disappointed that they had seen no sign of her about the streets. She kept to herself, locked indoors, it was said, because she was ashamed. Maybe she was pregnant again. But that did not reconcile with her grand entry. Other coteries in Blacklaw were of the opinion that Mirrin was just biding her time.

Those few who had the temerity to quiz Kate at the sorting troughs were given the blunt answer that Mirrin was indeed home for a short holiday before returning

to London. Those who had the courage to ruffle Mam
Stalker's feathers by enquiring after her middle daughter's health and welfare were sent off with a flea in
their lugs.

On the surface Mirrin's return made no difference
to Mam and Kate. The old woman continued with her
round on the baker's van, Neill Campbell Stalker, sitting up and taking more notice of his surroundings
now, still with her. Kate turned up for her shift each
morning, as always, on time, and called in on Willie
Kellock each evening on her way home. It was the
third adult member of the Stalker household who was
most shaken by her sister's return. She discussed its
implications thoroughly with her friend and mentor,
Mr. Randolph Newton, as they lay in bed in the hotel
in Glasgow that Wednesday night.

"Why are you so afraid, Betsy?"

"Mirrin's always been a dragon."

"I thought you said she had changed and mellowed."

"Changed but not mellowed. My brother and I
have never been held in much favour by her."

"That hardly surprises me. If your twin is anything
like you, Betsy, then he must rub your conventional
family quite the wrong way."

"Randolph, it isn't a joking matter."

"Do you think that she suspects—about our relationship?"

"It's . . . possible," answered Betsy. "Kate's been
very icy t'me this past few months."

"How the devil could they have found out?"

"God knows!" said Betsy.

For some time Randolph said nothing, lying on his
back staring at the ceiling. Abruptly he pushed himself from the bed and crossed, naked, to the table to
pour himself wine. Sipping it, he said softly, "It may
be time for us to part, my love."

"Yes, that had occurred to me, too," said Betsy.

"I shall miss you, you know."

"You'll find another mistress easy enough."

"But not one like you."

"I take that as a glowin' compliment."

"Do you regret what's happened?"

"On the contrary," said Betsy. "You've taught me a lot, Randolph."

"That *is* immodest."

"I don't mean just here, in bed," the girl replied. "You've taught me that daft inhibitions bred into girls like me from birth are nothin' at all. An' you've taught me that I can look out for myself too, without goin' to the dogs."

"Don't you feel like a 'ruined woman'?"

"Not in the least."

Randolph sighed. "I will be sorry not to see you again."

"A clean break is best. It was, after all, that kind of relationship, was it not?"

"Yes, I suppose it was."

Betsy sat up, hair bobbing, her face beaming with astonishment. "You *like* me. I never realised it before. It wasn't just what I gave you, was it? You actually like me? A man o'the world, like you."

Randolph laughed ruefully. "Yes, I like you. Not because you're beautiful and co-operative, and certainly not because you're nice."

"Why then?"

"Because you have no scruples at all."

"Thank you!"

"You're not reckless, or feckless, but you are strong, Betsy Stalker. Don't let anyone ever tell you otherwise."

"Is this to be the last time?"

"Yes."

"It's just as well," said Betsy. "I'm becoming too dependent on you."

"Now," said Randolph, returning to bed, "let's see what I can do for you, to honour my side of the bargain."

"You've given me quite enough."

"Edinburgh," Randolph said, "is an expensive city."

"My brother will look after me."

"No, no, my love," Randolph said. "You must learn to look after yourself."

"Come t'think of it, you're right again."

"I like to flatter myself," Randolph said, "that I have given you your start in life."

"And what have I given you?"

"Pleasure," said Randolph Newton.

"Has that been enough?"

"More than enough, I assure you."

Betsy sighed. "At least," she said, "we still have the rest of the night."

"That's true," Randolph said and, turning, took her tenderly in his arms.

Mirrin could not adjust to the narrow house. She felt constricted by it, imprisoned. Its snugness gave her no comfort. In her heart she knew that this period marked the end of her youth. Blacklaw was almost behind her, the old Blacklaw, the Blacklaw of her childhood. At last she had really put herself apart from it, beyond it. The admission made her just a little sad. It was a door she could not re-enter, that simple workaday existence with its upheavals, minor intrigues, strange rules and almost holy rituals.

Behind her too were all the roads she had not taken, all the opportunities that she had passed by. Life she supposed was full of such doubts and lingering regrets, too rich a thing in its essence to commit lightly to one course. Tom had tried to explain it to her, at the *Creagan* inn that distant autumn night, but she had not had sufficient experience to accept it then. "Each time I come home, the grip has loosened." That was true.

Never mind, Tom Dandy! If her trust in him was honoured, he would have a lifetime to explain it to her come the day of the hiring fair.

Mam, Kate, and Betsy too, seemed infected by the impermanence of things. Perhaps Mirrin's newfound poise disconcerted Flora, who had taken so long to adjust to the tomboyish qualities in her daughter.

Betsy was polite, curious about her time on the stage, but cautious, bearing out Kate's suspicions that the young girl was, perhaps, involved in an affair that had gone beyond the handholding and cuddling romances that were to be expected at eighteen. To Kate's chagrin, Mirrin did not broach the subject with her young sister.

During those first few days, apart from exchanging news with her mother and sisters, she touched not at all upon her reasons for her sudden return. As November gripped more tightly, and Mirrin showed no inclination to begin digging in again, Kate became anxious, and testy. She had expected Mirrin to cut through their problems like a sword. Such passivity, such patience, were unusual traits in Mirrin. Kate was irritated by them.

Neill was bathed and fed and put down in the cradle, by the hearth. Attentively his eyes followed the play of the firelight upon the brass smoke canopy and the flicker of the lamp upon the plates on the dresser. Kate knelt by the cradle, hand upon her nephew's shoulder. He liked that comforting touch in the minutes before sleep claimed him. Flora was seated in the upright chair that had once belonged to Alex, but which, under her weight, had sagged into bulging middle-age. The house was not so neat as it had once been; Flora had grown careless of things since she had taken the job at Kellocks and since Neill had arrived on the scene. From the dissolving crystal of the family, Flora too had formed an independent identity.

When Neill was fast asleep, and Kate and Mirrin had carefully carried the cradle into the bedroom and returned, Kate said, "You've never told us yet, Mirrin, why you've come back home?"

"Now's as good a time as any, I suppose," Mirrin said. "I've come home to marry."

"You?" Mam exclaimed, colour draining from her face. "Marry? Who? What . . . what man?"

"Tom Armstrong's his name."

"That tink lad you told us about?" said Kate.

"He's no tink now," Mirrin said. "He's goin' into farmin'."

"Where?"

"In these parts."

"But . . . but where is he?" said Flora.

"I don't know," said Mirrin. "I've to meet him at

Lanark Hiring Fair in January. We'll marry then—if he still wants me."

"Oh, God!" said Mam. "Our Mirrin marryin' a tink."

"Would you rather I'd married a coalmaster?"

Kate glanced sharply at her sister. "No, Mirrin," she murmured. "Don't."

"Why not?" Mirrin said. "I could have gone off with Houston Lamont, Mam. He wanted me, too."

"I don't want t'hear: I don't want t'hear," Flora groaned.

"Aye, Lamont," Mirrin went on. "It's because of him, in a way, that I'm here now."

"What are y'sayin', Mirrin?" Flora said.

Calmly, Mirrin went on. "What's so shocking about that? I had a love . . . a time of love with Houston; when I worked in the mansion."

Flora began to weep, but oddly there was no real hurt or shame in it. After a moment, wiping her eyes on her cuffs, she ceased shedding tears, and, instead, indulged a cautious curiosity about the daughter she had never understood.

Mirrin said, "It's no great surprise to you, Mam, I'm sure. You heard the rumors. Maybe you chose to close your ears t'them, but you knew that they were true in part."

"Why do you tell me now, Mirrin?" asked Flora.

"What I did then, I did for you, for all of you; Drew in particular," Mirrin said. "Och, it was no great act of sacrifice. I thought I was in love with Houston Lamont. I *was* in love with him—*then*. It wasn't the loving that drove the bargain, but the parting."

"Why didn't you tell me, Mirrin?" Flora asked.

"Because you wouldn't have understood."

"But you tell me now? Have I changed that much?"

"Aye, you have, Mam: we all have."

"Because of Neill?" said Kate. "That's your reason, Mirrin, is it not?"

"You were willin' to shield Drew by lettin' the lie stand, the lie that Neill was my child," Mirrin said. Flora opened her lips to protest.

"Maybe you didn't say it, but you didn't deny it,"

Mirrin continued. "I was safe away: I had a 'bad name' anyway. It was only Mirrin. It didn't matter much what folk thought of her."

"I never . . . never told a soul that Neill was your baby," Flora said.

"But did you ever, once, deny it, Mam?" Mirrin said. "Or you, Kate? Did you tell anyone the truth?"

"Drew's so young," Kate said.

"He's what we made him."

"We're finished with him now," Kate said. "I made that clear when I took Neill away."

"We're not finished with Drew," Mirrin said. "God help us, but I wonder if we'll ever be finished with him."

"Are you weddin' this tinker out of spite, Mirrin?" Flora asked.

"I'm marryin' Tom Armstrong out of love."

"Is he the best you can do?" Flora demanded waspishly.

"That's it, Mam: that's what's wrong with you, *and* this damned town. I'm pegged t'a station, t'a manner of behaviour. Well, I never could thole it. I had to leave to find out the truth. Now, I know what I am. I'm Blacklaw—yet I'm not Blacklaw. I'm Alex Stalker's daughter—yet I'm not like my Da'. I'm Flora Stalker's middle girl—but I'm not like you either. I'm all of these things, yet I'm an individual. I can choose t'be what I wish."

"A tinkie wife?"

"If you call him a tink again, mother," Mirrin snapped, "I'll walk out that door right now an' that'll be an' end of it."

"Is he a good man, Mirrin?" Kate asked.

"He's as good a man as I'll ever want," Mirrin replied. "He'll look after me."

"Is that all that matters?" Kate asked.

"Look, luv, I *picked* Tom," Mirrin said. "It's not like it would have been if I married Rob. That would have been because I had little or no choice. But choice is given t'all of us, if we're bold enough t'take it. Don't you see that yet? Don't you see that we're all of us drifting, that only when some terrible event rocks us do we ever consider change. Look at you, Mam."

"What have I done?"

"Changed."

"I'm old now, Mirrin, an' widowed. You've no right t'accuse me."

"I'm not accusin' you, Mam. You've got your job at the baker's, an' you've got wee Neill t'raise, an' love."

"Is that so dreadful?" said Kate.

"But you really didn't much care how you got him," said Mirrin. "Look round you. See them, the boys and the girls, my age, not so much older, aged already, beginnin' t'decay. But we Stalkers called a halt to that process, each one of us."

"Except me," said Kate, dolefully.

"Find out what you want, Kate, an' you can have it."

"I don't believe that."

"Pick, choose, change, decide, act," said Mirrin, with some of her former vehemence. "I'll have my Tom, my farmer."

"An' what about us?" said Flora.

"That's really why I came home," said Mirrin. "We're in debt, in debt t'each other. And in debt to Houston Lamont."

"But he *gave* us life-lease on the house?" said Flora.

"I want freed from that bargain, Mam," Mirrin said. "I'm not dishonest enough t'trade on a man's feelings or capitalise on hope any longer."

"What are y'sayin', Mirrin?" Flora cried.

"I'm sayin' that we must give up this house."

"My house? My home?" Flora struggled to her feet.

"It was too much, Mam: it cost us too much."

"You were born here, all of you. I came here as a young bride wi' Alex."

"It's dead, Mam. My Da's dead, an' all the house ever meant is gone. It was never our house, anyway. It was always Lamont's."

"But he *gave* it to us," said Flora. "He won't go back on his word."

"Aye," said Mirrin, quietly now, "I think he will."

"Why, Mirrin?" said Kate.

"Because he believes I've come back for *him*."

"But . . . but he's married," said Flora. "A married man?"

"What'll we do, Mirrin. How will we live?" Kate said.

"Honestly," Mirrin replied.

Flora said, "Aye, it's all very well for you, with this tink lined up t'give you a bed an' provide for you."

"I want t'be clean again, Mam," Mirrin declared. "I *won't* live like a hypocrite any longer."

"So for your own selfish reasons you'd see your mother an' wee Neill flung out . . ."

"Stop it, Mam," Kate said. "Mirrin's done more for us than we ever had a right t'expect. It's true what she says. We traded away the last of her good name in this town just t'protect Drew: aye, an' t'give us a baby, a child t'nurse. We're the ones who've been selfish, not our Mirrin."

Flora groped behind her and lowered herself into the chair.

"I won't abandon you, Mam," Mirrin promised. "I've some money saved. It's not enough t'give you a secure future, but it means that we don't have to rush into anythin'."

"It's not much we'd be askin', Mirrin: a roof an' a job," Kate said.

Mirrin chuckled ruefully. "That's the whole story in a nutshell, Kate: a roof an' a job. Well, there's one thing you haven't thought of."

"What's that?" asked Kate.

"Drew."

"Drew?"

"It's time our dear brother paid his debts."

"But Drew's only a student," said Kate.

"What can he do for us?" Mam asked.

"That," Mirrin replied, "remains t'be seen."

Five

THROUGHOUT THEIR FAMILY life together Mirrin and Betsy had hardly spent an hour alone and had certainly never engaged in such a frank tête-à-tête as occupied them on the journey from Hamilton to Edinburgh. Mirrin had been conscious of changes in Betsy, of how similar the girl had become, in many respects, to her twin brother. It seemed that all along shrewdness had been lying below Betsy's flightiness. Now they talked like women of equal experience. Of course, Betsy was thrilled to be invited to join Mirrin on a day-trip to Edinburgh, though she contained her excitement beneath a mask of indifference. As the train rattled through green fields beyond the edges of the coal-producing belt, Mirrin broached the problem which had so troubled Kate.

"That's a very pretty dress you're wearin', Betsy."

"Thank you, Mirrin. It's no nicer than yours, though."

"Was it expensive?"

"I daresay it was."

Winter sunlight, streaming through the compartment window, made Betsy's hair shine like spun gold. She was, Mirrin acknowledged, ravishingly beautiful, modish without being vulgar and with an assurance that even Drew could not better.

"Who bought it for you?" Mirrin asked.

"An admirer."

"Who?"

"That I won't say."

"Somebody in the shop?"

"Is it likely, Mirrin, that somebody in the shop

could afford a dress like this? No, a gentleman of my acquaintance bought it for me."

"Kate saw you in Glasgow one night."

Betsy did not bat an eyelid. "Did she now?"

"You worry her, Betsy."

"Kate's a born worrier. Besides it won't be for long."

"D'you mean that your man friend intends to marry you?"

"Don't be daft, Mirrin. You're a woman of the world, ain't you? He's married already."

"I see," Mirrin said. "I suppose I should warn you against men like that. But there doesn't seem much point."

"It's over in any case," Betsy said. "Amicably over. Kate won't spot me in Glasgow any more."

"How long did it last?"

"Long enough."

"Betsy, did you . . . ?"

"Of course. That's what it was all about."

"It's wrong, you know, promiscuously wrong."

"It's not wrong, Mirrin. There was nothin' wicked about it. Besides, I thought it was time to look out for myself. Nobody else ever does."

"Kate an' Mam . . ."

Betsy laughed. "I'm not the baby in the house, in case you'd failed to notice. They've no time for anythin' except Neill."

"Havin' an adulterous affair was dangerous, Betsy."

The younger woman shrugged. "No more dangerous than many of the things you've done."

"I can't deny it," Mirrin conceded. "I assume you've a plan for the future?"

"Edinburgh," Betsy said. "To be honest, if you hadn't asked me along on this outing, I'd have gone myself very shortly."

"With what?"

"I have a little bit of money saved, and some decent clothes."

"Where? Not at home?"

"The money's in a bank, and the clothes I keep in a friend's house in Hamilton."

"God!" Mirrin said. "Kate would have a fit if she knew what you'd been up to."

"Kate need never know. I think you and I understand each other now." Betsy regarded the passing landscape for a moment. "How many men have you slept with, Mirrin?"

"Only one. The difference is that I . . . I loved him."

"Yet you took from him, didn't you? From Lamont."

"Not for myself: nothing for myself."

"An' that makes it all right?"

Mirrin hesitated. "No, I don't suppose it does."

"I can't understand what you ever saw in Houston Lamont."

"I told you, I loved him."

"Aye, that's always the excuse, ain't it?"

"He taught you a lot about cynicism, Betsy, this gentleman friend of yours."

"Not just him: others in Dalzells' too."

"What?"

"No, no, not like that," said Betsy quickly. "By example, that's all. I did what Drew does: I copied others."

Mirrin shook her head. "It seems you've grown up without any of us realisin' it, Betsy. What do you hope to find in Edinburgh? A husband?"

"Of course."

"You're just as calculatin' as your brother."

"But I won't make a fool of myself."

"Meaning?"

"Meaning that from now on I intend to be very careful," Betsy answered. "For one thing, I'm *not* goin' to fall in love."

Mirrin sighed. "That's the big difference between us, Betsy."

"Hm?"

"I'm the kind that needs t'fall in love."

"Will you really marry this tinker?"

"If he'll have me."

"I just don't understand that."

"You probably never will."

"What d'you intend to do about me?"

"Not a blessed thing," said Mirrin. "From now on you're Drew's worry, not mine."

Drew Stalker could not imagine who the lady might be who wanted to see him. He had avoided the company of women since the outcome of his affair with Heather Campbell, and the words of the first-year sprat who brought the message sent a shudder of apprehension through him. Mercifully, on this occasion, he was crossing alone towards the gate that would take him to the library where, on Drew's instruction, Fraser McAlmond had incarcerated himself with a programme of study and from which, like a gaoler, Drew would release him now that the afternoon's voluntary lecture was over.

The summer had treated Drew uncommonly well. He had consolidated his position as a close friend of the McAlmond clan and had spent many weekends at Pearsehill. Under Daniel Horn's guidance, he had learned more about the under-workings of the practice of law than any idealistic student had a right to know. Havershaw had even paid him for jobbing that vacation, though the money was less important to Drew now. Fraser proved a generous friend indeed; Drew,' however, was careful to trim his own cloth and impose no undue strain on McAlmond's hospitality. He ate well at Fraser's table, bought neat, plain-cut clothes from his winnings at backgammon and, all round, had created a comfortable unostentatious mode of living for himself—and for Fraser too. Centered on the library rather than the tavern, the students' activity bore fruit. It now seemed distinctly possible that Fraser would one day ascend to the Scottish bar. The Sprotts and Hector Mellish, too, had sobered in their second year, egged on, though they would never admit it, by the example of young Andrew Stalker.

For a moment, there in the quadrangle on that bright November afternoon, however, Drew's edifice of scholarly respectability rocked. To that sprat he said, "Is this a joke? I warn you . . ."

"No joke. The lady's really there. A corker she is,

too. Knock your eye out, you lucky dog. She's waiting behind the chapel."

It was not until he was within a few yards of the elegantly dressed woman that Drew recognised his sister. His first reaction was one of admiration, bordering on awe. Apparently he wasn't the only Stalker who had risen in the world. The change Mirrin had wrought on herself was astonishing. Last time he saw her she was ungainly and shabby and unrefined, unmistakably a working-girl. Now—well, she was, as the sprat had said, a lady to the bone. Even her voice had changed. In her, fleetingly, he saw mirrored his own progress. He smiled expansively as he approached the rustic bench by the chapel wall. "Mirrin! What a surprise! I didn't know you were home? It's jolly decent of you to visit me."

"Hello, Drew," Mirrin said. She offered her hand. She was thinking how like his father Drew had become, the same breadth to the shoulders, the same dark intelligent eyes. But a coldness, an imperiousness that were all his own, gave him the appearance of a man already past the pleasant period of illusion which is the season of youth.

"You must let me give you dinner," he said.

"With your friends, Drew?"

"If you wish. Certainly they would enjoy meeting you."

"Perhaps they would not care to hear us talk of your bastard son."

The easy humour drained from Drew's face.

"Is that why you are here?"

"Partly," Mirrin said. "You didn't suppose it was because I craved your company."

"Let's walk, Mirrin," Drew said. "I'll show you round this fine building."

"If you like."

He guided her away from the populated parts of the university, out towards the arched gate beyond which lay the terraces, sheds and storehouses of the master of works. A walking path followed the low outer walls.

"Is there anything wrong at home?" Drew asked.

"No more than usual."

"The . . . the child? Is it thriving?"

"Considerate of you t'ask," said Mirrin. "Yes, the child's thriving. Don't you even know his name?"

With a surprised grunt, Drew admitted, "No, actually, I don't."

"Neill. Neill Campbell Stalker."

"Who picked it? Kate, I suppose."

"You disapprove?"

"It's nothing to me, to be perfectly frank."

"I'm glad we're bein' frank today, Drew."

"What is it—money?"

"For once, no, it's not money: not directly."

"What then?"

Tersely Mirrin told her brother of the situation in Blacklaw and, guardedly, of her intention to marry and become a farmer's wife.

"But what has this to do with me? Do you want my blessing, Mirrin? Do you want me to act as the man of the family and give you away?"

"I want you to renounce Lamont's patronage."

"I understand," Drew said, at once. "Square away one chap before you take on another."

"Be careful, Drew," Mirrin warned.

"Lamont's made no move to retract on his undertaking. Legally, I assure you, he is committed. The situation is in no way changed by your decision to marry this farmer fellow, nor by anything else."

"Not even by the fact that you fathered a child."

"I was under the impression that Kate . . ." Drew stammered just a little, flushed cheeks indicating anger at being involved in the timid fears and petty pride born in his womenfolks' minds. "Does Kate not care for him?"

"Well you know she cares for him. And, as you say, Lamont may be legally committed to sustaining your annual twenty pounds and the lease of . . ."

"Ah, the lease?" Drew said, relieved. "The *lease* is the problem."

"I want us out of Lamont's hands, Drew; finally and completely."

"Well, I can easily manage without his pittance now."

"Mam, Kate and your son—they can't. Like it or not, Drew, we're all in the same boat."

"I'd contest that, Mirrin. You, for example, are our highly privileged passenger. Your . . . friendship, shall we say, with Houston Lamont did that much for you."

Mirrin's face stiffened. "For all your brains, Drew, you've the instincts of a pit rat. Mam and Kate are no longer just my responsibility. It's your bairn they're looking after."

"I'd the feeling it would come to this," Drew said. "Exactly how can I help them?"

"*You* must tell *me*. You're the intelligent one in this family."

"You make it sound difficult, Mirrin," Drew said. "I can influence Lamont now, however. With Havershaw's assistance, I'm sure I could hold on to that lease, have it upheld."

"That is *not* what I want."

"So I gathered," Drew said. "I suppose I could borrow enough to rent them another house. But I'm reluctant to put myself in anyone's debt."

"Except ours?"

"Quite!" Drew said. "Very well, Mirrin. I'll do what I can to pay off your debt to Lamont. I'll find money. That *is* what all this pleading is about, is it not? Money —as usual?"

"It's about the welfare of *your* family."

"I require only one thing," Drew said.

"What?"

"Betsy."

"Aye," Mirrin said. "I thought as much."

"I'm sure she won't object."

"I know she won't," Mirrin said. "That's why I brought her with me."

"She's here, in Edinburgh?"

"Across the street in a teashop."

"I see you do mean business, Mirrin?" Drew said. "We've more in common, perhaps, than you realise."

"The same boat, that's all," Mirrin said. "And only for a little while."

"Come on," said Drew. "There's no sense wasting time."

The evening of Betsy's first day in Edinburgh was an overture to her future in the capital. First, there was her meeting with Drew. The effect of her beauty upon her brother firmed her in the knowledge that he was no longer master over her destiny, though he might, if she so decided, become its instrument.

After a strangely unemotional greeting, she was whisked to Gow Havershaw's chambers and there introduced to the lawyer. Breathless with appreciation of the honour bestowed upon him by his apprentice, Havershaw immediately invited Andrew and his sisters to dine. Politely Drew refused the invitation. Instead, he carried his sisters off again, by cab this time, across the city to Morningside where Fraser McAlmond, nursing his irritation at being abandoned in the library, had returned home.

Fraser's pique vanished at once when he clapped eyes on Betsy Stalker. If Betsy was impressed with the house in which Drew lived she gave no sign of it.

Fortunately the sisters were quick-witted enough to pick up Drew's hints that they must not perjure his present position by divulging the truth about his upbringing. Even Mirrin was sufficiently impressed by the tale that Drew had concocted out of bits and pieces of reality, to support his inventions and add a few embellishments of her own. It was as well, she thought, that Kate had never come here, had never met McAlmond. Poor Kate would have been like a fish out of water. She would never have condoned the fabrications that Drew had devised or the need for such hypocrisy.

They dined, the four of them, in a genteel restaurant in Allandar Lane. During the course of the dinner, Drew quickly set in motion the plan which would free his family from care and, more importantly, establish his own future more firmly in Scotland's capital city.

"And," said Drew, midway through the fish course, "do you think that you will like Edinburgh, Betsy?"

"It will do for the season," Betsy said.

"Have you found a place of residence to your liking?" Drew asked.

"That *is* a problem," Betsy said. "A young woman is not always welcome. Besides . . ."

Fraser who had been hanging on every word butted in. "A place to live?"

"Just for a time," said Betsy.

"My aunt . . ." Fraser began.

"Wouldn't dream of it," Drew said.

"But really, my aunt would be delighted. You've met Aunt Roberta, I believe."

"Have I?"

"At the mid-summer, in Pearsehill."

"Ah, yes, a most charming lady."

"She would be only too pleased to provide your sister with hospitality. What do you say, Miss Stalker?"

Mirrin answered for Betsy. "As Drew has perhaps indicated, Mr. McAlmond, our circumstances . . ."

Airily, Fraser dismissed that argument. "Pride, that's Andrew's failing too. Stubborn pride. You would favour my Aunt by giving her your companionship, Miss Stalker. She is a spinster lady, and the house *is* far too large for her."

"Where is the house?" Drew asked.

"In Queensferry," Fraser answered. "Please, Miss Stalker, at least allow me to make an introduction."

"Andrew?" said Betsy, ostensibly deferring to her brother's experience in the protocol of such arrangements.

"Now, Fraser, are you sure?" Drew said, with just the right degree of uncertainty.

"The sister of my best chum must be made as comfortable as possible. And my dear old aunt, whatever her foibles, keeps an excellent house."

Mirrin said, "It can do no harm, Betsy, to meet the lady. If she *is* looking for a companion, perhaps you may fill the bill."

"That's it," said Fraser. "When will you officially take up residence?"

"Soon," said Betsy.

"Before Christmas?" said Fraser.

"Probably."

"Then we must invite you to Pearsehill for the Yuletide. How marvellous!" Fraser enthused. "Lord, but the Sprotts and Hector will be pea-green with envy. If you would kindly consider me your friend, Miss Stalker, I would regard it as an honour."

"But I consider you my friend already, Mr. McAlmond. Drew has told me so much about you."

"By Christmas, then," Fraser said. "You will be one of us, Miss Stalker."

"In which case, I insist that you call me Elizabeth."

"Elizabeth." Fraser poured wine generously and lifted his glass, eyes shining with infatuation—as well they might, thought Mirrin. "A toast: to Miss Elizabeth Stalker."

Glasses clinked. Once more McAlmond poured, and toasted. "To Andrew. To Andrew and Elizabeth Stalker."

"No," said Drew, smiling modestly. "If we must impress the ladies with our convivial habits, Fraser, let's pick our graces with more care."

"What, then, young Stalker?"

Drew lifted his glass, and sighted carefully through the pale, dry wine. "To friendship," he said. "To friendships, past, present *and* future."

"Perfect!" Fraser McAlmond declared. "As usual, you've hit the nail on the head."

All four glasses touched.

Betsy lifted her eyes and studied Fraser McAlmond's handsome, moonstruck face. For an instant there was amazement, that childish rapture which Mirrin remembered as one of her sister's many seesaw moods. But then it was gone, replaced by a glint of pure speculation.

Whatever Drew planned for his sister's future, he would not find Betsy wanting.

Daniel Horn grinned wolfishly, and sank his teeth into the potato pie. Munching, he said, "Gone again so soon, have they?"

"It was only a flying visit," Drew replied.

"You're a devil, Drew."

Drew cut his pie into eight neat pieces and forked the first into his mouth. He sipped ale from the mug and said nothing. It was lunchtime in the city's taverns.

"When did they depart?" asked Horn.

"The last train last night."

"Young McAlmond accompanied you all the way to the station, I imagine."

"He did."

"Fell for her, did he?"

"Daniel! Must you be so blunt?"

"She really is a wee jewel, that sister of yours. Come to think of it, even the older one is something special."

"We Stalkers are just naturally handsome."

"The females are, at least. When is she comin' back?"

"Two weeks."

"Lookin' for a bed for her?" Daniel asked optimistically.

"She'll be staying with Fraser's aunt, if you must know."

"Lady Roberta?"

"That's the one."

"How long?"

"Throughout the winter," Drew said.

"I don't mean that: how long until the nuptials?"

Surprised, Drew looked up at his friend's vulpine countenance. "Nuptials?"

"You do intend t'marry her into the McAlmond family, don't you, lad?"

"Perhaps," said Drew, drily.

Horn's jaws ground to a standstill. He picked his teeth with his fingernail, head cocked. "You don't?"

"What good would that do *me?*" asked Drew.

"Fraser's brother-in-law," Horn said, conducting the crescendo with his knife. "Plenty of influence. Wealth. The McAlmonds always look after their own."

Popping another segment of pie into his mouth Drew said, "I'm tired of being looked after."

Brow wrinkled, Horn asked, "But what other way is there?" Abruptly, he slapped his forehead with the heel of his hand. "You don't mean . . . ?"

"Of course I do," Drew said. "I'm no lickspittle, Daniel. I will accomplish my objectives in my own way."

"What are your objectives?"

"A full partnership in Havershaw's."

"You mean, you'll encourage that lovely sister of yours to *wed* the old boy?"

"That," said Drew, "would be a dreadful waste."

"Aye, I couldn't agree more," said Daniel. "What then?"

"Betsy may break as many hearts as she chooses," said Drew, "provided that she warms old Havershaw's hopes enough to persuade him to take me into partnership with him. By that time, I'll have the Mc-Almond business in the palm of my hand."

"How long will this take?"

"Five years."

"Ouff!" said Daniel Horn. "You're even more cunning than I gave you credit for, Drew, m'boy."

"After that, Fraser's patience will be duly rewarded and Betsy will marry him."

"I thought I would wind up clerking for you," Daniel said.

"Once I have control," Drew said, "we'll have some profitable fun with old Havershaw's secrets; all legal and more or less above board."

"All this plottin' is based on the assumption that your sister's willin' to play along with your plan."

"Betsy," Drew said, "will do exactly as she's told."

Rosy cheeks glowing under a snug blue-wool cap Neill Stalker took stock of the world that Sunday afternoon with all the innocent wonder of a princeling. He was far too young yet to evaluate the passing scene, but his alert eyes were tickled by the colours of the leaves that littered the ruts above the Poulter's burn and by the ruddiness of sunlight on the school and stout kirk steeple. Besides, he was with his aunties, and, so instinct told him, quite safe and secure. His tummy was full and he was content, the very picture of happiness, quite unaware of the meaning of the words that were flung back and forth between the adults who carried his Moses basket.

Mirrin was saying, "All right. We're alone now, Kate, so suppose you tell me what's got into you. You've been like a bear with its ear in a poultice since last Thursday. Is it because Betsy's goin' t'Edinburgh?"

"I'm glad t'be rid of her, Mirrin."

"What is it then? You're actin' as if you were mad at me."

"I'm . . . I'm resentful, I suppose."

"Resentful?" Mirrin was surprised.

"You know where you're goin'. You always did."

"My travellin' days are over."

"Only because you've found somebody that loves you—or so you say: though, it's a damned funny suitor that never comes near, an' that we've never even met."

"Aye," Mirrin agreed. "It's not exactly a model Blacklaw courtship, but that's part of what Tom and I have in common. It's not the means but the end that counts with us."

"Have you . . . slept with him?"

"No."

Kate paused to tuck in the bottom of Neill's blanket and, smiling, to dab the baby's button nose with her forefinger. Neill giggled. The women walked slowly on along the field path, the basket swinging between them.

"There's no . . . no passion in my life, Mirrin," Kate said. "Never has been. How long should I wait for it?"

"God, how can you say there's no passion. Look at us, all of us. We're full of passion, us Stalkers."

"Aye, *you* are," said Kate, bitterly. "You're so sure of yourself that you'll drive the rest of us willy-nilly in your chosen direction."

"You think I'm bossy?"

"Bossy's not the word for it," said Kate. "I'm not even sure I trust you any more, Mirrin."

"Not trust me? Oh, Kate, how can you say that?"

"You got rid of Betsy. I wonder if you're tryin' t'get rid of Mam, Neill an' me in the same sort of way."

Mirrin controlled her anger. She said, "Betsy and Drew are far tougher than you are, Kate. Drew renounced us long since, an' Betsy openly despises us. Edinburgh's the proper place for them."

"You made a bargain with Drew, didn't you?"

"Not a bargain exactly," Mirrin said. "But I used him, I'll admit."

"Nobody uses Drew."

"He can employ Betsy's good looks the same way as he employed his own brains. Drew's never been an ordinary lad, Kate. You said yourself . . ."

"I said I wanted no more to do with him," Kate snapped.

"He won't show his face in Blacklaw again, I can promise you that."

"Maybe not," Kate said. "But you're gaining *your* freedom by puttin' Mam and I in Drew's debt."

"That's daft, Kate," Mirrin said. "Whatever he's done he's our own flesh an' blood and we're entitled . . ."

"*I want nothin' from him.*"

"Would you rather be in Lamont's pocket for the rest of your life?"

"What *did* you arrange with Drew?"

"I asked him to look after himself, that's all."

"He's been doin' that for years."

"To renounce Houston's patronage."

"Aye, an' what else, Mirrin?"

"To find the money to secure you an' Mam an' *his* bairn a permanent home. It's high time you were out of the house here. It's got nothin' for us now but bad memories, Kate."

"How will Drew do it?"

Mirrin shrugged. "How do I know? I left the problem with him. But he'll find a solution, never fear. Lord, Kate, if you'd only seen the way he lives, hobnobbin' with the rich, easy an' familiar."

"I've seen the way he lives," Kate said. "I've seen a poor dead girl on a filthy mattress."

"You won't forgive him for that?"

"You weren't there."

Mirrin sighed. "No. But listen, Kate, we can use him."

"What are y'saying, Mirrin? We're not like him, even though we are his sisters. I don't believe in usin' people."

"I want you settled," Mirrin declared.

"So you'd even force Drew t'do it for you."

"I thought . . ."

"You're as selfish as he is," Kate said. "Mam was right."

"I want little enough for myself," said Mirrin.

"Only this man of yours, this mysterious tinker."

"Aye, an' why not?" Mirrin demanded. "Do you think I *had* to come back here?"

"I think you did," said Kate. "I think the old Mirrin and the Mirrin you've become were at war in you, an' that's the reason you came home."

"I've no patience with you, Kate; not in this mood you're in."

"I've precious little patience myself, Mirrin."

"Don't take it out on me because *you* got left on the shelf."

"Is that what you think?"

"I'm sorry, Kate. I spoke without . . ."

Stooping, Kate set the basket down, forcing Mirrin to do the same. For a moment Neill was bewildered then, his viewpoint on the fields changed, he concerned himself with inspecting the bleached weeds at the side of the path. Glancing round, Kate pointed at the village spread out behind them.

"D'you see it, Mirrin? Blacklaw: my village, my home. I have that, at least."

"Kate, I didn't mean . . ."

"Go your own way, Mirrin," Kate said. "Find what you want for yourself. I wish you luck. But leave us be now, Mam, Neill and me. We can look after ourselves."

"But the house isn't safe?"

"Was it ever safe?" Kate said. "We can live with that if we have to. No, Mirrin, leave us alone. We want nothin' from you now, an' nothin' from Drew."

"Are y'throwin' me out?" Mirrin asked, swallowing her tears.

"I'll never do that. You'll always be welcome in our house, but it will be *our* house, not yours, not Drew's."

"I only meant . . ." Mirrin was at a loss for words.

For a strange silent moment there was between the sisters a new respect; then Kate bent and drew Neill from the basket, swaddling him expertly in the warm blanket and holding him against her breast, hand upon his back. The little boy swayed slightly then took balance and swivelled his head to peer across at Mirrin, frowning into the sunlight as if he too was an accuser.

"I'll carry him home," Kate said. "Bring the basket."

"Kate, please, don't let's fight."

Holding the baby against her body, Kate hesitated. Behind her the sun skimmed off the grimness of the pit and tinted the long drab rows to the colour of leaves that would one day brown and wither and feed back into the earth.

"Tell Houston Lamont," Kate said, "that he can have his damned house back."

"But why, Kate? Why?"

"Like you I no longer want to be tied."

It was very early. Farmers were still in bed, dayshift colliers deep asleep. Only the winding towers creaked in the small hours' uncanny silences, telling that men were burrowing in smokey black stalls far underground, their lifelines guarded by a handful of troll-like shapes that flitted across the inner reaches of the pithead yard.

Yawning, Willie Kellock came downstairs and entered the rear of the bakery. Conscientiously, he attended to his oven before he attended himself. He unlatched the iron door with his elbow to expose the glowing mound of embers that remained from the previous evening's sponging. Feeding in kindling, he hooked out the ash-pans with quick fingers and slid them across the floor. On to the crackling sticks he dropped lumps of small coal as delicately as a duke measuring out sugar lumps, then, while that caught, he sawed at the flues to loosen soot and open the apertures. It was not until the firing had been completed, the pans emptied into a sack in the yard, and the glass gauges checked for the first slight temperature rise, that Willie entered the tiny kitchen to wash his hands, put on his clean apron and set the kettle for breakfast.

To his astonishment the chores were already done. Tea steamed in a tin mug, a bowl of porridge and a toasted ham roll were arranged on a tray on the drop-leaf table. The lamp was lit in its nook above the old brick hearth and Kate Stalker, neatly dressed in a brown serge skirt and Sunday best coat sat on a wooden chair in the corner.

"My, what a fright y'gave me, Kate," said Willie. "Still, it's grand t'see you first thing on a Monday morn. What is it, though? What brings you here at this unearthly hour? Is it trouble?"

"I hope not, Willie," Kate said. "Here, eat your breakfast. I'm not wantin' t'keep you back from the day's work."

Puzzled, Willie washed his hands at the sink, then, rather nervously, seated himself at the table and lifted his porridge spoon.

"Kate, what is it?" he pleaded, as the woman put down a jug of milk.

"I'm thinkin' this is the best time for the truth," Kate said. "It's hard t'be deceitful at this hour."

"Kate, what is all this?"

"Are y'still of a mind t'marry me, Willie?"

"You know I am."

"It'll mean sharin' your house with me."

"I want nothin' more, Kate."

"An' givin' room too t'my mother an' my nephew."

"I've great respect for your mother, Kate, an' I would be a good . . . well, father t'the wee chap. I think you know that."

Kate nodded. She leaned forward and kissed the baker on the brow.

"All right," she said. "I'm ready t'name the day."

"When?"

"The Saturday after Christmas."

"You're sure?"

"I'm certain."

"Right," Willie said. "I'll post the banns tomorrow."

Six

To THE REVEREND Mitchell's gratification Blacklaw kirk was packed that Sunday morning, though the minister, a sheltered soul and not long come to the parish, did not understand the reason for the revival of interest in the word of God. Perhaps his elder, Mr. David Dunlop, who received banns of intended marriage, could have explained it; Davy had broadcast the news to the community in advance. Though other minor diversions coloured the precarious lives of the colliers, the Stalkers' affairs continued to intrigue all and sundry and, enlarged by malice, humour and imagination, the family's fortunes furnished a constant source of interest.

Though Flora Stalker could be encountered any day of the week, seated on her carter's bench, defended from casual approach by the big, untrustworthy horse, and Kate still worked her shifts at the troughs, Mirrin and Betsy were seldom seen in the village. The chance of a sighting of the two fashionable misses could not be ignored.

Mirrin and Betsy entered the church and walked together to the vacant pew close to the pulpit, a pew left unoccupied by the unspoken collusion of the congregation. The younger daughters were followed by Kate and Flora. Willie Kellock brought up the rear: a dirty old devil, some thought, who had wheedled himself into Mam's good books just to find a young wife for his bed. Not many miners held that ungenerous opinion, however: enough honest men and women were left in Blacklaw, in spite of Thrush's pernicious influences, to wish Kate happiness and to think to themselves that the girl was fortunate to have found a chap with a bit of siller tucked away and a tidy wee business to support her, even if he was old enough to be her father. Soon there would be no more troughs for Kate Stalker, no more grim winter days howking coal: she was lucky indeed.

Callum Ewing deigned to enter a church again, out of sentiment more than curiosity. Even Rob and his young wife, Eileen, had come together to attend. Rob seemed haggard and awkward in a serge suit and rimmed collar, his coarse fair hair slicked down with macassar oil. He looked like the one who was ailing, not Eileen. She was soft and pretty and gentle. It was difficult to credit that she had an illness at all.

Maggie Williams and other old school chums of Mirrin had dragged themselves from their beds or from the sticky demands of their bairns to trail along to the chilly kirk that Sunday, not only to hear with their own ears that Kate had netted the baker but to see what Mirrin and Betsy were wearing and in the faint fond hope that, at that public gathering, there would be some sort of telltale sign to substantiate the rumour that Mirrin was the mother of the Stalkers' bastard child and Houston Lamont the father.

If Willie Kellock was aware of the true sources of community interest in the formal announcement of his betrothal he gave no sign. He sat contentedly by his intended's side, dapper, smiling faintly, showing no hint of nervousness. Already he was planning how he would refurbish the house, how he would employ Mirrin— whom he liked—to help with the painting and cleaning that would be needed to make the bachelor rooms fit for Kate, Flora and Neill to live in. To his credit he did not now view his commitment with any sense of lost freedom. He had, he now realised, denied himself strength of feeling towards Kate in the expectation of rebuff. But now that she had named the day his love had blossomed, and he was impatient to enter again into domestic bliss. The house, even the bakery, seemed empty. His marriage to Kate would end his loneliness for ever.

Marriage was on the mind of several other gentlemen in the congregation, too. By chance, the Reverend Mitchell had chosen the Marriage at Canaan as his text, innocently abetting the irony of the apposition which put the Stalkers in one row and the coalmaster and his entourage adjacent to them, both households in full view of the miners' wives who craned and whispered and still hoped for a miracle of revelation or, at worst, a bit of a confrontation.

It was not to be though. The service passed without a stir, the usual ritual broken only by the reading of the banns and a murmur of sympathetic approval as Kate and Willie turned, involuntarily, and glanced at each other during the declaration.

For all that nothing much happened, Blacklaw's womenfolk considered church attendance well worth the effort.

By their clothes and bearing Mirrin and Betsy clearly defined the rise in the family fortunes, and there was, some claimed, that fleeting second when Edith and Mirrin, emerging from their seats after the Benediction, had met each other's eye, and, so it was said, looked daggers.

And there was the way Lamont himself looked, like a sick pony, head down and eyes staring, while Thrush courteously escorted both women, his sister and Lamont's wife, to the waiting carriage. But it wasn't much, really, and next day, before daylight, the old woman and her horse were out and about selling hot rolls and mutton pies, and Kate, in her dowdies, was back again shoulder to shoulder with her colourless workmates at the troughs, target for naughty remarks and recipient of good wishes, taking it all as any spinster might do, in good enough part.

The Stalkers' private confrontations were very private now, though any wife in Blacklaw would have given a year off her life to have eavesdropped at the meeting of Mirrin and Houston Lamont which took place that same Sunday evening in the mansion among the leafless oaks.

At that hour, she was their equal in every way. It was apparent in her manner, in the confidence with which she addressed Anna Thrush who, startled out of her implacability, kept Mirrin waiting upon the mansion's front step while a maid scuttled off to fetch the mistress.

"I did not ask for Mrs. Lamont," Mirrin said. "Is the coalmaster not at home?"

"Mrs. Lamont always receives our guests, even uninvited ones," Anna Thrush retorted.

"And her housekeeper keeps them waiting outside in the cold, I see."

"I have no instructions about the likes of you."

"And no proper manners, it seems," Mirrin said. "I'm not here to steal the plate, you know."

"Why are you here, if one may ask?"

"One may not ask," said Mirrin. "My business is with Houston Lamont, not his domestic employees."

"You were an employee here yourself once, were you not?"

"Aye, an' better at it than you are, I think," Mirrin said.

Anna Thrush's retort was stayed by a disturbance in the depths of the hall. Through the half-open doorway, Mirrin glimpsed a huddled discussion between Edith Lamont and a stranger—Sydney Thrush, she assumed—in the nook under the staircase. Obviously the pair had come from the back parlour, that large, musty room with its tuneless polished slab of a pianoforte flanked by two gilded music stands like embalmed dragonflies; never a note had Mirrin heard struck to dispel the room's pretensions of cultural refinement.

Thrush was more handsome than she imagined; the regularity of his features did not make him personable or attractive however. At the instant of sighting, his hand was on Edith's forearm, his head lifted alertly as if he had developed the habit of peeking in four directions at once and, even in moments of intimacy and agitation, he could not focus directly on his companion.

Edith Lamont's distress was palpable. The mantel of authority had slipped like a cloak from her shoulders and, briefly, she was exposed as unsure of herself, even in the sanctuary of her home. How embattled did she really feel, that small aggressive woman who, oddly, bore a slight resemblance to the Queen herself, the Hanoverian nose more prominent now that cheeks had fattened and the chin thickened into the throat?

Anna Thrush stepped back as her brother advanced, an expression of polite enquiry, perfectly suited to the occasion, engraved upon his long face. Edith hovered in the middle reaches of the hall, hands clasped, her expression one of injured propriety.

"Ah, Miss . . . ?" Thrush appeared to search for the name.

"Stalker."

"Of course," Thrush said. "If you're here in search of employment may I suggest that you call again, at the kitchen entrance, tomorrow, when my sister, Miss Thrush, will . . ."

"I take it, sir, that you are Mr. Thrush?" Mirrin interrupted.

"I am: manager of Blacklaw pit."

"As I've already informed your sister," Mirrin said, "I wish to speak personally with Mr. Lamont."

"Mr. Lamont has retired for the night."

"Has he now?" said Mirrin. "That's most unfortunate."

"Perhaps I may be of assistance?"

"I doubt it, Mr. Thrush."

"Deliver a . . . a message?" Thrush too was nervous, caught off balance, perhaps by the young woman's confidence.

"You may tell Mr. Lamont I called," Mirrin said.

"By all means, Miss Stalker," said Thrush. "May I give him an inkling of what business you wish to discuss?"

"Property," said Mirrin.

"Property?" Intrigued now, Thrush was reluctant to dismiss her.

From the safe island of an Indian carpet in the middle of the hall, Edith Lamont called out, "Which property, Miss Stalker?"

"Mr. Lamont's property," Mirrin replied, loudly. "However, if Mr. Lamont has retired . . ."

"Ask Miss Stalker to join us in the drawing room for a glass of wine," Edith said.

"Will you join us, Miss Stalker?" Thrush asked.

"Under the circumstances, I must decline," said Mirrin.

"Perhaps, then, you will allow me to accompany you to the gate?" Thrush stepped quickly across the threshold, buttoning his jacket against the cold whirling wind that clashed the brittle stalks of the ivy plants by the entrance. Without waiting for her answer, the manager closed the mansion's front door.

Pools of light from the porch lamps diminished on the gravel. The curve of the lawn was swallowed up by darkness. Thrush paused at the foot of the steps, studying her. Mirrin caught the smell of wine on his breath, sweet, like his tone.

"I fear, Miss Stalker, that you may not understand quite how drastically the situation has altered during the time you've been away."

"Oh, an' what situation is that, Mr. Thrush?"

"I feel I may speak plainly," Thrush said. "You have the reputation of being a forthright young woman."

"I've changed, too, Mr. Thrush."

Thrush nodded. "But you still care about Blacklaw?"

"Yes."

"We have that in common, as I'd hoped."

"Don't make Blacklaw an excuse for plain speakin', Mr. Thrush," Mirrin said. "I'm not one of your colliers now, but I've eighteen years of experience built into me an' I know your sort too well to be soothed by a few nice phrases. What is it? Why won't you let me talk to Houston?"

"He's not responsible."

"That's not what I heard."

"Do not misunderstand me, Miss Stalker; in all outward appearances Mr. Lamont is *almost* his old self again. But I know differently. He suffers—as his sister suffered."

"I don't believe you, Mr. Thrush."

"He spent the summer with you, did he not?"
Thrush put in bluntly. "You lived as man and wife,
shall we say, in Beale."

"Houston told *you?*"

"No."

"You spied on him, on us?"

"How I came by the information is immaterial,"
Thrush said. "My concern is with the administration
of Blacklaw colliery. I carry a major responsibility
now. I must be told why you came here tonight, and
what business you have with the coalmaster."

"Why?"

"I may be able to help you."

"In what way?"

"If you wish to . . . to go off, shall we say, with Mr.
Lamont, a friend, an intermediary, would surely be an
asset in making the way easier."

"What will you gain?" Mirrin said.

"Personally," Thrush answered, "I will gain nothing. But Mrs. Lamont, for whom I have the greatest
respect, will be happier freed from the burden."

"Losing her husband to . . . to another woman will
make her happy?" said Mirrin. "That's a strange statement, Mr. Thrush."

"She lost him years ago," Thrush said. "Now she
may even lose the pit too; her share of its profits."

"So I'm to be the whipping-boy," Mirrin said. "I'm
to persuade Houston to give up everything . . ."

"It would take little enough persuasion," Thrush assured her. "It's what he wants. You've quite bewitched
him, you know."

"No," Mirrin said. "I only filled a hollow in his life,
and that's over now."

"Even after this summer?"

"I'll have no part of this . . . this deal of yours,
Thrush. I'm sick to death of deals and bargains, and all
the self-seeking that goes with them. I didn't return to
Blacklaw for Houston. I'm here to tell him so, that's
all. Even colliers' lassies have some sort of honour."

"Honour!" Thrush exclaimed. "What can you know
of that? You lured the coalmaster into adultery, and
yet you talk of honour. What did you gain? You

gained money, favour, did you not? Very well, ask me for a favour."

"I ask you only for the favour of the truth," said Mirrin. "You must tell me why you want the coalmaster disgraced?"

Thrush snorted. "Are you a simpleton, girl? I want control of Blacklaw colliery. With Lamont out of the way I can have it."

"Blacklaw is all Houston has left," Mirrin said.

"He has you."

"Nobody 'has' me."

"Think of your family," Thrush said. "I can make life very comfortable for them."

"We can manage without that sort of help," said Mirrin.

"I can also contrive to make it very uncomfortable."

Mirrin said, "No, Mr. Sydney Thrush. You've no power over us any longer. You've lost your hold on this particular collier's family."

"I can ascertain that your brother loses his place at the university, that your sister is sacked from her job, that your mother and sisters are tossed into the gutter, homeless."

"Too late, Mr. Thrush," Mirrin said. "We are free of you an' your kind. We've escaped. All of us."

"You will never escape," Thrush said. "Come now, you're a woman of the world. Tell me what you want."

Disgust welling within her like a sickness Mirrin swung away. Thrush caught her by the arm.

Suddenly, Houston was there, stepping from the shadow of the porch, where he had been all along. His waistcoat was open and his shirt sleeves unbuttoned at the cuffs. His leather slippers made no sound at all upon the verge as he came, in a dozen rapid strides, to Mirrin's aid. Thrush had no opportunity to block the blow. Lamont's knuckles struck him full on the mouth, drawing blood. The manager fell to one knee, only to be hauled bodily to his feet and struck once more in the face.

Holding the sagging figure by the bunched lapels of his jacket, Houston said softly, "You will be out of my house by morning, Thrush: out of the village; you and your sister and all your bags and baggage."

Thrush gathered blood into his mouth and, jerking his head, spat on to the gravel. "How dare you, coalmaster."

"By morning."

"Mrs. Lamont may have something to say about that."

"Mrs. Lamont does not own Blacklaw," Lamont snarled. *"I do."* He flung Thrush from him, sending the man sprawling on to the grass.

Thrush was on his feet at once. "I can ruin you, coalmaster," he hissed. "I can bring you down."

"No, Thrush," Lamont said. "You can only ruin my reputation, and that's worth nothing now. *Get out of my sight."*

Still bleeding, Thrush limped towards the mansion and rang the bell. The door was opened by Edith. She was almost knocked aside as Sydney Thrush pushed past her and, in spite of her protests, slammed the door behind him.

Afterwards, Mirrin thought how strange it was that it should end there, in the pool of light cast by the ornate lamps, surrounded by a raw December darkness. She could sense the landscape around her, the direction of the town, cluttered and cramped, spooling out from the workings, and the river running black between its black banks, and the high clean moorland behind the house. The mansion seemed to soar out of it all, not solid, flat as cardboard, a creation needing passion to give it substance. Only Houston and she had solidity, like actors upon a patchwork stage in some provincial hall where the fantastic was made credible only by traditions, conventions, and pleasant deceits.

Houston said, "I thought that you had come back for me, Mirrin."

"No, I came to tell you that it is truly over."

"I heard your voice, and I . . . I hoped."

"I'm sorry that you should have to find out as an eavesdropper," Mirrin said. "I take it that you were in the study."

"I came out by the window," Houston said. "It's a farce, Mirrin, isn't it? It doesn't even have the trappings of tragedy, now."

"What will you do about Thrush?"

"Be rid of him."

"And Blacklaw?"

"That is mine: that, at least, will always be mine."

"Houston, I am engaged to be married. I will wed my man at Candlemas, or shortly after. I thought it right that I should tell you myself."

"Yes."

Houston's face was haunted by defeat, and yet there was a dignity to it now, a disquieting nobility like that of an emperor who has cast off at last the shackle of scruples.

"Is there nothing I can do, nothing I can say to keep you, Mirrin?"

"Nothing."

"Then it is really, finally over between us?"

"It ended in Beale, last summer, Houston."

"Who is he, this man you'll marry?"

"He's nothin' special," Mirrin said. "He's just a man who wants his life to be his own—like me. I've had enough of giving and taking, Houston. I want to *share* now, share joy and sorrow, happiness and grief."

"You know, Mirrin, that I will fight it."

"Don't," the young woman said. "Please, Houston, don't."

"Your brother, and the house: have you thought of them?"

"I'd hoped you wouldn't force me to say it, Houston," Mirrin told him. "But we have no need of you now."

"What you told Thrush," Houston murmured, "is that true of me, also. Must I own you to have you? Is there no other way?"

"None," Mirrin answered.

"But you did love me once?"

"Yes, Houston, I loved you once."

He nodded. "I will remember that. I will remember,

and wonder why I could not hold the things I treasured most. It seems that my life must be filled with second best, Mirrin. I can only thank God that in twenty years, or thirty, it will be over, the struggle ended."

"Houston, I wish . . ."

He took her by the shoulders, and brought his mouth to hers. Though his grip was strong and passionate, the touch of his lips was tender not forceful.

"I wish, too," he murmured, then turned from her, moving away while Mirrin stood helplessly at the mouth of the avenue that led down through the arched trees to the gate.

Houston hesitated, glancing back over his shoulder, his left arm raised in an incomplete gesture of farewell. "I wish that Thrush was wrong."

The coalmaster entered his house again and, after a moment, a maid appeared to extinguish the porch lamps, leaving Mirrin alone in the darkness to pick her way home as best she could.

The letter, the last direct communication they were to receive from Drew, came addressed to Mirrin. It contained a banker's order for the sum of fifty pounds. The implications behind the gift were obvious. The letter itself was curt, stating only that Lady Roberta Oakley had accepted her nephew's recommendation and would welcome Miss Stalker as a companion for the season. There was no question, of course, of Betsy being paid for the few duties that she would be expected to perform. Board, lodging and the facilities of the house would be recompense enough. It did not occur to Drew—or to Betsy either, for that matter— that there was anything unusual in a girl from a mining village, the daughter of a dirty, coal-howkin' collier, being given such a post in the centre of Edinburgh's haughty circle.

Drew did not enquire after his mother, his sisters or his son.

Kate took it upon herself to pen an answer,

an equally brief letter to accompany the banker's order on its return to the sender. She gave no reason as to why she rejected the gift. Drew would understand. If he did not, then Betsy would have leisure to explain soon enough. Betsy would not leave Blacklaw in search of herself. Unlike Mirrin, she had long ago fixed on her objective. Departure for the capital, for Lady Roberta's house and ingress into the McAlmond set were undertaken as if they were quite natural progressions. Skinned of the girl's possessions, the narrow house seemed even more empty than before, haunted by memories stirred up by imminent change and the Christmas season.

It would be a lean time again for most miners' families. But not for the Stalkers. They, it appeared, had finally escaped the grip of poverty, not by chance or mere good fortune but by design. There were those in Blacklaw who depised them, others who were envious, and a handful, Rob Ewing among them, who saw in the Stalkers the rewards of courage and foresight and who could not, no matter how they tried, condemn them for it.

Mam and Kate bid Betsy goodbye at breakfast. There was little room for sentiment among the teacups and porridge pots and the scamper to make Neill ready for the day. Even Mam's kisses and tears were almost perfunctory as she tucked Neill into his basket. Flora too had her own life to lead and Betsy was no longer a part of it.

It was left to Mirrin to escort Betsy to Hamilton station where a number of boxes and a small trunk waited to swell the quantity of hand luggage that Betsy had brought from the house.

To Mirrin's surprise a contingent of Dalzells' staff had stolen time off to bid farewell to young Miss Stalker. Mr. Gabriel Reeves was there, and even the doorman, the old sergeant, had nipped away from his post to wish the pretty young miss 'all the best,' in the campaign ahead of her. Mr. Sutton had despatched a letter of reference, via Mr. Gabriel, and there was also a 'character' signed by no less a personage than Mr. Anstruther Dalzell. It was certain that Betsy had not wasted her apprentice years and would never want for a job.

Mr. Gabriel Reeves was also the bearer of a gift, a tiny box wrapped in hollyberry paper which, when opened, revealed a filigree silver locket which Betsy had often admired in Dalzells' show-case. Though empty of any sentimental geegaw, the locket was accompanied by an engraved card which identified the sender as Mr. Randolph Newton. Betsy's quick, wistful grin as she tucked the card hastily into her reticule told Mirrin that, whatever her failings, Betsy was not quite as ruthless as her twin and gave in good measure for what she received.

Shortly, Dalzells' staff returned to the emporium, tactfully allowing the sisters a few moments alone before the train left. If Betsy was in any way apprehensive about her future in Edinburgh and her employment by Lady Roberta she gave no sign. She only wanted to be off, to be there, to plunge into the adventures that awaited her and tackle the tricky problems of 'fitting in' as they came.

Mirrin said, "I've nothin' for you, Betsy."

"I'm not a great believer in trinkets."

"But you like that locket?"

"Ah, yes. But I know how much that cost."

"Will you write to Mam, Betsy?"

"Of course."

Mirrin doubted it.

"And Kate's wedding, will you come home for that?"

"Not without Drew."

Mirrin shook her head. "I'd hoped you'd be our go-between."

"We're twins, remember. If Kate won't have Drew, then . . ." Betsy made a small apologetic gesture with her gloved hand.

"Best stay away then," Mirrin said. "It would only upset things if you brought Drew."

"Why do you hate him so much? Because of the baby?"

"God, no," Mirrin said. "That's the only thing he's ever given us, an' even that was hardly a gracious gift. I think Drew's the warnin' to all us Stalkers. Maybe we're all a bit afraid because he's our flesh and blood."

Betsy laughed. Even the laughter was controlled and careful now. "Tell me something, Mirrin; d'you really have a beau? I mean, is there really a romantic gypsy man just waiting to marry you?"

"Why should I lie about it?"

"To give yourself an excuse for getting out?"

"I don't want out, Betsy. I want in again. It's not for me the travellin' life, or the bright lights."

"I never really believed your tale," Betsy said. "You must be very sure of yourself, Mirrin, to set so much store by this rendezvous."

"I'm sure of Tom Armstrong," Mirrin said.

Betsy raised a quizzical eyebrow. "Well, if you ever need a dinner and a bed, I'm sure we can find a place for you in Edinburgh."

"Tom will provide what I need, Betsy."

The train chugged out of the siding and squealed to a halt at the platform. There was bustle among the handful of passengers and a deal of noise at the train's end where a Lanarkshire farmer was waiting to unload four bullocks from a cattle car. For an instant Betsy was forgotten, Mirrin lost in contemplation of the scene, engrossed in the realisation that soon she would be part of that hard, rustic life.

Even then, with Betsy's cynical warning still in her ears, it did not occur to her that Tom Armstrong would let her down. In two weeks, she too would be reaching out towards her goal, committing herself to a mode of living totally different to that which Betsy had chosen. The house, the hill, the herd, the pasture, those would be her limits. No matter how harsh, she could always console herself with the thought that at least she had fashioned the choice, and not been governed, as so many colliers were, by sheer necessity.

Betsy kissed Mirrin's cheek, and stepped into the carriage.

A minute later the train pulled out and, irrevocably, the sisters went their separate ways.

Seven

MANY YEARS HAD passed since Houston Lamont had betrayed any outward sign of vanity. Though always sober in appearance, he dressed to suit his rank and professional status, not to be a dandy to society ladies. That Christmas Eve, however, it seemed that he had gone out of his way to top his wife who, out of habit and boredom, had spent most of the afternoon preparing her finery.

When Edith emerged from her room and glided to the top of the stairs, she was amazed to see her husband waiting for her in the hall below; Houston resplendent in full evening wear, complete with a frilled shirt and black silk tie. Clean shaven, hair trimmed and groomed, he presented the aspect of a man about to attend an investiture rather than a provincial coal-master treating his wife to dinner at home. The garments were all brand new, and expensively tailored. It could not simply have been whim or irrational impulse that had caused him to wear them. Obviously, he had planned it.

Immediately Edith suspected some sinister purpose, some additional burden that she must bear along with the twists and shifts of temperament that had plagued her for two years and which, now that Sydney and Anna had been expelled from the mansion, she was obliged to face up to alone, without confidence or aplomb. She descended the stairs slowly, only the rapid fluttering of her fan hinting that she was not at ease. The doors to the dining room stood open, the table within set for two. Without emotion, Edith took her husband's arm. He did not smile, but in every other procedure his manner was perfect, formal yet relaxed as it should between husband and wife. Edith felt herself being escorted into the dining room, the door closed behind her, her arm again taken, her body conducted to the waiting chair. In the absence of a housekeeper, Houston drew out the chair for her, waited until she was comfortably settled, then walked down the length of the table and took his own place.

Pure wax candles burned cleanly in silver candelabra, plates gleamed, an ice-bucket glistened frostily, bottles, decanters and wine-glasses glittered; the table-cloth was snow white. Beyond the island of light, though, the gloom of the house made itself felt in the old, oppressive furniture. Even the bright fire was cowed by the heavy over-mantel.

Edith lifted a handbell from the tray by her right hand. She was anxious for the servants' fussing. It would be a relief to have even that sort of company to lessen the tension. She could not describe her emotion, would not admit that it was fear.

Houston said, "Please wait a little, my dear. I wish to speak with you."

How long since he had used an endearment? She thought she detected sarcasm in it, but that was not her husband's style.

"The dinner will spoil," she said mildly.

"I have given instructions that dinner be served at eight fifteen."

"Oh!"

"Tomorrow is Christmas, Edith."

"The fact had not escaped me, Houston."

"I have a gift for you; several gifts, in effect."

Edith's heart-beat increased. She was deathly afraid now. This was the height of lunacy, more disturbing, more dangerous than any drunken mood, any outburst of violent anger. She had never, ever quailed before his authority as she did that night. Gifts? What did he mean by gifts? In the ten days since Sydney and Anna had been sent packing, after the Stalker girl's appear-

ance at the house, Houston had hardly spoken two
words directly to her. Now he was using endearments
and offering gifts with a graciousness that, in other
circumstances, would have been quite touching.

Numbly Edith stared at her husband.

He slid his hand into his inner pocket and removed
a sheaf of official documents, fanning them between
his fingers like the oversized cards elderly ladies used
to play cribbage with.

"These are my gifts, Edith."

"P . . . papers, Houston?"

"First, notice of eviction served on the Stalkers, effective from January first."

"But . . ."

"Yes, the eldest daughter will be married then, and
they have already given notice of intention to vacate.
This document, however, will ensure that there is no
wavering on their part."

"Or on yours?"

"As you say," Houston acknowledged. He touched
the second document with his forefinger. "This is a
letter from Gow Havershaw. In it he informs me of
his intention to article the Stalker boy at once, to take
him into the business, in other words, and to meet
expenses during the young man's final year. He frees
me from my patronage."

"The impudence. We will take our trade elsewhere."

"Havershaw does little enough for us, in any case,"
Houston said. "But I agree: we will remove our business from his keeping and find another lawyer if and
when we require representation in the capital."

"What makes you suppose that these items are of
any interest to me?" Edith asked. "They are strange
gifts, indeed, for Christmas."

"I wish you to have, in your possession, written tes-
timony that I have . . . have done with that kind of
charity."

"It would seem to me, Houston, that 'that kind of
charity' has, rather, had done with you."

Tapping the third document, Houston went on un-
perturbed. "A letter; copy of a missive I sent today to
your ally Sydney Thrush."

Edith stiffened. Surely, now the blow must fall.

"I have offered Mr. Thrush a new contract, a per-centage share in profits, and a small plot of land on the lower part of the estate. He may build there, if he so wishes, or find another residence for himself and his sister. I wish to exploit his experience, but I do not wish to endure his company."

"And Anna?"

"No, Edith. I will not have either of them in the house."

"But . . . but, I don't understand this change in your attitude."

"I want profit from Blacklaw now, Edith: profit, and more profit. If I can have nothing else in this life, I will at least enjoy the fruits of material success."

"How do you propose . . . ?"

"Thrush knows how it can be done. I will work with him, hand in glove with him. That's all that con-cerns me now. It's my intention to leave behind a model colliery, and a mansion worthy of the name of Lamont."

"'Leave?"

"The fourth document, Edith—this one—is a deed of co-ownership."

Edith paled. "With whom do you intend to amalga-mate? Who'll be your partner?"

"You will."

"Me? But . . ."

"I have transferred forty-five per cent of the stock into your name. You own it. You cannot, however, sell it in my lifetime, nor can you overthrow my wishes in respect of policy. The clauses are quite rigid on that score, my dear."

Tears welled into Edith Lamont's eyes. "Your partner. I never dreamed that you trusted me, Houston. Oh, my love, how can I repay your generos-ity."

"It will not be easy," Houston said. "You are my partner, now, and I demand high standards. You will help me make decisions, those decisions which affect the prosperity of the pit."

"And Blacklaw."

Her husband's face darkened; the deep, tragic lines bit into his flesh again, his eyes were haggard with hatred. It was not madness now, not even revenge. The coalmaster's inbred authority had steeled into an urge for total domination, a hunger for power in material forms.

"I care *nothing* for this town: *nothing*. It has done no more for my happiness than it has been paid to do, bullied into doing. I own Blacklaw, almost every stick and every stone of it. I will turn those stones, and every soul clinging to them, to *my* service."

"They were always your people, Houston."

"They were *not* my people. Never let me hear you say that again. They are nothing; serfs, that's all. You rule them, or you are ruled by them. Do you see?"

"Yes, Houston."

Lamont dropped all the documents save one to the cloth, spilling them neatly, like the hand of a new card game. Perhaps it was a game, too, Edith thought. If so, it was one that she could play with ease, supporting her partner, her strong and powerful partner as never before.

The coalmaster leaned across the table and, stretching, dropped the last remaining parchment close to her plate.

"What's this, Houston? What more can you give me?"

"My last will and testament," Houston Lamont said. "When I am dead, you may have it all to rule or ruin as you wish."

"Houston, please, no. Don't talk of such morbid things."

"Do we understand each other now, Edith?"

"Is it over, Houston?" Edith asked, looking down at the will, not daring to touch it. "Is all the quarrelling over?"

Lamont did not answer. He lifted the other papers and passed them to her, physically transferring all the sullied fragments of the past, tied now and neatly docketed for the future. But the letter on top had wafted open and exposed, by chance, the name *Stalker* printed in a bold inexpert hand.

And when Edith saw him stare, and how in his eyes there was no triumph and, at that instant, no resolution, she realised that her victory had been won at terrible cost.

She had gained a business partner and, forever, lost a husband. The last faint possibility of love had, that Christmas Eve, finally been snuffed out.

No snow fell on the Christmas season. Grey cold numbed the town throughout the week, locked the land under neutral cloud so that the clamour from the long sprawl of yards and railroad sheds rang hollow, out of nowhere, like voices remembered only in the head.

The celebrations which marked Kate Stalker's wedding were strangely restrained. Even her workmates did not know how to handle the occasion. The japes and send-off merriment which normally brightened a bride's last shift at the troughs did not materialise. A gift or two, small hand-made things, were given over at the dinner break and there was some half-hearted singing when Kate left the colliery gate that night. But on the whole Kate's marriage made Blacklaw folk uncomfortable.

Why was it that the Stalkers, between them, had achieved so much more than any other family in the town by turning the daydreams of their contemporaries into reality? Nobody could understand—not the nature of it, nor the cost. All that the colliers' wives could see was escape—escape from the anxiety of the trade, the tied house, the daily grind of making ends meet, dread of injury, fear of illness. The baker's premises with their newly white-washed thick stone walls, and the small, tall house in the cul-de-sac smartened by Dalzells' best curtains and, so it was said, furnished like a palace, became a coveted haven of security and peace for many of the women and Kate Stalker the object of their envy. The wives understood what the hot young girls did not, that there was more to a man than the strength of his limbs and his ardour in bed. After a year or two, after the second or third bairn had been born, none of those 'intransient' virtues mattered very much. Maybe Willie Kellock was no spring chicken, but clearly he loved Kate Stalker and would lavish on her all the substitutes for vigour that an old man could provide.

Perhaps it was that love they envied most, a love quite safe from the demands of passion—and its pitfalls. It was unlikely that there would be bairns to distract the couple from each other. Besides, Mirrin Stalker had seen to that provision, in advance. Aye, they were nicely set up now, those Stalker women, with their future and the bastard bairn's future snug and secure. Betsy had always been apart from the community, being more than Blacklaw could handle or contain; Drew it had never understood and thus had feared; Mirrin it held in awe, for she had been where they would not dare to go, and had suffered not at all for her wilfulness; Flora was happy, with her hearth, her horse and her chatty contact with friends, casual and uncommitted, and a grandson to lavish love upon. And Kate, a spinster past her best, even she had managed to net a catch that, when all was said and done, was one of the best the town had to offer.

Aye, they were damned lucky, those Stalkers.

But the men, the colliers, colleagues of Alex Stalker, mates of his collier sons, they sensed the significance of the gossip in another manner, more diffuse, less personal. Even bawdy comments as to what the bride and groom would do that nuptial night to while away the hours covered a wistful sadness, a nebulous acknowledgment that times had changed, and that, in the close-walled community of Blacklaw, a whole era had at last dwindled to a close.

Where were they now, the hearty militants, the talkers, the planners, the dreamers? They were gone, or they were silent. Only the Stalkers had somehow wriggled from the crushing fist of circumstance and change. For the rest of them the grip had tightened to the point where poverty was not the principal enemy. Poverty at least had been familiar. What nagged the miners now was fear of their own selfishness and greed, qualities exposed by Thrush, utilised by Lamont, kept raw and vulnerable by a man's need to hold body and soul together in a lean world. So the past became the best time, a golden age; none of them had appreciated it before past became present, and the future was swallowed up in its despair.

Not many waited then at the kirk gate at four o'clock on that Saturday afternoon, two days before the year's end, to see Kate and her groom descend the steps as man and wife and troop across the top of Main Street to enter the cul-de-sac and the tall cramped house around which the satisfying aroma of bread perpetually clung.

The façade of the single lofted tenement was as white as flour now. Willie had hung holly over the lintel, mistletoe over the windows, and to announce his delight, had given away a tiny iced cake with each bag of rolls the previous day. The Stalkers were calm, even Kate, their happiness turned in upon themselves. If they were conscious of the thinness of the family ranks—with Drew and Betsy absent—they gave no sign of it. Flora held Neill, chattering, attentive, excited by it all. Mirrin wore her plainest gown and a sober hat, so as not to detract from the trim blue suit that Kate had chosen to be married in. No guests were invited to share the wedding supper, not even the Ewings.

When the door of the baker's house closed the spectators loitered aimlessly at the mouth of the little yard. They did not understand that the Stalkers, at last, had locked out the loss which had tainted their lives and almost brought them down.

Callum Ewing grunted.

"Well, that's that done," he said.

Rob nodded. "She looked bonnie, though, I'll give her that."

"Kate will make him happy," Callum said.

"Aye," Rob agreed. "Are y'for a pint then?"

"It's a gey thin weddin', though. Alex Stalker would . . ."

"Alex Stalker's long dead," Rob said. "An' a lot else besides, I'm thinkin'."

Father and son walked towards the welcoming door of the *Lantern*.

Rob said, "I wonder if it's true, about Mirrin?"

"The trouble is," Callum said, "that Mirrin Stalker usually lives up t'all the bloody rumours about her."

"Mirrin married t'a tinker." Rob shook his head. "What a pitiful waste."

"Unless she changes her mind."

Rob glanced furtively at his father. "Is that possible, d'you think?"

"I'd never wager money on what Mirrin'll do next," Callum said.

The younger man stopped. They were by the public house wall now, the weathered hoardings above them, the faint conspiratorial murmur of the bar beckoning them, as it beckoned most men, with its promise of companionship. Rob said, "I'm not sorry, Da."

Callum frowned, the sick, pinched flesh giving an anger to his expression, an emotion that was rare in him. If he had learned anything, he had learned stoicism; a dangerous philosophy, difficult to master, and, in the end, defeatist.

"Sorry about Mirrin, y'mean, son?"

"I was mad for her, y'know," Rob confessed. "I've never told anybody this before, but . . . but there have been times I've wished . . ."

"Don't say it," Callum advised gently. "Don't put it int'words, Rob."

"I feel so bloody guilty now."

"We've all wished for second chances at some time," Callum said. "A new job, a new wife, God, even a new pair o' lungs. But then, one day, without really bein' aware of it, the wishin's no longer a part of you. Instead, you're just thankful for what you've got."

"Last month," Rob said, "I would've called you a liar, Da, a bloody old hypocrite."

"But not now?"

"Not now," Rob admitted. "After all these months, I still love Eileen. It's the thought of losin' Eileen that made me want Mirrin; not . . . not . . . the other thing."

"Aye, lad, I taught y'politics but I can't teach you everythin'," Callum reached up and patted his son's shoulder. "Not even your old man can tell whether it's a worse thing t'need than t'be needed. Come on, we'll away in an' have a crack with our kind and a jug o' best draught."

Rob got as far as the door.

"No, Da," he said. "I'll pass it by for tonight."

"Why? Where else d'you have t'go?"

"Home," Rob said, "t'my wife."

The wind came from the Lothian hills, bringing a taste of snow from the high pastures, and hardship for ewes in lamb and beasts on scant winter grazing. Nourished by an unimpeded passage over the moor, it howled down the funnel of the Sheenan's glen to clatter slates and snap tackle throughout Northrigg, Eastlagg and Blacklaw.

Some found the wind invigorating. Some, snuggled warm in quilts and blankets against the drafts, were stirred to fantasise on the towering waves that threatened mariners and other hardy rovers, and imagine themselves braving the elements in some God-forsaken spot elsewhere. Some listened with a pragmatic ear, predicting damage across Scotland, an aftermath of floods or snowdrifts, and bemoaning the probable loss of trade. Up in Lamont's colliery, the coalmaster toured with Thrush, a phalanx of foremen around him, bowing and scraping like liveried flunkies, fervently promising that no mishaps would delay the flow of coal from the guts of the earth to the marketplace, no matter how bad the weather. Second-hand assurances no longer satisfied the owner. He had to see the work done with his own eyes. Gaunt and sombre in a half-tile hat and lined cloak, his presence whipped on the midnight and the January dawn.

Hogmanay, and many of its traditional sentiments, were blown away by the gale, abetted by Lamont and his manager, Thrush. The goodfolk of Blacklaw mainly stayed indoors, nursing their memories and sweetening their greetings to 1876 with a dream by their own fireside. Those hardies who 'popped out' soon enough 'popped in' again, dishevelled and chittering cheeks reddened by the scathing wind, not by alcohol.

In her new home in the cul-de-sac, Kate Kellock helped her husband lug in hay for Wallace's supper.